DAVID EBSWORTH is the pen name of writer,
and Regional Secretary for Britain's Transpo
was born in Liverpool (UK) but has lived fo
North Wales, with his wife, Ann. Followi
write seriously in 2009.

For more information on the author a
www.davidebsworth.com.

CW00494858

Also by David Ebsworth

The Jacobites' Apprentice
A story of the 1745 Rebellion. Critically reviewed by
the Historical Novel Society, who deemed it:
"worthy of a place on every historical fiction bookshelf."

The Assassin's Mark
A political thriller set towards the end of the Spanish Civil War.
"The characters are so incredibly vivid – there are characters you adore,
others that annoy you and all of these are so expertly devised that
you simply cannot help but miss them all when you finish the book,
and you will finish it; this is not a novel you will be able to put down."
– Rachel Malone, Historical Novel Society

The Kraals of Ulundi: A Novel of the Zulu War
Picks up the story of the Zulu War where Michael Caine left off.
"An accomplished, rich, beautifully produced and very rewarding
read that brings a lesser-known era of history to life."
– Cristoph Fischer, Historical Novel Society

Each of David Ebsworth's novels has been awarded the coveted
B.R.A.G. Medallion by the worldwide Book Readers Appreciation Group

The Jacobites Apprentice was a finalist in the
2014 Historical Novel Society Indie Book Award

THE LAST CAMPAIGN OF *Marianne Tambour*

A NOVEL OF WATERLOO

DAVID EBSWORTH

To Chris
With great appreciation
and
best wishes
from Dave

SilverWood

Published in 2015 by the author
using SilverWood Books Empowered Publishing®

SilverWood Books
30 Queen Charlotte Street, Bristol, BS1 4HJ
www.silverwoodbooks.co.uk

Copyright © David Ebsworth 2015

The right of David Ebsworth to be identified as the author
of this work has been asserted by him in accordance with
the Copyright, Designs and Patents Act 1988.

All rights reserved. No part of this publication may be reproduced,
stored in a retrieval system, or transmitted in any form or by any means,
electronic, mechanical, photocopying, recording or otherwise,
without prior permission of the copyright holder.

This is a work of fiction. Names, characters, places and incidents
either are products of the author's imagination or are used fictitiously.
Any resemblance to actual events or locales or persons,
living or dead, is entirely coincidental.

ISBN 978-1-78132-321-2 (paperback)
ISBN 978-1-78132-322-9 (ebook)

British Library Cataloguing in Publication Data
A CIP catalogue record for this book is available from the British Library

Set in Bembo by SilverWood Books
Printed on responsibly sourced paper

Dedicated to the memory of M M Bennetts, an astonishing talent, researcher and story-teller of Regency and Napoleonic tales

Preface

I loved writing this story. It was inspired when I read a factual account of French Napoleonic cantinière, Madeleine Kintelberger, who served with Bonaparte's 7th Hussars during the Austerlitz campaign and was caught up in fighting against the Russian Cossacks while protecting her children, who were also with her on the battlefield. Her husband had been killed by cannon fire and Madeleine held off the Cossacks with a sword that she had picked up, losing her own right arm in the process. She was slashed by sabres and speared by lances during the same engagement, as well as shot in each leg. Yet she was also eight months pregnant with twins. It seems nothing short of a miracle that she survived at all. The Russians took her prisoner and she eventually returned with her children to France, where she was received in person by the Emperor and awarded a military pension. But the most astonishing aspect of all this was the fact that Madeleine was only one of hundreds of women serving in such positions in the French army's front lines, many of them with similarly incredible tales to tell and yet largely ignored, both in fiction and non-fiction alike.

And then, almost immediately afterwards, I also came across the real-life exploits of Marie-Thérèse Figueur who in 1793 had joined the French revolutionary army in her own right as a woman and who served with distinction in various Dragoon regiments through most of Bonaparte's major campaigns until 1814 when she retired and opened a table d'hôte restaurant in Paris. Once again, her story was not particularly unusual.

So the proposition was simple. What if two fictional women, but based on the real-life characters of Kintelberger and Figueur, were brought together by something more than a simple twist of fate during Bonaparte's final campaign, in June 1815, that culminated in the Battle of Waterloo? And what if that "something" had a mystical element that would have been very typical of the age's flirtations between the scientific and the spiritual?

Like my other novels, this is a work of fiction, based on historical fact. I have knowingly strayed away from facts, however, on a few significant points. First, the Imperial Guard's 4th Regiment of Foot Grenadiers never possessed a Second Battalion in 1815, but I felt that its invention allowed me to tell some aspects of the campaign's history more clearly. Nor did the 3rd or 4th Grenadiers participate in the attack on Tongrenelle. In addition, the Second Regiment of Dragoons did not take part in the action at Quatre Bras, nor the pursuit of Wellington's rearguard to Genappes, and neither did they carry muskets in 1815. I also took some artistic licence with the role of the Dutch Hussars and Light Dragoons at Quatre Bras. Finally, there is still considerable dispute about the precise nature of the discussions that took place over Bonaparte's 8.00am breakfast at Le Caillou (The Pebble) farm on the morning of Sunday 18th June, largely due – as Andrew W. Field tells us – to "the many discrepancies and contradictions in time and detail between them" from the later recollections of those who took part in the meal. But they are well-trodden by historians and I simply wanted to give a flavour of them here, so deliberately composited and compressed the accounts in a way which, I hope, will not cause too much distress to students of these events. Those students will know, too, that the Emperor's carriages actually remained at Le Caillou throughout the battle, rather than as I describe them. But, for the most part, I hope that the story will give readers an accurate though perhaps different (for English-language readers, at least) perspective on the five formative days of that campaign.

In addition, since I was thinking about the battle from a French perspective, I began to consider bringing into the tale some of those characters from French literature who also have a Waterloo connection. So you may find the Thénardiers (from Hugo's Les Misérables) or Fabrizio del Dongo (from Stendhal's The Charterhouse of Parma) wandering through these pages also. I hope you can forgive their intrusion and my presumptions! Indeed, if you should notice any other cameo appearance that may or may not resemble an additional literary figure or two, I hope you might forgive that also.

And, lastly, I should mention that, since this story is told from a French perspective, I've chosen to use translations of some more commonly known French place names in an effort to convey what those names would signify or convey to French-speakers. So, for example, the inn and farm from which Bonaparte viewed part of the Battle of Waterloo is always referred to as La Belle Alliance, which translates readily as The Beautiful Alliance. And since that name has a certain relevance to the plot, that's what I've used – and I've used the same protocol for other locations, such as the Pebble Farm (Le Caillou), or the Holy Hedge farm (La Haye Sainte) though left town and village names in their normal format.

But what about the background?

In 1789, the people of France threw off the shackles of a feudal monarchy and tried to establish a meaningful constitution. Their European neighbours, however, feared that this revolutionary spirit might spread and insisted that the French should return King Louis XVI to the throne. This sparked a declaration of war against Austria and Prussia, but also a Reign of Terror against supposed counter-revolutionaries, as well as the execution of Louis and his Queen, Marie-Antoinette.

In 1795 a new constitution was agreed and, soon afterwards, the armies of France began to achieve success against the enemies now threatening them (principally Austria, Prussia and Britain). And among the French Republic's crop of new generals, one name stood out above all others – the young Corsican, Napoleon Bonaparte, with his victories in Italy and elsewhere. But the political situation in France itself remained unstable, with Bonaparte leading a coup against the governing but divisive Directory in 1799, and declaring himself First Consul. This effectively ended the Revolution itself, although Bonaparte continued to introduce at least some progressive reforms, which included laying the foundation for Europe's modern legal system by establishing the Napoleonic Code.

In 1804, however, he abolished the Consulate completely and crowned himself Emperor of the French. The country was at war with many of its European neighbours for the next ten years but, following the disastrous Russian campaign of 1812, and then defeat by a coalition of his enemies at the Battle of Leipzig, he was forced to abdicate in 1814 and was exiled to the island of Elba.

He returned in March of the following year with no more than 1,000 men but, despite the ravages of almost continuous war for the previous twenty years, such was the magnetism of the glory that Bonaparte had heaped upon the nation, within three months he had assembled an army of almost 280,000 men without having to use conscription. Pitted against him was a coalition of 850,000 troops on four separate fronts. But the most immediate threat, in Bonaparte's eyes, came from the Anglo-Allied army commanded by the Duke of Wellington (110,000 men), with his headquarters in Brussels, and the Prussian army of Marshal Blücher (117,000 men), based at Namur.

Leaving the bulk of his forces to prevent the intervention of the Austrians, Russians and Spanish-Portuguese threatening his other borders, the Emperor marched north with 125,000 soldiers in an attempt to destroy the numerically superior armies of Wellington and Blücher on Belgian soil.

David Ebsworth
November 2014

Chapter One

Wednesday 14th June 1815, 2.00pm

The boning knife flashed from the left, flensed the lower buttons from Marianne's coat in the instant she jumped back, a reflex from the strange gift of premonition – or perhaps it was a curse – that she possessed.

The other woman, Lomballe, had come at her from the cover of a pig-shed, as Marianne picked her way between the outbuildings of a roofless and tree-grown ruin, seeking to avoid the road itself, busy and clogged with horse-drawn guns or their long ammunition carriages, supply carts, straggling units of horse or foot. And now the assassin recovered from her failed charge, was making another.

'Bitch!' screamed Lomballe, as Marianne, swinging the precious brandy cask hanging at her side, deflected the blade coming for her in a sabre grip, point first, in the manner of the Sicilians. But she registered this quickly, all her concentration focused on flight.

Recovering the small barrel, Marianne gripped the strap to keep it tight against her stomach and rolled against the low wall alongside, clumsily throwing herself across the tumbled stonework as the knife slashed the air behind her. She landed in nettles on the far side, recovered quickly and stood, grasping a smaller slab and hurling it almost blindly at Lomballe. But it was enough to make her attacker flinch, to draw breath. For the wall was now between them and the odds no longer so unequal. Yet Marianne could not afford to waste the opportunity for survival, so she kept moving, keeping to her own side of the barrier, panting slightly, her gaze locked to that of the other woman. Stooping fast to collect another manageable rock, she hefted it in her hand as Lomballe followed, keeping pace on the other side.

Marianne reached the corner, feinted back the way she had come, for she did not want to leave the wall's protection. Not yet. There was a chastity knife tucked inside her bodice, the little *salvavirgo* she had acquired in Spain, but she knew it was no use to her now. She had seen people attacked with knives many times before, had considerable experience of the thing herself. Yet she could count on the fingers of one hand the number of times the victim had enough time to draw a weapon of their own. The soldiers often bragged about knife fights, though knife attacks were stabbings, not fights. There was no such thing as a knife fight. When people came at you with a knife, they meant to murder you, not fight you. And it mattered not one jot how fast you were, for you would never be quick enough to beat somebody who already had a blade in their hand. You could only beat somebody to the draw if your opponent was incompetent or afraid. And Lomballe was neither of those things. If you were lucky, you learned these lessons when you were young. If you did not, you were dead. So Marianne knew that in the time it would take her to fumble with the remaining jacket buttons, Lomballe would be across that wall and finish her.

'You won't get the commission back whatever happens,' said Marianne. 'You know that, *cornade*?'

She had previously served as canteen-mistress with a line battalion. Yet that was all before the Emperor's exile, of course. Before Fronsac's transfer to the Guard when the Emperor had returned from Elba. Then, since this new battalion's canteen-mistress, Lomballe, had lost her husband, it had seemed perfectly reasonable to Marianne that she should herself make application to the Regiment's Administration Council, proposing that the commission pass to her. After all, a canteen-mistress without a commission was a woman without an honest penny to her name, a woman reliant on her husband's already modest rations.

'You think not?' snarled Lomballe. 'Battle tomorrow. Or the next day. You think they'll not want their dainties?'

The Council members had been reluctant, however. Lomballe's husband was a popular fellow. There was sympathy for his widow, for without her income she would likely die by the roadside. And although they reasoned there was every chance she might marry again, they could not escape the regulation requiring each canteen-mistress to be wed. If an alternative had not arisen, of course, they would doubtless have let matters lie. But faced with Marianne's application, her reminder of the rules, her experience, her own marriage to Fronsac, they had no real option except to grant her, with evident displeasure, the commission she sought.

All she had to do was stay alive long enough to enjoy it. She weighed Lomballe carefully now. Not entirely ugly, despite her mastiff's face. A tall and strong woman. She must have been to haul her cart all the way to Moscow and back. Well, perhaps not all the way back, but she always pulled her own cart, that was the thing. Never used horse nor donkey, they said.

'Fronsac will kill you for me,' Marianne yelled, wondering how those others, who moments before had been all around her on the road, had now disappeared so efficiently.

Lomballe set her free hand – her right hand – on the wall, as though she would try to vault it, but Marianne swung her own arm back, hefting the small slab and threatening to let fly. At the same time she tried to look behind her, to work out how far she would have to run, to see whether there was any escape route there for her at all. *There must be a door,* she thought, but she had not noticed one. Only fallen roof timbers, saplings that had taken root alongside the still intact chimney, the rustling spread of summer leaves against brick, a stink of soldiers' piss.

'Afraid to fight me yourself, bitch?' Lomballe replied. 'Let me come in there with you and we'll settle this properly. You must have a pricker of your own, eh? Where is it, sweetie? Inside the jacket?'

It was a trick, of course. The result would be the same. Marianne would step back and go for her own knife. But she would be dead before she had its grip. She met a Spaniard once who tried to teach her about knife fighting. It was a joke. He was teaching her how to fight a duel. Toe to toe. Like the fencing rules of gentlemen. Except the *gitanos* were no gentlemen. Though they still had their bloody rules. Their so-called honour.

Knife fights aren't like that! she thought. The very last thing you wanted to do when somebody attacked you was to fight. It was hard to resist, of course. It was a human thing, after all. To see whether you had what it took. But in practice it was usually better to run away. And once you made up your mind to run, your instincts would safely take over. Even when you thought you were cornered. Amazing how easy it was to wriggle your way out of the most impossible jam. Yet the one thing you must not do was dither. Dither and you were dead too. Never let pride and ego blind you to your death. If you had the upper hand, kill them. If not, then run.

'Fair enough! Let's do it,' she laughed, lowered the stone to her side, took a pace back, saw the wicked smile on Lomballe's face as the woman shifted her weight, hitched her skirts and set a foot on the wall. There was the smallest instant when her eyes went down, to check she had a decent grip, and in that instant Marianne flung the rock with every ounce of force that she could muster. Lomballe caught the movement, her head jerked down and to the left. And Marianne was unsure whether her own aim was luckily misplaced, or if she had genuinely calculated that her enemy would flinch that way, in the direction of the hand she favoured. But in any case, she heard rather than saw the impact of stone on flesh, the small scream of fury from Lomballe's broken lips and rotten teeth. She heard them as she ran.

It was no demonstration of athletic prowess either, but a clumsy scramble, impeded in part by the pair of woven *reticule* pouches that she wore beneath the nankeen trousers to guard her daily takings. At the same time, she was forced to keep one nettle-rashed hand on the brandy cask, the other seeking a steady purchase on the collapsed beams that barred her way, causing her to clamber onto their lower ends. Then she saw the doorway, part concealed by rampant shrubs. It offered escape to the road beyond, and sanctuary among the traffic which, she was sure, must still be thick upon its rutted path. Yet there was no time to dwell on that. She was over the timbers, scrambling over a mound of masonry, wrestling with the scratching shrubbery, turning to see Lomballe's filthy blood-smeared face behind her.

Marianne almost fell as the branches finally yielded to her frantic pressure, allowing her to jump down into a ditch. And then she was heaving herself on hands and knees up a bank on the other side, clogs scrabbling for a purchase until she tumbled onto the road itself, lacking all dignity, her cheek pressed in the dirt as she stared directly into the hooves of cavalrymen heading north. She rolled over, out of their path, dusted herself down and seeing no sign of Lomballe, she winked her eye at the astonished captain of Dragoons leading the squadron.

'Lomballe's promised she'll cut out your heart, Marianne,' said the Artisan Battalion's Master Carpenter some time later, and waved his chisel at her.

'She's already tried that,' she replied, 'on my way here. Anyway, we all die some time.' She held her breath, gripped the clay pipe tighter between her teeth, painted the final strokes on the end of the small barrel gripped between her knees.

The man shaved the final slivers from the spoke on which he was working.

'Finished?' he asked, when she stretched her neck to study the effect, the neatness of her handiwork.

'What do you think?' She set a hand on each side of the barrel, fingers touching the iron bilge hoops that held the bulging belly staves of the cask in place, lifting it to show him the head. Simple enough, those few black letters on the freshly painted blue beneath, but they sang to the world that she was now officially commissioned as canteen-mistress of the 2nd Battalion, 4th Regiment of Foot Grenadiers. Nothing else was necessary. For there was no other such battalion or regiment except that which served the Emperor as part of his Imperial Guard.

'I think that when Lomballe guts you, she'll see it as a pretty inheritance.'

'No doubt you'll assist her by painting over my name and replacing it with hers?'

'She doesn't have your eye, Marianne. And how could I refuse if she asked me? It's a fine cask. Though that new splash of blue makes the rest cry out for a touch-up, does it not?'

Marianne turned the barrel sideways. He was right. The red on the opposite end, on the front face and back as far as the forward bilge hoop, was faded to pale rust, though the spigot had been freshly seated and was dry as a bone, conserving every drop of the precious brandy within. The belly of the cask was tidy enough too. The central white stripe was somewhat discoloured, but she had replaced the cork bung that stoppered the fill spout on top. So it was just this other end that was lacking, supposed to be blue, naturally, but now largely flaked to the grey beneath, apart from that flash of fresh colour that she had used to erase the number of her previous regiment. *It's passable enough*, she thought. *At least, until we've settled with the Prussos and the English Goddams.* It was all she had for a uniform, after all – the cask's tricolour design. And the *tonnelet* was also all she possessed for concealment of her fortune, the modest accumulation of gold coins she had garnered through a lifetime's toil and now packed behind the false rear face of the cask, together with her one souvenir of Maman Cholet – the slender gold chain and locket.

'They'd told me Lomballe was good,' she said. 'With a knife, I mean. Didn't seem much like it to me.'

'I saw her in Russia. She saved the Colonel's life. Sliced the throat of a Cossack, pretty as you please. She needn't have bothered, of course. The old man froze to death two nights later in any case. But,' he sneered, 'you wouldn't know anything about that, all cosy and warm in Spain.'

'Warm it was, indeed!' Marianne replied, drew on the pipe, felt the tobacco bite on her tongue. 'But cosy?'

'Well, it wasn't bloody Russia,' said the carpenter. 'And look at you. Landed on your paws now.'

'Landing on your feet is one thing. Keeping them planted firmly on the ground after you've done so is another.'

The carpenter turned from his bench, ran his hand along the curve of the new spoke, brushed the scent of freshly cut timber in her direction, blew the finest cloud of sawdust across the fingers of early afternoon light that probed through the holes of the workshop's makeshift canvas awning.

'Fancy yourself some sort of philosopher then?' he said.

'Just an old-fashioned Daughter of the Revolution, Jacques,' she laughed.

He laughed too.

'What else?' he said. 'With a name like Marianne. But Tambour? That for real?'

'On the day the people took the Bastille, they also took the Invalides. Remember?'

'I remember,' said the carpenter.

And how could he not? she thought. The fall of the Veterans' Hospital was more significant than the taking of the Bastille itself, for without the muskets and cannons stored in the hospital's basement, how would they ever have taken the prison?

'Well,' she continued, 'that's where they found me.' She knocked the dottle from the bowl, put the pipe in her pocket. She was not the first to be born at the Invalides, of course. Marie, that they called Woodenhead, canteen-mistress with the 1st Regiment, had been born there too, though not abandoned. 'Whether Maman ever meant to come back for me,' she continued, 'is another thing. Not that it matters much to me. They say I was only a couple of hours old. But they found me lying on top of a drum and I've been Marianne Tambour ever since.'

It was not quite true, of course. She had simply been Marie, or maybe Anne, back at the beginning. But by the time both she and the Revolution were three years old, the name Marianne had come to symbolise the entire Republic. The folk of Provence sang of *Marianne's Cure*, a hymn to Liberty and Reason. And there were legends. About the woman of the barricades, wearing red cap and clogs, pike and musket in hand, leading the common people to their destiny. So those who had found her, drunk on their new-won freedoms, had eventually given her this more suitable name – the name by which that female personification of the Revolution was now known. Marianne.

'Well, Citizen Tambour,' said the carpenter, 'watch out for Lomballe. She'd take great delight in skinning you alive and presenting your hide to the drum corps for their repairs. She has that sort of humour.'

Marianne adjusted the buckles on the cask's worn leather strap, checked that it ran freely through the retaining plates and slung the barrel over her shoulder, setting it to rest comfortably on her hip, keeping the wet paint away from her patched russet jacket, her black apron, her nankeen trousers. The clothes were as worn as the army's uniforms but the gulf between campaign wear and tear on the one hand, and careless neglect on the other, was inestimable.

'I'll be careful, Jacques, never fear,' she said, though casting an involuntary glance at the road and knowing that it was a fair step back to the bivouac she shared with Fronsac.

They had been on the march for a week, moving silently out of Paris in the same way that the other Corps had slipped from Metz or Lille, Valenciennes or Mezières. Quite a trick, with each Corps replaced quietly by units of the National Guard. Nothing to arouse the suspicion of the enemy's spies. For there were plenty of those. Not just Goddams and Prussos either. But some of their own. People still loyal to Fat King Louis, though they must have been sleeping as the Imperial Guard marched north until, at last, today they had come within reach of the Belgian border, the head of the Guard's infantry column at Beaumont and its tail, their Artisan Battalion, at this mill and hamlet where the Chimay road crossed the River Hantes, a kilometre to the south.

The rest of the army was spread along the border both west and east. 125,000 men, they said, with the centre here while, across the border, twice their number of Prussians and English. And when the Emperor had done with those, there were still the Russians, the Swedes, the Austrians, all to be driven from French soil.

I don't want to know how many more they have, she thought. *But he'll take them one at a time. Divide and destroy. That's what he's good at. But I'll not be with him. Not then. We'll settle with the Goddams, then I finish with all this.*

The carpenter told her to leave the brush on the bench.

'I'll need it soon enough,' he said.

'Good fortune, Jacques,' she replied, setting her leather bonnet in place and tying its ribbons beneath her chin.

The road climbed slowly from the river towards the wooded hill on which Beaumont stood, a steeple rising from its centre, the square bulk of a fortress tower on its higher, western edge. The road itself was still packed, so that Marianne chose to join those following the field edge and flattening an ever-widening margent around the waist-high wheat. Still, those around her – the local villagers and traders, as well as the military's lame and lost – provided a sense of security. She could not say that she feared Lomballe, for she thought that she had never truly experienced fear in the way others might know it. Her first meaningful recollection was being jostled in the basket panniers on one side of Maman Cholet's horse, wedged among the sutler's goods that Cholet – Marianne's adopted mother – supplied to the Revolutionary Army. For it was the Cholets who had found her, taken her into their care that day at the Invalides. So she had passed her childhood on the battlefields of Europe, amid the din and death that allowed no furrow for ordinary fear. The Cholets had made all reasonable enquiry, they said, to discover her blood relatives. But there were so many families divided that year, so many displaced and abandoned, set upon the roads as France heaved herself from the swamp of slavery.

Yet she could not dwell on thoughts of Maman Cholet, though she longed to do so, briefly felt the warm condolence of mingled memories. But she knew that beneath this layer of temptation there was a deeper pit. The nightmare waiting to trap her, though pushed aside here by a new and growing rumble of excitement. Blue uniforms surging towards her from the tented encampments on the track's farther side. Arms pointing, shakos being raised, men running.

She looked back, scratching at the rash on each hand in turn. Still no sign of Lomballe, but from the south came the sounds of horsemen, with the soldiers' clamour now hurting her ears. *But then*, she thought, staring down the track in that direction, her pulse beginning to race, *it's always like this. When the Emperor's among us.*

The imperial entourage was almost upon her before she knew it. No advance guard, but the Emperor himself at the cavalcade's head, riding the white horse and wearing his grey campaign coat despite the summer afternoon's heat. But close around him were his generals; his Adjutant-Commandants and their assistants; a jostle of orderlies and pages. Marianne recognised the ever-loyal Grand Marshal, Bertrand. For, by Christ's Nails, she had seen him often enough during those same battles of the previous year in which her husband had also made a name for himself. Bertrand had been with them, always with them. Not like the other one. And yes, she recognised him too. That jutting cleft chin. Soult. The wretch. He may have given Wellesley a bloody nose at Toulouse but he must have made himself dizzy this past year, he had changed his coat that many times. But here he was, back in favour again, this so-called Duke of Dalmatia, now the Emperor's Chief of Staff.

They were almost level with her, other soldiers crowding around her, or clustering on the other side of the road, so that the Imperial Escort, the green dolmans of the Guard Horse Chasseurs, spurred ahead to provide a belated cordon as the cheering began.

'Long live the Emperor!'

Over and over until it formed a rhythmic chant, a war cry that made Marianne's heart pump faster in her breast despite herself. She felt like a child. She always felt that way, whenever she was caught up in the fervour. And though at one level she resented the man himself, believed that he had betrayed so many of the Revolution's principles, its egalitarian promise to women like herself, she experienced these as a child might come to first recognise that a beloved parent was perhaps less than perfect after all.

She glanced around, checking that Lomballe had indeed disappeared, realised that the Emperor had halted, removed his cocked hat, was waving it above his head.

'Soldiers of France,' he cried, 'your Emperor salutes you!'

And they chanted still louder, tears streaming down the cheeks of raw recruits and grizzled veterans alike.

Bonaparte's steel-grey eyes blazed, his gaze sweeping the crowd on one side, then the other, until they settled on Marianne. He pointed at her cask.

'Let me see!' he yelled, gesturing for her to reverse the thing, barely able to make himself heard.

She grasped the small barrel, turned it so he might see the letters she had painted there. He nodded, called for a page to fetch his cup, waved his hat some more while the young fellow allowed Marianne to fill the ornate goblet. Then the Emperor sampled her brandy, lifted the cup in a toast to his troops.

'To the glory of France!' he yelled.

'Glory!' they howled back at him. 'Glory!'

And Bonaparte tossed back the rough spirit, raised the goblet once more – this time to Marianne Tambour.

'How much will this rotgut cost me?' he called.

'To you, Shaveling,' she replied, using the affectionate nickname that only the Guard dared use, even to his face, 'let's say two francs.'

'Expensive!' he replied.

'We always over-charge the officers, Sire,' said Marianne. 'You'd expect nothing less, I think.'

The Emperor nodded, gestured for one of his Aides to toss her the money.

'Pay her,' he called, and she caught each of the spinning coins deftly, one with the left hand, one with the right. 'You are canteen-mistress to my Guard Grenadiers,' the Emperor said to her. But was it question or statement?

She smiled. *Oh, foolish vanity*, she thought. *Where is your resentment of him now?*

'I am, Sire,' she replied.

'Then, madam soldier, I suggest you straighten your bonnet and wash your face. You look like you've been dragged through a hedge. It will not serve.' The Emperor laughed. 'We're not Wellesley's infamous rabble, after all.'

And he was gone, the Horse Chasseurs pressing a path for him towards the Beaumont ridge.

Chapter Two

Wednesday 14th June 1815, 4.00pm

'Defenestration,' said Fouché, 'is an especially inadequate word for such brutality. Distinctly architectural overtones.'

'And only applicable, I think,' replied the woman, 'when a victim is actually thrown from a window by means of deliberate assassination. For one's victim to fall accidentally, a mere by-product of the day's endeavours, it can hardly qualify.'

Fouché snorted with laughter, grotesque and phlegm-laden.

'Semantics, madam,' he said. 'You put proposals to poor Berthier that put him in fear for his life. He suffered a heart attack. He fell from his window. Four storeys, was it not? And he naturally died as a consequence. I can think of no other word which sufficiently describes the deed. Defenestration. Not perhaps in the classical style of the Bohemian Protestants of Prague, but close enough.'

'In fear for his life? Yet they were hardly threats,' said the woman. 'I delivered the message exactly as you instructed. That it was still not too late to declare a Regency on behalf of Bonaparte's son. That Berthier should act as Regent. That France – or, rather, Fouché – expected him to play his part. As he has always done.'

Fouché peered at her down the substantial length of his nose, querying her over-familiarity.

'For many,' he said, 'Fouché's expectations have been more than sufficient to foster such fear. And his response?'

'He said,' she replied, remembering to allow her tone some additional respect, 'that Bonaparte would never agree, even if it was acceptable to the Allies, which he doubted.'

Fouché smiled. He had been handsome once, though now the eyelids hung so heavily in his cadaverous skull that he – the Emperor's Minister of Police, the Duke of Otranto – seemed permanently in danger of drifting into sleep.

'Oh,' he said, 'I confirmed the arrangements with Wellesley himself. Though I suppose he might consider the agreement to be somewhat negated now that my lord and master has taken the offensive. So far as Bonaparte himself is concerned, he still needs this new Chamber of Representatives. It is a pretty enough sop to throw against those who choose to brand him as a tyrant. The

Senate is a slightly different case, of course. They were instrumental in forcing his abdication last year, were they not? And with Cambacérès as President, they will have even more bite. The author of the Emperor's Civil Code can hardly be ignored, despite his proclivity for young men. But tell me, Madam Dumont, did you go to Berthier dressed in that fashion?'

The woman looked down at her riding clothes, the russet jacket and the buttoned cloth overalls that she wore to protect her breeches.

'I rode seventy-five leagues,' she replied, 'to bring you the news from Bamberg. What did you expect, Your Grace? My dragoon's uniform? That would have gone down well with the Russians and Prussians, don't you think?'

There was that lack of reverence again. It would get her killed one day, she knew. Yet she also understood that Fouché prized this quality in his agents.

'You passed through their lines safely?'

'In truth,' said the woman, 'I saw none except when I was with Berthier himself. There were Russian horsemen. He went to the window to watch them pass the end of the road. Clutched at his chest. And then he fell.'

'Who else was in the house?'

'Only his Governess, Gallien. But she will say nothing. She's been well paid for her silence.'

Fouché went to the window of this other room, gazed out from the Residence of the District's Sub-Prefect, so recently occupied by the Emperor, to the wooded valley below Avesnes.

'Alas, poor Berthier,' he said. 'He would have made such an eminently suitable Regent. Respected by all factions of the Senate – the Revolutionaries; the Bonapartists; the Royalists. I've never heard a bad word against the fellow from any of them. Never militarily the most brilliant of Bonaparte's Marshals, as you know. Yet as his Chief of Staff, to serve the Emperor in that capacity for eighteen years without a break. Remarkable! But I came across him long before. I was on the Committee of Instruction.' *Difficult days*, she recalled. *The Church to be taken apart. So-called counter-revolutionaries to be executed. So many executions.* She recalled them with bitterness, dragged herself back across the twelve intervening years. 'And Berthier,' Fouché smiled, 'had already made a name for himself. Such intellect. Fastidious attention to detail. Total reliability. And tireless. Utterly tireless.'

'Ultimately not so tireless, it seems!' said Dumont

'You must explain to me, my little Liberté,' he said, 'why these powers to which you lay claim are incapable of divining such a momentous outcome. Did your visions hold not the merest hint that the encounter would result in Berthier's death?'

'If you had wanted a seer, Your Grace,' she replied, 'you should have chosen Madam Lenormand.'

'That ugly toad?' said Fouché. 'A charlatan, like all her type.'

'Yet when I arrived, you asked for my opinion of Nostredame. Does your strategy rely in any measure on those half-prophesies?'

'Strategy?' snapped Fouché. 'I said nothing about...' Then he paused, lifted his head so that he could stare directly down into Dumont's gaze. 'Well, why not?' he continued. 'In all these past twenty-one years, I have never been so unsure about the future. You should not dismiss Nostredame so readily. Some of his predictions correlate so precisely to our recent history, and to that of the Emperor in particular, that I cannot ignore them.'

'I have studied them, Your Grace,' said Dumont. 'They lack clarity. Indeed, it seems unclear to me whether those supposedly relating to Bonaparte have any relevance to him at all.'

'But,' said Fouché, 'there is this. "*From a simple soldier he will aspire to Empire. From a short robe he will aspire to the long.*" From lieutenant to Emperor. From consular cloak to imperial gown. There is a quatrain to fit every period of his career. Toulon. Italy. Egypt. The victories against Prussia and Austria. Spain. The Russian disaster. And now this. In the First Quatrain. "*In the third month, at sunrise, the Boar and the Leopard meet on the battlefield. The fatigued Leopard looks up to heaven and sees an eagle playing around the sun.*" Is this not the third month since his return? Is the Boar not Paris? Or Bonaparte himself? And the Leopard is Wellesley, surely? Bonaparte has often enough referred to him thus.'

Dark shadows filled the room on this northern side of the building, cold despite the month. Yet it suddenly felt colder still and a silence dropped between himself and Liberté Dumont. Then it was ripped apart by the sudden beating of a demon's wings above his head. Fouché started, buried his face in his hands as the dove flapped raucously from its hiding place in the rafters and found its escape through the open window. He turned to see Liberté Dumont staring at him.

'Spies everywhere, Your Grace,' she smiled. 'But so far as that Quatrain is concerned, it could mean almost anything. Or nothing. If Nostredame had written them sequentially, made clear that they all refer to the same piece of history, the same person, they might have more credibility. Yet they are scattered throughout his writing. No obvious link between them except that which the beholder may choose to make for his own purpose. These are, after all, a record of Nostredame's dreams and visions. But a record that more closely resembles the faecal mess of a madman.'

'I set no real store in the misguided mysticism of Madam Lenormand. Nor in the scribblings of Michel de Nostredame for that matter. But a person in my position must gather all the coins that he is able, then weigh them collectively. That is the true art of prediction, sweet Liberté. To forge a vision of the future, the widest range of alternative endings, no matter how strange the source, and then to open options which may deal with them, keeping as many ajar for as long as possible, closing each only with reluctance that we might achieve the optimum benefit.'

'For our personal gain, Your Grace, or that of the nation?'

Fouché's features registered a measure of shock.

'My dear,' he said, 'I have caused men to suffer unspeakable agonies for lesser imprecations. Yet I am more stunned that you should believe any separation to exist between the interests of Fouché and those of France herself. I stand only for the long-term ideals of the Revolution. Heads of state may come and go, and we must sometimes bend to accommodate the winds of change they bring. But when each of them has passed, the ideals still remain. The Republic resounds to their song.'

'It is a refrain,' replied Liberté Dumont, 'that I have never fully understood.'

'You were lucky,' said Fouché. 'Fighting for the Federalists, for the counter-revolutionaries, was so nearly a fatal mistake for you. How old were you? Nineteen? And far too beautiful for the guillotine. But you bent with the wind too, did you not? Accepted my little proposal. Gathered such skills. Probably the best female sword-sharp in France. A deft fingersmith in the bargain. And this mystical ability – you truly believe yourself capable of conveying your spirit through the aether?'

'Astral projection, Your Grace. Though I am merely a minor adept.'

Fouché suppressed his amusement.

'You must demonstrate for me on some occasion when we have more leisure,' he said. 'Or perhaps I should find you a task which would allow you to exercise the function?'

'I sense that you mock me, sir,' she said.

'Not so! Not so! The whole subject fascinates me inordinately. And it must surely have contributed in no small measure to your glittering career, has it not? You have met the Shaveling how many times now?'

'Three,' she replied. 'Once at Toulon, after I was wounded. Then a dinner invitation after he became First Consul—'

'The third occasion in March,' Fouché interrupted. 'At the Tuileries, I recall. You must have found him much changed?'

'Thirteen years is a long time. And he has been Emperor for most of those.'

'Does that enhance or diminish the man?' said Fouché.

'How can it not enhance him, Your Grace? He curbed the excesses that the Revolution brought in its wake, restored something that at least resembles a monarchy, the natural balance.'

'Ah, sentiments now so much back in vogue. You must be pleased to see the Revolution brought so low.'

'I think you understand me better than that, sir,' she said. 'My father and the Federalists simply saw the Revolution on a different road. But our hearts were as filled by its principles as those of any on the Committee of Public Safety. I was named anew for the first of them, after all. And I fight for them still, those values that have set France free.'

'Then you are fortunate, madam. In my eyes, Bonaparte violated the Revolution in the most brutal way by subsuming it to his imperial ambition. Then compounded his crime by establishing a family dynasty. I have warned him so many times, supported him only where his actions matched the needs of our people. But at this point I can discern neither the needs nor the outcome.'

'Yet he trusts you. Despite your part in forcing his abdication, the way you welcomed the King back as soon as Bonaparte was imprisoned on Elba.'

Fouché's laughter bore no hint of humour.

'Trusts me? Because he made me Minister of Police again on his return? His philosophy has always favoured the devil he knows. He understands there is nobody else who can perform those duties like Fouché. And, in the end, those duties for a Police Minister are to serve the state, regardless of whoever happens to be its head. I must be here to perform them long after Bonaparte has gone again – and nobody would understand that better than the Emperor himself. So there is a different sort of service that I seek from you, Dumont. For my most trusted agent, a double endeavour.'

'Yet you cannot be certain that he will be gone.'

'Of course not. And when we have weighed the possibilities, kept open our options as long as possible, exhausted them, and still do not see the future clearly, there is only one course still available to us. We create the future for ourselves. We act. So far, Wellesley has been deceived into believing that Bonaparte's campaign will not begin until early in July. He may just now be waking up to the fact of that deceit. But, in any case, we will assist him somewhat.' Fouché crossed to the writing case that lay on his bed, unlocked the walnut box and hefted a sealed pouch of documents in his hand. 'These,' he continued, 'are my personal dispatches to the English Duke. They contain the precise details of the Emperor's strategy. They are enciphered, naturally. But Wellesley has the key already.'

Liberté's astonishment elicited a glimmer of amusement in that tiny segment of Fouché's eyes visible beneath the half-lowered lids.

'You want me to help you betray the people of France?' she whispered.

'Do you know the true traitors, Liberté? They are the same that always betray the people. The arms dealers. The bankers. How many muskets has France purchased this year? No, let me correct that. How many have we purchased since the Emperor's return from Elba?'

'I have no idea,' she replied, though her voice betrayed a weary belief that he was dissembling.

'The answer, my dear, is forty thousand. And from whom did we purchase them?'

'Our enemies, I imagine.' Her response lacked true interest.

'Exactly,' said Fouché. 'Made in Birmingham. Perfect copies of the Charleville-pattern. The parts shipped to Belgium with the butt plates uniquely marked and the guns assembled at the Liège factory before being shipped across the border to our own arsenals. And how might we have paid for them? Can you imagine?'

'English finance?'

'Almost,' Fouché smiled. 'I believe that *international* finance might be more accurate. Let us take the Rothschilds as an example. One brother, based in London, provides almost ten million British pounds to England's allies. A subsidy loan, naturally. And I understand that the latest will be closer to forty millions. Other consortia provide loans to England herself. Meanwhile, another Rothschild brother, Jacob, provides similar loans to our own Government. It is a game, is it not? But the vested interests involved in prolonging this war are incalculable. Bankers make huge profits from this military financing. Exchange-rate transactions. Commissions. Risk-free debt. Meanwhile, there is bond-price speculation. Bankers like Ricardo, dozens more like him, are stockpiling bonds as quickly as they can lay hands on them. The price is at rock-bottom, of course, and can only rise. British government bonds. Consolidated annuities. French government securities. And when they rise, private fortunes will be made.'

'Yet you provide the Emperor's plans to Wellesley,' Liberté frowned. 'It must aid them to profit more quickly. With Bonaparte and France defeated, British bonds rise in price again.'

'Of course. But think how much more they may gain by a prolongation of the war. Those fortunes will look like chicken-feed compared to the returns on the subsidy loans. Unimaginable wealth. And not only the financiers. But the weapons manufacturers. The victuallers. The horse-breeders. The clothiers. The boot-makers. The wagon-builders. There is no end to it. Here. England. Sweden. Russia. Austria. Prussia.'

'Yet it is surely governments, monarchs, that wage war, one upon the other?'

'Do you think so, madam?' said Fouché. 'I have to tell you that on this subject, if on no other, I am entirely in accord with the Emperor. These speculators are no better than common gamblers except that unlike common gamblers, these scoundrels have the ability to guide the destiny of all Europe to achieve their aims. They employ invention, false rumour, disfigured intelligence. Anything they need to secure the ear of councillors, cabinet members, ministers, ambassadors, the monarchs themselves. They mislead public opinion. A public always more thirsty for lies than the truth.'

'A public that enjoys its own speculation too!'

'Indeed! Bonaparte said as much himself. That trading in securities seems to be the business of every second Parisian.'

'And you think it preferable that we give Wellesley an easy victory?'

'There is no such thing as an easy victory, Liberté. Have you ever seen one? You have served with the Eagles for over twenty years. Egypt. Italy. You must have fought on a dozen battlefields and are a unique treasure, my dear. Not one of those breech-clad bawds that occasionally enter our regiments disguised as a man. A soldier in your own right. Gifted soldier too. I may not have much time for mysticism, but I recognise your special talents. And so does the Emperor. It's the reason that he released you to my service so readily.'

Fouché caught the faint sound of scratching from the wardrobe that stood in the corner of the room.

'Damned vermin,' he said. 'Might as well be sleeping in a menagerie.' He snatched up the walking cane propped against a bed post, hobbled quickly to the piece of furniture and threw open its doors. More scratching and scrabbling, a mouse leaping from the lowest shelf and running circles upon the floor until Fouché, with one deft two-handed stroke of the cane, caught the creature a fatal blow that flung it against the wall. His chest heaved with the exertion.

'Did the Emperor know you would use me to betray him?' said Liberté, as though there had been no interruption.

'Betrayal is a filthy little word,' said Fouché. 'As inadequate as defenestration. I doubt there is any other living soul who has spent as much time as myself exploring Bonaparte's mind. So I shall tell you a secret, Liberté. The answer to your ironic question is no, my dear. He did not know that I would employ you in this way. But let us imagine a variant of your query. Would the Emperor be *surprised* at my plan? Indubitably not. And might he actually *endorse* it? That is the conundrum. He may have betrayed the Revolution, yet he loves France as deeply, as surely, as myself. If he could stand outside his own body – that same gift of which you claim to be capable – would he not relish the thought of an honourable and speedy end to all this? Besides, these documents are more than they seem, a conundrum within an enigma.'

'A lesser man than yourself, Your Grace, might have settled for a share of the bankers' game.'

'Life has treated me well enough. For the son of a modest ship-owner I have prospered. But always as a just reward for my efforts, my dear. It is too late for me to learn the arts of corruption now. But we do need some financial safeguard.'

'The double endeavour you mentioned?'

'The Emperor himself is unusually circumspect about the outcome of this campaign. Do you know how this circumspection is evident?' Liberté shook her head. 'He carries always in his dormeuse,' Fouché continued, 'a strange assortment of personal comforts. But this time he also carries with him a king's ransom. An emperor's ransom, to be more precise. Diamonds, dear Liberté. Because he believes that if things go badly, he might escape to his friends in America. Commence afresh there.'

'But if he is captured?'

'Exactly. A significant portion of France's wealth will fall into foreign hands. A foolish risk, and I have told him so. Yet that hardly seems enough. So here is your task. In the battles to come, you will stay close to him. And if there is the slightest threat of danger to the Emperor... No, let me phrase that differently. If there is a threat of danger to the Emperor's dormeuse, you will liberate the diamonds and return them to me. They are apparently hidden in a tea caddy. Beneath the sleeping box.' Fouché took another document from the writing case. 'Here,' he said, 'this carries my personal authority, a safeguard for the bearer.'

'Does the Emperor know that I carry this duty?' said Liberté.

'He does not.'

'And my reward?'

'If you had re-joined your regiment in March,' Fouché replied, 'you would have received the imperial bounty, would you not?'

'Fifteen hundred francs,' she said.

'Then I shall match that figure. For the safe delivery of my documents to Wellesley. And so long as the Emperor's diamonds are still in safe hands at the end of this present campaign.' Fouché returned to the wardrobe, hid his precise movements from her, though she could hear the happy jingle of coins. 'For the time being, I'm certain that a small advance might be in order?' He closed the wardrobe door, turned to present her with five gold Napoléons. 'Shall we say a hundred francs?'

'How will you know that I have made the delivery to Wellesley?' Liberté asked him, pulling the thin leather strap that secured her purse safely inside the waistband of her breeches, and depositing the coins.

'Oh, by the outcome, dear Liberté. By the outcome. This plan has certain risks, of course. We reveal the Emperor's plans to Wellesley. Simplicity itself. Tell your enemy the truth and he is certain not to believe you. He will therefore act in a contrary fashion, and be humbugged in the process.'

'And in the unlikely event that Wellesley takes the documents at face value, Your Grace?' Dumont's skin began to crawl with uncomfortable possibilities. Fouché had a certain reputation, after all. So if the English took his bait, it might indeed help the Emperor to defeat them more quickly. Yet what a momentous outcome that would be! For a victory against such odds could surely be seen as nothing but the most monumental evidence of Bonaparte's destiny. Entirely feasible too. For there was no simpler way to deceive one's enemy than to tell him the truth, then simply leave him to conclude that it must be a deception and make the wrong moves. But what about the alternative? And yes, they included victory for the English, a return of Fat Bourbon Louis – a victory for which Fouché could still claim some of the credit. "*There,*" he would say, "*did I not reveal to you the Emperor's plans?*" Or the middle ground, defeat for the Shaveling but the Allies' acceptance of the four year-old Napoléon François under a Regency. The boy had already been Emperor, after all, for just seven days in the previous April, as Napoleon the Second, following his father's abdication. In either case, Fouché would be unlikely to want a witness around in the aftermath.

'Then perhaps we must put our faith in God, after all,' said the Minister of Police.

'I had never appreciated that the Emperor had such spiritual tendencies,' said Liberté.

'Oh, he does not!' Fouché snorted. 'He has always made his views on the subject very clear. That all religions owe their origins to man, not God, and seek to indoctrinate with the morality of the men that invent them. He is fond of saying that he would believe a religion only if it could demonstrate its existence since the beginning of the world – or at least from the time that man first set foot upon the path of civilisation. He has a fair point, do you not think so, Liberté? It is difficult to understand how God could have made himself known to us only so late in our human history as the age of Plato. Then to have repeated the introduction, ever with differing messages, to Moses, to Christ, to Mohammed. Goodness knows how many others besides. And when it is all over, your missions complete, and the years of war behind us, what will you do?'

'A cabaret, of course. Highest quality. Somewhere on the Rue de Grenelle.'

'Then I shall patronise your establishment, Liberté. But first there are the practical matters. A decent mount, for example?'

'I have one, Your Grace. Two, in fact, if I count my Percheron mare. But I assumed that you would not wish me to be conspicuous, whatever the task. I have a mule that will serve admirably.'

'And a fish tale to cover your activities?'

'With the army on the march, I hardly need one. There is always a shortage of one thing or another. I have some saddle baskets packed with a selection of trade goods. That's the only cover I need. If I leave soon I can catch them quickly enough.'

'And the same ruse will see you through the English lines?'

'You can rely upon it, Your Grace!'

Liberté Dumont crossed the cobbles to the stable block, emerged moments later with a fully laden mule and walked him back towards the gate where she swung right onto the Charleroi road. But just before she did so, she turned quickly, saw Fouché duck back from the window where he had plainly been watching her. She understood that she might never see him again and there was a moment of regret. She knew that she was, indeed, one of his best agents. Valued. To a certain extent. But she was not indispensable. She knew that too.

Chapter Three

Wednesday 14th June 1815, 6.00pm

He had been forced to abdicate, of course. Marianne followed the dust of the Emperor's dormeuse carriage all the way back to Beaumont, remembering the agony of that previous year. Forced to it. By his useless generals, the very Marshals of France that he had personally raised from the gutter and who had repaid him with weakness and vacillation, fame and fortune corrupting their loyalty. Oh, they would have been inventive in their excuses, playing upon the clamour of traitors elsewhere, the agitators both within the army and without. Those who had whined about twenty-five years of war. Those who were fond of inventing figures for the fallen. Almost two million Frenchmen, they claimed. And that was just the soldiers, they would say. What about the ordinary citizens of France? The innocent victims of war. What about them? As though they gave a damn!

For they had forgotten what it was all about. The rich had become richer, of course. But did they not always? Yet at least the slavery practised by the old aristos was dead.

We could at least talk about liberty, she thought. *Listen to each other's dreams. Read about freedom, if we were fortunate enough to have the gift.* Half of the country's men gained the right to vote. Only half, and no women. But a beginning. Even those without voting rights – women included – now had legal protection for their belongings, for their liberty, through the Emperor's Civil Code. Not for the colonies, of course, or the colonies' own slaves, yet that would come too, in time. For now, the walls of feudalism were torn down, never to be built afresh. Imprisonment without trial, without appeal, gone forever. Legalised torture too. And the seeds of revolution were spreading. Why else would all the old régimes of Europe have massed against them? Because Bonaparte was a tyrant? It was laughable. There was barely a ruler among the enemies of France that was not himself a despot. Though they had done France a favour, united her in a way that she had never been united before.

'Did you see them?' shouted a soldier alongside her, removing his oilskin-covered shako and mopping his brow. His greatcoat had once been brown but was now stained and bleached to pale ochre but it still sported the remains of a torn green epaulette, from which she placed him as one of the Young Guard's light skirmishers.

'Arse lickers, all of them!' she replied, assuming that he, too, was reflecting on the quality of the Emperor's generals.

'And that bastard Soult the worst of the bunch,' said the soldier. 'It's the last thing we needed. All the old buggers back. We want young generals. Fire in their bellies. Hungry for a Marshal's baton. Like the old days.'

'This lot were all happy to see Fat Louis back as soon as the Emperor was out of the way,' she agreed. 'At the point of foreign bayonets too.'

And it was true. After the disaster in Russia, their enemies had closed for the kill. The Russians themselves. The Prussians, Austrians, Swedes. The English, of course. Along with the Spanish and Portuguese – the *manolos*, as she collectively thought of them. Yet even outnumbered by those impossible odds, the Emperor had beaten them many times more. Dresden, they reckoned, had been one of his finest moments. But then there had been the defeat at Leipzig, followed by a brief and final moment of glory in the defence of Paris before its fall, the Emperor forced to abdicate and sent into exile on Elba. Marianne had still been in the south, of course, where word of the abdication did not reach them until they had fought one last battle. At Toulouse.

By the Host, she thought, *we gave the bloody English something to remember that day!* As it happened, Soult had been their commander. But he could not claim much credit for the thing. The whole army knew he had missed a golden chance to wipe out Wellesley altogether, had settled for a tactical withdrawal, while credit for holding the Calvinet Heights was due purely to the tenacity of those Divisions posted there.

'Well,' laughed the skirmisher, 'we'll blunt their points for them soon enough, pretty one. This is the best we've been for years! Now what about a sip of that brandy?'

He was right about their readiness, though he seemed too wet behind the ears to speak with such conviction. But everybody understood that this army was a far cry from the weakened thing that had failed them at Leipzig. That had been filled with raw recruits, conscripted to replace the 300,000 lost in Russia. But the Emperor was done with conscription. He had learned his lesson. So when he came back from Elba, he had simply called up those on leave, or the many who had refused to serve Fat Louis. And, by Christ's Nails, they had flocked to join him. Half a million men. And why not? Fat Louis and the Bourbons had only been back in power for a year, yet it was like they had never been away. The aristos back in control again, the new laws all ripped up, treating the people like slaves. Like shit.

As though the Revolution had never been, she thought. *As though our blood hasn't nourished it these twenty-six years past.*

Thus, they flocked to join the Emperor again. Some for love of the man himself. Some for their love of France. But most from pure hatred of their enemies. Hatred of the Bourbons. Hatred of the foreign powers, like England, that had set Fat Louis and his cronies on the throne again. Hatred of defeat, of humiliation, of occupation. Louis was no longer there, of course. He had fled pretty fast when he found out that the Emperor was back on French soil. He had run like a bloated rabbit, so quickly that even those who might not have been great supporters of the Emperor welcomed the Shaveling home with tears in their eyes and, by the time he reached Paris, it was like he had never been away.

'Do you have no canteen-mistress of your own, soldier?' she shouted. He was not a bad-looking boy, this one. But the sort that would want mothering, she imagined.

'Not one as handsome as you, darling.' He laughed, slapped the back of a companion. The normal banter. 'And they say the Grenadiers get better brew than the rest of us.'

Handsome? She grimaced. *And how old does he take me for? He calls me 'pretty one' – but what does he see? What's the gap between us? Two years? Three? I bet he thinks it's a dozen or more.*

Marianne looked up and down the ranks around her, checked for any sign of Lomballe. But the woman seemed to have entirely disappeared.

'You're right, Jacques,' she said. 'Only the best for my Grenadiers,' and she placed a hand under her now almost shapeless bosom, hefted it provocatively. The soldiers laughed, obliged her with some lewd gestures of their own.

'We'll maybe see you again, little pearl,' shouted the skirmisher as she waved them farewell and turned along a narrow track which led to the chapel around which her battalion was camped. It had started to grow chilly, Marianne noticed, a cold wind coming up and bringing light drizzle with it, a real change from the fine weather that had favoured them all the way from Paris.

She found Fronsac easily enough, playing dominoes – the bone set he had carved on the English hulk – with his good friends, Marle and Argonne, sharing a pipe beneath the small canvas shelter they had rigged from the side of the chapel to the raised shafts of her cart. Their pony, Cocotte, was hobbled and grazing alongside, a pair of Marianne's goats tethered just beyond.

'You were supposed to get the canteen tent up,' she snapped at Fronsac.

'That's your job,' he replied, tugging at the gold ring with which his ear lobe had recently been pierced.

'I've been working, husband. Look!' She produced the pair of one-franc pieces. 'From the Shaveling himself.'

'He dropped by for a drop of dog-dog, I suppose?' said her husband, and his friends laughed, nodded as they imagined the scene. 'Anyway,' Fronsac continued, 'if this weather gets any worse, we'll have to shift round to the other side, out of the wind.'

Marianne looked about, searched for their daughter, but could not see her.

'Where is she?' she said, pretending at a lack of concern but suddenly afraid for the girl. She had not made an earlier link between the threat from Lomballe and Florisette's own safety but she recognised now that such a thing was not beyond a creature like that. Yet her instincts told her that such a possibility was remote, and she relaxed.

'Playing with Argonne's kids,' Fronsac replied. 'Can't you hear them?'

Cutting through the permanent background noise of wagons on the road, the hooves, drums, troops on the march, cooking pots being unloaded, came the singing. There was always singing. Songs for marching. Songs for drinking. Songs of love and loss. Songs from the Vaudeville. Marianne kept a few ballad sheets herself, and the tune she could hear now was an old friend – Florisette's thin voice piping at the chorus. The words changed with every campaign, and those inside the chapel had already turned them to their present situation.

'Ah, they will remember, la lira,' they chanted, *'the march to Charleroi.'*

It could just as easily have been *Song for the Fall of England* or *The Brotherhood Hymn*. Florisette knew them all. Except nobody called her Florisette; the whole battalion knew her as Poppy.

'She sings as badly as you, Fronsac,' said Marianne. He picked at his bulbous nose, slapped down a double five. His time on the hulks at Cádiz had not done him any favours, his deeply lined face was blotched with liverish spots.

'You can't have everything, Marianne,' said Argonne. 'You end up with the best-looking fellow in the battalion and expect that he'll perform opera too?' Fronsac appreciated the compliment, smoothed down the mustachios he had been growing enthusiastically since his promotion to the Guard.

'It would be nice if he performed at all!' she sneered. But she regretted the biting sarcasm almost immediately. Fronsac may have escaped from the hulk itself, but never quite from its effects. Besides, she needed to tell him about Lomballe and now felt as though she had lost the opportunity.

'If you're so worried about the kid,' her husband snapped, 'why don't you go check on her?'

'And you can keep an eye on those brats of mine,' said Argonne, 'while you're at it. Here, you want a pull?' He offered her the pipe, but she shook her head.

'If push comes to shove, Argonne,' she replied, 'I think those kids could look after themselves better than you sorry bunch!'

So they could too, whether it was foraging for food or firewood, helping with the laundry. And they knew everything, or seemed to. As though each batch of newborn arrived with a better measure of sense than the one before. Those that survived, of course.

Marianne counted her own losses. The girl stillborn. The boy with no roof to his mouth so he could not take her milk. *One out of three*, she thought. *I've been more unlucky than most!* But only just. In her experience there was little more than an even chance of campaign babies reaching Poppy's eight summers, and the odds not much better among the citizen population. But for the ordinary citizen there was this crumb of consolation, that they could keep their grief close, a marker in the local graveyard, while the army's infant dead warranted nothing more than the meagre mounds that marked their marches. From Moscow to Lisbon, Dunkirk to Cairo.

She picked her way around stacked muskets and knapsacks to the open chapel door, looked into the gloomy interior where the cloying stench of incense wrestled with the unwashed body odours of its occupants, their stamping feet carving out a battle beat of the familiar refrain.

'Ah, they will remember, la lira...'

Poppy's clog was keeping perfect time, her mucky little hands clapping less precisely. She had Marianne's own colouring, the same red-brown hair, grease-smeared, the same upturned pug nose.

What will become of you, little one? Marianne wondered, though the thought was almost redundant. Most of the army's working women were themselves daughters of others with the same professions. *But I should be thankful, I suppose, that you won't go for a soldier, as the boy would have done.*

The girl's gaze turned to the doorway and her dark eyes blazed, then dulled with doubt, for her mother's arrival was generally a harbinger of further chores to be done. Marianne beckoned to her, saw the dawning of defiance, repeated the gesture with greater vehemence.

'Now!' she mouthed, and the child obeyed, though not without sharing a conspiratorial shrug with Argonne's wife. The woman had been making mischief more or less continuously since the march began, and while it was true that Fronsac would have revenged Marianne if Lomballe had killed her, and while Fronsac and Argonne might be firm friends, it would have been Catherine Argonne – regardless of her missing leg – seeking the retribution if any harm befell Lomballe herself. The two women had been close, and there was nobody in the Battalion who resented Marianne's acquisition of the canteen commission more than Catherine.

'You were told to gather firewood,' Marianne snapped, catching Poppy's wrist and dragging her the final couple of paces through the door, for the girl had stopped to wave yet another farewell to Argonne's clutch of six. She reached down and used her sleeve to wipe a smear of snot from her daughter's upper lip before the evening's work began. Thirty minutes or so for Marianne to erect the canteen tent, with Fronsac providing assistance only when he could finally drag himself away from the dominoes and helping only to hammer home the guy ropes, while Poppy scooped out a fire pit, filled it with the driest kindling, sparked a small blaze, then fanned and fed its flames.

'You should have pitched on the other side,' grumbled Fronsac as he drove home the last peg.

'If I'd been here,' she replied, 'that's exactly what I would have done. But I was busy, as usual, and while you were enjoying yourself, that Spanish sow you fancy so much managed to rig her tent on the best spot.'

Juanita Bufanda was the Battalion's second and senior canteen-mistress – Marianne's competition in more ways than one. She was married to the Third Company's Corporal Cluny. At least, nominally married. But Bufanda had the morals of a village cat, which could be a dangerous trait. There were enough hazards for the army's women from the enemy – as Marianne had good cause to know – without making themselves easy prey among their own men. But, like the rest of them, Juanita had her own reasons for being with the Eagles.

There were four women in the Battalion, the number strictly prescribed by the War Ministry. Marianne and Juanita Bufanda served as canteen-mistresses, while Catherine Argonne and the heavily pregnant Breton girl, a mulatta, Suzanne Prairial, were officially listed as Sutler-Laundresses. On paper it was an ideal complement, though in practice the services they provided were hardly so clear-cut.

'It's the soup that makes the soldier!' Poppy beamed with each ladle of stew that she later slopped into the mess tins of their customers, queuing at the tent's entrance. It was a phrase that was a favourite of the Emperor, of course, but Poppy had adopted it as her own.

Marianne watched Fronsac approach the girl.

'What about an extra ration for your old man?' she heard him whisper.

'Only if he pays for it, Florisette!' shouted Marianne. 'The bugger will eat away all our profits if you give him half a chance.'

Poppy looked uncertainly from her father to Marianne.

'I'd be better off eating with the boys from the mess,' snarled Fronsac.

'Be my guest,' Marianne replied, serving a glass of brandy to another fellow and unburdening him by the sum of two sous. Like every man, Fronsac had nine sous deducted from his pay each week towards the collective pool of money that allowed the eight soldiers of his mess to draw their daily meat, bread, rice and beans ration and turn them into some semblance of food. But, as Marianne's husband, he also enjoyed the great fortune to benefit instead from the normally superior meals cooked up by the canteen-mistress at one franc, ten sous a throw, bread and drink included. Yet her rules for Fronsac were clear. One free portion only. If he wanted more, he bloody-well paid for it like everybody else. 'You choose,' she continued. 'But if you prefer it, go and eat those slops that pass for cooking with your messmates. Either that or you could always break into whatever little luxuries your knapsack holds. When Marianne Tambour is around, Fronsac, even the Little Shaveling pays his way.'

Fronsac grimaced at the very thought of the emergency rations, the dried horseflesh and hard biscuit buried deep in his pack.

'Oh,' he said, 'I suppose you've been chatting with the Emperor while you were out and about.'

She smiled to herself.

Perhaps I'll tell him afterwards, she thought, *when things have settled down a bit. And about Lomballe too.*

But the pots and pans were no sooner scrubbed and stowed than Assembly was beaten by the drum corps, the Battalion's five hundred and fifteen souls gathered tight together around their supply wagons with the unit's major, old Beltaine, at their head – though he did not address them directly. There were captain-adjutants for that, those with the loudest voices, and this one was balancing on a tailboard.

'Soldiers of the Second Battalion,' he roared, 'be silent and heed these Orders of the Day, delivered at the Imperial Headquarters, Avesnes, on this Fourteenth Day of June by Napoleon, by the Grace of God...' Marianne, like many others who had renounced the Church, spat upon the ground as she always did at this point, while the Captain-Adjutant continued, '...and by the Constitution of the Empire, Emperor of the French.'

There was cheering, shouts of 'Long live the Emperor! 'And when silence was restored, the officer began to read the Shaveling's own words. The crowd pressed forward even more, the rancid smells of sweat and garlic, tobacco and damp wool washing around her until Marianne could no longer see the officer for the shoulders that bunched above her. But she could still hear him well enough.

'"Soldiers! This day is the anniversary of Marengo and Friedland, which twice decided the destiny of Europe. Then, as after Austerlitz, as after Wagram, we were too generous! We believed in the protestations and in the oaths of princes, whom we left on their thrones."'

'Better to have taken their heads,' Marianne muttered. *And I was at both those bloodbaths*, she recalled. Just eleven years old at Marengo, helping carry water to the soldiers of the Revolution as they liberated the Italian states from the Austrian yoke, Bonaparte so recently established as First Consul in the Year VIII, by the Revolution's calendar. And the 22nd had earned its first battle honour there. Friedland was seven summers later, of course, though Marianne was still serving her apprenticeship with Maman Cholet then. Friedland. Preceded by a hacking and burning campaign through East Prussia, their Division's mauling at Heilsberg that left them looking more like beggars than conquering heroes. But a mauling that also left 20,000 Russians dead or wounded on the field – 20,000 that would be not available to their enemies for the decisive battle at Friedland itself a few days later.

'"Now, however,"' said the Captain-Adjutant, '"leagued together, they aim at the independence and sacred rights of France. They have commenced the most unjust aggressions. Let us, then, march to meet them. Are they and we no longer the same men? Soldiers! At Jena, against these same Prussians, now so arrogant, you were one to three, and at Montmirail one to six!"'

Marianne touched Fronsac's arm. He was standing just ahead of her.

'We missed Jena,' she said.

'But not Montmirail,' he growled, craning his head so he could see her. 'You should have brought a crate!' Fronsac winked at her. Montmirail had been his finest hour. A hell of a fight – though she doubted the odds were ever actually one to six. And was it only last year? But yes, it was. Their backs to the wall. Or, rather, their backs to Paris. Four battles in six days, and the Emperor won every one of them. *And then his bloody generals lost their nerve*, she thought. *Well, we haven't got our back to the wall any more. And what we could do then, we can do now as well!* It was not that she felt contempt for the Prussians. They were decent enough fighters in their way. But, having beaten them so many times in the past, she resented the fact that they should be back here again, once more threatening the precious soil of France. It was almost a personal insult.

The officer was still reading.

'"Let those among you who have been captive to the English, describe the nature of their prison-ships, and the frightful miseries they endured."'

She pushed Fronsac in the back.

'Go on,' she said. 'You heard him. Describe them.'

After East Prussia they had marched to Spain. And what a bitch of a march that was! Then all the horrors of the Peninsula and badly led in the bargain, with the Emperor back on the Danube. But there was this triple blessing at least. First, that one of the regimental laundresses was taken by the damned Spanish. *No blessing for that poor girl herself, of course*, thought Marianne, whose nightmares still featured images of those tortured remains alongside visions of Maman Cholet's wicked death, both high in a lifetime's catalogue of horrors. But the awful death left a vacancy, and Marianne would have been a fool to miss the opportunity. Fronsac had shown a respectful interest in her for some time, seemed almost like an old man to her though he was barely thirty. So she married him, picked up the vacant commission as her dowry, worked her fingers raw with mending and scrubbing, pooling her pay with the Cholets.

Poppy was the third of her blessings, naturally, though it may not have appeared so at the time, assumed a different significance once her fortunes changed for the worse. It was march and counter-march. Burning summers and biting winters. Bad food and illness. More pregnancies, each a miracle in itself given the rarity of her bleeding, the first child delivered dead from her womb, the second unable to feed. And then, in a minor skirmish with the Spanish army, Fronsac had been captured, disappeared. She had given him up for lost, but within a year he had returned. He had been sent to the stinking, disease-ridden hulks of Cádiz that both the Spaniards and the English used as prison ships. Tens of thousands of Frenchmen had died on hulks like those, either from neglect, or starvation, or disease. But Fronsac had escaped, helped to cut the ship's moorings and drifted her to the shore – though an English vessel fired on them without mercy and turned the hulk's decks into a shambles.

'Describe them?' said Fronsac. 'I wouldn't know where to start. But I owe those English pigs!'

And I owe them too, thought Marianne. *For Maman Cholet*. She might resent and hate the rest of their enemies, but the English, she believed, were beneath contempt.

'"Madmen!"' the Captain-Adjutant recited. '"One moment of prosperity has bewildered them. The oppression and the humiliation of the French people are beyond their power. If they enter France they will there find their grave."'

If she was honest, Marianne did not fully understand the first part of this reference. Who had been bewildered? she wondered. But a movement to her right also distracted her. It was almost nothing, but that sixth sense, which had always served her so well in the past, made her turn quickly, in time to see Lomballe's wicked face – scratched and bruised from the rock that Marianne had thrown – alongside that of Catherine Argonne, before each of them disappeared again within the forest of deep uniform blue. Marianne cursed. She was trapped here and bloody murder was just too easy in a crowd like this. She thought about Poppy, feared for her, instinctively began to press back in the direction of the cart and canteen tent, then realised that while she would put nothing past that wicked bitch Lomballe, Poppy would be safe so long as the Argonnes were around. They were her appointed Protectors, after all, the revolutionaries' alternative to godparents. And they took their duties seriously. So Marianne reversed her route, pushed instead towards the Battalion's front and their gathered officers.

'"Soldiers!"' the captain-adjutant was crying. '"We have forced marches to make, battles to fight, dangers to encounter; but, with firmness victory will be ours. The rights, the honour, and the happiness of the country will be recovered!"'

She forced her way through the press of male bodies, some of which yielded readily, allowed her through, while others resisted, hands pushing at her, snarling recriminations. But these were helpful too, for Marianne did not need to turn to know that she was pursued. There was almost an echo of her own passage in the wake that she left, the same angry voices repeating their curses only fathoms behind her. And she was angry herself. Angry that she had allowed Lomballe to choose the ground for a second time. Angry that, once more, she could not readily reach the *salvavirgo* hidden in her bodice. Angry that she had allowed herself to be caught like this.

Marianne was almost at the front, so close that she could now see the captain-adjutant easily, reading the Emperor's final message.

'"To every Frenchman who has a heart,"' the officer paused for dramatic effect, then ended with a flourishing roar, '"the moment has now arrived to conquer or to die."'

She was almost lifted bodily from her feet as the Battalion responded.

'For France!' they screamed.

'For Glory!'

'Long live the Emperor!'

And somewhere away to their right, the uproar was echoed as another battalion received the Order of the Day in similar fashion. Then another. And another. Until all the fields around Beaumont, and the town itself, was tear-filled with it.

Marianne burst out, at last, into relatively open ground, the few feet of limited respect that separated the Grenadiers from their officers. She turned then to face her attacker. *Let her dare now*, she thought, and loosened the remaining buttons of her russet jacket, felt inside to finger the handle of the deadly dagger.

'Long live the Emperor!' she yelled, and lifted her bonnet, waving it in the air. An invitation. A challenge. Until, suddenly, she found herself hauled into the air. There was a moment of panic as she reached in vain for the knife, dropped the bonnet, turned her head, looked up into the grinning faces of the captain-adjutant and a lieutenant as they dragged her up beside them onto the wagon. She laughed, turned back to the uniforms, the faces, the shirtsleeves below her, scanning their ranks until, finally, she saw Lomballe. It had been a close thing, she realised, as the woman mouthed some twisted profanity at her, then slipped backwards and was gone from her sight.

'Conquer or die!' yelled Marianne Tambour.

Chapter Four

Thursday 15th June 1815, 1.00am

'Wake up, woman, for pity's sake!' Fronsac was saying. He seemed to be shouting it loudly, from far above her, but as she heaved herself from this pit of dreams, she realised that it was merely a whisper, and that he was shaking her shoulder. She shrugged herself free of his grip, pulled the blanket closer around her shoulders, barely awake, still sobbing but Poppy at least tucked safely within her arms.

'That bitch Lomballe tried to kill me,' she said.

'Just a bad dream,' he replied. 'Go back to sleep.'

She almost smiled. *In the morning*, she thought, *I must tell him*. But Marianne was still in that limbo between slumber and wakefulness, afraid to return to the nightmare that hid waiting for her in the blackness, not Lomballe, but Saint-Sébastien. So she played through the things that she must do before first light, half-listening to the sounds of an army at night, never fully dormant. The restless groaning. The gagging snores. The farts. The belches. The lice-scratching. The murmured conversations of those that sleep evaded. The more distant whicker of a horse, or hoot of owl. The comforting crackle of the cook fire's embers that still lived just outside the canteen tent flap.

She slipped back into slumber in the usual way, a slow blurring of the edges between present, past and future. For, suddenly, there were drummers with their hands ablaze, the beat chaotic, hammering out some folk dance that Marianne had learned in her youth, though the rhythm was now impossibly fast. And then Marianne was performing the steps herself, standing on top of a drum, at the Veterans' Hospital in Paris, at the Invalides.

Or maybe it was Salamanca, for there was an English soldier cavorting around the place, waving a pole that bore one of the precious Eagles. The same that was taken from the 22nd during the battle, she imagined, though thankfully not the Eagle that belonged to her own battalion. But the drummers and the dancers all shared the disgrace of its loss. And, oh, the ignominy of losing it to the English!

She stopped dancing, began to sob, for she did not want to think about the English. They had no place here, did they? There was always something fearful that followed behind them. Marianne looked down at her arms, at the wrists, scratched and bleeding. But Poppy was there, rubbing a salve into the wounds. A younger Poppy, who smelled of late summer afternoons and mown hay.

'How old are you child?' asked Marianne, feeling guilty that a mother might not know the age of her own daughter.

'Five, Maman,' Poppy replied, stretching the nostrils of her pug nose.

Marianne placed a hand on the girl's head.

'That's a dangerous age,' she said.

The Emperor stood in Poppy's place, though Marianne's hand was still upon his head.

'You think that I'm too old for this?' he asked. 'I hate becoming old.'

'Growing old is something to relish, Sire,' she replied. 'It is a privilege denied to so many in our army.'

Bonaparte held her two lost babies in his arms for a moment.

'Like these?' he asked.

'These, or a thousand young men that I have known by name,' said Marianne, and the babes were gone. The Little Shaveling was offering her a sip of brandy from the cask slung across his imperial shoulder.

'This is the best dog-dog I've tasted all week,' she smiled at him.

Poppy was back.

'Why is it called dog-dog, Maman?' she asked. It was their favourite game on the march, inventing reasons for the liquor's nickname.

'We must wash your hair, young lady,' said Marianne. 'Try to get some of that grease out!'

'Ready for the battles, Maman?'

'Ready for the battles.'

And she was flying, with Poppy at her side, gripping tight to her fingers so she might not fall. They were following the stars southward, above carpets of blackened land, across the snow-peak barrier of the Pyrenees to the plains of Léon. To a small mound where she had left the stillborn. And then there was a walled town, with clover sprouting from the fields around its outskirts, and blind harpers playing maudlin melodies.

'For the Irishmen?' asked Poppy.

'There!' Marianne replied, and pointed to the breach they had made in Astorga's fortifications. The breach was filled again, with the same wild young men of the Emperor's Irish Legion who had perished in their forlorn hope to take the thing. Though they seemed happy enough now, despite the music's melancholy.

Marianne searched for the boy child here, for she had hidden him safely beneath some of Astorga's stones. But he was nowhere to be seen.

'They were good to me, the Irishmen,' said Poppy, and her voice choked, tears scraping thin tracks down her cheeks.

'Yes,' said Marianne. 'Good boys!' And she took Poppy's hand again, sailed with her on a gathering breeze, up and over the Guareña River, across the battlefields of Castrillo and Salamanca itself. But she did not wish to go further. She refused to go further, struggled to fly higher, seeking the light, then realised that they were pursued. Lomballe, mounted on a grotesque black cat. Leading a whole legion of harpies. Marianne turned and twisted, fear clawing at her guts.

'Maman!' screamed the girl. 'Don't let me fall!'

Yet Marianne could not help it, felt the small fingers slipping from her grasp, knew that she would lose her in this place as she had lost her once before. In that chaos about which none should have to speak, the horror that nobody should have to visit a second time.

'Mami!' The child's breath was hot in her nostrils as Marianne struggled to ascertain whether she still slept or had returned to the real world. Though that was not quite how she thought of it. More like a return to the present. For she knew that these journeys she made were more than simple dreams. They were too real. Yet, whatever they might be, it was plain that she was now in the canteen tent. A simple proof. Because the kid's breath never smelled so bad in her imagination as it did in the weft of a waking night.

'What is it?' Marianne sat up suddenly, responding to the urgency in Poppy's voice.

'You were squashing me,' said the girl. 'And making noises.' She pushed herself free of her mother's arms and rolled over, snorting straight back into sleep.

But Marianne had no desire to follow her. She knew what happened next and would avoid it. For tonight, at least. So she fumbled quietly for a candle stub, her flint and tinder box, her sewing kit, wriggled to the tent flap and, by the spluttering tallow-light, stitched a couple of spare buttons back upon her jacket until, inevitably, the needle slipped from her fingers and her chin slumped upon her chest.

She found herself in Saint-Sébastien's main square, in happier days. A carnival atmosphere. A bull fight in progress and Marianne hovering above the action, while the townsfolk pushed and jostled in the makeshift *tendido*, behind timber barricades that lined the square's arched cloisters, or sipped wine in the Town Hall's *grada* seats and presidential box, or hung from the windows rising above every side, each window permanently numbered and the rooms hired by the day to provide the *andanada* grandstands.

Then silence, the wind rising again, the beasts all gone and the *Plaza Mayor* deserted except for a rapidly drifting spectre of smoke and dust, the nauseous vibrations of a bombardment begun afresh. There was nothing here except an abandoned light field piece and all its accoutrements – drag ropes, handspikes, sponge-rammer, bucket, wormer, a wooden case of firing tubes, priming iron and port-fire. That was all. Yet Marianne searched here all the same, trembling with fear and uncertain of the thing she sought, weaving in and out of the archways, past shuttered bodegas and out into the narrow streets, away from the cannon and mortars that not only pounded the rampart walls but also dropped their ruin within the town, tearing at the thin fabric of its dwellings to reveal their nakedness, their internal intimacies.

There were churches, packed with those who sought salvation. The *manolos* and their women, sackcloth poor even by the standards of Parisian slums, three thousand of them foolish enough to have stayed when they had been given the chance to leave. So they slept on the streets now, as far from the attack as they could manage, huddled in the northern quarter with all the poor possessions they could carry, a convenient though unwitting service to the looters who would come behind the flames. And somewhere here was the thing Marianne had lost.

Too late! She could hear them at the breach, though she had hoped that this time the English would not break through. And perhaps they would not. For she hung above them as they climbed the fausse-braye with their backs to the Urumea, then up the scarp and the curtain face, wave after wave, and each wave ploughed into the ground by the churning fire from front and flank, until at last they reached their summit – to find a yawning chasm at their feet and further progress barred, retreat a suicide. So they cowered, pinned among their cluttered dead within the meagre cover of the collapsed wall, the attack stalled, each survivor curled like a foetus behind stone or timber beam.

Perhaps there will be time, thought Marianne, *to search again*.

She floated high, back across the battlements where General Rey's meagre garrison poured lead upon their enemies. And there she saw Maman Cholet.

'You cannot stay here!' Marianne pleaded, panic and guilt seizing her.

'Where else should I be?' Cholet replied, a sympathetic smile playing on her lips and in her eyes. She was serving water to men of their battalion who queued for the kindness, and Marianne recognised each of them in the line – though surely these were lads who had died elsewhere.

'I have misplaced something,' she said, and a section of the curtain wall's crenellation exploded in shards of stone and steel that swept away a score of defenders, smearing them across the rooftops behind.

'Look!' said Maman Cholet, 'the devils are firing over the heads of their own men.'

It was a risky strategy for the English, since the many shells that fell short would kill those still sheltered within the rubble of the breach.

'Then come away, Maman,' cried Marianne.

And there was Poppy, laughing at Cholet's side, the wind blowing her hair, holding up a sprig of jasmine.

'Where have you been, girl?' Marianne demanded. 'I've been searching for you.'

The ramparts ran with blood now, crumbling section by section, until all resistance from the French fell away, leaving only the two women and the child, as the English below negotiated their way down the steep drop and swarmed up, forcing openings into the town – the town that was now blazing from the bombardment. And, further north, the Portuguese had succeeded in crossing the estuary in force at low tide, taken advantage of a smaller breach in the walls, while the wind that rattled tiles, that fanned flames, carried Marianne, Cholet and Poppy swirling through the streets like tossed leaves as house after house was consumed, eaten by fire, the defenders fighting desperate rear-guard actions towards the *Plaza Mayor.*

French soldiers, most of them wounded, struggled through those same burning alleys and lanes, flinched and stared wildly about them, confused, as a second bombardment began. But this was a different thunder, heavy storm clouds blowing in from the bay, bringing false night, creased by sheets of lighting, drenched with squalls of rain, though it did not seem to trouble the drummers. They were here again, their hands still ablaze yet now with bandage and wads of linen waste with which to pack the wanderers' wounds.

'I must help,' said Marianne, though she knew that this was the very thing she should avoid. Her daughter and Maman Cholet looked at her with misplaced trust while distant drums and bugles sounded Retreat.

'They're falling back to La Mota,' said the regimental assistant-surgeon, Mongé, his shirtsleeves rolled as he splinted a shattered leg, supervised the application of a tourniquet, rain pouring in rivulets down each lens of his spectacles. 'Can you help with that one?' He pointed to a youngster, propped against a wall, his right heel blown away.'

Marianne sent Poppy for a bandage from Mongé's drummer boys, began to examine the wound, pouring water to wash away some of the filth, heard screaming in a foreign tongue, not the babble of the *manolos* but English, she thought. Guttural. Harsh. She tried to find the source as she applied a pad of charpie to the gaping wound, secured it above and below, around the foot, though the young soldier seemed barely to notice as she helped him to the handcart serving here as Mongé's flying ambulance.

'Time to go!' the assistant-surgeon was shouting.

'There are English prisoners?' yelled Marianne.

'Around the corner,' said Mongé, 'in the old convent. And to hell with them!'

'They are burning,' Marianne told him.

'How do you know?'

'I always know,' she said, and they were outside the convent's abandoned wing that served as a prison for the English and Portuguese captured earlier in the siege. Smoke billowed from the upper windows and flames gnawed away at roof timbers, licking from beneath the roof tiles until a triumphant, demonic roar, showers of spark and burning clay, told them that a section had collapsed inwards. The prisoners on the lower floors screamed louder and a hundred arms stretched through the ornate window grilles, fingers clawing for purchase at the heat-laden air outside.

Mongé moved quickly to two French soldiers sprawled in the lane, checked in vain for signs of life with the first, lifted keys from the guard's belt and handed them to one of the drummers.

'Here,' he said. 'Let them out, if we must. These fellows must have been hit by the same blast that fired the roof. But hurry!' He moved to the second sentry, who seemed to be clinging to a cobble, his last purchase on life. 'This one's still alive. Bring the cart.'

Marianne and Poppy helped to wheel the handcart closer, collected the men's muskets, while Maman Cholet ran with the drummer boy, took the heavy key ring from him when he fumbled at the lock.

'They may be pigs,' she shouted, 'but we can't let them roast to death!'

And she disappeared inside. Moments later, while Marianne was lifting the unconscious guard onto the ambulance, the prisoners began to pour out of the convent. Most of their uniforms, where they still wore any, were threadbare. Many showed the stomach-clenching, fouled nether garments and scabrous dry-lipped languor of dysentery sufferers, or the shivering fevered embrace of malaria, each of which had taken a greater toll of both armies than any battlefield injuries. Among them, Cholet and the drummer were helping to support a small man in the brown uniform of the light skirmishers that the Portuguese called *caçadores* – hunters, chasseurs. He was still alive, but barely, his face a bubbling mess of sizzling flesh and, as soon as they settled him on the ground, Maman Cholet looked quickly at the upper storey, snatched the keys and began to run back inside.

'No, Maman!' yelled Marianne, yet looking further down the street, where the first familiar signs of an army out of control were beginning to show themselves. Scarlet jackets, windows being smashed, yelling, *manolo* citizens dragged out of hiding places, officers yelling unheeded commands. She had seen it before, of course. From their own regiments in a dozen campaigns. Or the word of survivors after the surrender of Badajoz and the savagery of English reprisals. But Cholet was gone inside the prison once more, while batteries of French drums, bugle calls, beat and sounded the Retreat once more, urgently this time.

'Time to go!' said Assistant-Surgeon Mongé, and they gathered those they could, pushing the cart north towards the wooded bulk of Monte Orgull and the castle's sanctuary.

'How can a place burn like this in such rain?' murmured Marianne. But the answer was obvious, for the riotous looters, drawing closer now, could plainly be seen at work there, heaving furniture to stoke the flames, and the flames in turn fanned by the winds. Closer still, Maman Cholet emerged at last among a second group of released prisoners. Yet here was the thing that Marianne had feared in her demented dreaming, the reward for generosity of spirit, her misguided insistence on helping, on leading her family into even greater hazard. For Cholet was dragged from the convent by a redcoat. He wore the down-pointed triple chevrons of an English sergeant, yellow facings at his cuffs and collar. She thought at first that he was burned for the right side of his face was livid purple. But he showed no other evidence of being wounded, an arm tight around Maman Cholet's neck, using the woman as a shield and forcing her forward on the tips of her toes, pointing at Mongé's fleeing company and bellowing at his fellows, spittle flying from the black maw of his mouth.

'Maman Cholet!' Poppy cried, as her mother seized one of the muskets rescued from the sentries, fumbled with the lock, checked that it was primed, and dragged the hammer back to full-cock. The frizzen and pan seemed soaked but these Charlevilles were reliable enough in most weathers.

The English sergeant was almost upon them, yelling at her, choking Cholet with his forearm, and close enough for Marianne to see that it was no burn on his evil face but a birth mark, the size and shape of a cauliflower.

'Let her go!' Marianne screamed, not caring whether he understood her or not. But she dared not fire at the man. The others, cowering around him, were a better target, though she could only take one of them. And there was Poppy to think about. She moved back towards the cart, found the assistant-surgeon at her side, the second musket levelled at their pursuers. Yet it was still hopeless. 'Take care of my daughter,' she said to Mongé. 'Get her out of here.'

'They'll take you too,' he said.

'One or more of them will pay for the privilege,' Marianne replied, and she levelled the musket, aimed, fired.

A shirt-sleeved Englishman was thrown into the arms of a man behind and the pursuit faltered, the former prisoners all shouting now, their focus suddenly on their fallen friend. And Marianne snatched the opportunity to grab Mongé's gun.

'Get her away!' she told him again, as she cocked the Charleville. Though she never did fire the second shot. Instead, a whole volley ripped down the thoroughfare, carried away each of the Englishmen apart from the sergeant, who was now falling back very fast, while Marianne turned to see Fronsac and a few others pounding down the road towards them.

'Go and get her,' Marianne screamed.

'There's no use,' said Fronsac.

'Then take the girl,' she said, 'I'll fetch her myself.'

She left Poppy with Fronsac, began to follow.

'You can't!' shouted Mongé.

'No,' said Fronsac, 'he's right. You can't go down there. Show some sense for once.'

'Maman,' sobbed Poppy, 'don't let them take Cholet!'

'No,' said Marianne, 'I won't!' And she snatched a bandage from one of the boys, began wrapping it around and around her head, leaving only her eyes, quickly smearing dirt from the floor, blood from the dead Englishmen, across the linen.

Fronsac grabbed her arm.

'Don't be a bloody fool, woman!' he shouted into her face. 'She's gone.'

But Marianne pulled her arm away, ran back to the wounded Portugee who was still sprawled outside the convent door. He was bigger than her, but not by much, and though she struggled to get him out of his jacket – he tried feebly to resist, after all – she was soon running down the alley, buttoning the brown coat, looking always in the direction taken by the English sergeant, back towards the *Plaza Mayor*, through the growing throng of rabble who must pass for soldiers in Wellesley's army. Not patriots these, she thought, but the scum of England's streets, rolling puncheons of Spanish wine from every bar and bodega, the air stifling despite the continuing downpour.

And here were the first of the horrors. A girl not much older than Florisette, carved open from purple grey crotch to scarlet throat. An ancient *manolo* held helpless by each of his arms, weeping like a child while a soldier violated his black-garbed wife. Another woman dead, her throat slit, and the English using her body for a bed on which they humped a youngster, perhaps the woman's daughter. The men who had been shot, or hacked to pieces, when they had tried to defend their womenfolk. Mounds of bodies, the stink of blood, shit, burnt clothing and burnt bodies. Deafening noise, the drunken fury of these heroic victors, the screeching agony of their victims, the gut-wrenching groans of survivors. There were English officers here too, one of them also sobbing with frustration as he tried to pull his troops from their rapine. But, overall, it was a hell like none she had witnessed before. Something worse too. For she saw these creatures in their dotage, knew that many would look back on this day each time they tried shamefully to hold the gaze of their own wives and daughters, knew how different they would be at their homeland hearth, knew the genuine heroism – almost divine in nature – that could equally carry men like these, of any nation, through the most unbelievable adversities, like classical gods while, here, turned to satanic demons within their flames of Hades.

It was burning. All burning. Yet when she thought that she had witnessed the worst of the depravity, Marianne finally turned the corner into the main square itself, found Lomballe waiting for her. There was no logic in dreams, when all was said and done, so she took Marianne's hand like some helpful guide.

'Look,' said Lomballe. 'See my linen line.' Spectators were hanging from each of the numbered *andanada* windows once more, though every one of these was dangling from the end of a rope. 'My dirty laundry,' Lomballe smiled, a sweep of her arm taking in the further heaps of dead and dying, the acrid smoke, the screams and pleas for mercy. 'The offal and lights for our next stew...'

There was a priest, his head broken like a dropped watermelon, the grey sludge of his brains forming a halo around the shattered skull, his arms still enfolding the babes he had died trying to save.

'No more!' whispered Marianne. For she knew the rest, did she not? That this madness would last for days. That from the six hundred houses of Saint-Sébastien, no more than a few dozen would survive the conflagration. That from the three thousand Spanish souls who had elected to stay here, more than a third, and almost all of the women, would be butchered by this English rabble – which claimed to be the *allies* of Spain. That, ironically, with order finally restored, surrender of the fortress finally unavoidable, the French garrison would be permitted to march out with their honours flying high, their drums beating.

'But you were searching for Cholet,' Lomballe reminded her.

Marianne shook her head.

'I want to go now,' she said, though she knew it was not yet time.

There was the English sergeant again, laughing at her through rotting teeth, his face unmistakeable with the birthmark. There was the abandoned field piece, though its drag ropes now served other purposes around the *plaza*. There were the accoutrements, or some of them. And there was Cholet, spread-eagled over the gun's barrel. Defiled, naturally.

Does it matter, Marianne wondered, *how it happens? Or for how long the torment endures?*

It was a stupid question. For she had known women who had been raped and lived to tell the tale, who seemed able to build some semblance of normality again after the event. Never fully themselves, but the spark of their life still alight, either through hatred or an undeniable instinct for survival. A lesser spark, but a living spark still. Then there were the others, the irrevocably ruined that the deed would destroy, later if not sooner. And after these others, there was this...

Desolate screeching death.

For besides any other form of filth that the English – that English sergeant with the birthmark – may have practised upon her, the final violation had not been with brutal flesh, blood and semen but with other things. Things. Like the wad-screw, that artillerymen call a wormer, upon which Maman Cholet was still impaled.

Chapter Five

Thursday 15th June 1815, 5.30am

They beat the *tra-ta-tra* of the Diana at half-past five o'clock for the Grenadier battalions, though Marianne had already been awake for some hours by then, a score of cockerels crowing and the silent, ghostly spectre of a barn owl wheeling past her head through the mist and thin drizzle. The nightmare had disturbed her as it always did, left her confused and trembling as the first smudge of pale grey lightened the sky just after three, and she finally shrugged herself free of her blanket at four-thirty, careful not to disturb Poppy, when the Young Guard were roused in the front line of the bivouacs. She had re-kindled the cook fire, ignoring the order – as did everyone else – to mask the flames in hollow pits. For the clouds above had been stained orange all night, a clear beacon to mark their location for any enemies with eyes to see. So she had hung the camp kettles to boil by the time those junior units were on the road at five, just as the Diana was hammered out again, nearer now, to awaken the Guard's Foot Chasseurs.

It was a familiar pattern, this mobilisation and dispatch by Divisions at half-hourly intervals. Always a fine plan on paper. To get the army on the move with fluidity. A necessary thing when, as now, there were over a hundred battalions of infantry, the same number of cavalry squadrons, two hundred and fifty cannon, five hundred transport wagons – almost eighty thousand men in total – spread across a front of thirty kilometres. By the time their own Corps was fully on the march, they would be stretched out in a snaking line stretching almost twelve kilometres from end to end, just one of four or five such columns.

'What sort of cock-up will it be today?' said Suzanne Prairial, pausing to sniff at the thin soup, supporting her swollen belly with one hand, then holding up a batch of woollen socks with the other. 'Hey!' she shouted. 'You men who wanted socks darning, you'd better pay me if you want them back.' Her Breton accent was so thick that it was sometimes impossible to understand her. But they got the message this morning, as they rolled blankets, shivered in greatcoats, muttered that she was a mercenary bitch.

'The same as usual,' Marianne replied. 'One over-fed general or another will have missed the Diana completely, or misread the orders, or headed off on the wrong road. The normal bollocks. In a couple of hours we'll be bunched up, thousands of us, all trying to cross some bloody river at the same time. And you can bet that at least one of the pricks will have betrayed us by sunset.' She pointed with a ladle towards Prairial's awkward bulge. 'How long?'

'Worried you'll miss the big event?' the pregnant mulatta replied. 'I heard Lomballe was on the prowl again last night.'

Yes, thought Marianne, recalling the nightmare yet again. *In more ways than one.*

'Don't fret, Suzanne,' she laughed. 'I'll still be around to pull that little bastard of yours free. A boy too, from the way it's hanging.'

Prairial, handing out the darning and collecting a few centimes in return, swung towards the second canteen tent where Juanita Bufanda and Catherine Argonne, assisted by a nest of children, were slopping out gruel to those stupid enough to pay for it. It was some distance away, fifty fathoms or more, but Prairial's fish-wife bawl covered the gap comfortably.

'Hey, Catherine!' she bellowed, hooking a thumb towards Marianne. 'What d'you reckon? Will this one be around to see my babe born?'

Argonne used the single shaft of her crutch to deftly swing around that other cook pot, kept the padded crosspiece tight under her right armpit, but lifted the fingers to make a slicing gesture across her throat.

'No way!' Argonne shouted back.

Prairial suddenly lost her sense of humour.

'Don't do that,' she murmured. 'I think it's bad luck to wish somebody dead when the babe's so near.'

They were a superstitious bunch, these Bretons, thought Marianne. And Prairial was worse even than your average. *Probably the savage in her blood*, she imagined, though Prairial was barely darker than the rest of the weather-scoured women. Yet the mulatta had spent the entire march fervently praying that there should be no cannon-fire before the child was born lest the sudden noise should cause it disfigurement; or scared witless when a hare had jumped in front of them, certain that the incident would result in a deformity of the infant's lip; or avoiding direct eye contact with the moon in case madness, lunacy, might develop in her offspring; or curbing her desires, her cravings, for it was well-known that satisfying such pangs would surely set a witching mark somewhere upon the baby's body – and Prairial had been beset with the worst of longings at this time of year, for wild strawberries.

'Why doesn't Argonne use the wooden leg?' said Marianne, in an effort to distract her.

'It's her pension,' replied Prairial. 'She has to keep it safe.'

Marianne shook her head. She feared Catherine Argonne, but could not help admiring her. A ball had taken away her left leg below the knee and, some time later, she had been fitted with a wooden peg. Then she had applied for a pension, though the War Ministry had turned down the claim. Technically not a soldier, they had said. And her husband still alive, on full pay. Marianne had not actually seen the letter, of course, though legend had it that the War Ministry ended their missive with a recommendation that Argonne should be grateful for the stump. So the woman had simply decided to continue working.

'Look at her, leading the invasion,' Marianne murmured to her daughter three hours later as they watched from the roadside when Catherine Argonne, perched on the side of her noddy cart, crossed into Belgium by the border that was marked by more than a stream's trickle and the sudden flood of loyal tricolour flags flying from the scattered dwellings beyond. There was hierarchy and precedence even among this element of the army, and it was Juanita Bufanda – as senior canteen-mistress – who was more properly entitled to head this rear-most section of the Battalion. And they were always at the rear, naturally. Eating the unit's dust in summer, slogging through its sludge during the winter. Yet they had a motto of their own, Marianne and her like. The worse the weather, they would say, the better the business.

'She's my friend,' said Poppy, shifting on the sacks and casks of their own modest wagon.

'And a good one to have!' called Suzanne Prairial from the tailboard.

The mulatta might not like me, thought Marianne, *but she's not too proud to accept a lift now she's the size of a whale.*

'All the same,' she answered, 'Bufanda had no right to let her take the lead. And you're going to tell me what a bad enemy she makes too?'

All the goods and tools of Prairial's own trade were stacked on a dolly, hauled and goaded along by several of Argonne's lads, including the one they called Onion. Normally she would have hauled the handcart herself, but these past few days had been too much for her.

'No,' said Suzanne. 'I was only thinking about friends. That last time we marched through here, we had a better reception.'

'Aren't we still in France, Maman?' said Florisette.

'Well, it depends how you look at it,' said Marianne. With Argonne now safely ahead of them, she flicked the reins, clicked her tongue at Cocotte. The fly-bitten pony broke into a walk, set the goats to bleating as their tether to the back of the tumbrel began to tighten. 'This is Belgium. The Spanish had it once, they reckon. Then Austria. But we freed them. Made them part of France. Then, last year, the English Goddams plotted with the Dutch to make them part of some so-called United Netherlands. But from this moment, Poppy my love, these lands are safely French once more.'

'They're friends too then!' said Poppy.

Suzanne laughed.

'Short memories,' she said. 'Lots of them now pressed to fight for the English, they say. Though God alone knows what sort of soldiers they'll make!'

'So can we loot them or not?' asked the girl.

'Loot?' said Marianne. 'We don't loot, child. Though it's necessary to requisition from time to time.'

They crossed the border without incident or contact with the enemy, but as they made their slow way towards Thuin, still on one of the roads to Charleroi, rumours started to run down the column, most of it from a Regiment of the Line that had been re-routed and then forced off the lane to make way for the Guard, to salute them as they marched past, those salutes extended – though with some good-natured mockery – even to the women's carts.

'The road's safe, girls,' shouted a corporal. 'The Prussos' outposts were driven in hours ago. They've all turned tail for Charleroi.'

'We'll catch up with them there, then,' Marianne replied. 'No need to rush there yourselves, boys. The Guard will sort them out for you.'

The soldiers around the corporal laughed.

'That'll make a nice change,' he called. 'They're usually too busy keeping those pretty white stockings clean.'

'You're only jealous,' said Suzanne Prairial, her hands folded protectively over the dome of her stomach. 'You need a fair pair of legs to look good in those stockings.'

'What happened this morning then?' shouted another soldier. 'Were they up too late to get them smoothed?'

And then they were left behind, Marianne looking ahead, along the companies of the Guard's Grenadiers in their order of march, away into the distance, a regimental band playing *The Black Musketeers* while the men sang their own coarse words to the tune, and the sound of a Jingling Johnny carried back to her on a summer grass breeze. They might not have quite the polish of the Old Grumblers, and their headgear might include the occasional bicorne, shako or forage cap, the cotton stockings swapped for a market stall motley of campaign nankeens in grey or blue, but they were still an impressive bunch of buggers, she thought. The tallest men of the army, made taller yet by the high bearskin caps worn by many, resplendent and unique in their style of long-tailed coats, blue also, each man distinguished by his powdered pigtail, the gold ring in his ear. But these were no parade ground toy soldiers. They had fully earned their reputation as the most tenacious of Europe's fighters. And, by Marat's Ghost, Marianne was proud to be part of them!

She slipped from the cart, easing the pony's load for a while, walking at Cocotte's head.

'Well, old friend,' she whispered in its ear, 'there may be action today. Need to hold our nerve, eh?' She reached into her pocket. Time for a pipe of tobacco, maybe. But the stem was snapped, and too close to the bowl to still be useful. She cursed. It must have been broken during the night. *And I need to watch for Lomballe too*, she thought, but privately hoping the woman might have given up the chase by now, the ardour gone from her thirst for revenge. Marianne moved the cask strap on her shoulder, settled it more comfortably, then realised that it kept whispering the same leathered words to her with each step, breaking the silence once, and then a thousand times. It was always this way on the march, when the conversations dried up, when the singing stopped. Just the quiet creak and babble of the equipment. *English*, she thought it said. *English, English, English.* Over and over, maddening her. Yet she hoped it was a promise. She had respect for the Prussians, though she was convinced they would be beaten easily enough. But she had none for the English. And it was with the English that they had the most scores to settle.

'Well, you were right about this at least,' said Suzanne Prairial, waddling from one side of the cart to the other. They were selling water, slices of smoked meat, to those among the Battalion who would pay their price.

They had been here for two hours, and many of the other units much longer even than that. Yet there was good news and there was bad. For the latter, Marianne's prediction had been entirely accurate, since several of the columns had arrived at these wooded slopes south of the Sambre at the same time – and there was only one bridge that crossed the river from the scattered houses of the southern suburbs into Charleroi itself. Worse, the Prussos had thrown up a stout barricade across the further side and fortified the houses just behind, as well as some remnant of the old walls.

'But the fools have left the bridge itself intact,' said Marianne. This was the good news, though it seemed inconceivable to even the greenest private soldier.

'They're still holding us up though,' said the mulatta. She placed her hands on the small of her own back, rubbed at it to provide some relief.

'Not for long,' Marianne smiled. 'And it could have been a damn sight worse!'

Indeed it could. It seemed a lunacy to her that the army had not crossed in several different locations, outflanked and surrounded the enemy. Yet, on the other hand, with the French all trapped here together on the southern bank, it would have been equally easy for the Prussians and the English to trap them with a pincer movement. It was not as though their manoeuvres had gone without notice, and there had been a succession of spectators on the farther bank of the Sambre, mostly to the west, beyond its many meanders and tributary junction. The strangest of them had been a tall rider in a tattered green tunic and sporting a brown tricorne hat who sat watching them through a telescope, a large dog at his side, until a troop of Dragoons appeared to chase them away while here, on the French side, swallows danced and darted for their own prey. But, as things stood, there was no sign of Wellesley and the bridge remained in one piece.

'Why don't they attack?' asked Prairial, pointing to the flat ground where squadrons of Hussars were taking their ease, horses cropping at the grass and the troopers themselves lounging around, smoking their pipes, as though this were some Sunday outing in the Bois de Bologne.

'Not a job for those pretty boys,' snarled Corporal Cluny – Bufanda's man, an ugly brute with a scar running the length of his face. From a Russian sabre cut at Borodino, he claimed. 'And our precious leaders will be drawing lots for which of us lucky sods gets the honour of leading the attack.'

He nodded towards the dark blue dormeuse carriage that stood on the road to the right of their ranks. The Little Shaveling himself had ridden up on his favourite horse earlier, at the head of a growing entourage, and almost immediately received a succession of increasingly agitated gallopers. Significant news it seemed, for when the dormeuse finally arrived, the Emperor had entered the vehicle with his most senior staff and had not been seen since.

'No?' said Marianne. 'I think you're wrong. I told Prairial earlier that some prick of a general will have deserted us.'

'Yes, of course,' replied the corporal. 'Like you'd know.'

But within ten minutes she was proved correct in this prediction also. At least, so far as the latest gossip ran. A couple of line regiments were moving towards the right wing where, it was said, General Bourmont had gone over to the Prussos. Threw away the tricolour cockade from his hat, they reckoned, and set the Bourbon white in its place. *And will have taken the Emperor's battle plans with him no doubt*, thought Marianne Tambour.

'Bastard officers!' said Fronsac, loudly enough for their own lieutenant to hear. 'Can't trust any of them.'

'Those lads are almost as pretty as the Hussars!' laughed Fronsac, pointing down the hill towards the bridge. It was true. Even in their campaign dress, the Marines of the Guard were a colourful bunch, blue trousers and blue tunics, these decorated with yellow facings that matched the cords and reinforcing bands of their shakos. 'And it makes sense to use them, I suppose. There's a bridge. And under the bridge, a river. Rivers mean water. So who else but the Marines to clear the way for us?'

But the companies of Marines were not alone in the task, for they were flanked by the Guard's helmet-clad Engineers, more than a hundred of them. And the Emperor himself had emerged from his carriage to watch the operation.

'I'll never take the piss out of those boys ever again,' grumbled Cluny. 'You should have seen them at the Berezina. It was Eblé's Bridge Builders and the Sappers that saved us. Trapped, we were, with the Russians at our backs and the bridges home all collapsed. But those poor sods got in the river up to their necks. The end of November. Loads of them just froze to death. Or got their heads caved in by great blocks of floating ice. But they got the pontoons built so we could get across. Say what you like about generals, but don't let me ever hear a bad word about Eblé. He's a diamond, he is. Him and his bloody Sappers.'

'But these are our own lads, aren't they?' said Fronsac. 'Not Eblé's men.'

'Makes no difference to me,' growled Cluny. 'No bloody difference at all. Sappers. Engineers. Bridge Builders. Great lads, that's all I'm saying.'

'There's no arguing with that, I suppose,' murmured Fronsac, and he winked at Marianne.

The Marines were approaching the Sambre in two files, one on each side of the road, using the ditches, the cottages and a slight embankment to shield them from the worst of the enemy's fire, though Marianne could see them fall, one here, another there. To their rear, the companies of Engineers stood in their ranks, tough fellows, brass helmets with high black combs, enormous axes as well as their slung muskets. Harsh brutes to a man, she knew. And they were taking casualties too, stoically, dispassionately, until the Marines had reached the bridge's parapets. After that it was simply routine. They laid a murderous fire that forced the enemy back, allowing the Engineers to march in support, a slow and deliberate menace that would have kicked any remaining fight from the foe.

'Why don't the Prussos support their own men?' said Marianne, stupefied that there were no more infantry here to oppose them, no artillery, no cavalry.

'The bastards will be waiting for us to get stuck on the bridge,' said Cluny. 'Half of us on this bank, half over there. Then they'll bring up the big guns. Fight us house to house.'

Marianne could taste the tension here. She saw the Little Shaveling gesture towards the waiting Hussars, and there were trumpet calls, horses snorting in anticipation, their troopers mounting, sergeants harrying squadrons into formation. On the bridge, the Engineers were hard at work, hacking through ropes and timber beams that held the barricade together, pitching wagon beds, wheels, pillaged furniture and filled gabions into the Sambre while the Prussians took off in full flight up the steep street beyond.

Bonaparte was sprawled on a chair, one leg stretched out and his left hand resting upon a small table outside the forge of Puissant the Blacksmith on the rue de la Neuve-Église in this lower suburb of Charleroi, not far from the recently captured bridge and across from the decayed ramparts of the old walls. There was barely a window here that had failed to fly the red, white and blue of the Revolution. Of liberation. Wildflowers strewn upon the road.

'Somebody said he's eating the breakfast that old Puissant was going to serve the Prussos' general,' said Prairial.

'No way!' Marianne snapped. 'You won't catch the Shaveling making do with sauerkraut and greasy sausage. German pigs!'

'Oh please, don't,' Prairial replied, her face become a shade paler. 'I feel bad enough already. It's so hot.'

She's sweating like a pig herself, thought Marianne, remembering the discomfort of her own pregnancies, especially in these final days. And she was thankful that Prairial had made clear her desire for Argonne to help with the birth, for she no more enjoyed the agonies of others' labour than she had the racking torture of her own. All the expectation that, despite the pain, there may be no child at the end of it.

Marianne pushed the thoughts aside, watched as, from time to time, the Emperor would turn from the Marshals at his left shoulder, his attention caught by one unit or another as they marched past, shouting a greeting to this fellow or that as he recognised old comrades-in-arms. His honour guard of Horse Chasseurs stood rigidly on each side while, on this nearer edge of the small square, a company of the Old Guard's Grenadiers stood equally rigidly to attention. Marianne's own battalion was already assembled up in the Place Charles Deuxième, but she had taken the opportunity of coming back down, through the narrow celebrating streets, to follow up a rumour that there might be a cache of tobacco stashed away in one of the shops. Besides, it was hard to resist watching the Shaveling when he performed his magic with a crowd – and there was certainly a crowd here, gathered in hundreds to catch a glimpse of the legend, to bestow bouquets and garlands, to chant obscenities about the detested Prussians, and pressed back by a cordon of Gendarmes, the military's policemen, so that the advancing army could at least make some progress.

But the crowd was so packed behind this cordon that there was no chance of conducting any business here, and Marianne was about to tell Prairial they would give up, try again later, when she seemed to experience one of those unworldly frozen moments that often dogged her life. For she imagined she was looking at herself on the opposite side of the road. There was a tightness in her chest, a lightness at her brow, as though she might faint. And several baited heartbeats passed before reality dawned upon her, that the woman she could see may have worn a similar russet jacket to Marianne's own, the bonnet might be familiar, a clay pipe gripped between the teeth, but the face belonged to another woman entirely, older than Tambour and with the features of a weather-blown hawk, eyes fixed on the Emperor. Or, rather, on the Emperor's carriage, his dormeuse, its rear wheels protruding from a coaching yard attached to the smithy.

'Look,' said Prairial, in her ear, 'isn't that...?'

Marianne needed no more than the briefest glance to weigh the situation. Hawk-face had her face turned, would not have understood the danger in any case for, behind her, and insinuating her way through the noisy throng was Lomballe, a livid bruise on her cheek, right arm across her chest and the fist tucked tight below her left armpit. And Marianne had no doubt about the thing that Lomballe gripped there.

I could wait, she thought, *and watch Hawk-face die, hope that the Gendarmes might pick up that bitch Lomballe*. But she knew there was little chance of that happening and, in a split second, she had begun to press between the townsfolk, edging to the right, away from any possibility that Lomballe might notice her, realise she was stalking the wrong prey.

Marianne's own hand was loosening the jacket buttons, reaching inside to her bodice and the *salvavirgo*, a firm grip on the wire-wrapped wooden hilt but keeping it hidden. The best killers, she knew, kept their weapons concealed until the last possible moment. *You don't use a weapon to fight*, she remembered. *You use it to win*. And there was little defence against a determined attacker who simply moved straight in with no aim except one – to gut their target as quickly and efficiently as possible. She had seen some fancy handiwork in her day, those *navajeros* from Sevilla and Málaga with all their sly deception. And she had seen them gurgling on their own blood at the hands of a simple brawler who declined to play the game by its rules, who moved in quickly, grappled them to the ground and finished the thing.

She kept her head low, risking a look only rarely to get her bearings, to time her crossing of the road just ahead of some drummers as they beat the March. She swung the brandy cask from her side so that it sat more comfortably in the small of her back, then slipped easily through the cordon of the Gendermarie, into the second mass of spectators. There was singing here, the strongest smells of onion and cheese, sweat and fire smoke, but it was easier to pick a path to the rear, veering towards the direction in which Lomballe had been moving.

'Make way, citizen,' she growled. 'Give way there, Jacques.'

And the crowd parted before her as though she had the plague mark. That was good. For it was the ability to move that usually determined the outcome of a knife encounter. If she were lucky, she would come up behind Lomballe with enough time and space to slash her tendons, hamstring her, cut her enough so she would bleed plenty, let her bleed out. After all, and above all, you just needed to be a survivor. To do what it took. For yourself. For your daughter. Whatever made you want to stay alive. And the harder your life, the more you learned the skills to survive it. She just hoped, by the Host, that her own life had been harder than Lomballe's.

Marianne was behind her now, a couple of fathoms, no more, silent and camouflaged by the noise of those around her. She could see the back of Hawk-face's bonnet too, the head turning slightly, something about the dormeuse that fascinated her. *Why the carriage?* wondered Marianne Tambour, the gap between herself and Lomballe closed to a single fathom, no more than a *toise*. Her sabre grip tightened on the knife handle and she began to slip it clear of her breast, to stoop a little, to close behind Lomballe's legs. Then she saw the bitch stiffen.

Tambour straightened, saw that Hawk-face had turned, that Lomballe realised her mistake, her own survival instincts racing to deal with this reversal, forcing her to check for the danger that she seemed to sense may threaten her instead. There was a flash of surprise as Marianne's eyes met those of Hawk-face, then Lomballe was spinning around, trying to move back, to make her own space in the crowd, the long blade lifting towards her foe. But the chastity knife was already in play and there was no time for anything else now.

Marianne stepped inside the swinging arm, caught the free hand that Lomballe lifted to ward off any incoming strike, swept the hand aside and pushed the wicked steel hard into the bitch's neck, twisting it sideways as they both fell.

Chapter Six

Thursday 15th June 1815, 12.30pm

Liberté Dumont grabbed for the leather belt of the woman's tricolour-painted brandy barrel, wishing that she could take a tot right now, dragging her upright. But that first contact sent a jolt through Liberté's arm, much worse than the one she had received from the electrical generator on show at the Natural History Museum in the Jardin des Plantes, a bone-jarring jolt like those she experienced when linking her soul to the spirit records. At the same time, her mind was filled by strange and terrible images that, she was sure, emanated from this woman's deepest nightmares.

'We have to move!' she yelled. 'For the love of Our Lady, the Gendarmes...'

And not the Gendarmes alone. There had been screams among the crowd, space opening around them as the citizens of Charleroi distanced themselves from the blood, eyes turned from the marching column, the Emperor's honour guard called to the alert.

'My knife!' snarled the woman.

'To hell with your knife.' Dumont seized the collar of the killer's coat, realised that it was almost the twin of her own. Who was this? There was something familiar. A face not unlike her own. Plain enough. Hard. The hair neither red nor brown but somewhere between, straight and grease-smeared. The nose and features small, more stubbornly rounded. Handsome enough, Liberté supposed, beneath the grime. But where had she seen her? There could be no doubt that she must be another of Fouché's agents though in all the time she had served him she had never been face to face with one of them – at least, not so far as she knew. She pushed the woman through the townsfolk, out into one of the alleys that led from the Rue des Remparts.

'Let go of me,' the knifer hissed, shook herself from Liberté's grip. 'And leave me alone. Get back to whatever business brought you here.'

'Not until you tell me who she was.'

'Who? That bitch Lomballe? This isn't the best place to gossip, lady.'

And she was right. A man was shouting from the lower end of the lane, pointing up at the two women. Then the rattle of boot studs sparking on cobbles as a pair of Gendarmes rounded the corner, bounded up the steps towards them. But by the time Liberté looked back, her saviour was gone. An open doorway across the alley, the clatter of a clumsy fugitive within the dark interior. Dumont followed, plunged into the building, ignored a gloomy and noxious staircase, felt her way along the mildewed passage. A courtyard. A second hallway. A maze of even narrower streets, lined with huddled cottages, and Dumont chose the thoroughfare that ran, more or less, straight ahead.

She hugged the walls, came to the next junction and pressed herself around the corner, peering back in time to see the Gendarmes make the wrong choice, turning north, taking the lane that climbed towards the old fortress. Glancing around, Liberté found herself looking down a series of broad steps, hovels on both sides, and each step almost a terrace, stone and dirt from which stunted trees grew, showing little foliage despite the height of summer. Yet they bore their own fruit, long warps of woven wool soaked in dyes and draped to dry on the branches. Most towns had their street of tenters and this one was busy today, the weavers taking full advantage of the decent sunshine, women and children carrying wooden troughs from their houses to the trees, suspending the long warps carefully, leaving the troughs below to catch the precious dripping remnants of brown and red, ochre and indigo that they would use again for the paler shades. A good place to cover her tracks, but how would she now find the agent who had saved her life?

Dumont untied the ribbon of her bonnet, secured it to the waistband of her breeches, having removed the overalls and left them with the mule packs. So she removed the jacket too, rolling it into a bundle under her arm and making sure that the inside pocket, the one that held her prized lock-picks and Fouché's authority, was properly fastened. Then she started to descend the steps. She was sweating, unfastened the neck button of her linen blouse, wiped the sleeve across her damp cheek.

So, she thought, *now what?*

An assassin had tried to kill her. Here, in Charleroi. What could that mean? So far as she knew, nobody but Fouché himself knew about her mission and, therefore, surely nobody but Fouché could have wanted her dead. But so soon? Her mission so freshly received? And it hardly explained the second woman, the one who had saved her. The same logic applied, did it not? Another agent watching her back could also be nobody's handiwork but Fouché's. Things had changed, of course. She had realised as much immediately on hearing word of Bourmont's desertion. He had gone over to the Prussians, apparently taking all the Emperor's campaign plans with him. But did that mean Fouché's first task was now completed? He had been very specific. The plans, the enciphered dispatch, must be delivered to Wellesley. The Prussians had barely featured in their discussion. And a return to the Minister of Police for further instruction was out of the question. He would be long gone by now. On his way back to Paris, she thought. To spin yet more webs of intrigue in which the possible future destinies of France might be caught. But one thing was certain: whatever the future might hold, Fouché himself would come up smelling of roses. He always did.

Liberté stopped to get her bearings. This tenters' street was now curving away to the west, but the terraced steps still dropping towards the Sambre. She had left the mule somewhere down to the left, at a livery on the Rue de Dampremy, but this district was like a rabbit warren. Still, if she kept going, it should not be too hard to find, even if she had to double back some little distance. Yet she had taken no more than a few more paces when she froze, slipped into the shadows. More Gendarmes below her, climbing the lane, checking houses as they passed them. And when she turned, slowly, to retrace her route, there were a further two above – the same pair, she thought, that had pursued her earlier.

And why, exactly, am I the one who's running? she wondered. There might be difficult questions, of course. Enough to delay her mission. Not that she was sure about how that mission should proceed just now, but it would all become clear, she was certain, once she had taken time to draw breath.

If I am brazen enough, she thought, *I may simply stroll past them, simply deny any knowledge if they stop to question me.*

Liberté Dumont headed back up the slope. Or, at least, she had that intention. But then she was pulled sideways, strong hands gripping her arm, that same jolting shock.

'Oh no you don't, lady!' snarled the knife woman and hauled her through the door of a weaving shed. The women within the cramped interior simply ignored them, continued their endeavours even when Liberté dragged herself free, raised her voice to its sternest pitch.

'Hands off,' she threatened.

The coldness of her demeanour would have daunted most people, yet she saw it reflected precisely, degree for degree, in the eyes staring back into her own. Exactly as she might have expected, of course, from somebody who could kill with such equanimity. Fouché's agents had a tendency to brutality. Naturally they did. But if this woman was also truly a canteen-mistress, well, they were a particular breed, especially hardened like most of those who followed behind the battalions from less reputable professions – the locals who hoped to earn a few sous by acting as guides to otherwise unknown paths; the military cowards who feigned injury to keep themselves always at the rear of the action; the pillagers of the dead; and the vendors of sin.

'You followed me,' said the woman. 'Then decided you'd dab me. What for? Thought there'd be a reward?'

'I had no idea you were here,' Dumont replied. 'And why would I turn you in? That would have jeopardised both of us, wouldn't it?'

The Gendarmes were shouting to each other now, drawing closer. The woman ignored her, smiled at the weavers, put a finger to her lips, then passed around the tables, the tenter frames and their tension hooks, pouring each worker a shot of brandy from her cask, filling up their small tin cups before crouching in the darkest corner, where Liberté Dumont joined her.

'Hey!' she whispered to the knife woman. 'You can pour a shot for me too, eh?'

To her utter surprise, she discovered that this canteen-mistress, who called herself Tambour – a clever code-name, Liberté considered – possessed not only a husband but a daughter too. It was a wonderful cover, though difficult to maintain, she imagined.

The battalion in which Tambour apparently served – the Second Battalion of the Middle Guard's Fourth Regiment of Foot Grenadiers – was at ease, sheltering from the sun in the shade of the fortress walls, close to the upper town's main square and awaiting its turn to form column of march at the allotted hour. There was that odd sense of charged boredom, which so frequently foretold impending action; the gambling, the snatched opportunity to doze, the forced good humour, the irritable grumbling at the trivial, the prayers and the superstitions, the distracted effort to eat and drink.

'You don't need a fortune-teller to measure how soon there'll be a battle,' said Liberté, watching a Spanish woman – they called her Bufanda – reading palms. 'Just measure the quantity of cheap brandy you can sell.'

'You've seen a battle?' replied Marianne Tambour. She was doing a brisk trade, a queue formed around her cart, the young girl, Poppy, collecting the coins and wiping cups, while a heavily pregnant dark-skinned assistant served bread and cheese. The woman was probably as close to giving birth as Liberté's own mother had been on the day she left their apartment on the rue de Grenelle and disappeared. The day the Bastille had fallen. Liberté had been fifteen.

'A few,' she told the canteen-mistress.

'Well,' said Tambour, 'the Prussos are just over there.' She flicked her head towards the northern side of the square. 'So you'll get to see another soon enough.'

Liberté looked around the Grenadiers. *Yes*, she thought, *there's always that smell. Fear? Excitement? Anger? All of those things? And that other essence for which there is no word.*

'Oh, I won't be hanging around that long,' she said. 'It's like you told me. I need to get back to my own business.'

Tambour did not look at her, kept pouring the rot-gut, moving the queue along, playing the line, each soldier remembered by name, a familiarity here, a bawdy comment there, all punctuated by her exchange with Liberté Dumont.

'And what might that be?' said the canteen-mistress.

'I think you know I can't tell you that,' Liberté replied. 'After all, we both serve the same master, do we not?'

'I only serve the Revolution, lady.'

'The Revolution – or the Emperor? Or the Emperor's Ministers, perhaps?'

'His Ministers?' Tambour laughed. 'There's not one of them I wouldn't send to the Razor.'

'Those days are gone, Our Lady be praised.' Liberté remembered her own narrow escape from the blade. How long ago? Twenty-two years. Astonishing. Pure luck. Fouché's intervention. 'Now we simply all serve France. And there are many ways in which to serve.'

'Only one way,' Tambour replied. 'Destroy her enemies. Our enemies. And if you want to get your own business done, you'd best learn to take better care of yourself. Think yourself lucky I was there.'

'That's exactly what troubles me, my dear,' said Liberté. 'How was that exactly?'

'By the Host!' Tambour snarled. 'How many times?' She stopped serving, turned to watch her assistant a moment, only continued when she was satisfied that the pregnant woman was fully engaged. 'And this isn't the place for me to call witnesses,' Tambour continued. 'You'll have to take my word for it. It was *me* that Lomballe was hunting. Just a case of mistaken identity. Now let's leave it that way. But remember, you owe me one!'

Indeed I do, thought Liberté. *But maybe there's still more that she can help me with. And if she wants to keep up this charrado about the attack, that's fine.* Yet she recalled the shock she experienced each time there had been contact between them, a sense of something shared. It must be explored. But first there was the initial mission to complete.

'I think I can promise you payment in full,' she said. 'But you may have to wait a few days to collect. Until after my business is settled.'

'Leaving us so soon?' said Tambour, the words spilling sarcasm but dripping into oblivion, drowned out by a new clamour in the square, a mounted staff sergeant, several of his red-breast Elite Gendarmes at the run, a tail of curious citizens and, at their head, a one-legged woman with a crutch.

'Well, it's certainly been an eventful day,' said Liberté, as the queue around Tambour's cart suddenly evaporated. The common soldier might mock the Guard's Gendarmerie for their immortality – they were rarely exposed to serious fighting – but even Grenadiers kept a respectful distance when the Elites' distinctive uniforms and bearskins were in evidence.

The staff sergeant clattered to a halt, waited for his men and the one-legged woman to reach him. And while he waited, he delved inside the flap of a saddle holster, drew out a cloth-wrapped bundle, opened it gingerly, carefully avoiding the dark dampness of the material, to reveal a small but wicked blade.

'Show me!' he shouted.

Liberté saw Marianne Tambour tense, take a step back from the cart, mutter an obscenity beneath her breath and then give the crosspiece of her cask tap a defiant twist. Tambour ran her finger across the spigot spout, catching the drip that had formed there and, looking straight at the staff sergeant, she lifted her fingertip and licked it dry.

'That one!' cried the crippled crone, extending her free arm to point at Tambour.

'Arrest her,' said the sergeant, and his men moved towards the cart.

'On what charge, citizen?' called a Grenadier who had come forward to stand at Tambour's side, placing a protective hand on the shoulder of the woman's child, Poppy. Tambour's husband, Liberté assumed, but an ugly brute, face like a spotted pig.

'Stand down, soldier,' the sergeant replied, 'if you know what's good for you.'

'Yes,' said Tambour, as two of the Gendarmes grabbed her arms, 'stand down. Think of the girl, Fronsac.' And the girl screamed.

'Let my mother go!' she yelled. 'She has done nothing.'

'She has committed affray, mayhem and murder in the presence of the Emperor,' the sergeant announced, for the benefit of all that could hear. 'Under the Penal Code, this is a capital crime.'

'A military court?' said Tambour.

'You know the regulations,' the sergeant sneered. 'You're no soldier. You'll be held here in Charleroi until the new administration is properly established, the courts operating fully under French law once more. And then...'

'And then the guillotine!' cried the one-legged woman. 'You murdering bitch.' There was a murmur of approval from the civilian crowd, more sobs from the child as the Gendarmes began to drag her mother away.

'Sergeant!' Liberté Dumont shouted, her voice carrying clear authority around the square. 'A moment, please.' She hurried forward, taking the jacket that she still carried, unfastened the inner pocket that held her valuables. The staff sergeant turned to study her, gestured to his men that they should proceed.

'What is it now' he snarled.

'A civil matter, you say?' Liberté asked. 'Then you should see this.'

She handed him the personal authority, signed by Fouché himself.

'This is a safeguard for the bearer,' said the sergeant. 'That's you, I take it?'

'Indeed,' said Liberté. 'And signed by the Duke of Otranto, as you will see,' she continued, more quietly now.

'Oh, I can see well enough. But what concern is this, precisely, of Minister Fouché?' Yet there was apparently sufficient potential for the sergeant to countermand his own orders while he gave the matter further consideration. 'Halt!' he shouted to his men.

'Like each of Minister Fouché's concerns,' replied Liberté Dumont, 'a delicate one.'

'They say that the canteen-mistress bared this very blade within pistol-shot of the Emperor, killed some other woman in his plain sight.'

'And if I told you,' whispered Liberté, 'that this canteen-mistress did so in the Emperor's direct service?'

'How so?'

'If the *carte blanche* from the Emperor's Minister of Police is insufficient for you, Staff Sergeant, I doubt that any more words of mine would help.' She held out her hand for Fouché's letter of authority. 'Perhaps better if I sought an audience with the Emperor himself.'

'Our Lady be blessed that an audience with him was, in the end, not necessary,' said Liberté, patting her mule's neck as they approached the crossroads, the left turn heading north to Brussels, the lane to the right driving north-east, carrying a traveller – or, in this case, much of the Emperor's army – to Fleurus, Sombreffe and the Prussians. She pulled a pipe from her pack, her tobacco pouch, filled the bowl but put it away again unlit.

'Our Little Shaveling must snatch his sleep where he's able,' replied Tambour, smiling with unrestrained affection towards the miners' tavern, the *Belle Vue*, that flanked the junction, and where Bonaparte lay slumped on a brace of dining chairs, chin on chest and dead to the world in the afternoon sunshine. He had not long returned from a reconnaissance of the forward positions, atop the local windmill, returned with a tail of adoring townsfolk to whom he had made a very public pronouncement – that he had come to wage war against the English and Prussians, not the Belgians. For the Belgians, he said, had always been faithful and would, from that moment, once again be French.

The canteen-mistress flicked the reins of her own pony, clicked her tongue, urging the cart onwards, and Liberté recalled the three occasions when she had met the Emperor in person, idly wondered whether he would have remembered her if the staff sergeant of Gendarmes had called her bluff.

'Will you bide a while?' she said. 'Catch up with the column a little later? For there are things about which I must talk to you.'

'An explanation maybe? The credentials you showed the red-breast sergeant?'

'I have no idea what you mean. No more than you seem able to tell me about that assassin.'

Tambour shook her head – feigned frustration, Liberté thought.

'Well I'm glad you were there,' said the canteen-mistress. And at least the *salvavirgo* had been returned to her, nestled once more in her bodice.

'Two lucky escapes between us in one day. Fate, d'you think? And your one-legged friend? What's the story?'

'Argonne? No friend of mine. She was Lomballe's. Never happy that I'd taken her commission. Swore to avenge the bitch if anything happened to Lomballe.'

'And repeated her oath this afternoon,' said Liberté. *Well*, she thought, *she has a quick mind, this one. Inventive.* The old woman had been livid, demanded to know what was going on when Liberté had shown Fouché's letter to the sergeant, quietly explained that they were both about the Minister's business, that the dead woman was an *agent provocateur.*

'For a minute, I thought it was Argonne the red-breasts were going to arrest,' said Tambour. 'Whatever tale you spun them, it must have been a good one. And now? You're heading north?'

'With the Left Wing, yes.' Word was abroad that Ney had been given command of the Left, and the decision had generally been well received. 'For a little way, in any case.'

'The English lie that way, do they not?' the canteen-mistress replied.

'You sound as though you long to see them.'

'To see the English? I saw enough of those bastards in Spain to last me a lifetime. But there's one of them I'd sell my soul to meet again.'

'Scores to settle?' said Liberté, though she barely heard Tambour's echoed response. Instead, she found herself fainting away, blown upon the wind, her head spinning and nauseous. There was a walled town on a crescent bay, yet most of the houses within those walls all ablaze, a fortress on the hill beyond. And among the burning houses, in the streets and alleyways, in the squares and on the steps of churches, there was atrocity at a level she had never seen, despite her soldiering in a dozen or more campaigns. But she was drawn particularly to one scene, a matter of such brutality that she gasped for want of air while, at the centre of that scene, there was a face that Dumont knew was projected by Marianne Tambour – the face of a redcoat sergeant, his ugly features marred by a distinctive birthmark.

'Florisette, my cask!' She heard Tambour's voice echoing through the darkness into which she had fallen, opened her eyes just as the canteen-mistress slapped her cheek with a blow that almost knocked her senseless once more.

Liberté Dumont struggled to sit, looked around to see the pregnant woman holding her mule, the child Poppy climbing down from Tambour's cart with the tricolour brandy cask, and Tambour herself peering at her.

'A simple spill,' murmured Liberté. 'Nothing more. The heat, perhaps.'

'By the Host, lady,' said Tambour. 'You're not fit to be let loose.'

'Am I not?' Liberté whispered, as Tambour took the cask from her daughter, unhooked a tin cup and poured a measure of the dog-dog. 'Well, I have seen your Englishman, Marianne. The one with the purple face.'

Tambour's hands began to shake, spilling the brandy, and she waved her daughter away.

'Take the cart,' she said. 'Keep up with the Battalion. I'll find you later.'

And the girl obeyed, while the pregnant mulatta, Prairial, handed back the mule, joined Poppy on the cart. There was bad blood here, Liberté had noted. For while this Breton wench travelled with Tambour, it was clear that her friendships lay elsewhere, and especially with the one-legged woman, Argonne. There had been hot words between them after the Gendarmes abandoned the arrest, though in the end it was Tambour's cart that the mulatta had followed. It jolted away now just in time, clearing the crossroads as a cavalry division began to move through, taking the Brussels road, the brazen helmets and green jackets of Dragoon regiments, the scarlet facings and a few familiar faces of the Second.

'Come on,' said Liberté, keeping her head down, pulling the mule behind her. 'Let's get off the road. Quickly.'

'Don't want to be seen?' laughed Tambour. 'You look as guilty as sin!'

'My regiment,' Liberté replied, not really knowing why she should bestow so much information on this other woman, regardless of whether she might have saved her life.

'What?' said Tambour. 'Going to tell me you're a canteen-mistress too, I suppose? What did you do, steal the regimental silver?'

'Nothing like that,' Liberté told her. 'Just better if they don't see me. Besides, we need to take some shade.'

Tambour gripped her arm suddenly, venom in her eyes.

'Is that so?' she snarled. 'And this Englishman you claim to know so much about. This purple-face. You say you've seen him. But that's shit. Who told you about him? Was it Poppy?'

'I've seen him right enough. And I've seen him the same way that *you* see him, my dear.'

'Dreams,' said Tambour. 'I see him in my dreams. Nightmares, maybe.'

'Dreams?' Liberté Dumont smiled. 'Is that what you call them? I think you know better. What sort of dreams are they that play out details in such a way? And not just once, but time and time again. It's more like living the past all over again. Isn't that it?'

'You're no canteen-mistress, are you?'

'We are each more layered than the world might suppose,' said Liberté.

'In our dreams perhaps,' said Tambour.

'They're not always filled with that English sergeant then?'

Tambour regarded her with undisguised mistrust.

'Not always,' the canteen-mistress replied with apparent reluctance. 'But he is there more often than anything else. And, by the Host, one day I'll be face to face with that creature.'

'No other ambition?'

'Plenty,' said Tambour, though she did not elaborate.

'Let me guess,' said Liberté. 'Poppy? You do all this so your daughter won't have to follow the army too.'

'All this?'

Liberté laughed.

'Very good,' she said. 'His Grace would be impressed. But Poppy won't be a girl for much longer. And then you've got all those dangerous years. All those men,' she nodded towards the now distant column, 'that are presently happy to play the uncle...'

There was a flash of anger in Tambour's eyes.

'What of it?'

'These things that you call dreams, my dear. What if they were, indeed, something else? Let us suppose they were pathways. And that by following those tracks, we could find our way to the fellow at their farther end.'

'That's nonsense,' said Tambour. 'Isn't it?'

'And what if there was also a way for you to earn more gold Napoléons in a week than you could make selling rot-gut for the next five years?'

Chapter Seven

Thursday 15th June 1815, 4.30pm

Marianne watched the fully laden mule until it became indistinguishable from the mass of other mounts and their riders that crowded along the Brussels road.

Mad as a hatter, she thought, then turned her own steps towards Fleurus. The woman had resembled nothing so much as a mature bird of prey, for her eyes and nose, the tight set of her mouth, could indeed have belonged to a hawk. There was a lightness of movement too, so that the woman appeared to possess the gift of winged flight, and even the hair had a feathered quality, though black as night, flecked here and there with the beginnings of grey.

Marianne fell in, alongside these other Grenadiers, men of the Guard's First Regiment, the Old Grumblers, the Emperor's finest, bringing up the rear of the column. Her own battalion was some distance ahead now, but she should not have too much trouble catching them. Yet it would take some time, and time alone on the march filled a body's head with all manner of nonsense, waking dreams that were difficult to ignore. So the crazy witch-woman's words played themselves to her, not once but a dozen times.

Much of it she had not even understood, but when Marianne had pressed for an explanation of her claim that she had seen the purple-faced Englishman, she had been rewarded with a gibberish lecture about the mysteries of the mind. Something that Hawk-face had learned in Egypt. Somewhere like that. The soul's ability to fly free. Well, that was nonsense enough. Religious nonsense that Marianne had forsworn with the Revolution. But then there had been all the rest. The brain a storehouse of memories, of all things that have happened, of all things yet to come. All the thoughts, the deeds, the activities of each person. And the words, the lines of those patterns were not written in ink on paper, but were woven into all the fabric of life. So, beyond the rest, the final lunacy. That there were those born with a gift to free their souls from their bodies, to reach inside the fabric, to travel the track of dreams.

'And you, Marianne,' the mad woman had said to her, 'you also have that gift.'

How else, she had said, could Marianne so regularly revisit the scenes of her past tragedies? How else could Hawk-face have shared her visions, her deepest secrets? When they had touched, the woman claimed, she had been able to see inside Marianne's own soul journeys, to experience them too. Yes, it was a lunacy. But there was something about it that warmed her. This idea of life's fabric. Something that she had almost sensed already for herself. It surrounded her now. The idea of two worlds running side by side. This contrast between the rhythmic tramp of the Grumblers' boots to her right, the crushed grasses and crops of their passing, the swaggering chorus of their equipment, the sweating heartbeat of their marching song, and the sweet summer music of this Belgian afternoon to her left, the sun-drenched virginity of its flower heads, the lazy background hum of its insects, the sweet waft of its pollens. If she half-closed her eyes, she could almost see herself absorbed into that other world, floating through its essence – its aether, as Hawk-face had called it.

And what if I could do that? She thought. *What if I could, indeed, find the Englishman, pay him in kind for what he did to Maman Cholet? Would that ease my guilt?* The damned woman had presented her with just too many temptations. Not just revenge, but wealth too. Yet for what service?

'Very well,' Hawk-face had said, 'you play the game well!' Though Marianne had no idea what she meant. 'Then let us suppose that we each have our own duties to perform.' *Fair enough.* 'But that His Grace...' *There she goes again.* 'But that His Grace has purchased a second fire-mark against the possibility of a certain loss. So far as the Emperor's dormeuse is concerned, that is. It would, after all, be eminently sensible to site such an extra insurance here, within the Imperial Guard itself, would it not? Somebody with the ability to move freely in the confines of the Imperial canton. Do we understand each other?' *Not a single word*, Marianne had thought, but the mention of split rewards had caused her to smile enigmatically, to raise her forehead, stretch her lower lip, as though she were giving the matter serious consideration. And she was no fool. The woman might be mad, but there was no doubting that she carried important documents, sufficient to secure Marianne's freedom from the Gendarmes. Deluded she might be about Lomballe's intentions, yet the woman clearly held a genuine belief that it was she, rather than Marianne, who had been the target of attempted assassination. And she must, therefore, also have some inner belief of her value as an assassin's mark. Then there was her claim that she belonged to a regiment of Dragoons. It was not unknown, women among the ranks. Common enough during the early years of the Revolution, less so now, but not unknown. So a picture formed. A woman soldier. Probably a good one if she was with the Dragoons. A deserter? Unlikely. And claiming to have her own duties. Carrying credentials, or such like. Talk of fire-marks, insurance. An agent of the security services then? But which? Or did it not matter? Hawk-face had either decided to take Marianne into her confidence for some hidden reason of her own, or else – and this would be hilarious – she had assumed that the canteen-mistress might share her profession.

'Fine,' the woman had said. 'That's settled. I'll try to get back to you as soon as possible. Better two heads than one for this little business. You can say that we're related maybe. Come to help you with the canteen. And we share the rewards. Agreed?'

Marianne, doubting that she would ever see her again, smiled to herself.

A few extra Napoléons would have come in handy, all the same, she thought. *And yes, a future for Florisette?*

But the beat of hooves brought her rapidly back to the present. She turned and, for the second time in two days, saw the Shaveling himself riding up the line, was caught up in the roar of the Grenadiers as their Emperor passed them. He glanced at her, though there was no sign of recognition, no hint that he remembered paying her those two francs for her rotgut just the day before. Yet she found herself, for the very first time, less fascinated by Bonaparte himself than by the procession that followed behind him, and particularly by his carriages. First, the open Landau. Then the dark and gleaming blue of his dormeuse, with its gold ornaments, lamps at each corner, the windows louvered and the shutters cracking against the glass with each jolt of the wheels over the rough ground, the driver denied the road and trying to find the smoothest route, while the postilion clung to the rear and, also on the box, the Emperor's Mameluke. Not the famous Roustam, of course. No, the Armenian, they said, had buggered off when the Shaveling was sent to Elba. So this was some new boy, elevated to act as the Shaveling's valet, to wear the baggy trousers, the turban, the Turkish finery. But guarding what? Why should an agent of the security service, the Ministry of Police perhaps, be so interested in this dormeuse? It was the Emperor's home very often, on campaign, of course. Legend had it that the vehicle carried the imperial privy pot, a wardrobe of spare clothes, an iron bed, his personal treasures. Yet what other secrets did it hold?

The cannon opened fire just before Marianne came over the final rise, passing the church, the isolated barn and stone enclosure that marked the northern extremity of yet another nameless Belgian hamlet. Ahead of her, the road dipped slightly, crowded with the battalions and regiments of the Guard infantry – the nearest Grenadier units still moving from column of march by platoon to column of attack – and then dropped to a ridge that rolled and meandered from west to east. Squadrons of cavalry, Dragoons and Hussars, spread along the ridge for perhaps a kilometre in each direction with a more substantial village to their front, a single row of houses on both sides of the road, massed ranks of line infantry, smoke from the artillery batteries drifting lazily to the right, towards a windmill where the staff officers had gathered and, further again, the dirty smudge of coal mines interspersed with still more large formations of the Emperor's horsemen.

Along the valley's bottom ran a rivulet, though it was too slight to present any major obstacle. The road crossed the stream just before it passed through another modest cluster of houses, and there seemed to be a barricade there.

The Prussos certainly love their useless barricades, thought Marianne, for she could see signs of the enemy there, uniforms so dark that they appeared black at such a distance. Then another ridge, climbing steep and high, up to the skyline far above, much of it wooded, blocks of Prussian infantry visible on the open ground, spread between some church buildings – an abbey perhaps – to Marianne's left, and a château or village beyond a cleft in the ridge to her right. She could not immediately discern their artillery until a white pall obliterated the trees at the Prussian centre. The thunder of the guns reverberated between the slopes and their balls tore up the ground in filthy clouds just in front of the leading French positions.

Marianne passed another canteen-mistress whom she knew a little: Maria Chactas, busy serving the men of her battalion.

'Where are we?' she shouted to the woman – a Tuscan, she recalled, who had come from Elba with a soldier of the Emperor's bodyguard and taken the soldier's name.

'Christ knows!' Chactas replied. But a grizzled sergeant heard the exchange too.

'It's Gilly,' he said. 'The village. They call it Gilly.'

'It was the guns, Maman,' Poppy shouted.

Around their own cart, chaos reigned, some of the fellows from Fronsac's squad – Bloc, Lejeune and Daubanne – fussed and fumed, while their corporal, Poncet, cursing and swearing, tried to get them back in line. Prairial was folded over her dolly barrow, screaming profanities in that Breton tongue of hers, a small puddle of wetness at her feet, Florisette gripping her skirts and yelling that the woman must breathe deeply. It was advice beyond her years, Marianne knew, for childhood is an elusive shrew, short-lived for those spawned among the Eagles. But at least she found the cart easily enough. It was the advantage of Fronsac being in the Fourth Company, always at the Battalion's backside where the women were also supposed to remain.

'I wasn't expecting them,' cried Prairial. 'Oh, God forgive me. They made me jump.' She clenched her teeth, squeezed out a protracted groan of agony, panted at the contraction's passing. 'Our Lady protect us,' she said. 'Let the child be whole. The water...'

'Don't be a fool,' Marianne told her. 'It takes more than a few of the Shaveling's Beautiful Daughters to forge a crippled child. And that water's nothing but the first flow. Now, where's Argonne? Isn't she supposed to be helping you?'

She looked around. Argonne's noddy cart was present, though at the opposite end of the rear files, at the farther end of the Fourth Company's Second Section, beyond which the Guard's own artillery, its horses, limbers and caissons, rumbled forward. But there was no sign of Argonne herself, only Bufanda there to look after the canteen goods, along with Argonne's kids. Marianne called to them over the background clamour of hoof and harness, song and salvo, asked where their bitch of a mother might be, but received only disinterested shrugs by way of response, a gesture from one of the smaller girls that she should go shaft herself.

'I think it's near,' Prairial hissed.

'And what d'you expect me to do about it?' Marianne replied.

'You know what to do,' said Prairial, 'if anything goes wrong.'

Marianne ignored her. Prairial had made some sly comment after Argonne had confronted her in the square, let Marianne know that she had kept quiet about seeing Lomballe, about Marianne going off to follow her. After all, she had said, it was not really any of her business. If the red-breasts were satisfied, well, that was good enough. But it had not been good enough for Argonne. She had fallen out with Prairial about it, apparently, called her a snake.

'What have I missed?' said Marianne.

'The Shaveling came past a while ago,' Corporal Poncet told her.

'I saw him.'

'We watched him cross the stream down there,' Poncet pointed to a house on the opposite slope. 'Bloody close to the Prussos. But they soon pulled him back. He's at the mill. Over this way. Other than that, there's nothing much to tell. We missed the start. By the time we got here, the horse boys had cleared the village and the Prussos were formed up across the way. Where you see them. Up there. The guns have just kicked off, and so has your mate, it seems.'

'She's no mate of mine,' Marianne replied.

'You know the drill though,' said the corporal. 'You all do!'

'Yes,' said Marianne. 'We keep you from starving when the rations run out. We dodge bullets to bring you water and dog-dog when you shit yourselves with thirst. We stitch and darn your socks. Then we do the same for your worthless flesh when you're too daft to stay out of harm's way. We cure your fevers and your pox. And you expect us to deliver your bastards too?'

But they did, of course. And she had watched Cholet do the deed more times than she could count, had once spent three days and three nights with some poor cow whose babe was stuck fast, coming by the head, but stuck fast. The child still alive too and the mother racked, tortured beyond endurance, screaming herself hoarse until she bit through her own tongue, getting weaker by the hour until somebody sent for a black-robe priest. Cholet wanted to use her crotchet to get the head out, save the mother. But the priest had said it would kill the infant, condemn Cholet to eternal damnation. So she waited until he had administered the last rites and gone, then she used the crotchet anyway. Hooked it just so, while Marianne and a few others pinned the mother down. Hooked it in the eye socket, then eased the head free. By the Host, it took an age. Yet they both lived, the child at the cost of an eye, the mother at the cost of her tongue. Lived, all the same.

Then there had been the feet-first and buttock births, and Cholet had never lost even one of them. All manner of tricks, she employed, for dropping them out. But always one rule. Never touch the babe itself until the head was clear, lest the poor mite should be enticed to gasp and drown in the mother's water. And women had come to Cholet from miles around, not just for the delivery but for general advice too. There was nobody who knew more than Cholet about how to keep a man from straying when his wife was heavy with child. She had known every position in the book, and then more besides.

But Cholet was no longer there. She had been raped to death with a barrel wormer in the flames of Saint-Sébastien. And Marianne thought again about Liberté Dumont's promise of revenge.

'Maman!' shouted Poppy, as Prairial let out another scream of outrage.

How long had that been since the last spasm? Marianne wondered. *Three minutes? Less?* Too close for comfort, in any case, and still no sign of Argonne.

'Dammit,' she said. 'You'll owe me for this.' And she cupped a hand under the spigot spout, turned the handle to catch some of the rotgut, washed her palms and fingers. Another of Cholet's strictures. At the same time, she counted out the seconds of Prairial's pain. Sixty seconds. Maybe seventy. But no more. 'Get me a blanket,' she told Florisette. Then, 'No. An old one, you silly girl.'

And if the guns really set her off, she thought, *how long ago was that? A half-hour?*

'Anything we can do?' asked Corporal Poncet, but in that tone of voice that begged a negative answer.

'Not yet,' said Marianne. 'Just get her down on the blanket while I have a look at her. Oh, and do your best to keep the Prussos away, eh?'

But there seemed little danger of anything beyond the continuing artillery exchange, a permanent thunderstorm background now, and the balls falling far away. Too early for anything else. Units still moving up to the front. Four squadrons of green-jacketed troopers cantered past the rear of the Grenadiers' position, heading east to avoid getting tangled with the advancing guns, still manoeuvring off to the left. Marianne glanced up at them as they shook the ground, wafted odours of dung, sweat and leather in her direction. Fine mounts, the men's horsehair helmet-crest tails flying, black, behind them, and the panther skin bands around the lower portion of their headgear marking them clearly as the Guard's Empress Dragoons. Behind the first squadron rode a group of staff officers and, at their head, a General that Marianne recognised as Letort. She had last seen him at Montmirail, a good-looking fellow, tall in the saddle with a full head of dark curls. A great cavalry leader, one of the best, they said. He surveyed the scene, urged his beast out of the column, was followed by a brace of his staff officers, and reined to a halt alongside Marianne's cart.

'We're to have a new recruit for the ranks, canteen-mistress?' Letort said to her.

Prairial was suffering another contraction but the presence of the horsemen had distracted Marianne from her count. She crouched, pulled the woman's skirts up, pushed her legs apart.

'And sooner than you might think,' she replied. Prairial's pale coffee thighs were slick with sweat, the hair-framed, pouting lips of her placket slimed, the slime smeared with blood, and the lips parted as wide as Marianne's clenched fist. Not yet, but not long.

'This is a good omen' said the General. 'I have a baby also. Three months old now. Her name is Fanny. My wife is English. Is that not strange? We shall fight the English too. Tomorrow, or the next day.'

'And not a day too soon,' shouted Marianne, so that the men of Fronsac's squad took up the usual cry of 'Long live the Emperor!' that spread through the company, the section, and then to the whole Battalion.

Letort smiled down at them, unfastened the buttons of his single-breasted surtout so that the braided gilt cords of his aiguillettes fell, swinging loose from the shoulder. Reaching inside to the pocket of his vest he drew out three gleaming gold Napoléons.

'Here,' he said. 'For luck. One for the mother.' He tossed a coin to Florisette, who slipped it into Prairial's hand as a comfort. 'And this for the infant.' He threw a second coin. 'And this one for the birthing-wife.'

Marianne caught the thing with one hand, dropped it into the *reticule* purse within her waistband.

'Marat be with you, General,' she said. 'Good fortune.' And she croaked out the first line of the '*Ah! Ça ira*' until this, too, was carried through the ranks.

'Oh, it'll be all right, be all right, be all right,
Hang the aristocrats from on high,
Oh, it'll be all right, be all right, be all right,
The aristocrats, we'll hang 'em all!'

By the time Prairial's contractions were coming at intervals of much less than four minutes, and the screams lasting for a good quarter of that time, Letort was long gone. In the intervals, Marianne had done her best to soothe the woman, pleased that she had at least been rewarded for her efforts. A Gold Napoléon would, after all, have been Fronsac's pay for three weeks.

'Well,' she said to him, as he stood in line, 'I suppose we should be thankful that the Battalion's not moved.'

They remained in reserve as befitted the Imperial Guard while, below them, three broad columns of line infantry – two battalions in each – moved forward, past a farm, cleared the Prussians from the sharpened stakes of the abatis they had thrown up across the road and to each side of it, while away on the far right the French cavalry were sweeping up towards the distant cluster of dwellings and the château, which could be seen rising above the surrounding woodland.

'They're falling back,' Fronsac replied. His thumb delved within the cavity of his nostril as he stared across the valley. The Prussian battalions, their artillery pieces, were climbing to the ridge's upper reaches, their retreat covered by skirmishers. 'Hadn't you better get back to her?' he asked.

Marianne looked towards the cart.

'She's got a while to go yet,' she said, then noticed the figure of Argonne and her crutch, away at Bufanda's canteen, way down the line. 'Ah! I wondered when the old bitch would show up.'

'D'you miss them?' said Fronsac. The other men of the squad, the *peloton*, were sharing out tobacco, and Marianne felt guilty that she had not followed up her quest for further supplies in Charleroi. Wished her own pipe was not broken.

'Miss who?' she replied, though she knew fine well who he meant. He was always like this, before a battle.

'We should have named them,' he said. 'What if there's a heaven, after all, woman? And the poor little sods are wandering around there with no names. Lost?'

Well, thought Marianne, *in that unlikely event, if Hawk-face is right, they'll be written into the tracks of life somehow or other. Names or no names.* But she did not think so. Not really. And she choked back something dark that rose in her throat.

'We're born,' she murmured. 'We live. We die. That's it, Fronsac. Maybe leave a memory or two behind us if we're lucky. And I can remember them just fine as they are. Now go and fill your pipe. I'd better go find Prairial's man. Give him a progress report.'

Chapter Eight

Thursday 15th June 1815, 5.30pm

'Your man doesn't seem to be much excited at the prospect of being a father,' said Marianne.

'He thinks the baby will be black,' Prairial replied, the parody of a smile flickering across her face.

'Didn't he think of that before?'

'He didn't know, not when he married me. My mother was dark too.'

Marianne could imagine. It was true for lots of Bretons that she had come across. An ancient folk, older than time, some of them.

'Your mother never told him? About you being a mulatta?'

'Why would she? It was only the commission that she passed down to me. Not her husband. After she died, it all seemed to make sense. Wybicki's a sergeant, when all's said and done. They might have challenged the commission. He needed a new wife. That's about it!'

'That Pole's old enough to be your grandfather,' said Marianne, but Prairial made no reply, bit back another scream as the latest spasm shook her rigid.

Less than two minutes since the last, thought Marianne.

'Feel like I'm going to shit myself,' the mulatta groaned, began to writhe, try to get up, panic pressed into her features.

'That's normal,' Marianne told her. 'It won't be long now.' She turned to her daughter. 'Poppy, wash her face.'

Their own company sergeant, Flambert, came by to find out how things stood.

'Can't you hurry her up?' he said. 'She's frightening the lads.'

Marianne swallowed a shot of her own dog-dog. She would need to give some to Prairial before too long, she knew, but she needed this last break from it all, to clear her own head, remember all the things that Cholet had shown her – though it was far from easy with all this going on.

Across the valley, things were warming up. She had no idea how many Prussians were facing them, but somebody had said there may be twenty thousand. Not their whole army, of course, but enough of the buggers to pose a serious threat. And a good position too. So why were they abandoning it? They must have orders to fall back, to even better ground, and join up with the rest. Everybody knew that the Shaveling was facing two separate armies, each likely to be as large as their own. The Prussos here and the English somewhere close, but off towards Brussels, away to their left. If those two joined up, there would be hell to pay.

She watched the enemy battalions climb higher up the opposite slopes, trying to keep their formations tight while the artillery duel continued, though with apparently little effect on either side apart from the noise and smoke. Then, below her, she saw French cavalry, Dragoons, crossing the stream, riding up past their own infantry regiments that had come to a halt after clearing the Prussian barricades. Three large squadrons and a fourth straggling behind, as though the whole thing had not been formed properly before moving to the attack. Green jackets, almost certainly the same Empress Dragoons who had passed the Battalion so recently, Letort at their head. But they were shifting now, sweeping diagonally up the hill towards a forest in an effort to prevent their enemies from reaching its protection. Yet they were too late – at least so far as the Prussians' leading units were concerned. Their skirmishers were out, tiny figures stinging the horsemen with their musket fire. Not much, but enough. So that, within moments, company after company of the Prussians had been swallowed by woodland.

Two other battalions, however, were still half a kilometre from this same safe haven, and the French Dragoons did not even pause to draw breath but curved away from the trees, starlings flocking at twilight, reaching out to strike at the more exposed enemy below them. And they were joined now by still more squadrons of their comrades, mixed units, more Dragoon green, Lancers' pennants of white and red. A dark line of Prussian skirmishers simply disappeared as the horses rolled over them, folded around the hollow square that the infantry beyond had formed to protect themselves. An imperfect square though. A square torn between defending itself and reaching the trees. Creeping uphill, over broken ground.

Poor bastards! thought Marianne, as the inevitable unfolded. It was an involuntary reaction for, while she had no sympathy for these German invaders, there were few worse ways to go than being butchered by the horse boys. So she winced as one of the Prussian companies detached itself from the square, held off one or two charges, while the rest of their battalion struggled on. Then they broke, were drowned, hacked, sabred and speared, their fate repeated, company by company, until they were visible no more.

The French cavalry were not yet done, of course, for there was still one more battalion of Prussians left on open ground, though this one seemed more steady, better composed, remaining intact and edging ever upwards, two hundred paces to cover, while the French cavalry ran round and around, push after push, seeking an opening which, Marianne thought, they would not find this time. It was a rare thing for cavalry to break an infantry square. Not unknown, if the cavalry had a leader like Letort. But rare.

*

Suzanne Prairal's screams, her curses, had punctuated that other, more distant struggle, but Marianne now recognised the intensity of the woman's current contraction. She poured a further cup of rotgut, passed it to Poppy.

'Here,' she said, 'give her this.'

And she knelt, pushed the mulatta's shaking knees apart again. There was almost no need, for she could have guessed what she would find. The flesh around Prairial's placket had swollen out; the lips now opened to the width of Marianne's two fists, side by side. Within this pulsing mouth the baby's crown domed out like the rolled tongue of a gargoyle, deep purple and matted with scabrous clots.

'Can you see it?' Prairial gasped.

'Help me turn her, girl,' Marianne told Poppy and, between them, they persuaded the young woman to move onto all fours.

'More dog-dog?' Poppy suggested.

'To hell with that,' said her mother. 'She'll have to manage with what she's had.' Prairial screamed, lifted a corner of the old blanket and stuffed it in her own mouth. 'The priests used to say that pain when dropping babies is God's punishment for women. Eve and the Forbidden Fruit. That sort of thing,' she panted.

'We don't believe in priests though, do we, Maman?'

'Don't push yet,' Marianne yelled at Prairial. 'Not until you can't hold it any more.'

'Eve be damned,' Prairial snarled. 'It's my bitch of a mother whose sins I'm paying for. Oh, Holy Lady spare me.'

'Her mother?' whispered Poppy.

'She did the business with a black man, didn't she, Prairial? And out popped a little brown Prairial.'

The mulatta screamed again.

'No!' Marianne yelled. 'Don't push when the pain is worst. Wait until it eases. Then you can push.'

Prairial groaned, a deep racking sound, puffing and blowing for all she was worth.

'Can you see yet?' she asked. 'The colour?'

'Push now,' Marianne replied, remembering the threads of information that she had extracted from Prairial during their many leagues on the road. The mother's unfortunate liaison with her American sailor in Lorient, the young Suzanne farmed out to a family in Quimper, given a new name – *Prairial*, for the month in which she was born – while her disgraced mother fled to Paris, followed the army, a string of husbands. The most recent, Sergeant Wybicki.

'The colour?' she grinned. 'Blood red of course, sister! Now push again.' Prairial, meanwhile, had grown up in the Cornouaille, Lower Brittany – *Breizh*

Izel in the Bretons' own tongue – and was apprenticed to a seamstress. Until last year, that was. 'Bet you wished you'd stayed in Quimper now,' Marianne laughed.

'No choice,' Prairial whispered. 'The bitch. She was wounded. Sent for me.'

'And after she died,' Marianne told Poppy, 'our Prairial married the good Sergeant Wybicki herself. He didn't waste any time either, did he? And push! Third time lucky.'

But the head had not budged. Marianne frowned at the purple crown, and Florisette crawled towards Prairial's raised buttocks, peered around and blanched.

'Oh shit,' said the girl, 'what a mess!'

'On your back,' Marianne told Prairial, though she did not wait for a response, manhandling her and pushing the woman's knees up hard into her chest. 'Now,' she said, 'every time there's a spasm, push again. Push bloody hard!'

'I don't know how *she* feels,' Marianne told the Spanish girl, Bufanda, 'but I'm bloody exhausted.'

When the head had finally emerged, the cord wrapped around its neck, Marianne had been careful to pull on neither the head nor the cord itself, but lifting the blue and purple beating rope as gently as she was able, slipped it free. And no sooner had she done so than the mite turned its wrinkled face to one side so that, with Prairial's next push, a tiny shoulder emerged. Marianne helped ease the other shoulder down and out. The rest followed simply enough, slithering forth like a jellied eel. She had caught and held it, tilted downwards, checking that it breathed properly.

'Whole and healthy,' she had said. 'And a boy.'

'But what colour?' Prairial insisted, though she had been limp, dripping sweat.

'Black as a Cossack's heart,' Marianne had lied for, in truth, the child seemed much the same as any other.

Bufanda looked down to where the child now rested, head on his mother's shoulder, feet on her breast, while the men from the squad – indeed, most of the section – were given leave to gather in groups, to demonstrate proud and collective fatherhood.

'He is so...' said the Spanish woman, as though she was struggling for the correct word in French.

'Small?' suggested Marianne.

'A little *Moro*,' said Bufanda, but she glanced nervously back along the line.

Marianne peered again at the babe she had delivered, wondering whether Bufanda had seen something in its colour that she, herself, had missed.

'Worried that Argonne will catch you conspiring with the enemy?' she said.

'It is between you and Argonne,' Bufanda replied. 'For me, it's simple.

Lomballe would have killed you.' She shrugged. 'You killed her instead.'

'The red-breasts were satisfied.'

'They say you had a friend in a high place.'

'Friend?' said Marianne. 'Who needs a crazy woman for a friend? But stay with Prairial, will you? There's no afterbirth yet, and I should go tell her man he's now a father. And you, girl,' she called to Florisette, 'watch the cart!'

She managed to draw herself another shot as she made her way forward to the First Company, but word had spread, and there were cheers, jibes from each rank that she passed. They seemed to have lost interest entirely in the battle across the valley, for it was obvious that the Battalion would not be needed this day. Yet that was not true for the line infantry over there, blocks of them now taken over from the cavalry, pressing up against the tree-lines as they gradually pushed the Prussians back into the woodland. The outcome was inevitable. No less so than Prairial's struggle. Though with its own birthing pangs. The contractions as the enemy volley hit them. The moment of respite. The push to gain another fathom or two of ground. The cannons were all silent now but the crackle of musketry drifted back to her in ceaseless spasm. She wondered how they could even hear drum or bugle call, surrounded on all sides by oak and beech, birch and elm, their ears deafened by their own fire. And the French horse boys? Marianne could see them too, taking a long and leisurely ride around the farthest edges of the woodland, hoping – she imagined – that when the Prussos emerged from the farther side, they would be there waiting for them.

It took her almost ten minutes to reach the Battalion's head, its First Company, and then to locate the section for which Wybicki was a sergeant. She did good trade here while she broke the news to him.

'He has your eyes,' she told him.

'All goes good!' Wybicki replied. Sarcastic, she thought, though his French was so heavily accented that she could not be certain. But, in truth, he was darker even than Prairial herself. Something Jewish in his features, brown eyes, the long hair and drooping moustache snow-white, like many of those haunted souls who had gone into Russia with the Great Army three years before, and come back out again, lived to tell the tale. He was heavily scarred too, reminded her of an old badger.

'In fact, Sergeant,' she said, 'he's the very image of you.'

'You done all good,' he told her. There was no smile of appreciation, however, and she hoped that he was clearer in commands to his men than his limited French seemed to imply. But she was suddenly proud of her achievement. More so since the First Company's soldiers heaped praise upon her, for this had been the company in which Lomballe's husband had served. She had been their girl. But yesterday's girl. Now, it was Tambour this, and Tambour that. More tots of brandy sold until the cask ran dry and Marianne's pouches jangled with coin.

'I come later, see boy,' said Wybicki, after she tried to explain her need to get back to his wife. He looked at her strangely, without comprehension. An army wedding, of course. No ceremony, no lawful licence for Prairial. Just the uncertain affections of this reluctant and possibly temporary protector. 'All goes good!' he nodded.

'Yes, all good,' she echoed, then fell in alongside a couple of Dragoons flanking the first straggle of Prussian prisoners. Militiamen. Greatcoats and blankets rolled around their chests, short jackets in faded shades of blue, flat caps – though most were bareheaded. They seemed in decent enough spirits, though. The lucky ones. Still alive. Few of them wounded. Out of the fighting. Still cocky. *Typical bloody Germans*, she thought, as one of them shouted to her.

'How much, Fräulein?' he laughed, made an unmistakeable gesture to show that he was not referring to her rotgut.

'Up yours, Fritz!' she called back, and gave him the sign of the horns for added emphasis.

'Rub her here,' Marianne told her daughter, placing the girl's hands firmly on Prairial's stomach, just below the belly button. 'Press down. And rub.'

'Holy Mother,' yelled the mulatta. 'That hurts.'

'Stop whining. It'll slow the bleeding.'

'Is he coming?' Prairial asked.

'Your man? Yes. And you seem to have done me a fair favour after all. A gold Napoléon from Letort. Then, all the crap I had to put up with from the First all forgotten, it seems. They couldn't give a fig for Lomballe now.'

'Argonne won't forget though,' said Prairial. 'Oh, Sweet Lady, what's that?'

Her face registered a new fear, and Marianne lifted the blanket she had thrown loosely over mother and babe, saw the cord – paler now, no longer pulsing, almost milky clear, snaking out with a squirt of fresh blood, followed by the afterbirth mess.

'Well,' said Marianne, 'it seems we have fresh sausage for your baby banquet. And you can let me worry about Mistress Argonne.'

She tied the cord tightly in two places, one near the child's belly, then again a few inches lower, gripped the slippery rope as firmly as she could manage, then used the *salvavirgo* to saw slowly through the surprising toughness of its flesh. When it was done, she covered them both again while, just beyond the cart, the Battalion's Adjutant-Major, Captain Vicquot, leaned down from his horse in conversation with Sergeant Flambert.

'Tambour,' the captain called, meeting her glance, 'the Major's had word we'll be on the move again soon. How long before she's fit to move?'

'Only to move, Captain? Marat be praised! I thought you'd want her back at work.'

Laughter in the ranks, some bawdy banter.

'How long?' insisted the sergeant.

'Do we get a cart to carry them?' Marianne asked.

'You've got a cart,' said Sergeant Flambert. 'So's she. Now get it sorted!'

'And I've seen the child now, Tambour,' Captain Vicquot told her, 'so no need to bring it for the Declaration. Just meet me later, when we bivouac. Either you or the father. That's Sergeant Wybicki, isn't it?'

Marianne nodded.

'And the place of birth,' she reminded him. 'What shall we say?'

'Oh, Gilly, I think,' said Vicquot. 'Seems like we have our first significant victory of the campaign. But tell Prairial to sort out some decent names for the kid. Something to match the day.'

'An auspicious day, sir,' said the sergeant.

Auspicious? thought Marianne. *That's a good word. For a strange day.* Lomballe. Hawk-face. The crazy woman's tempting promise of revenge. Letort's gold coin for luck. Cholet at her shoulder during the birth. The tiny wonder of the child.

'Auspicious?' Captain Vicquot replied, an echo of Marianne's own thinking. 'It would be if we hadn't lost our best cavalry commander.' He noted the surprised expressions around him. 'You haven't heard? General Letort's been shot. Stomach wound. Not expected to survive.'

Chapter Nine

Thursday 15th June 1815, 6.00pm

Liberté Dumont had fully digested the size of her problems long before she caught up with the army's Left Wing, little more than an hour away, at Gosselies.

By the time she had gone a few hundred metres, perhaps six or seven *arpents*, crossed the Ravine and its twin rivers by way of the Lodelisart Causeway, she had licked all the way around the edges of Bourmont's desertion, its implications – not Bourmont alone but a whole clutch of other officers besides – and details of the Emperor's plans that they would carry with them. For her own part, she was acting on behalf of Minister Fouché, and it was not for a mere agent to gainsay the machinations of the government that brought her here. She had fought too long for France to happily see her country defeated, even for the greater good of the people. But she had seen enough of life to know that things are seldom as they seem at the moment of their passing. Allow a week, a month, a year to pass and it was sometimes difficult to believe that you were looking back on the same event. For all she knew, the documents she carried might indeed be a rich subterfuge, part of the game, the bluff and counter-bluff, in which both the Emperor and Minister Fouché were such formidable players. So she would fulfil her orders. Because she owed a debt to Fouché for her life.

But, as the journey had taken her twice that distance again, to Lodelisart itself, its crossroads, the track east to Gilly – nostalgic sounds of battle from that direction now heavy in the clammy evening air – Liberté had bitten down hard on the confused images of her own early history. Family roots at Arcachon. When the Estates General had been convened to deal with the crisis in '89, her father was elected as Delegate for the district's bourgeoisie, travelling to Paris with his three children and pregnant wife early in May that year. They took an apartment on the rue de Grenelle that they occupied for much longer than expected, through all the constitutional turmoil of those two turbulent months. And then, in response to the rumour that Marie-Antoinette was sending the army's foreign regiments against the citizens, the people of Paris, fifty thousand strong, had marched on the Invalides for weapons, then the Bastille for powder. Deputy Dumont had gone with them and later in the day, Madame Dumont – Liberté's mother, close to giving birth – had followed after him. Despite protracted searching, they never saw her again. The shattered remnant of the family returned to Arcachon, stayed there in a mixture of hope and mourning as the country was plunged into war by the foreign powers and their industrialist paymasters, those who feared the potential spread of the Revolution's ideals. The family remained in Arcachon as the strategy of their country's enemies began to work: as the army's defeats caused each of France's factions to turn one against the other; as the mob lost confidence in all of them and developed their own faction; *sans-culottes* unleashing the Terror to purge the country of its traitors, its aristos, its counter-revolutionaries. Moderate groups, like those to which Major Dumont belonged, rose in a federalist revolt against the Committee of Public Safety – and the Committee responded by unleashing its considerable powers against them. Liberté had stood beside her father and his comrades at the barricades of Bordeaux, and though the whole rising ended with a relative whimper, three hundred of the so-called rebels had been selected for transportation to Paris and the guillotine, Liberté among them. And only saved by Fouché's direct intervention. He had seen something in her that he assumed may be useful. Just pure luck. Unlike the rest of those selected from Bordeaux. Another three hundred from Marseilles. Two thousand butchered in Lyons over many months under Fouché's direct supervision, that city re-named.

From Lodelisart, the Brussels road ran further north, two kilometres, forty-five *arpents*, to Jumet. She had watered the mule there, balanced the beast's load afresh – a variety of trade goods; food and a decent bottle; a fodder bag; the large valise that kept her Dragoon uniform; the strong sack in which her helmet was so carefully wrapped and oil-skinned; and the rolled canvas awning that concealed both straight-bladed sabre and a pair of Year Thirteen-pattern pistols. She must find a safe home for her kit long before she reached the enemy lines.

'You fought for the Federalists, for the Girondins,' Fouché had said to her, 'so the price of your life, sweet girl, the price of your family's liberty, is that you now fight for me. For France too, of course. Whenever I need you!'

It seemed a fair bargain, though she would not have been Liberté Dumont had she failed to squeeze as much as possible from the deal, persuaded Fouché – then out of favour, no longer holding any official position, but still with a considerable influence and covert networks – to help find her mother. Yet all to no avail. So she had fought. At Toulon. Then with the 15th in Egypt.

Ah, Egypt! she recalled. The mystic Nile had unlocked something in her, a force that had at first confused and frightened her as little else in life was capable of doing. It had drawn her, irrevocably, to the group of natural philosophers who were so central to young General Bonaparte's expedition staff.

Italy had been her next campaign, reassigned to the 9th. Captured once, by the Austrians, and escaped. Wounded four times at Genola. Captured a second time. Paraded around the Austrian lines as some sort of freak – though, in truth, there were plenty of other women serving in the French ranks. A lengthy captivity, but eventually another escape. Followed the regiment back to Paris, now listed in the changed and incongruous politics of the day as a "gentleman volunteer."

The same incongruous politics, she recalled, *that had by then brought Fouché back from obscurity, installed him as Minister of Police, utilised him to eradicate the very Jacobin Club whose ideals he had so long espoused.*

Liberté had chewed on all this as she rode the final fifteen minutes to the sun-bruised spires and ancient towers, the long-shadowed mills and town thoroughfares of Gosselies. She had endured the sabre scars of Genola, her transfer to the 2nd, the slaughter of Vitoria, the ignominy of Leipzig, a dozen dangerous missions for Fouché in Spain and elsewhere, yet she had never felt so much at risk as she did now, in the aftermath of the attempt on her life in Charleroi. She would deliver the Emperor's plans to the enemy, come hell or high water. Then she would return to the main column, try to complete the second part of her instructions. Either that or she would seal her own fate with that of the army she loved. But, for now, she would focus on this greatest of her problems – that somebody wanted her dead. And, more important, that she had not seen it coming.

There were bodies to be buried. They had been sprinkled along the Brussels road like marker stones, Prussians mostly, from the skirmishing that had dogged their retreat northwards. The grotesquely hacked heads and fractured faces of a cavalry pursuit, which brought back memories of her earlier battles. And here, at Gosselies, the markers were become small cairns, modest mounds of darkest blue, splashed with splayed flesh. The enemy had stood here, though they had not stood long, been driven out at the point of Reille's bayonets.

And, clustered around the dead, each attended by his personal consort swarm of angry blow-flies, were the maggot mourners – the degenerate scavengers who followed behind every army, cleansing the ground with shallow graves for the fortunate, filled ditches for the rest, taking whatever loot they could glean by way of funeral fees. Sometimes they were locals, supplementing their meagre incomes by a few sous here and there, at others they were professional carrion crows.

By this time there was gunfire up in the direction of Brussels too, a balanced echo of the eastward volleys and salvos – the whole army, it seemed, now engaged in a front of lesser scuffles that spread across several leagues.

'The Prussos went that way!' said a fellow, looking up from his work with a pair of pincers and extracting teeth from a corpse's mouth, though he seemed to have shattered more than he pulled. Alongside him, a scabrous younger woman scraped and sweated in the field's margent soil at the town's outer limit. She had a tiny baby swaddled against her back and seemed pregnant with a second. The fellow's thumb jerked over his shoulder, away to Liberté's right.

Fleurus, she thought.

'How much are they fetching now?' she asked.

'The pearlies?' he replied. 'It's a bloody disgrace. State of the economy. I'm lucky if I can get a couple of francs for most of them. An écu for the pointed ones. But they reckon to fetch five times that much in London.'

Liberté looked back to the almost naked corpses that lay close to the man's feet.

'Well, there'll be a good supply soon,' she said. It was an obscene trade, but Europe's wealthy were now paying huge premiums for sets of natural replacements when their own teeth became sugar-rotten, and you could hardly blame even gutter-rats like this one from cashing in. She turned her gaze to the road that ran straight ahead, south to north, between the houses of Gosselies. 'And that way?'

'That way's the English,' the fellow replied. His skin was sallow, a phlegm-green cast to his cheeks, and his eyes tinged with febrile yellow. He regarded her with the predatory curiosity of the entirely lawless, bone-sharp, ricket-ridden. Yet, when he had pocketed his loot, he stood, reached down and grabbed one of the dead men's wrists, dragged him effortlessly to the hole's edge, tipped him over with the toe of a Hessian boot.

'You've served in the ranks?' said Liberté, admiring the quality of his fine footwear, yet assuming that, in truth, the boots had more likely been recently stripped from a hapless Hussar.

The man followed her gaze, began to cough violently.

'Until the lung disease caught up with me,' he gasped. 'Heaven help me, eh, lady? That it's come to this. A real fall from grace. Sergeant too. Ninth Light Infantry.'

'You've a pension then?' she asked.

How old is he? she wondered. *Forty perhaps? A bit less?*

'Pension?' he said. 'For the likes of poor Thénardier? You must be joking. But I know you, lady. I saw you earlier. In Charleroi. You were mixed up in that bit of blood-letting, were you not?'

'It is you that's mixed up, friend,' she replied. 'You've confused me with somebody else.'

Thénardier grinned.

'To each his own place and season, lady,' he said. 'Isn't that what the blessed Saint Augustine taught us? If you say it wasn't you, that's good enough for Thénardier.'

He shifted his grip on the shovel, placed his hands together as though praying, his previously upright military bearing becoming suddenly more bowed, penitent, priest-like.

'And Marshal Ney,' said Liberté, 'in which direction did he go? Do you know?'

'Ney?' the fellow sneered. 'Oh, he never goes anywhere without confiding in old Thénardier. Sergeant, he says to me, I'm off towards Brussels to chase the

English Duke and if any high and mighty mule drivers come looking for me, feel free to send them on behind.'

On a different day, she thought, *and in a different place, I'd teach this scum some respect*. But now she simply smiled at him.

'Well,' said Liberté, 'it's good to know that the Bravest of the Brave has such reliable servants to watch his back. I'll make sure to pass on your regards if I catch up with him.'

'You do that, lady. And I'll look forward to hearing what he had to say for himself, next time our paths cross.'

'You think we'll meet again?' she replied.

'Oh, you can rely on it, lady,' said Thénardier.

Waves of warming wheat lapped away into the insect haze so that, at times, Liberté Dumont would almost forget she was travelling through a war zone. And while the eastern evening still popped and crackled with pyrotechnical celebration, there was comparative tranquillity in her present direction and a dearth of the dead, now that the Prussians had veered away, towards Fleurus – or wherever their seventy-three year old commander, Blücher, might be consolidating his forces.

There were stragglers, naturally, a veritable jam of carts and wagons blocking the next crossroads, Mons to the left, Sombreffe and Namur to the right, and it was a half-league further again until she reached the next concentration of the French Left Wing, at the modest village of Frasnes, with its ancient chapel and crumbling château. Just ahead of her, parties of French Lancers collected casualties, finishing horses that were now beyond help. Imperial Guard Lancers, square-topped czapkas, scarlet jackets of the old "Dutch" 2nd, the blue tunics and crimson facings of the Polish 1st. All one regiment now. Beyond them, running from left to right, crossing the road on this side of the village, ran an extended tangle of fallen foot soldiers.

But whose? she wondered. The uniforms were dark green, though that did not always mean very much. Yet this was clearly a killing ground. And it was impossible that the Guard's Lancers would have attacked their own men. Conclusion? That the dead were allies of the English. Newly-turned Dutchies, perhaps. Or the bloody Nassauers. In either case, these uniforms belonged to enemies, and their destruction told its own story. They had formed up here, not in square but in the thin line formations that the English favoured, even though they were suicidal against cavalry attack. So the Lancers had driven them away at little cost to themselves and the front had moved on yet again, battalions formed up and either advancing to reach it or waiting to march.

Liberté Dumont surveyed the units that she could see: the blue regiments of Line Infantry, mottled with greatcoats in tan or faded grey; the green jackets and frogging, the fur caps of the Guard Light Cavalry Chasseurs; and, furthest away, more green-jacket horsemen – Dragoon squadrons including, she guessed, her own 2nd Regiment. She had thought about this long and hard on the road. It was clearly preferable for nobody else to know her business, and especially her cavalry comrades. They were inquisitive enough at the best of times about her comings and goings. Yet she needed to leave her uniform somewhere, and she could think of nowhere safer than their regimental quartermasters. Besides, she had not reported to her commanding officer since receiving the summons from Fouché. And Colonel Planzeau was not a man to easily accept dominion over his troopers being undermined by a civilian authority, even when that authority was the Minister of Police. Better to appease his vanity if possible, for there was always the possibility that she may need to quickly scuttle back to the ranks if all else failed. She owed Planzeau that respect. It was not a word that she used lightly, and she had no respect for the officer class in general. But finally? She would pay her grudging respects to Planzeau because, in doing so, she might also visit Lucette.

'This explains nothing whatsoever!' the Colonel snarled. He waved Fouché's authorisation letter at her. He was perhaps a year or two older than Liberté and held his left arm permanently in a thin sling due to a wound he had received two years previously – two years before he had assumed command of the 2nd, just a few weeks earlier, in May.

Planzeau dismissed his squadron commanders as soon as Liberté sent word that she needed a moment of his time, then had her escorted to the campaign table at which he was taking wine while his companies took their own ease, smoking, gaming and chatting in the lazy June heat.

'It's not possible for me to dictate the contents of Minister Fouché's missives, sir,' she replied. 'He requires me to fulfil duties on the Emperor's behalf. And armed only with that document, Colonel, I'm afraid.'

He passed it back to her as though it was distasteful to his touch.

By the Host, she thought. *I could do with a stiff drink.*

'And how long?' His accent betrayed Planzeau's Provençal origins. Marseilles, she thought. 'We need every man...' The Colonel scratched his forehead. He had never been comfortable with her. Indeed, Planzeau enjoyed the celebrity of being the fifth Colonel of the 2nd Dragoons in the past two years alone – and none of them had been comfortable with Liberté Dumont's presence among their responsibilities.

'I hope to complete my mission before we confront the English, sir,' she said, then gestured towards the village. 'And those? Part of their army?'

'Sachsen-Weimar's men. Dutch regiments, filled with Germans – Nassauers to be precise. Some Belgians too. Fought like buggers. Caused a new problem.'

'Looting?' she said.

He looked up at her, surprise etched into every creased and frowning feature.

Yet it was a simple deduction. It was hard enough to stop men, accustomed to foraging for their survival on enemy territory, to break the habit in more friendly lands.

'As soon as they found out there were Belgians with Sachsen-Weimar,' said Planzeau, 'dozens of them chose to entirely forget that this is now France once more. Some of the townsmen came to trade for fresh carcasses. But it would have caused a riot. Anyway, we'll need all the horsemeat we can find, before long. Speaking of which, you've taken care of your own mount, I take it?'

She had, indeed. Easily enough, too. Lucette tended to stand out in the horse lines, a fine dappled grey Percheron mare and not far short of sixteen hands. The farriers had confirmed that the greasy heel was now all but disappeared, so she would soon be fit for riding again. *I'll have to make sure I get back for her,* thought Liberté, *before she gets snatched for a remount.* Lucette had transferred with her when she came to the 2nd, an unusual arrangement and only permitted because her former unit had been converted to a Lancer regiment and Lucette was simply too tall, too heavy, for a Light Cavalry mount.

'They all seem to be in good condition, sir,' she replied.

'Well, I'm not sure how anybody in this damn'd regiment would recognise good horseflesh, Trooper Dumont,' Planzeau snapped. 'When I arrived last month, you men...' He paused again. 'The horses were still being turned loose at night in fields of green grain. Clover too. Colic everywhere.' The distant sound of gunfire came to them from away in the east. 'And there,' he continued, 'just my luck. Stuck over here when all the action's with the Prussos.'

'We'll engage the English soon though, Colonel, will we not?'

'You think so? I doubt it. We'll drive off old Blücher at some stage. Tomorrow, or the next day. Then Wellesley will run for the Channel. What else can he do? Two-thirds of his men are Dutch, or Germans, or these bloody turncoat Belgians. They won't stand. So it's not to confront the English that I need you back, Dumont. No, the Prussians will head for the Rhine, wait there for the Austrians and Russians to join them. And then there'll be a reckoning. We'll pay those bastards back for Leipzig.'

But, just then, there was a rumble of cannon fire northwards. Close too. Planzeau jumped to his feet as a galloper came in, the Colonel's Aides and squadron commanders returning quickly to his side while Liberté Dumont quietly moved away, heading for the horse lines where she had left her mule. The English were still close, it seemed, and she had a mission to complete.

She walked the beast – a more contented mule now, with its lightened load – back through the fields where Sachsen-Weimar's men had tried in vain to hold off the Lancers. It might only have been an hour before, but the stench of the charnel house was already gathering here, blowflies again. And the dead mounts that Colonel Planzeau hoped would help supplement the army's diet on its march to the Rhine would not take long before corruption began to set in. Local cattle were gathering around them, sniffing curiously at the carcasses. She had seen it many times before. A horse will avoid dead things like the plague. But cows? They had a morbid curiosity for death, it seemed. And not the cows alone, of course. But the body-followers too. More of the locals and the scavengers, searching among the pockets of the fallen Nassauers, stripping their uniforms.

'Hey!' somebody shouted to her as she crossed the road towards a small chapel, hoping to skirt the rear of the village, avoid the crush of companies marching north. She turned in some surprise to see that the fellow she had met earlier, at Gosselies, was already here and, once again, supervising his woman as she worked. 'I told you we'd meet again,' Thénardier smiled.

'Wouldn't surprise me, with this heat, if there was a storm,' he said, keeping pace alongside the mule. 'What d'you think, my dear?'

'It might help if you'd carry the kid a while,' replied his woman.

'I'm carrying the shovels, aren't I?' said Thénardier.

'Then maybe this kind lady would take her up for a little ride?' suggested the wife.

Liberté had been trying to shake them off since Frasnes, ten *arpents* back. It felt like the longest fifteen minutes of her life. But she halted the mule all the same. Something about pregnant women. The shade of her mother's soul. She had felt the same around Tambour's companion, the Breton mulatta. The vestiges of maternalism, even though Liberté knew that she, herself, would never now bear an infant of her own. She had not bled for a dozen years. Nothing uncommon for women on campaign, for women at war, to lose the bleeding, often for months on end, but with Liberté it had become a permanent state long before she reached thirty.

'What's the child's name?' she asked, as she stripped to her shirt, rolled the russet jacket, tied it safe and tight behind the cantle crosspiece.

'My little treasure?' said the scabrous woman. She untied the large shawl that held the babe to her back, found a suitable space among the sacks of trade goods and fodder bags that hung from the mule's wooden saddle frame. 'We call her the "Little Mare". Isn't that just the thing? Her name is Éponine.'

Fifteen tortuous minutes later found them close to the army's left flank, where the Guard's Light Cavalry was drawn up at the foot of rising ground topped, on the west side of the road, by beech forest that spilled down towards them, a stream running diagonally from its lower reaches through open nearer meadow, fields of rye, and a large farm with gardens and orchard. Stretched along the ground above the farm it seemed, and across the treeless ridge to the right, was the English army. Reille's infantry battalions were drawn up across the road and, further still, the rest of the French Horse. The artillery had come up too, unlimbered and began to return the English gunners' fire, great gouts of smoke and flame bursting from the barrels, though shooting impossibly uphill, while the enemy had the advantage of height and were finding their range.

'Well, you promised us a storm, husband,' cackled Madam Thénardier as the putrid sulphurous smoke drifted past them.

Yes, thought Liberté, *there they are*. The English. But was Wellesley with them? If so, could she reach him? And how much of the English army stood across their path? It was impossible to tell. But a fair climb. The sort of position the English had chosen so frequently in the early days of Spain, they said. And the higher ground extended as far as the eye could see, sloping away both east and west. Difficult. A march in either direction to attempt a move around the enemy would badly expose Ney's flank.

No, she thought, *he's too good a general for that*. She had not been in Russia, but the Marshal's reputation, already solid, had become legend there. That god-awful retreat from Moscow. And Ney in command of the rear-guard without which none of those ice-rimed survivors would have reached the Niemen. Ney, a Marshal of France, wrapped in rags and knee-deep in snow, leading his tatterdemalion band with musket and bayonet, day after bitter day against the Cossack devils. It was rumoured that something of his soul had been left behind in those Russian wastes, and he had certainly wavered while the Emperor was in exile, then again after his return. But Ney was back now, bold as ever, surely. And so trusted by the Emperor that he had been given command of this entire Left Wing of the army. *So what will he do?* she wondered.

'Poor little mite will need feeding soon,' said Thénardier, lifting the shovels from his shoulder and leaning his weight upon them.

'Me too,' replied his wife. 'And not much to do until the lads start killing each other, eh?'

The infant began to wail, not for the first time, and Liberté jumped down from the mule.

'Here,' she said, 'you'd better take her back. Our paths part here, I think.'

'You hope to make a few sous, lady?' sneered the woman, moving cautiously around the beast and beginning to unstrap the baby. 'You've got a cask of dog-dog in there somewhere?'

Liberté wondered how Tambour was faring. She found herself experiencing genuine concern for the woman.

'I leave that to the canteen-mistresses,' she said. 'I don't carry anything so pricey. Just a few ounces of tobacco. Clay pipes. Mess tins. Threads and patches. That kind of thing.'

'And all that stuff you off-loaded with your Dragoon friends,' said Thénardier. 'As well as that neat little letter you showed to the red-breasts back in Charleroi, of course.'

She looked over the top of his insolent head to the rising terrain and inn,

Le Balcan – they had turned off the road there – a few hundred paces away to the rear, near which several French senior officers were gathered, examining the enemy position. The English guns were firing in rolling salvos now, the long-fused shells exploding in filthy clouds and raining deadly swathes of iron shards down onto the infantrymen's heads. It was obvious that the French could not stay there much longer and must advance soon if they wanted to take the hill.

He must do so, surely? thought Liberté. For though the English artillery was well-served, the guns seemed few in number, and while that might be a ploy, it must more likely be an indication that whatever stood upon those heights, it could not be the whole of Wellesley's army. Yet as this thought struck her, there was a strange echo to the gunfire here. Another cannonade in the distance. To the east again. There had been no din of battle in that direction this past hour and anyway, this sounded as though it were more distant still, far beyond the forest that framed the horizon behind Frasnes. But where, and what did it signify?

'You've been spying on me?' she said, returning her attention to Thénardier and realising that he must have also been in the square when the one-legged crone had led the Gendarmes to them. But as she spoke the words, a chill ran down her spine. *Could it be?* she wondered. *Is this another one?* It seemed improbable, yet the best agents were sometimes those most skilled at playing the buffoon. And if Tambour could hide herself behind spouse and child, might this fellow not be doing the same?

'That's a filthy word to use, lady, when all we've done is befriend you on the lonely road.'

Another exchange of shot here, a further rumble away towards Sombreffe, and the French trumpets blared as Ney's gallopers finally began to carry his orders forward to the regiments. *Now we shall see*, thought Liberté. Yet as the commands were conveyed to the rearmost units, they were not answered by any of the drum calls that would normally signal preparation for attack but, rather, by the rattling rhythms of the March, a sure sign that Ney's army – valiant and heroic Ney, the Bravest of the Brave, Prince of Moscow – was falling back.

'I'm sure that you must have been accused of worse,' she said. In truth, she was surprised but relieved by the threat. She could now make her way up the road in relative safety, straight into the English lines. For profiteering pedlars, with no loyalty to anybody but themselves, were usually welcomed by all sides. There were risks, naturally, but...

It took her another moment to realise that Thénardier's wife had been a long time fetching the baby, and she turned quickly, as the woman snatched her hands away from Liberté's russet coat, still strapped behind the cantle.

The bloody documents! she thought, spinning back towards Thénardier, just in time to catch the blur of movement, a dark thing that filled her vision, that swung towards her face and exploded inside her head; shards of white-hot light, a ringing metallic bomb that stunk of iron and blood.

Chapter Ten

Thursday 15th June 1815, 10.00pm

'You lucky bunch!' Sergeant Flambert shouted to his Company. 'That nice Captain Vicquot says you can bivouac here after all. So break out the canteen, Tambour. I bet the lads could do with a glass or two.'

'Well, that's bloody good of him,' grumbled Fronsac. 'How many times have the buggers marched us to that sodding abbey and back again? I've lost count.'

So had his wife. It had been two hours since the Emperor passed them on his own way back to the headquarters in Charleroi, while Tambour had driven the cart up and down the road. More accurately, the pony, Cocotte, had pulled them one way, then the other, as Marianne snatched some sleep at the reins, with Florisette curled beside her while, somewhere else, some fool of a general tried to decide where they should camp for the night. And they were disturbed slivers of slumber too, from which Marianne had been jolted by her own open-throated snores, or by scalding reproaches from the ghost of Maman Cholet, or most often by some sense of pain that she knew emanated from the hawk-faced woman so that, on waking, she also understood perfectly well that Liberté Dumont was again in danger.

Behind them, two men of the Fourth Company, Second Section, *Peloton* A, had bounced Prairial's own dolly over the lane's ruts and rocks, the cobbled road around Soleilmont Abbey, while the mulatta and her new baby vainly tried to rest within the barrow's confines after their ordeal. But they too were now awake, the woman crying to be fed, like one of the seagulls from her Breton harbours.

'So,' said the sergeant, 'any other problems, my boys? Any moans, groans, beefs or bones?'

'If the bastard says that once more…' Marianne muttered, shaking Poppy by the shoulder. 'Come on, girl,' she said. 'Help me get the canvas up.'

'Maman!' the child complained.

'Don't tell me,' snapped Marianne. 'We're all bloody tired.' How long had she been on the go? Eighteen hours. Nothing unusual about that. But it was not every day that she had to kill a bitch like Lomballe. Nor bring another brat into the world. As it happened, she was not even sure that the tent would be needed and she was too tired to worry about it. On warm nights like this one, the lads generally preferred to sit out in the open. But there was something about the streaked cast of the darkened western horizon, more imperial purple than sunset red, that promised a turn in the weather. Yet it was clear enough still, the sky overhead and to the east dusted with stars, clear and black because the half-moon, which had risen at noon, was already set.

'Alright!' she relented. 'Let's just get the stuff off the cart. In case. We can put it up later, if we need it.'

So the nightly routine followed its safely predictable pattern. Fronsac's corporal, Poncet, consulted his simple list, determined that it was Senent's turn on the squad's rota to track down the supply wagon, draw their rations, while Firenzo gathered wood, lit the cook-fire, and confusion reigned until somebody remembered that Cazajus had handed the mess-pot to Trinquart because he had been helping push Prairial's cart. But once the cook-fire was lit, at least they could all get their pipes filled.

And all this, thought Marianne, putting a burning sliver of wood to the bowl of the pipe she had borrowed from Fronsac, *repeated in the second of the Section's platoons, both sections of the Company, all four companies in the Battalion, each of the two hundred battalions scattered from here to Marat knows where. Six companies in each of the Line and Light battalions. How many fires is that?* she wondered, as each stack of kindling sparked into life, reflecting the celestial glory a while until, in the end, even the stars were drowned in the artificial glow of four thousand flames.

'You want help with the fire?' said Fronsac.

'Only if you have some sudden urge to cook,' Marianne replied. 'The lads will have to make do with rations tonight. They'll have worked up a thirst though, eh? So we'll break open a new keg.'

'We'll lose business then,' her husband snarled. 'Argonne's got a pot boiling already. Down by the Second.'

'A few of the lazy buggers might waste their money on Argonne's swill,' said Marianne, 'but most of the Battalion knows that she waters her dog-dog. Let them feed there if they don't want to share their mess rations. But they'll come here for a decent swig afterwards. Anyway, looks like even the Spanish slut's abandoned her.'

But she instantly regretted drawing Fronsac's attention to the approach of Juanita Bufanda, who had come swaggering through the lines, paying her second visit to Prairial and the baby, and the muscles around Marianne's jaw tightened as her husband's gaze followed each sinuous movement of the Spanish girl's hips.

'Hey, *nena*!' shouted Bufanda. 'How it goes? *Madre de Diós*, the kid is whiter than you now. I thought...'

Prairial cursed her, some Breton oath that sounded like she was vending fish on the wharves of Lorient. But Marianne barely heard. She was thinking about Hawk-face again, another vision of her facing danger, a recollection of the strange things she had said about travelling the dream world.

Captain Vicquot – that same nice Captain Vicquot who had finally given them leave to stop tramping the Belgian countryside for the night – summoned her half-an-hour later. So she left Poppy and Fronsac to look after the shop while she stumbled back down the lane to Gilly, yet again. She was unhappy about entrusting Fronsac with the brandy but there was nothing else for it. She could not really expect Prairial to help, and Bufanda was too frightened of Argonne to do any work for the competition. And at least Fronsac would keep an eye on Florisette.

Marianne had been right, for once the individual platoon messes had fed themselves and cleaned their kit, many of the men had gathered at Tambour's tumbrel and blaze, bought shots of her cognac and begun a raucous sing-song. Good-natured enough. All the old favourites. The *Carmagnole*. *It'll be fine*, naturally. *The Onion Song*. And *The Departure*. Muhler knew all the words to that one, the official anthem of the Empire, twin to *The Marseillaise*. And everybody could do the chorus.

'La République nous appelle...'

But she had noticed the way, as the rotgut flowed, some of the men had looked at her daughter. *By the Host!* she thought, as she made her way towards Gilly. *Not so soon. She's not even nine yet.*

Marianne could have chosen any number of routes rather than the one that might take her past Bufanda's canteen, where Catherine Argonne had been left hard at work. But it was difficult to resist the temptation, almost immediately rewarded by the cowed way in which the woman followed Marianne's approach, though without raising her head from the labours in which she was engaged, the crutch carefully angled outwards to provide balance and free both hands for the work.

'So, old woman,' Marianne shouted to her, as she drew alongside, 'you've been left to clean up the slops? Bufanda and your brood all abandoned you?'

Marianne knew the answer very well, for in a curious reversal of yesterday evening's events, Argonne's six youngsters, even the smallest, were back at the Tambour canteen's campfire, singing as lustily as the Grenadiers themselves.

'You'll laugh on the other side of your face, lady, before the week's out!' Argonne replied. Yet there was no venom, nor anger, just a straightforward statement of fact, and all the more chilling for that.

'You should give it up, *cornarde*,' said Marianne. 'Lomballe's been gutted. A coincidence, really, since she was about to do the same to me. Or *thought* she was! Just her bad luck to mix me up with somebody else. Gave me the edge. And all your hobbling about to set the red-breasts on me, dear Catherine, was wasted

– you should have saved your strength for this scrubbing maybe.'

The woman shifted her weight, tossed the handful of cleaning straw back into the burn-blackened cauldron, and wiped the back of her wrist through the sweat and grime on her forehead.

'Bollocks to it!' Argonne replied. 'It's not my job anyway. And I was looking forward to seeing you topped. But perhaps you're right.' She gripped the crutch shaft, jerked herself upright, turned to face Marianne more fully, meeting her gaze with empty eyes. 'Time's too short, eh? And they say you made a decent job of the mulatta's babe. A life for a life, I suppose. That how you see it? Well, Our Lady be praised that you had the gift.'

'I piss on your Lady Whore,' sneered Marianne. It vexed her that after so many years of revolution, folk should have slipped back so easily into that nonsense. 'It's no gift. You learn these things from the old ones. The same women that your black-hooded preachers have so often caused to burn.'

Saying that, she felt the wind-rush again, was swept back to Cholet in Saint-Sébastien. The horror. But then, instantly, from Cholet to Hawk-face, somewhere still close, the danger again. It was a confused and mixed emotion. Who was she? Why this connection? Secret agent perhaps, yet the woman was living some strange delusion, was she not? Believed herself charged with some nonsensical missions she had promised to share. Something about the Shaveling's dormeuse? The promise of gold as reward for Marianne's participation in her schemes. Well, it was tempting. Maybe just the chance she so desperately needed to lift Florisette out of this life and into a better one. And then there was the madness. The glimmer of hope that, through Hawk-face, she might somehow, absurdly, find a way to exact revenge against that evil bastard who had butchered Cholet.

'Well,' said Catherine Argonne, crossing herself, 'may the Lord have mercy on you for that blasphemy. But you have no need to fear any hurt from me, Tambour.'

No? thought Marianne. *Well, that makes me feel better.*

'They're in good voice tonight,' said the captain. He was quartered in a windowless cottage at the nearer end of the hamlet, a candle flickering on the table.

'It's going to be a long session, Captain, more's the pity. I could do with some sleep.'

'Ah, the baby. It must have been tiring,' said Vicquot. He was probably thirty, with all the appearance of a man famished in most aspects of his life. 'Did she name it?'

'Josef, after the father,' Marianne replied.

'Fine. Then I'll write up the Declaration later. But if you were expecting to bed down for the night, Tambour, you'd have been disappointed, even without the singing. I need you to go back to Charleroi.'

Christ's Hooks, she thought. *He can't be serious.*

'You've run out of tobacco again, Captain?' she sighed. Yet perhaps it was no bad thing. All that nonsense with Lomballe had prevented her hunting down more supplies and she had no idea when she might next have the opportunity.

'Well,' Vicquot replied, 'you can pick me up a few ounces while you're there. I'll have to owe you the money, of course. Usual terms?' Marianne nodded. Loans to the officers were a regular part of her business. A part at which she excelled. She acted as a bank for the rankers and lent from its vaults – the false compartment at the back of her cask, in truth – with appropriate interest, the rate depending on how much she liked the officer in question. The profits were all her own, of course. She had not yet built up the level of trust with her new battalion that she had earned over many years with the 22nd, though it was getting there. 'But that's not really why you're needed back in town,' continued the captain. 'You know that General Letort's been wounded, of course. I understand he spoke with you.'

She could almost feel the weight of Letort's gold Napoléon in the *reticule* laced about her waist.

'That was before the fight,' she replied. 'He still lives?' There was suddenly renewed hope for the man. They could ill-afford to lose those good ones they still possessed.

'Surgeon Blondy is with him. But he needs somebody to help look after his patient. Since you already seem to be acquainted…'

'It was Prairial who caught the General's eye,' she said. 'He has a soft spot for babies, it seems. Has a brat of his own? So I think you need to find somebody else, Captain. I've still got work to do.'

'Generals don't have brats, Tambour. And you're all we've got at the moment. Besides, I heard all about poor little Lomballe. I had a soft spot for that girl.' *Soft?* Marianne wondered. *Or a hard one?* She smiled to herself. 'You may have been lucky with the Gendarmerie,' he continued, 'but that doesn't put you in the clear. If we'd been in depot, it would have been different. Very different. A Battalion Court of Justice, with the wrong fellows on the Bench?'

'Fine,' said Marianne, 'you've made your point. I'll start walking again.'

'No need,' Vicquot smiled. 'We've got some more wounded going back to Charleroi. An ox wagon and an ambulance, I think. You can catch a ride. Report to Surgeon Blondy, will you? You'll find him, and the general too, at the house of Notary Delbruyère. By the river. Somebody will point you in the right direction.'

It was impossible to credit that such a modest passage of time could cut so effectively between the heroic halls of a man's past and the inglorious garrets of his present. The General's flesh had lost its weathered wealth and sunk to the waxen tallow of a shrunken candle stub. The hair that, just hours before, had been a feast of healthy curls was now reduced to the consistency of stewed cabbage. The eyes, earlier so brazen with summer's blaze, were now the cold grey ash of winter's spent fuel reserves. He was propped upon his side in the bed that Notary Delbruyère had presumably once occupied, the General's white midriff wrapped in bandages that wound down to his buttocks and the soiled, wet drawers that covered his upper legs and his modesty.

At least, thought Marianne, setting down her cask, *as much modesty as may be maintained with a strip of oakum through your lower gut that stinks of piss on one side, shit on the other.* It must have hurt like buggery when the surgeon had poked it into place. She had seen oakum used to drain wounds in the past, but rarely at such close quarters.

'Will it help?' she said. 'To drain the poisons?'

'We can only hope so,' said Surgeon Blondy, prematurely grey, loosening his spattered apron and slipping into his green Dragoon officer's jacket. 'But it's not that which troubles me.' Letort's body spasmed, forced a scream from between his clenched teeth. His right hand groped towards his crotch as his groin convulsed, only easing when a tiny fresh patch appeared within the existing cotton dampness. 'It's that!' Blondy pointed. 'He needs to pass water every few minutes. Yet never anything but a few drops. His kidneys, I fear. I removed all the splinters of hip bone that I could find. But the kidneys...'

'And what d'you expect me to do about it?' asked Marianne.

'The regiment has other men coming in,' said the surgeon. He hung the apron behind the bedroom door, picked up his rosewood Instrument Chest and matching Dressings Box. 'And God knows we're only at the start, already over-stretched. Short of doctors and orderlies. I need to make sure that everything's sorted. Though I won't be long. They tell me you've handled wounds before?'

Marianne shrugged.

'What can I tell you? I threw my first stitches into a flap of some fellow's face when I was eleven. At Marengo. My first splint for a shattered leg the same year, at Goito. Waste of time, of course. It had to come off anyway. Then I picked up stuff about laudanum compresses from a Moor kettle-drummer. When was that? Heilsberg, I think. Maybe Friedland.' She remembered East Prussia. That forsaken hole! Their gear all shredded and looking like a bunch of beggars. And then there had been the fevers. The typhus. All the others.

'For pity's sake,' snapped the surgeon, 'it's not an examination for the Paris Faculty, Tambour. I was just checking that I can leave you alone with him for a few minutes. His valet is below, if you need any help, though the man is worse than useless.'

General Letort's clothes and equipment bore evidence to this, heaped in a corner of the room so that, while he lapsed back into unconsciousness, she took it upon herself to tidy, brought the boots neatly to attention, folded the blood-soaked breeches and holed shirt, examined the blue jacket with the absurdly precise oval missing from the crusted cloth above the left skirt front. The aiguillette that he had worn so proudly and the fringed gold epaulette to which it had been attached, both were now absent, and so was his bicorn hat.

But the sword was still there, propped against a mahogany side chair, along with a small saddle valise. The purse, however, from which he had gifted his coins, was also nowhere to be seen.

He screamed again, his eyes open and staring madly once more, while his body writhed – so far as its weakened state allowed. The spasm lasted longer this time, ended with a new trickle of urine. She thought to clean him, knew it was futile, settled instead for taking a damp cloth from the bedside porcelain to sponge his forehead.

'Did we break them?' he murmured.

'Like twigs, General,' she smiled. 'Bloody Prussos! Never could stand their ground.'

'Prussians?' he said. Then again, 'Prussians.' He looked up at the ceiling. 'Where is this? Jena?'

'No, General. Not Jena. That was nine years ago. But you broke their bastard squares there too. And you'd better get back on your feet! There'll be more squares to smash. Tomorrow. The day after. Prussos and Goddams both.'

'English?' he whispered. 'Yes, the English. My wife is English.'

'You told me.'

He peered at her, struggling for recognition.

'Father brought her to Paris. When she was a baby.'

'What was he? Another English profiteer? Banker?'

Letort smiled, a weak twitching of his pale lips.

'Revolutionary!' he said. 'Come to support us.'

Ah, she thought, *the British Jacobin Club*. Hard to remember now how many of them had crossed the Channel, thrown in their lot with the National Convention.

'He stayed?'

'And died,' said Letort. 'Would you do something for me?'

'If I can, General.'

He directed her to his valise, to a pocket edition of *Le Ministre de Wakefield*, begged her to read a passage for him.

'You can read?' he said. 'I never learned English and Sarah's French is perfect.' He panted as the pain returned. 'So I have to read *Monsieur* Goldsmith in translation. Do you mind?'

'And your baby?' said Marianne. What did you call her?'

He smiled.

'Fanny,' he replied. 'Fanny-Rosalba.'

The book fell open at a well-thumbed page. A poem. And she read for him.

'*When lovely woman stoops to folly,*
And finds too late that men betray,
What charm can soothe her melancholy,

What art can wash her guilt away?
The only art her guilt to cover,
Hide her shame from every eye,
To give repentance to her lover,
And wring his bosom, is... to die.'

'Oh, Christ...' said the General.

His fists and facial features clenched tight, so that Marianne gripped one of his hands, looked around for something to push between his teeth.

'Sarah!' he screamed, and tears squeezed from between his eyelids.

'It will pass,' said Marianne, though on this occasion it did not. Not for a long time.

Letort's agony became worse, the torture more extreme, so that he would at one moment lapse into pain-induced stupor, the next be jolted awake again by the self-same torment. The cries became louder until she was certain, first, that they must surely deafen her and, second, that he must surely expire. His back was arched, despite the wound that pierced his lower abdomen, and she marvelled at it. For she knew that this was the worst of all wounds. She had seen pain in every form, but she had never seen pain such as that exhibited by men shot in the lower gut. So she could not imagine the sheer brutality of stretching and testing that wound with his current contortions. She still had the *salvavirgo*, back within her bodice, and for a moment she thought about ending his miseries.

And then they stopped.

A cold sweat drenched every inch of Letort's exhausted body as a jet of piss finally flowed free, soaking his drawers afresh but spreading, too, a blossoming scarlet flower.

'Oh, God in Heaven!' the General panted. 'What was that?' He sobbed. 'What?'

Marianne was frightened now. This was beyond her. So she thanked everything she held dear that Surgeon Blondy chose that moment for his return.

'What's happened here?' he demanded, setting down his matching cases, though Marianne could not rightly tell him. The surgeon crossed to his patient, eased up the bandages and pulled down the front of Letort's undergarment. He pointed to the Instrument Chest.

'In there,' he said. 'Second tray. Bullet extractor.'

Marianne unbuckled the fastening strap, lifted the lid and removed the upper section, finding the lengthy forceps beneath.

'These?'

He snatched them from her, probed within the general's drawers, and lifted out a hard lump, the shape of a small shrimp, black-crusted.

'You passed this?' Blondy asked the General. Letort licked his lips, barely managed to nod a response. 'Well,' said the surgeon, 'that's one problem solved.'

'What is it?' Marianne whispered.

'This, Tambour, is the missing piece of his coat, driven into the poor fellow's kidney. Well, at least he should rest now. Will you watch with him a few minutes more. I need to make one more call. I'll try to find some fresh drawers for him. Then we can at least get him cleaned up. Fresh dressings too. It will be quite the thing.'

'So…' Marianne paused, hope filling her again as she whispered. 'He will live?'

The surgeon looked over her shoulder, saw that Letort was sleeping, then looked at her with exasperation.

'Don't be a bloody fool!' he snarled.

Damn the man! she thought, furious with herself that she had allowed Letort to affect her so much. Tiredness, she told herself. Just that. It was almost midnight as she climbed the winding cobblestones of Charleroi's main street, still with the prospect of another thirty minutes' walk and then, perhaps, a few hours' sleep. And at least she had found a local trader willing to part with a decent stock of tobacco and clay pipes before leaving the lower quarter. She heaved the leather carrying strap of the *tonnelet*, set it more snugly on her shoulder and plodded forward, though the slope made each of her legs feel like lead. But she pushed the journey along by mentally counting the cache of coin and Maman Cholet's chain and locket, wedged and wadded silent within the cask's hidden confines. She knew each gold Napoléon intimately, could account for every source. Nineteen in total. The equivalent of 380 francs, a year's pay for Fronsac, four times the amount paid to a line infantryman. *But how much do you need,* she wondered, *to secure a daughter's future?* More than 380 francs, she supposed. And this, she decided, was an even greater problem. That even the humblest gutter-snipe, the poorest street urchin, lived close enough to normal society that they would understand the length of the ladder, however daunting, they must climb to escape. Yet, from Tambour's perspective, trapped within the cloistered confines of the army's institution, she could not even imagine the lowest rungs. Well, she would find out.

She breathed a sigh of relief as the weight fell from her thighs and she reached the levelled expanse, the rutted carriage slabs of the upper town's square. It was busy again, some townsfolk dancing on this nearer side, lanthorns and braziers lit, the cooking fires of the First Grenadiers, flaming torches blazing in soldiers' hands, deep shadows flickering across the surrounding walls, wood smoke and horse dung, while outside the miners' tavern, the Emperor's small grey Arab stallion stood saddled, striking sparks from the stones with its fore-hoof. *Marengo again!* she thought, as though the horse's nickname was an omen.

Well, she smiled to herself, *at least the Little Shaveling seems to have snatched some sleep.*

'What's happening?' she asked a sergeant of the Old Grumblers, who had removed his bearskin and was untangling the ceremonial cords and polishing its copper eagle-plate on his uniform sleeve. 'He's on the move?'

The old sergeant shrugged.

'It was all panic ten minutes ago,' he replied. 'Bloody couriers and Aides running in and out, knocking over musket stacks by the minute. But it seems like the Prussos and the Goddam bastards are in flight everywhere, running like dogs. His Majesty's gone back inside for his dinner. Pleased with himself, I'd say. So it looks like we get some rest. The word is that tomorrow night we march on Brussels. We should be there early Saturday morning. And that's it! Not much of a campaign, eh?'

Chapter Eleven

Friday 16th June 1815, 5.00am

Across an ocean of time, Liberté Dumont saw herself, once more, aged fifteen, in the apartment on the rue de Grenelle, though the image was one drawn from deep within the memories of her mother. She felt the burden of an unborn child in her womb, the weight of her worry about a husband, Liberté's father, who was all too often the source of her greatest concerns. And she heard, through her mother's ears, the distant storm that she knew was no natural thunder, but the famished beast of the Parisian people, unleashed at last.

'No, my dear,' she heard her mother's voice say, as if it came from her own mouth. 'You must stay and care for the little ones. I have to find your father.'

'But Maman,' that other Liberté replied, 'the baby!'

At fifteen, the sharp features that would lend her the handsome aquilinity of later years were already evident, but strange to observe them through another's eyes.

'The baby's not ready yet.' She felt the muscles of her mother's face frame a smile, her gaze flicker from one to another of the younger children, tasted the hidden terror that, at her age, another birth was almost suicidal folly. But, laced throughout, she could smell the powder in the air, the scent of a revolution that had its heart in Paris, not in the National Assembly. The Districts were organised now, furious with starvation, fired by the appeals of Camille Desmoulins to take up arms.

And I must be out there with them! thought Liberté's mother.

She left the apartment, descended the flake-painted staircase to the yard, then ducked through their wicket gate to the street beyond. She turned westward, towards the Invalides, still the closest sounds of upheaval, though the cannon fire now seemed to be coming from the opposite direction and across the Seine. It was an hour past noon and, in better days, she had known this thoroughfare heavy with fresh baking, sweet and sharp with family stews, cheeses and roasting meats. Yet the grain crop failures, the systematic hoarding of food to force up prices, had led to widespread starvation so that, today, there were simply the vapours of hunger, seasoned with the sweat of July's white and blinding heat.

Her feet felt every fiery embrace as she cradled her swollen belly, balanced its bulk and kept to her own shaded side of the road, past the enormous stone and marble fountain – its twin spouts typically devoid of water – and the modern elegance of the Galliffet mansion. Outside the Carmelites' convent, a group of men, women and children, all rags and ribbons, were hauling a field piece, pushing an ammunition cart up the road.

'Where are you going, citizens?' she called, as they drew near.

'To the Saint-Antoine!' they yelled. 'To the Bastille!'

She asked whether the Invalides was still held. And yes, they told her. Strongly held. But they had no news of Deputy Dumont. The crowds grew thicker, more raucous, the closer she came to the Veterans' Hospital and arsenal, frequent clashes between the workers from the faubourgs and the middle-class militiamen who seemed to think they had a duty to patrol this centre of more bourgeois revolt, to protect the area from looting. For there was no sign of the army, not even the foreign regiments with which they had earlier been threatened. So, had the troops joined the Revolution perhaps? There were rumours to that effect, that those close at hand, both in the Military School and stationed on the Champ de Mars, had simply stayed in their quarters, while the people – armed with little more than cudgels and makeshift pikes – had stormed the Town Hall, filled the Place Louis Quinze, crowded into the Invalides.

Their debris filled the foetid moat that formed the building's boundary, littering the short bridge that crossed from street to esplanade, the bridge that was now packed with a modest throng attempting to free an enormous and ornate siege gun, the wheel of which had become firmly jammed around a gateway bollard on the farther side. A horseman cavorted back and forth, one of those fellows always on hand to assume authority at such times but who, invariably, succeed only in augmenting the confusion and chaos.

'No,' he yelled. 'Use the handspikes. The handspikes!'

Liberté's mother again tried to ask the citizens about her husband, but they were all too occupied to bother with her. So she felt compelled to follow the path further, across the esplanade's lawns to the entrance portico of that many-windowed façade, framed by the glittering dome of the St. Louis chapel beyond. But as she tried to move on, to cross the bridge, that fool on a horse sidestepped his mount towards her. It seemed to come from nowhere, looming up, monstrous large, until she could see nothing but the coarse hair of its withers, her nostrils filled with the smells of hay and dust, stable timber and manure, leather and saddle sweat. Its shod hooves drummed and skittered on the stones, so that she danced her feet away, fearful of being kicked or crushed. And as she tried to move away, her own shoe caught on the lower step of the gatehouse. She fell heavily, cracked her head on the roadway's paving blocks, shrieked as intolerable pain jolted through her spine. Liberté Dumont felt that agony, all those years later, through the mists and torments of her own injuries, and was almost returned to her present. But she was close this time, closer than she had ever been before to discovering Maman's fate. She struggled to remain in their shared past, concentrated her will until her mother's eyes opened once more, allowing Liberté to see through them again.

The horseman spared barely a glance despite the scream that forced itself from between her mother's gritted teeth as she clutched at her stomach, looked down to see her skirts soaked in blood.

'Help me!' she moaned, though the crowd had the siege gun on the move now, were trundling it across the bridge. But there was a woman, ragged, wearing a soldier's uniform jacket, who had been hauling on the wheel spokes, using her weight to help turn the wheels. Their eyes met, and the woman left the cannon and her comrades, walked back across the bridge. She stood with hands on hips, stared hard at Liberté's mother while, through her mother's eyes, Liberté returned her gaze, feeling the fire in her own belly, shocked to find that she recognised this person, a familiarity that she could not explain.

But how do I know her? she thought, as the pain tore once more through her innards, coalesced into a tunnel of blackness into which she was slowly dragged, brought spinning back from that ethereal plane.

Liberté Dumont lay sprawled down the bank of a shallow ditch, her head caught in the lower branches of some shrub. Consciousness ebbed and flowed, largely through her own volition for, in truth, she had fought hard to cling to her mother's presence, the link to that fragmented imprint of her spirit.

She lifted a tentative hand to her aching face, though careful not to move the head itself, since her skull throbbed intolerably, the slightest twitch bringing fresh waves of nausea. Her cheek was swollen, angrily sore, and crusted. Blood, she thought, as her fingers probed a cut at the base of her ear lobe. The flat of a shovel, she remembered. Our Lady be praised that it had not been its edge. She closed her eyes, rested a moment more, inhaled the odours of grass and earth, savoured the dampness in her shirt as it soaked up the dew, a grey morning mist rising from beneath her and filling the surrounding countryside. She listened for bird-song through the ringing in her ears. But there was nothing. She could hear nothing.

It was the horsemen who finally roused her again, for she felt the vibration through her whole body. It forced her to move, more by instinct than anything else, though the effort was crippling, and the next few minutes saw her succeed simply in rolling to the bottom of the ditch. She rested again, her shoulders against one slope, her legs stretching, inelegant, up the other. Yet she could at least now take stock. The mule was gone. Her jacket was gone. Fouché's letter of safe passage was gone. Her lock-picks were gone. Her pipe and tobacco pouch were gone. Her purse was gone, its leather retaining strap cut from the waistband of her breeches. And those thieving Thénardiers were gone too. But the encoded documents, meaningless and worthless to the casual observer, were discarded along the bottom of the channel. She had wondered whether the couple might be yet more agents, but she dismissed the idea now. Chancers, nothing more. And they had seemingly dumped her near the spot where they had attacked her. She cursed herself for a fool. How in the name of all that was holy had she let her guard down so badly?

The earth trembled again as she levered herself up the bank to see more clearly. Horsemen, as she had supposed. Fifty of them, perhaps, and close. And must be the enemy, for they were trotting down the slope in extended formation to screen groups of green-coated skirmishers advancing behind them. These latter could easily be more Nassauers, Germans in Wellesley's service. But the cavalry? Hussars clearly. Heavily braided dolmans, dark brown; waist girdles barrelled red and white; grey overalls; shakos protected by oilcloth covers. Yet from where? It occurred to her that they might also be some remnant of the Prussian force driven off towards the east last night. Simple enough to be cut off like this. But, whoever they might be, they were coming up fast and the troopers on their right flank, those nearest her ditch, were already pointing in her direction. She was seen.

A section peeled off, spurred their mounts, and one of them drew a curved sabre. He was plainly intending to take no chances. Liberté looked to the right, back towards Frasnes, but could not properly see the village for the mist, for the rolling ground, and for the pulsing at the back of her eyeballs. She had no idea whether the French army was still at hand. Ney had fallen back to where? Gosselies? All the way to Charleroi? By the easy manner of these Hussars, Ney might have been twenty leagues away.

She finally managed to heave herself out of the ditch, just as the horsemen halted, laughing, on the other side. The fellow with the sabre pointed the tip of its lethal blade in her direction. He mouthed something at her, though she could not hear him, regardless of the language he was using. She put her hands to her ears, pressed with her fingertips, though gently, in an effort to clear them. The cavalryman was saying something else, his lips moving slower, with more deliberation. Asking what she was doing here, she assumed. Or was he? For he was now putting a hand to his own right cheek, patting at it, then pointing to her own injury. *Ah*, she thought, *he wants to know who did this*. So she pointed towards Frasnes, spat on the ground.

'The French!' she said, confident of being taken for a Belgian.

He mimed the word, apparently in her own language, then raised a quizzical eyebrow.

'Yes,' said Liberté, stooping to collect her documents and pleased to note that a few sounds were now distinguishable, beyond the whistling deafness. '*Ja!*'

The Hussar's voice came to her at last.

'French,' he said. 'Where?'

Some of the enemy skirmishers had taken up positions above her, at the edge of the tree line, around the farm and down into a field of rye, but the rest had reached the bottom of the slope, also in no great hurry, halting near a small chapel while the rest of the Hussars were spread from here, across the cobbled road, then past Le Balcan. But they had no sooner arrived at the inn than they were wheeling back, a trumpeter sounding Recall while, beyond them, a mass of lance pennons seemed to float into view, hovering above the low-lying mist at the nearer edge of the village. And then, bursting onto a patch of clear farmland, horse artillery, each team carving a tight circle that spun their guns to bear against the Prussians and unlimbered, ready for action.

'There!' said Liberté, trying hard to keep the sarcasm from her voice, the pride in her army from showing on her face, though the Hussar was barely paying her any attention now, a sergeant shouting guttural orders to their section. They trotted away, making for the road, where the squadron was re-grouping, but the fellow turned back, just once.

'Stay!' he shouted to her. *'Abwarten!'*

The fortunes of war change so quickly, she thought. For, just a moment earlier, she seemed to have found her perfect passport to penetrate the enemy lines. The Prussians would surely have been willing to convey her to Wellesley's camp. It seemed an ideal time, for the main Prussian force was, indeed, in retreat and the English genuinely in danger of being cut off from the coast. So if Wellesley could have been persuaded by Fouché's documents that this was all going perfectly to the Emperor's plan, that perhaps the numbers facing him were greater than the reality, the campaign might be won without undue further bloodshed. But now? Now she must wait to see how this particular twist of fate would resolve itself. Or think of an alternative plan.

From the higher ground to Liberté's left, the enemy's artillery was opening fire, iron shot whistling through the air, while the Nassauer skirmishers started to fall back, in good order, on the farm, watched nervously by the Hussars. Liberté understood their concern, for the ghostly pennons had now materialised into a solid body of the Imperial Guard's Red Lancers, the same that she had seen earlier. Two full squadrons, it seemed, and the Prussian horsemen already outnumbered when a further unit of French cavalry – Guard Chasseurs from their green braided dolmans and black fur colpacks – ambled casually into view on this opposite flank.

If the Prussos don't fall back soon, she thought, *they'll end up with their arse in a vice*. But she knew also that they would stand as long as possible, to cover the skirmishers' retreat. Yet they did not stand. They were outnumbered, and they faced lances: almost three metres of heavy blackened ash shaft, tipped with a wicked steel point beyond the red-over-white swallow-tailed pennon, and secured to the trooper's wrist by a strap of Hungarian leather. She had fought Lancers herself. Only Austrians, it had to be admitted. But Lancers all the same, and she had no fear of them. The sight of those steel tips coming at you was daunting, for sure, but once you were inside the reach of the lance itself, the man wielding it could be cut down easily. But against superior numbers? That was a different story. So she was amazed to see the Hussars begin to Forward Walk in response to their trumpets, to hear the grating screech as sabres were drawn and sloped, the more strident notes of a Trot March, blades at the Guard, the ring and chime of horse harness, and then the urgency of the Charge, swords now Advanced. She could almost feel the amazement within the opposing squadron, but the Red Lancers answered soon enough with their own rapid and more familiar succession of trumpet calls, and they launched forward, while the artillerymen hurled round-shot and canister back and forth, though with apparently little effect, apart from the awful din, the smoke, the clods of earth tossed into the sky.

This is only going one way, Liberté decided. *And I'm damned if I'll end my days trampled by our own lads.* She could envisage the momentum of that charge, carrying the Lancers through the thin Prussian assault and, despite the slope, rolling them up to the tree line. Besides, she needed to be up there too. To find Wellesley. She could make a detour, of course, skirt this entire area, but she suspected that the English Duke would be somewhere straight ahead. It's where the Emperor would be, after all, if their roles were reversed. So she began to edge up the gradient, aiming for that ripple of yellow crops flowing downhill, connecting the large walled farm at the forest edge with a similar but smaller collection of buildings on the flatter ground to Liberté's left.

I just hope some trigger-happy bugger doesn't take me for a target, she thought, keeping low and trying to focus past her pounding head and heart. *And if I reach the top, what then? How long to find Wellesley's position?* It would have been so much easier with the mule. Nobody bothered you if they thought you were a trader. Well, she would find the beast in due course, settle with the Thénardiers. And then? With the first of her duties done, she would find Tambour again. Or try to fathom these clues about her mother's mystery.

The cannon fire had intensified, shot screeching between the opposing batteries, explosions shaking the hillside but, thankfully, none on this section of ground, though they also held no great terror for her. A dozen major battlefields had taught her fatalism. The only thing for a soldier to fear was fear itself. And she looked back to see how close the Prussian Hussars had now come to their own annihilation. Yet they surprised her once more, for they had shifted into an echelon formation, a thin column, its meagre sections widely spaced, angled obliquely at the nearest corner of the Red Lancers' squadrons. It was certain death for those at the echelon's head, including the officer who led them. He was speared quickly, among the clamour of steel and scream of horse, along with six or seven other troopers, but the sacrifice had the effect of drawing the Lancers around in an attempt to find a target against which they could concentrate their lance tips more efficiently, to surround the foe, though in practice, it allowed the dispersed echelon to swing outwards so that it was they, instead, who fell upon the French flank. But they did not stop to mêlée, simply kept riding, slashing at the unprotected scarlet sleeves and shoulders, the faces of the Lancers, whose weapons were now almost useless in such confined conditions. The result was a turning wheel, spinning anti-clockwise, with the Prussians clinging to their own section of the rim until it had made a full half-turn and the Hussars allowed themselves to be catapulted back towards the slope, while their opponents, their impetus lost, struggled to turn about and organise themselves for the inevitable pursuit. It had been a desperate manoeuvre, but one that had purchased time for the Nassauer skirmishers. And the Hussars took full advantage of the Lancers' confusion, hurtled up the road, past the tiny chapel, their numbers thinned, heading for the safety of their own guns – at least, so long as they could also outrun the Chasseurs galloping to cut off their escape.

Liberté reached a narrow track, golden rye waving along the length of its far side, and she followed the rutted path up to the farm's gates and flaking walls, from which the young faces of more green-coated Nassauers peered down at her, curious, laughing, making bawdy gestures.

No more than boys, she thought, gave them a couple of gestures in return, shouted a few obscenities, then ducked around the side of the barn that formed this nearer perimeter of the property. A stream ran close to the rear, a patch of ground where more soldiers were busy gathering the last of the farm's hens. They stopped as she turned the corner, caught in the act, perhaps a moment of guilt, then remembered where they were. More raucous shouting that she simply ignored until she found what she wanted. A discarded shoulder yoke and a few battered buckets. They would not fool anybody for long, but she felt they would lend her some anonymity, some substitute for the mule and her trade goods. So she splashed some of the rivulet's water into a couple of the buckets, hung each of them on the yoke's hook ends, settled its central curve, the worn grain of its grey timber around her neck increasing the pounding in her head. The Nassauers carried away their plunder and Liberté followed them, slowly passing behind eight further companies of Line Infantry, still more Nassauers, that stretched away to the edge of the woodland, their artillery just below them on the ridge top and now firing canister at the French Chasseurs and Lancers still milling on the ground above the chapel. The Prussian Hussars, those who were left, were now safely behind their own lines and trotting towards a gathering of senior officers grouped at the roadside on the highest rise.

Liberté could see that behind the ridge the terrain and the Brussels highway flattened again to yet another farm, before rolling once more to somewhat higher ground, perhaps a thousand paces away, where the road reached three or four buildings on the distant skyline. To her left, the trees and thick undergrowth ran all the way to that settlement behind more narrow fields of tall rye and corn, which also filled the rolling fields and all the ground east of the road. And that road was anxious with its own concerns, moving a thin trickle of citizens north, local farming folk, families displaced, as usual, from the sparsely scattered hamlets, yet shunting them regularly aside, their carts and belongings, giving priority to the English army's units moving south.

Still moving south! she thought, and was astonished at the paucity of enemy troops holding this ridge. She had assumed, on the previous evening – as, presumably, Ney must have assumed – that the English army was here in force. And yet there were, here, no more than a battalion, a few extra companies, a squadron, a couple of batteries, and all of them belonging to the forces of

Oranje-Nassau. Not a redcoat regiment in sight, for even those advancing down the highway were more of these Dutch-Germans.

So where is Wellesley? Not with the senior officers gathered on their hillock, that was certain. She decided to slip past them, hurrying to catch the closest group of fugitives, a ragged family with a palsied child, an older woman pushing their handcart of teetering possessions. Liberté, only a couple of *toises* behind them, kept her head down, while also peering through the corner of her eye at those commanders, their Aides and, in particular, the fellow at their centre. She had never seen him before but she could not be mistaken in his identity. It was, after all, her job to know such things. So, a simple deduction. Immaculately and extravagantly attired in hussar uniform, a scarlet dolman, jet-black pelisse edged with sable fur, both richly braided in gold thread. He pointed with his plumed bicorn hat, explaining the French positions to the young men around him. And they *were* young, for it was said that he favoured young men. Boys, in fact. He sat tall and slender in his saddle too, his high, domed head showing premature hair loss. 'Thin William', the French named him. Not yet twenty-three, this Prince Willem van Oranje-Nassau, and already a Major-General by the grace and favour of the English. And here on this ridge because he had a personal interest. Liberté understood this. For, with his royal father, the King of the Netherlands, he had been driven into exile as an infant twenty years earlier, when Dutch and Belgian patriots had risen up, and following the French example, had demanded an end to the absolute monarchy, sought help from France's revolutionary army. But the royal family was back now, restored at the point of Prussian and Cossack lances; Belgium once more part of Thin William's Netherlands fiefdom.

Well, young sodomite, she thought, *let's see how long you can hang onto it.*

She was almost past, joined the main Brussels road, risked a glance back towards Frasnes to see whatever the Dutch Prince was observing, and there she saw that while the morning mists were quickly dissipating, they did so only to reveal a different fog: the grey smoke of a hundred French cooking fires, squadrons of cavalry reorganised among the trampled cornfields and, being drummed from the direction of Gosselies, still more columns of Ney's infantry.

Keep coming! she willed them. *And you will simply walk all over these boy soldiers.* And, meanwhile, she would play her own part, find Wellesley, deliver Fouché's documents.

But she suddenly found her path blocked. A horse stomped and clattered onto this cobbled highway and she found herself gazing at the soft black leather of a Hungarian-style boot toe in its iron stirrup; steel spurs; the leg of grey overalls, buttoned and cuffed; a black fur shabraque saddle cover with red wolf's teeth edging; a forage bag and mess tins; an ornate red sabretache; sword slings and sheath; barrelled girdle; brown dolman; and the stern face of the Prussian Hussar who had spoken with her earlier.

'*Fräulein?*' he said. '*Halten Sie hier, bitte!*'

Chapter Twelve

Friday 16th June 1815, 8.00am

'I was instructed only to deliver the documents to the English Duke,' said Liberté, standing before the long and time-worn table. 'To your Commander-in-Chief. Only to Wellesley.'

The commandeered kitchen occupied the west-facing ground floor of the pitch-roofed, two-storey farmhouse, perhaps a hundred paces from the Charleroi-Brussels highway and in the lower ground of the Gémioncourt stream's fording place. The farm buildings themselves, mostly solid barns and vehicle sheds that matched the size and design of the house, stood around a central courtyard, their outer walls loop-holed and forming a perimeter, like that of a small fortress that had stood for hundreds of years, she guessed. It was ancient, gated on the far side of the yard where a cobbled track joined the main road.

'I am in command here, madam,' replied Thin William, his French predictably impeccable, perfectly petulant. 'Do you *see* any Englishmen? No, there are only our stout Netherlanders, standing to defend their own lands.'

'Is that so, sir?' she laughed. 'They tell me that most of them are pressed. That, given the option, they should prefer to fight for the Emperor.'

'It is a strange envoy,' said the Prince, 'who brings dispatches allegedly for our benefit but who so clearly despises our cause. Do you not say so, Rebecque?'

The young men who also occupied the kitchen – his catamites, as she now thought of them – sharing a breakfast of bread, cheese and ham, were plainly amused by the Prince's wit and sagacity. But his Chief-of-Staff, this Rebecque, was more focused on Liberté herself, and she wondered whether he could see the same familiarity of features in her that she could perceive in him. They could almost have been twins. The same sharply angular nose and chin, straight lips shaping a permanently cynical smile. And he would be about the same age, too, almost twice the age of these others, these boys. *Like looking in a mirror,* she thought. But there the similarity ended.

'Encrypted documents?' Rebecque replied. His uniform coat was well-cut, though modest compared to that of the Crown Prince, dark blue with a single row of gilt buttons, collar and cuffs black, piped with scarlet. 'A gift from Fouché? It is almost absurd enough to be credible.' Swiss, she recalled, and famously survived the massacre of the King's Swiss Guard at the Tuileries back in '92, or the Year One of the Revolutionary Calendar. He had been in the service of the Dutch Royal Family ever since.

'And why should we need this Greek gift from Fouché when I already have Rebecque, madam? He is perfectly capable of predicting Bonaparte's intentions without any outside assistance. And predicting much more besides. Indeed, it seems that he is better informed than the Duke of Wellington himself. If it had been left to Wellington, we would have abandoned this ground last night. And then where would we have been? But, fortunately, my bold Rebecque had the presence of mind to countermand Wellington's orders. Had he not done so, I expect that Ney would have been in Brussels by now. Or at least in command of the road that links us to our Prussian friends.'

Rebecque bowed slightly, acknowledged the compliment.

'And where is your proof that you act on Fouché's orders, madam?' he said.

'I carried his safeguard,' Liberté replied, 'until it was stolen from me.'

'How convenient,' said Thin William. 'And the encryption?'

'I am told,' she said, 'that Wellesley is in possession of the codes. That Minister Fouché has already discussed the matter with him. I am merely the messenger. A humble soldier, sir. We follow the orders of our superior officers.' In the revolutionary army, of course, this was only superficially true. 'If my Colonel instructs me to convey documents on behalf of Minister Fouché, I merely assume that I must do so without delay and without particular enquiry.'

The Prince began to speak in Dutch, then remembered himself.

'A soldier, you say?' he repeated, this time in French. 'You hear that, gentlemen? We have a veritable Amazon in our midst. And what regiment would that be, madam?'

'Oh,' said Rebecque, 'I'm certain the lady would not divulge such information to her enemies, Your Highness.'

'She'll answer as I damn well require, Rebecque!' The petulance again. 'Well, she bores me now, in any case. Her precious documents are useless unless you can decipher them. You are able to do so, I assume?'

'I can decipher most things, given time, Your Highness,' said Rebecque.

'Then we shall leave you to your endeavours,' said Thin William, 'while I go and take another look at madam's comrades-in-arms. They tell me it's Ney we face down there. Is that true?' Liberté made no comment. 'Well, it matters little,' continued the Prince. 'They still haven't made a move, although the odds must now be three-to-one in their favour. They must know that, surely. Their light horse has been up and down our lines a dozen times already, between last night and this morning.'

'Ah,' said Liberté, 'the Red Lancers, you mean? Did you not know that most of them used to be Dutch or Belgian too? A few Poles. But mostly French now. And every one of them would gladly die under Bonaparte's banners than see themselves under any tyranny of your own.'

She watched as young Thin William stood from the kitchen table, fury etched across his face, his fists clenched and pressing down on the oak surface.

'So why do they not attack?' Rebecque interceded. 'Or is that the secret of your dispatches, perhaps? That we are missing something obvious?'

'Perhaps they understand,' said the Crown Prince, 'that here they face a foe determined to defend its own land, regardless of those renegade red devils. I have fought the French in Spain, madam. Your godless hordes hold no fear for me. And each of my men is worth ten of Bonaparte's.' He snatched his plumed hat from the table and made for the kitchen door, while his young Aides hastily gathered up sabre and shako, sabretache and satchel. 'Make sure she tells you everything we need to know, Rebecque,' he called back from the threshold. 'I think we can already safely assume that she is a spy from her own admission. And, if so, she will pay the appropriate price.'

'You should not have goaded him, madam,' said Rebecque when they were alone, apart from a pair of sentries just outside in the yard. She could see their blue uniforms when she looked over her shoulder, though she winced with the movement. 'His Royal Highness was heavily engaged until the early hours.' Liberté tried to recall whether there had been fighting late last night but, if so, it must have taken place after Thénardier attacked her. When she looked back, she noticed that Rebecque was also staring at the doorway. 'But I would advise you not to think of escape,' he said. 'The consequences would be dire. And, in any case, you seem to be in no fit condition to wander far. Painful?' He lifted a hand, fanned it against his own cheek.

'There was another action?' she said.

'Ah, you mistake me, madam,' laughed Rebecque. 'It was the Grand Ball, in Brussels. The Duchess of Richmond. Sadly, I had the unfortunate duty to spoil the evening. A midnight dispatch of my own, madam. To inform the Prince that your fellows had already pushed north this far. It rather spoiled the affair, I fear, though His Grace, the Duke of Wellington, seemingly took the news with sanguinity.'

Only the decadent English could dance a quadrille at such a time, thought Liberté.

'Perhaps you should send these to him as well,' she said. 'He is likely to be less than sanguine if he knows that important documents have been withheld from him.'

'I still think we should have one of our surgeons examine your face,' Rebecque scowled. 'It looks nasty. At least sit yourself, I beg you.' But his attention had strayed again to the bundle of dispatches. She remained standing, watched as he laid the tips of his fingers to the paper, his eyes half-closed. There was something intimate in the thing, something she recognised. He sat like that for an entire minute, then another. And when he looked up at her once more, slowly, as though seeing her for the first time, the recognition that passed between them was palpable, a solid thing that she could not mistake. A certain hunger in his eyes.

*

Marianne Tambour had paid another visit to the Artisan Battalion's Master Carpenter.

'Well, look at you!' he said. 'Lived to tell the tale, after all. Who'd have believed it?'

And he had insisted on every detail of Lomballe's death before he would even listen to her request. But she was back at the cart now, the pony impatiently trying to graze, flicking its head and stamping a forefoot each time she attempted to fit the new rig that the fellow had produced for her. It was a crude and simple crib with a frame that would fit Cocotte's pack saddle, leave baby Josef's cradle hanging on one side from a wicker hoop gimbal and slung ropes that would keep the infant reasonably stable on the march.

She had been awake, as usual, at first light, long before four o' the clock, the summer sun's first rays freeing her from the usual nightmare. Saint-Sébastien, naturally. Though it had been different tonight, for the other woman, Hawk-face, had stood alongside her in her dream when she had found Maman Cholet's brutalised body. The rest of the Battalion, meanwhile, Poppy also, the other canteen-mistresses and laundresses, Prairial's baby, had all slumbered on in contented respite. There had been no *tra-ta-tra* of the Diana – at least, not until a couple of hours later when the church bells of Charleroi and the surrounding villages began to call the faithful to their prayers and their labours. And, by then, Marianne had lit her fires, boiled up the cooking pots and begun to wonder just how hot this day would finally become, hardly noticing Fronsac's approach until he patted her playfully on the rump, repeated the same intimacy with the pony, Cocotte.

'We should have another one,' he murmured. 'I told you we should.'

It had started last night, the bristly nudging at Marianne's shoulder, the nonsensical whisperings in her ear when he thought nobody would notice. Then his closeness under their small square of canvas, the hardness of him pressed against her spine until she finally turned on her back. He had babbled about babies for most of the following few minutes, while Marianne counted stars in preference to the hairs that proliferated from his nostrils. There was no chance of another child, of course. Not while they were on the march. For in this, at least, her body was reliable as clockwork. Regardless of the point in her monthly cycle, her bleeds would stop as soon as they left depot, and would not commence again until the campaign was done, the danger past. But Fronsac did not need to know that. And, in the end, after those first few minutes, she had rather begun to enjoy herself, made him pull out while she turned herself over, onto all fours. That way she could enjoy the moment without any distraction.

'Well,' she said to him now, 'you certainly did the business last night!'

Fronsac looked pleased with himself. And why not? There was another battle coming. Maybe today. Or tomorrow. You just never knew the moment.

But it will not be long, she thought, as the regimental band struck up a tune just in time for the Shaveling himself to ride past, though at a leisurely pace. The men stood and cheered, of course, continued to do so through the ringing of curb chains, the clatter of hooves from the generals, the Aides, the equerries, the couriers and the Chasseurs, and then the rattling rumble of the imperial carriages, with the famous dormeuse bringing up the rear. Marianne regarded it now with fresh interest, for she had sensed that there was something else about the dormeuse. Something that Hawk-face had not bothered to share with her.

'We'll be on the road ourselves then,' said Fronsac, for where the Emperor went first, the Guard's Grenadiers would surely follow soon afterwards. Her husband stroked a rough finger down the nape of her neck. 'But there might still just be time...'

She shrugged his hand away.

'You can have too much of a good thing, Fronsac,' she replied, and was still amused by the disappointment on his pig-spotted face when, half an hour later, with the Fourth Regiment's Second Battalion formed and ready to hit the road, their own dear Captain Vicquot rode down the line, summoned the women together, issued each of them with a satchel and instructed them to distribute the proclamations they would find inside to every farm, hamlet and village that they passed on the way.

It was rumoured that the Prussians, under the command of their decrepit Field Marshal von Blücher, had gathered around Sombreffe, much to everybody's surprise. After the thrashing they had received at Gilly – the loss of two thousand men, half of those taken prisoner, with only ten dead among the French – it had been generally rumoured that they were now well on their way back to the Rhine. There was poor General Letort, of course, within that otherwise modest French casualty list but, overall, a satisfactory result for the Emperor.

'And how *was* General Letort, Tambour,' said the captain, 'when you left him? Improved, I hope?'

'Oh much,' she replied, for it was a fact. His dreadful pain had subsided with the passing of the cloth fragment from his kidney, and General Letort would now suffer infinitely less while he waited to die.

'Captain,' said Juanita Bufanda, 'am I reading this right?' Her spoken French was good, but she often struggled with the written word. But that was true for most of the Battalion. 'Is this not tomorrow's date?'

She held up a copy of the broadsheet proclamation that called on all Belgians liberated this day by the Emperor's forces to join his victorious army.

'That's tempting fate,' said Suzanne Prairial, and the mulatta crossed herself.

'Nonsense,' said Vicquot, 'it's simply an indication that the Emperor's plans have come to fruition earlier than he had expected. It was thought there would be more resistance from the Prussians.'

'But they're waiting for us at Sombreffe,' said Catherine Argonne, shifting herself on her crutch. And, as if she had Marianne's gift of occasional premonition, her words were punctuated by the pop of musketry away to the northeast, in the direction of Sombreffe itself.

'And if they wait just a while longer,' Captain Vicquot replied, 'they'll be drowning in their own blood by nightfall. So by then, my lovely beauties, these local Walloons will indeed be liberated and have those proclamations safely in their fists, I trust.'

But they passed few Southern Belgians after the march began across the rolling plains of that region. The Battalion was not restricted by any need to follow the road, so the ranks spread on either side, trampling the shoulder-high crops, kicking up the parched earth, fourteen or fifteen men abreast, and most of them stowing their uniform jackets in favour of their greatcoats. To a casual observer it may have seemed a strange choice, given the murderous heat, but the garments were much looser than the jackets, lighter to wear than to carry. So the wide column, mostly blue-coated, slogged through the sunshine, sweat dripping from beneath their bearskins, or whatever headgear they had been issued.

It's easy for the bloody men, Marianne cursed to herself as she moved from squad to squad, selling a shot of dog-dog here, offering a swig of water there, to clear the choking grit from a parched throat. *All those buggers have to do is get themselves from this place to that, to put one foot in front of the other.* She spent some time giving Prairial a break from the endless task of swatting flies and drifting dirt from the baby, or helping Poppy keep the goats under control, simply to keep them moving as they bleated along behind the cart.

I was never this hot, even in Spain, she thought, and looked ahead into the reddish cloud of dust thrown up by the units ahead. *And Marat be praised that we're no further back. Nor have any further to go.* For, with the bands playing, the drummers beating time, they had marched less than two leagues, carved a flattened swathe across the wide plain of shoulder-high crops stretching from horizon to horizon, when Sergeant Flambert pointed to the cluster of dwellings ahead and announced that it must be Fleurus.

'And remember,' he said, 'we are here to liberate these people, not loot them. Is that understood?'

It was indeed, and a halt was soon called so the column could close up.

'I just heard somebody say that Gérard's Corps has only just crossed the Sambre,' grumbled Fronsac's friend, Marle.

'That wouldn't surprise me,' replied Catherine Argonne's husband. 'The silly bastards probably got themselves lost somewhere.'

'They reckon we'll be here for an hour,' said Fronsac. 'Maybe more.'

'In this heat?' the squad's corporal, Poncet, complained. 'Better put together the old *sombrilla* then.'

It was a trick they had learned in Spain, taking every kerchief, every neck cloth, any spare shirts or undergarments and tying them together to form a reasonable netting, suspending the finished shelter from the butts of their muskets which, in turn, had been spaced in a ring, bayonets fixed and the blades dug deep into the ground to keep the weapons upright. There was just room, within, for the fifteen men of *Peloton* A, Second Section, Fourth Company, to crawl carefully inside and seek some respite from the harsh sun that was now nearing its zenith. And there was time to use a tinderbox, to get a pipe going, pass it around. Marianne, Poppy, Prairial and her brat found their own shade beneath the cart, where the Breton girl exposed her nipple and let the baby feed, much to the entertainment of the Cuirassier regiments that came thundering ponderously up from the rear and churning up even more filth. These were the Emperor's Big Brothers: the heaviest cavalrymen, with the heaviest boots, mounted on the heaviest horses, almost carthorses. The Russians had called them the 'Iron Men', for they were armoured front and rear like the warriors of Jeanne d'Arc, with breast and back plate, strapped together and buckled at the waist, scaled metal clasps at the shoulder, this cuirass worn over a blue coat with facings of either scarlet or yellow, orange or rose, depending on the unit. Their peaked steel helmets carried a fluted metal crest from which a long black horsehair tail hung down behind. It took a long time for them to pass.

'Milhaud's Division,' Corporal Poncet yelled across to them when the dust had finally settled again. 'How about some dog-dog, Marianne?'

So she wandered across to the squad's *sombrilla*, squatted to one side and began to sell brandy, helped one of the fellows write a letter home, pale ink on coarse paper.

'We've been here before,' said Trinquart, one of the old hands. 'You remember?' he asked Senent, another of the long-service men. 'Fleurus. When the hell was that?'

They counted up the years. Remarkably, it had been twenty-one. The enemy then had been Austrians and Dutch, trying to kill the Revolution before it took root elsewhere.

'Twenty-one years?' said Fronsac. 'And what have we got to show for it?'

'A fine wife, of course,' Marianne snarled, though she knew what he meant. 'And what's left of the Revolution.' She was not sure whether she entirely believed that any more, understood instinctively that in any war, the soldiers are simply pieces in a much bigger game.

'I thought we were just doing it to make every other bugger rich,' said Trinquart.

'Personally,' Corporal Poncet told them, 'I just do it for you boys. Because I love you!' And he puckered his lips, blew stupid kisses at them. 'Anyway, carry on with the story. What about Fleurus?'

'Christ, it was a bugger,' said Senent. 'Fifteen hours of the worst fighting I ever bloody saw. Look, it was like this.' He reached into his ammunition pouch, drew out a handful of cartridges, set them out on the flattened rye.

'Here. That useless sod, Marceau, on the right wing. Smashed by the Austrians. Daft bastard, Montaigu, on the left. Smashed by the Dutchies.'

'And the balloon,' laughed Trinquart. 'You remember it? The first time anybody ever thought to use a balloon in a battle. What was it called? The *Enter*-something-or-other?'

'Who gives a piss what it was called,' Senent replied. 'We'd lost both wings, but those balloon boys were still able to let Jourdan know where the other side's weak spot was. Saved Jourdan's bacon. Mine too. Now *there* was a general. That Jourdan! A gem. He sent Kléber in to save the day. Like this.' He swept some of the cartridges through the centre, at the very moment that columns of real Line Infantry came into view behind them.

'At last,' said Fronsac. 'Maybe now we can get out of this hellhole. Find a breath of air.' The firing in the village seemed to have stopped too, indicating that the French skirmishers had cleared the Prussians from Fleurus. 'This is worse than being on that English hulk,' he continued. 'I owe those bloody English. Oh yes, I owe them big-time.'

'Well,' Trinquart said, 'maybe there'll be a chance to settle old scores with them when we've sorted the Prussos. But you've not finished the story, Senent. Kléber saved the day. Then the Austrians and the Dutchies ran like rabbits. Christ, where did we catch them again? Some god-forsaken little dump up the Brussels road, wasn't it? But I'm damned if I can remember the name.'

Senent's already wrinkled brow creased in concentration, he tugged at his moustache, then smiled.

'Got it!' he said. 'It was a village. And it was called Waterloo.'

Senent pronounced the name carefully, in the manner of the local Walloon, as *Vaterlô*, the "wet clearing" – but something about the very word itself made the hair stand up on the back of Marianne's neck.

Chapter Thirteen

Friday 16th June 1815, 11.30am

The Englishman, Wellesley, was in a foul temper, which Liberté Dumont had at first attributed to last night's interruption of his festivities at the Duchess of Richmond's ball. But she soon realised that it was the condition and location of his army that inspired his rage.

Or is it fear? she wondered.

Rebecque had brought her to this second farm, almost the structural twin of that at the Gémioncourt stream – except that this was a more modern construction, probably only twenty years old – when word first reached him, an hour earlier, that Wellesley was in Quatre Bras, just to the north. This turned out to be a rather insignificant place, though it was doubtless a strategic goal for Ney and the Left Wing since the *Four Arms* that gave this hamlet and its crossroads their name led, directly and respectively, to Brussels in the north and Charleroi in the south; Nivelles and Mons to the west, and Namur in the east, so that any commander wishing to move his forces easily around the region should, logically, have access to each of those roads, with Quatre Bras as their central pivot. They had come up the wide verge, the horse avenue of packed sand from the many small quarries that dotted the countryside in those parts, and that avenue ran alongside the main paved Brussels carriageway, edged with fields of crops on either side, the woodland still just beyond them on the left, a smaller farm to the right and the hamlet's dwellings on the rise ahead. But she had been less than impressed by its appearance. There was the large house of La Bergerie, with its gardens, perhaps two hundred paces south of the crossroads but beyond that, in the south-east angle of the roads, there were no buildings at all. In the opposite corner, the northwest segment, there was simply an inn, incongruously identified and illustrated from its hanging board, as the *Three Arms*. Across the Nivelles road, along the southwest angle, stood a few humble dwellings, while the farm took up the whole of this northeast quadrant.

'And you, madam,' Wellesley said to her, 'is it true that Fouché sent these?'

She was surprised at the precision of his French, even if it *was* that strangely accented version spoken only by the English, as though their tongues were somehow trapped between their hind teeth. But it was only a momentary surprise. French was, after all, the language of culture and commerce everywhere from St.

Petersburg to Québec, the Latin of this New Age. And there was something else of Classical Rome about this notorious Englishman. She had never before seen him in the flesh, but he reminded her of an engraving she had once examined, the Emperor Augustus Caesar, she remembered.

How old? she tried to recall. A few years older than herself, was he not? Mid-forties, Liberté decided, then realised that she knew precisely. For he shared the same birthing year as Bonaparte himself. So, forty-six.

'He told me the encryption would be familiar to you,' Liberté replied.

Wellesley made a coughing noise at the back of his throat, which she translated as acknowledgement that she could not have known this unless the Minister of Police had told her so. He was holding a dark and dust-stained cape close about him, seemingly to protect the scarlet dress uniform that occasionally revealed itself beneath the cloak as he moved, a fine though sweat-soiled white neck-cloth at the throat, white buckskin breeches, similarly discoloured by his time upon the road, and Hessian riding boots, also coated with a fine layer of ochre grime. He had set a large cocked hat upon the table, and even his thin brown hair hinted at the Roman fashion. Wellesley was a man with a reputation for plain attire, few military trappings, so the fussing about his ceremonial red coat spoke to Liberté of one risen prematurely from his bed, perhaps somebody who had not slept at all, who had dressed in the first thing to-hand, the same finery he had worn to the ball. He turned to an Aide who reinforced her view, for this fellow still sported silk stockings and buckled dancing shoes. And only a single Aide too. What sort of commander was this?

'Percy,' said the Duke, addressing the younger Englishman also in French, less a courtesy to her than an affectation, a statement of superiority. 'In my holster, the left one. There is a small notebook. Green leather cover. Fetch it, would you?' Wellesley turned to Liberté again. 'And our good Baron Constant-Rebecque tells me that you are a soldier, madam. Is that so?'

She should have guessed that Rebecque would be yet another of these aristos, but she was also watching Percy as he made his way out into the yard, unfastened the leather flap of a saddle holster hanging from the shoulder of an elegant chestnut mare. She admired the beast.

'I have the honour to serve the Emperor as a gentleman volunteer of the Second Dragoons, sir,' she told the Duke, for it seemed as though the occasion required some riposte to his boastful flirtation with her language. Outside, meanwhile, Percy was producing handfuls of writing implements, maps, scrolled papers and assorted small books from the holster, like a street entertainer pulling rabbits from a Phrygian cap.

'I suppose I should think of keeping a pistol in there,' muttered Wellesley, 'but there is so little space available to carry the tools of generalship.' Then he bellowed, 'That one, Percy! Green leather cover. Did I not say so?' He looked at Liberté with fresh eyes. 'A gentleman volunteer?' he smiled. 'I have heard of such things. And I interviewed another lady trooper such as yourself after Salamanca. She was badly cut about. But she'd fought with distinction. Your Third Hussars, I think. Fascinating concept. Often wondered whether women might make more prudent and intelligent commanders, though I would not say so too loudly beyond these walls. Do you mind if I ask how long you have been in service, madam?'

He took the notebook with which Percy had now returned, and began to turn its pages, finger them while referring frequently to the document text spread below his left hand.

'About as long as yourself,' she said, 'unless I'm much mistaken. I picked up my first piece of lead in Egypt fighting the Mamelukes, my first sabre slashes at Savigliano. That was the Austrians, of course. And I was taken prisoner there. They couldn't believe their luck, stripped me just to make sure that I really was a woman. Then one of them thought it would be clever to slice off the tip of my breast. This one.' She placed a hand over her heart, uncertain why she was telling him any of this. To shock the bastard, she supposed. 'For a trophy,' she said. 'Well, I managed to get away eventually, crawled back to our lines. I took some trophies of my own from the Austrians after that.'

Wellesley coughed once more.

'Did you, by God? Well, a soldier fights for his country – *her* country in this case, I suppose – right or wrong, eh?'

'Indeed, sir,' Liberté replied, 'and Our Sacred Virgin of the Rosary be praised that in my own case, I have always been able to fight on the side of right!'

'For the Revolutionary Terror?' said the Duke. 'And then for the tyrant, Bonaparte? How can you say so, madam?' But Liberté could see that he was becoming frustrated by the cipher's complexity. He snapped a question at Percy in English. For privacy, she thought, and Liberté had insufficient grasp of that barbaric tongue to follow the exchange properly. But she caught the word *intelligence* twice, and she imagined that he might be wondering why he had no Intelligence Officer available to help him with the document. Percy offered the Duke a lengthy response that simply earned him a scowl of reproach, with Wellesley glancing often at Liberté, as though trying to discern whether she understood. It was time to strike back.

'And you, Milord,' she said, 'what do you wear on that fine scarlet jacket? The Star of This? The Order of That? Rewards from the grateful bankers whose interests you protected in India. The fat English merchants for whose wealth your men died in Portugal and Spain. My own medals are all carved into my living flesh, sir. All except one.'

'The damage to your face, I assume,' said Wellesley.

Liberté lifted a hand to her cheek.

'No,' she said, 'I am ashamed to say that this was caused by a French-bred thief. But each of my battle scars was earned for the people of France. You want to see them? No, I thought you might not. But you should know that I fought against the so-called Terror also. My father did too. It was an awful time. But why did it happen? Because the rest of Europe could not leave France to her own destiny. And not the *people* of Europe, Milord, but the rich, the rulers, the landowners who both feared our Revolution and wanted to wage war against us. To wage war and to profit by it. A war that drove our citizens mad for a while.'

'Quite the philosopher you've brought me, Baron,' Wellesley said to Rebecque, in French again, an amicable enough comment, though Liberté could see a vein twitching in the Duke's jaw. Rebecque shook his head at her, though it was a barely discernible caution. 'And Bonaparte too, madam? Your revolutionary principles dictated that you should go through all that blood simply to put a despot on the throne?'

She shrugged. *Christ's Hooks*, she thought, *I'd give anything right now for a swig of dog-dog and a decent smoke.*

'I suspect that, once again, the outcome would have been different had we been left in peace to find our own path to a New Age,' she said. 'But I do not take lectures on tyrants from an Englishman who answers to half-mad German George, sir. And who serves the cause of that champion of serfdom and slavery, Tsar Alexander. Or any of the other inbred bastards who rule Prussia, Austria and the rest. But Bonaparte? Our wars may have cost us dear. But most of them have been thrust upon us by our enemies. Yet the people, the soldiers, still cheer their Emperor to the rafters. To the rafters. Each time he passes by. Have you any idea how much we all grieved when Fat Louis was back upon the throne? And how quickly we ripped the royalists' emblems from our uniforms at the merest hint that Bonaparte might return. And each time I've met him…'

'You've met Bonaparte in person, madam?' asked Rebecque.

She smiled.

'Three times,' she replied. 'The last occasion only three months ago, in March.'

'And I suppose you were about to tell us,' sneered Wellesley, 'what an affable fellow he is.'

'He is the Emperor of the French, Milord,' she said. 'Affability always hides inadequacy. And Bonaparte is anything but inadequate. I was about to tell you that each time I've met him, I have always been surprised that such a man, despite the burden and corruption of greatness, should seem so essentially practical. His eyes betray the presence of neither saint nor sinner, neither gentleness nor cruelty. A practical man, Milord. That is how I would have described him.'

'And you met him in March, madam,' said Rebecque, 'because…?'

'Ah,' Liberté replied, 'the one award that I carry upon me rather than within me.' And she fished within the tied neck of her linen shirt, fetched out a red ribbon from which hung a medal, the five radiating white swallowtails, the Legion of Honour. 'He made the presentation at the Tuileries. For some action at Brienne last year that I can scarcely recall. And there were many others awarded at the same time. But he remembered me. Or said that he did. Even though our previous meeting was many years earlier. A celebratory dinner after he became First Consul. Still, perhaps I was easy to remember. There have only been three other women who had the privilege of wearing this, after all.'

She was about to name them, including the nun but, across the yard, a solitary rider was entering the farmyard's double gates, trotting ceremoniously over the cobbles, the *clop-clop* of his horse's high-stepping hooves drumming the announcement of his arrival. Another scarlet tunic, though one that seemed to have been upon the road for some time.

'Ah, Grant!' Liberté heard Wellesley exclaim, as he slapped his hand on the table, though she could not follow the rest of his English. A Dutch-Belgian soldier came forward to take the newcomer's mount, and the rider climbed slowly from his saddle, pulled at the crotch of his breeches and stretched himself. He squinted briefly into the glaring sun, as though calculating the hour, then walked stiffly into the kitchen, pausing to allow his eyes some adjustment to the relative gloom of the interior. He saluted Wellesley with brisk formality, even though his insignia marked him as a senior officer too, a colonel perhaps, thought Liberté. And there was time to study the fellow while he made some report to his Commander-in-Chief though, from the despairing arm that he waved in the direction of the Nivelles road, it seemed more like a string of complaints. This incited yet more anger in Wellesley himself, who quickly barked some new instruction to his Aide, who hurried towards the open door until Percy had the presence of mind, and the good grace, to turn on his heel at the last moment and salute both Liberté and his commanding officer, so that Grant seemed to notice her for the first time.

'Madam,' he said, as if it were a question, and he offered her a courteous bow. She wondered idly why none of these French-speakers had yet thought to enquire whether she might, in fact, be a *Miss* rather than a *Madam* but she concluded that it was a politeness, on their part. Related to her age perhaps. So she simply offered this Grant fellow a nod of acknowledgement, once again noting the similarities between him and Wellesley, for Grant could easily have been taken for the Duke's brother, though a dozen years younger, the mouth softer.

'Yes, indeed,' said Wellesley, turning to her. 'Allow me to name Lieutenant-Colonel Colquhoun Grant, madam. He commands my Corps of Guides and serves as my Head of Intelligence. And this, Grant, is...'

Wellesley halted, realised that he could not recall her name.

'Trooper Dumont, Your Grace,' said Rebecque. 'It was remiss of me not to name her earlier, sir.' But he had done so, of course.

'*Trooper* Dumont?' Grant exclaimed.

'Of the Emperor's Second Dragoons,' Liberté told him.

'Though currently working, Grant, on behalf of your friend Fouché,' said Wellesley. 'Or so it appears.' He paused once more, seemed to consider whether he should proceed in their own tongue, but then continued in French. 'The lady brings us this document from the Minister, or so she claims. I have the first section. Simple enough. Confirms that Bonaparte is already on the move, with immediate effect rather than in July. It's dated… what? Four days ago? Fouché must surely have realised that Bonaparte would already have humbugged me on this score by the time Trooper Dumont delivered it. So why send me the news now, when it is too late?'

'And you would have had the news earlier too, Your Grace,' Grant explained, following Wellesley's lead and using excellent French. 'I left my own dispatches with General von Dörnberg two days ago at Mons. But I assume they never reached you?'

This time Wellesley did indeed abandon his French in favour of a form of English that, Liberté imagined, would have passed muster in a dockside tavern or among the fore-mast jacks of Crazy King George's benighted British navy. She almost laughed out loud. What might the English and Prussians have done if they had, indeed, received this intelligence two days earlier? United around Charleroi? Prevented the Emperor's passage of the Sambre as a single, unified force? *They are fools*, she decided. But Wellesley, she realised, was not such a fool that he would allow a moment's anger to possess him, whereas she knew very well that the Emperor's rages were legendary and, despite her earlier words about his pragmatism, she had witnessed one such prolonged outburst towards the end of the Tuileries event. Indeed, it had brought that very event to a premature close.

'Well, madam,' said the Duke, 'it seems that this first section of your dispatch is worthless after all. And this second section. What do you make of it, Grant? These are troop dispositions. Bonaparte's general deployment plans. But do they look accurate?'

Lieutenant-Colonel Colquhoun Grant consulted the cipher book and document once more.

'Yes, Your Grace. They are accurate enough. Bonaparte's Army of the North. 130,000 men. The broad intention to maintain three wings, but each closely connected. The reserve wing marching to support whichever of the other two might be fighting the principal engagement while the remaining wing holds the second of our Allied armies at bay.'

'And why would your employer send us this?' Wellesley asked Liberté. 'Why now?'

'It is not for me to know, sir,' she replied.

'Did you know that your Minister of Police has already made overtures to me on Bonaparte's behalf? Offering the possibility of a Regency, with your Emperor agreeing to permanent exile if his infant son is recognised as his natural successor when the boy comes of age. I was still considering the possibilities when the good Baron brought the news to Brussels that your precious Emperor had entirely different intentions.'

'A Regency?' said Liberté, feigning surprise.

'With old Berthier as Regent,' Wellesley continued. 'But poor Berthier came to a sad demise shortly after the offer was made. A strange coincidence, don't you think?'

Liberté saw Berthier once more, his arms outspread, flapping like a wounded pigeon, surprise and horror mingled on his face as he fell. He had been more feeble than she imagined and it had taken the merest nudge to tip him over the balcony rail. She had been shocked at the alacrity with which Berthier had accepted Fouché's proposal, as though it were somehow his due to reign in the Emperor's place, even if only as a surrogate until four-year-old Napoléon François could rule in his own right. It was unthinkable. For Bonaparte was France, and France was Bonaparte. The fate of one inextricably linked with the other. So when Berthier, hearing the Russian cavalry at the end of the street, had gone to the window, it had seemed like the most natural thing to take matters into her own hands. She had not thought of it as 'defenestration', but when Fouché had later criticised that word's inadequacy, she had privately disagreed with him, considered it perfectly apt in the circumstances. Pushed from an open window and a drop of four storeys. Well, *there* was an end to ambition.

'And is this figure correct?' Wellesley asked Grant. 'Ney has twenty thousand men out there? To cut us off from Blücher?'

'That seems about right, Your Grace,' Grant replied.

'And we have nothing with which to hold him but your Dutch-Belgians, Baron,' the Duke said to Rebecque. 'How many do you have?'

'At the moment, Your Grace, less than five thousand. Eight if we succeed in bringing down the whole Division.'

'That should be enough, don't you think? Ney may have twenty thousand, but he seems to have no intention of using them.' He turned to Liberté. 'Then this final section of Fouché's document, madam. It talks about General Lamarque. Does it make any sense to you, Grant?'

'There are two things, sir,' Grant replied. 'First, there is this paragraph implying that Lamarque's Army of the West has twenty thousand men and is marching up the coast to cut off your retreat to Ostend. If that were so, we should be caught like rats in a trap, Your Grace.'

'And no alternative except to abandon Blücher and make a run for it while we may.'

'Quite so, Your Grace. But I have seen Lamarque's forces already. They number less than half that number. Nine thousand at the most. Bonaparte sent them to the Vendée to put down a Royalist revolt there. It should have been a simple task. Allowed him to then continue up the coast and threaten our flank. But I happen to know that the Royalists have shown more than their usual level of strategic common sense on this occasion. They were grouping around

Rocheservière when I left them. Autichamp, Suzannet and Saint-Hubert. If they can keep themselves from falling out for a few days, they may just give Lamarque a run for his money. At the time Fouché penned this, he cannot have known that Lamarque would be so delayed. I think we may safely assume that his document is a well-intentioned attempt to ingratiate himself, Your Grace.'

'Then we have a chance,' said Wellesley. 'We can assume that Ney will continue to sit on his hands. When the rest of our Divisions finally get here, we can swing east, catch Bonaparte between the Prussians and ourselves.'

Has that little exchange all been for my benefit? thought Liberté. *Else no need to talk so openly, nor in French.* And, for confirmation, she believed, Wellesley switched to English, spoke with Rebecque for a moment, almost mumbling his words, and then stood from the table, led Grant by the elbow and took him out into the yard, where their conversation resumed, deep, intense.

'I assume I will be kept here?' Liberté said to Rebecque.

'For the foreseeable future, I suspect,' Rebecque replied.

'And you, Baron?'

'I am required to find Prince Willem and ensure that we hold here. If we can bring up the rest of our battalions, of course.'

'A problem?' she asked, as innocently as she was able.

Rebecque regarded her sternly, then smiled, as though asking himself where the harm might be in an honest answer.

'The English, it seems,' he said, speaking like a conspirator, 'have something of a traffic problem on their hands. Baggage wagons jammed solid along the Nivelles road. So we must pin down your Marshal Ney on their behalf while they sort out the mess. I regret, therefore, that any business you may have is likely to be somewhat delayed.'

'And Wellesley?' said Liberté.

'He rides to Blücher,' Rebecque replied. 'To share the news, revise our plans.'

But Wellesley did not do so without returning to the kitchen once more. He spoke to the Baron in English again. Rebecque answered in the same language, then switched briefly to French.

'And what should I do with Trooper Dumont, sir?'

Wellesley seemed dismayed by the question, glanced briefly at Liberté.

'Why,' he said, 'keep her safe until I get back. I doubt we shall hear anything of General Lamarque ever again. And Grant has just reminded me that this lady is a self-professed French soldier of Bonaparte's army, who has infiltrated our lines in civilian dress. That makes her a spy, does it not?'

Chapter Fourteen

Friday 16th June 1815, 2.00pm

The Second Section's A Platoon was restricted to just three files wide and five ranks deep, yet there was still barely enough room for them to squeeze through the deep sable shadows of this Fleurus back street.

The men were singing, not through any sense of occasion, nor to relieve the boredom, nor to lift their morale but, rather, for the sheer joy of having their voices boom and rebound around the walls of the stone-grey canyon, three storeys high on either side. And any melody or lyric was lost, in any event, among that other babble which shouted and cheered each of their steps from every doorway and open-shuttered, flag-flustered window.

'Death to the Prussos!' howled an old crone while, in the narrow entrance to a courtyard, children danced in a tight circle while chanting some rhyming thing about killing pigs.

At the end of the street they followed the tail end of the Fourth Company's First Section as it swung right, their eyes suddenly dazzled, blinded by the glare until they turned left again into a dung-strewn lane even closer, darker, than the first.

'This cool enough for you now, Fronsac?' yelled Marianne, as she led Cocotte, the cart with its gimballed cradle, and the brace of goats along behind.

'It's either famine or feast with this bloody army,' he called back over his shoulder. 'But this is more like it! Keeping us in the dark and no clue to where we're headed.'

But of course they knew. Their old enemies, the Prussians, were waiting just the other side of Fleurus with unfinished business to settle. Their commander, Blücher, had been badly mauled by the French at Jena, returned the favour at Leipzig. And then, last year, with the enemies of France closing around Paris, the old goat had almost been captured at the thrashing the Prussians received near Brienne. They were beaten again at Vauchamps. But Blücher had survived to see the Eagles narrowly defeated at La Rothière, and more decisively at Laon. So now it was time to decide the thing, and the Imperial Guard needed to be where the Guard was always stationed, at the side of its Emperor. The shortest way of getting there was through the middle of town, except that there was no road large enough to carry them quickly, so each of the regiments had been split into its component battalions, companies, *pelotons* and sections, using every available thoroughfare so that, whenever they reached a junction and could look either left or right, there they would see yet more snaking lines of bearskin bonnets, of blue-coated Grenadiers or Foot Chasseurs, and always bathed in the adulation afforded them as liberators by the townsfolk.

They halted briefly at the main square, across from the crouching bulk of the parish church. Only a short stop, Corporal Poncet assured them, while the Young Guard sorted themselves out, just ahead.

'You're full of shit, Poncet!' Marianne laughed, for it was rare that anybody in authority should confide very much in the poor fellow.

'It's true,' he protested. 'But just enough time for a swig of dog-dog. What d'you think, Marianne?'

She poured him a cup, took his two sous, and saw Catherine Argonne come hobbling up, waiting until Poncet had gone again before she approached, hefting an animated and raucous sack from her shoulder, and inviting Marianne to peek inside.

'Grateful citizens,' said Argonne. 'And I've no use for the thing.'

'You were given it personally?' Marianne reached inside the bag, grabbed the bound, scaly shanks of a hen and drew out the fine bird so that it dangled from her fist, flapped its mottled wings and cried in abject outrage at being treated thus.

'Well, by one of the lads in the Second,' Argonne replied. 'Somebody told him a bird this colour was bad luck and that's why it had been given away. Any other day and he would probably have taken a chance. But with the battle coming up… Anyway, I happened to be passing and said I'd take it off his hands. What about it? Peace offering. But just between us, eh? Can't stand having salt rubbed in the wounds. You know?'

Bad luck? thought Marianne. *Is that what she's doing? Passing it on to me?* For she felt a sudden sense of fear, though it was a confused sensation. Part premonition of evils still to come; part filled by an impression of Hawk-face, unexpected concern for her safety, wherever she was, somewhere away to the west; part fragment of her Saint-Sébastien nightmare; and part her constant worry about Florisette's future.

'Did you see my daughter?' she said to the other woman.

'Yes, of course,' said Argonne, surprised at the question. 'You sent her over with the mulatta, didn't you? They brought the stuff you sent for Bufanda. She's helping the boys, I think.'

Poppy and Suzanne Prairial had been busy bargaining for tobacco, cheeses, hams and wines from the locals. Just what the Breton girl had needed. Get her back on her feet, but nothing too heavy. Not today, at least. And a good haul. But Marianne had made sure to add a modest mark-up before selling the surplus on to that Spanish bitch. *Five per cent supply charge*, she had decided. *And another five for the way she waggles her arse at my man!*

'Since when have speckled hens been unlucky?' she said, knowing how much Fronsac's squad would have valued this prize.

'Well,' shrugged Argonne, 'it was that platoon in the Second with the bunch from Gévaudan who claim to have seen the Beast. Marat be praised that they'd never run away from shot or shell, but just let a black dog cross their path and it's a different story!'

Marianne stripped off the russet jacket again, pulled the peak of the leather bonnet a little lower to keep the pitiless sun out of her eyes.

'Hey, Marianne,' shouted Fronsac's friend, Henri Marle, 'where did you get the bird?'

She tapped a thumb against the side of her nose.

They were formed up once more, the various units gathered back together again in battalion columns and the Grenadier regiments straddling each side of the road that ran north-east from Fleurus and, somewhere ahead, according to those who knew the region, cut the highway that, beyond the skyline, linked Nivelles to the left and Namur to the right.

'Isn't this where they sent the balloon up?' she heard Trinquart ask.

'It looks like the same mill,' Senent replied. 'But who knows? It's been twenty years.'

'And one mill looks pretty much like any other, doesn't it?' said Marle.

'Well,' Fronsac smiled, 'this one doesn't. Not any more.'

Work was still taking place on the windmill that stood just to the west, and Marianne could see her old friend, the Artisan Battalion's Master Carpenter, directing the crew that had already dismantled the sails, fashioned an observation platform around the upper part of the structure and knocked through a doorway that gave access to the decking from inside. And the platform was already packed with Bonaparte's generals and staff officers, the Emperor himself surveying the troops gathered around the mill. On the farther side of the building stood the Infantry Division of the Young Guard while, on the nearer side, were the four regiments of the Guard's Foot Chasseurs. Behind the Grenadier regiments, the Imperial Guard's artillery was lined along a slight rise. Beyond the guns, the giants of the Heavy Cavalry – the bearskins and blue tunics of the Horse Grenadiers and Elite Gendarmes, the green coats and leopard-skin lined helmets of the Empress Dragoons, then the gleaming armour and black horsehair crests of Milhaud's Cuirassiers. Behind the mill, the Emperor's carriages and that bloody dormeuse with whatever mystery Hawk-face thought it contained.

A band was playing but otherwise it was remarkably quiet, peaceful as a *piquenique*, the drowsy hum of insects filling the air now that the army was in position, and Marianne climbed onto the cart for a better view of the field.

Ahead, the swaying crops sloped gently down to a steep-banked stream that meandered through the bottom of a shallow valley and was studded with stone-built settlements, each with its own church tower. To the left, three small hamlets in succession spanned a section that ran southeast. Then the brook swung to the northeast and passed through a larger village – Ligny, somebody said, and it stood almost directly opposite the Guard's position, another church at its heart – before winding south and then east through several more hamlets. Beyond the stream, the fields of rye rose up again, with a church tower and another mill prominent on the skyline, and it was on this opposite slope that most of the Prussian regiments had formed in an impressive array, cavalry on each flank, solid masses of infantry brigades between, and their artillery to the fore, while the brook's hamlets appeared to teem with their skirmishers.

'How many of them, Maman?' Poppy asked her, though it was a casual question, merely an eight year-old's curiosity.

'Flambert reckons they have eighty thousand,' said Marianne. *And we have just three-quarters of that number,* she thought. But three Frenchmen to four Prussians? Those were fair odds.

'And will Papa fight them?'

'I don't think so. Normally, the Prussos take one look at his ugly face and run away without firing a shot.'

Marianne ruffled the girl's hair then squeezed the pug nose between finger and thumb. She was glad that peace seemed to have broken out between herself and Catherine Argonne. The Argonnes were, after all, her daughter's Protectors. If anything should happen to Marianne herself, or to Fronsac, or to both of them, the Argonnes would bring up the girl as one of their own. *But can they protect her as she grows older?* she wondered, one of those morbid, pre-battle musings.

'Are those the Prussos on the other side of the stream?' asked Poppy.

'Yes,' said her mother, climbing back down from the cart, 'that's the buggers.'

In many places, the line of the stream was marked by willows and thick bushes that grew along its banks and especially near the settlements with their ditches and hedges while, elsewhere, the ground was dominated by the yellow patchwork of wheat and corn. The French line, however, seemed to curve around the enemy, as though to envelop them, green-coated Light Horse Chasseurs out to the left, then column after column of infantry, a full Corps and an extra Division; the Guard here at the centre and southern-most point in the curve; then another Corps, two dozen battalions or more; and, finally, the bulk of the cavalry flung far towards the right – more Cuirassiers; eight regiments of Dragoons; a couple of Lancer regiments. Between and around these units, broadly following the same curve, the Emperor's artillery.

*

Marianne heard the riders before she saw them, and it was only because it had previously been so restful that the hoof beats prompted her to look around. Another pair of red-breast Gendarmes, when they finally came into view around the edge of the unit to the rear. Like those who had tried to arrest her in Charleroi, but these in company with a civilian sporting a red, white and blue sash, a revolutionary cockade in his hat, and an old couple puffing and panting alongside. They all halted on the road just behind her and the pair of overfed ancients began an urgent and breathless conversation with the mounted citizen, the Mayor of Fleurus, fresh-sworn to French allegiance, Marianne imagined. She also fancied that this pinch-nosed fellow cast a furtive glance or two in her own direction before addressing himself to the Gendarmes, one of whom spurred away up the line. *What now?* she thought, trying hard to make an association between these old folk and Lomballe, but she had still not fathomed a link before the red-breast returned with Captain Vicquot, Sergeant Flambert running alongside.

'Come forward, citizens!' Vicquot called to the old couple then turned to Marianne. 'Tambour,' he said, 'where did you acquire that hen?'

For a moment, she considered thumbing her nose at him, as she had done with Marle. But she knew it would be unhelpful, and she could already sense the net closing around her. *The bloody hen!* she thought. *I should have known.*

'A gift, Captain,' she told him.

'From?'

There was a bad taste in her mouth.

'A friend.' She spat, her teeth twisting the word round and around.

'These people say that they had a speckled hen stolen from them,' said Vicquot. 'They told the Gendarmes that the culprits were Grenadiers.' He turned to the old couple, pointed to the bird that clucked and squawked from the back of her cart, as though the damned thing knew that its reprieve was imminent. 'Is this the creature?' Vicquot asked them.

The old peasant woman wrung her hands, while her husband kept his gaze fixed upon the ground.

'It looks the same, lordship,' the woman replied, trying hard to avoid catching Marianne's eye.

'Can you not be certain?' said Vicquot and then to Marianne, 'And you, Tambour. You had no such bird last time I passed your cart, I think?' Marianne untied the hen's shanks, bit her tongue and held out the now frantic creature. 'So you admit the theft?' Vicquot sneered.

'I do not, Captain,' she replied. 'I was given the hen in good faith, as I told you. But, as they say, a bird in the hand is worth two in the bush. If these good people have been deprived of a hen, they're more than welcome to mine. And I trust that the reward for my generosity, my good word, will be that the matter may now be forgotten.'

'You're impudent, Tambour,' said Vicquot, as the old woman took the hen from Marianne's hand and backed away with her husband, both of them bowing and scraping.

'Justice, it seems,' said Marianne, 'has been done. What more is there to say?'

'The names of the fellows who stole the bird in the first place,' Vicquot replied. 'I issued a warning, did I not, that looting would not be tolerated?'

'It wasn't looted,' said Marianne. But she did not sound convincing, even to herself. There was no doubt about it. That cow, Argonne, had arranged for a couple of likely lads to lift the hen and she, Marianne, whether she liked it or not, had subsequently received the stolen goods.

'It's always the same,' said Vicquot. 'I get more trouble from four women than forty men. You know the penalty for receiving looted goods?'

'I know there can't be any punishment without a verdict, and no verdict without a Battalion Court of Justice. What are you proposing, Captain? That we ask the Shaveling to delay for a while, so that I can be judged by the Bench?'

But there would be no delay. Not now.

Away in the valley, drums were beating and, as she turned, Marianne could see the entire central Corps of the French army, Gérard's Corps, lurch forward towards Ligny village. Trumpets sounded in response and, just discernible, Prussian Lancers, the *Uhlans*, materialised from almost nowhere, swept across the path of the French infantry as they quickly formed squares.

Behind her, a twelve-pounder cannon shattered the air, shook her eardrums with a signal blast. She spun around, just in time to see a second sulphurous billow erupt from a barrel's mouth, split by a gout of yellow flame, in time to hear another explosion as the olive green Gribeauval gun carriage bucked backwards between its smoke-ghosted gunners. And then a third bronze barrel completed the opening salvo.

Cheering broke out all around.

'Long live the Emperor!'

And there was another regimental band somewhere, playing *The Departure Song*.

She looked back to see what Captain Vicquot wanted to do now, but he had gone, of course. Back to his position at the Fourth Company's head. Yet she caught Poppy's worried glance, tweaked the brat's ear playfully.

'Long live the Emperor!' she screamed.

Liberté Dumont heard the triple cannon shots, all the way over at the Gémioncourt farm, and she was not alone in her confusion that, somehow, the signal guns had a relevance for them here, at least a couple of leagues from where they had obviously been fired. For, as their distant echo died away, the quaking thunder of another cannon salvo shook the ground all about her, shook through her feet and knees, her hips and belly. And this battery must have been within musket shot for there was barely a breath between detonation and impact, the walls of the barn, thick and solid as they might be, groaning and trembling with the concussion, dust and small stone fragments, birds' nest debris, falling down on the defenders. The place had already been showered with howitzer shells, though there was so much cover that the Dutch militiamen had taken little harm from them.

Rebecque had left her here some time back, before the French advance had begun, when the Dutch militia had been advanced here under fire. But she no longer enjoyed the comfort of the farmhouse. It seemed that her new status as an apprehended spy warranted no more than accommodation in the large barn that ran along the southern side of the yard. The seating was adequate – a large and well-filled forage sack – but the hospitality was lacking, since Rebecque had ordered her hands tied, with no concession whatsoever to their mutual attraction. She had made sure, naturally, to clench her hands, flex her wrists, allowing herself as much freedom as possible while they bound her, but she was more concerned with Rebecque's second instruction by which, she gathered, he had given leave to the blue-coated Dutch officer to shoot her if she attempted escape. This officer spoke some French and, initially, had been civil enough, although his civility had evaporated when, half an hour back, all hell had broken loose. The attitude of his men had changed too, their original curiosities, pities or desires now turned to contempt or total apathy as their attention was absorbed by the developing chaos. In the closed and shadowed limits of the barn, it was hard to know exactly what was happening, though it was easier to fathom the general flow of things.

Ney's assault had been opened with an artillery barrage and followed by the *pop-pop-pop* of French skirmishers, wave after wave of them, approaching from the south and east, with the Dutch-Belgians, Jägers, pouring back before them, crowding in through the arched and tile-roofed gatehouse. Then the entrance was closed and barred, the walls manned, the loop-holes and ventilation slits filled with their muskets.

And not an Englishman among them, she thought, as the battle became that which battles often become, a closed and personal struggle for a specific piece of turf. Yet here it was more closed than usual, the entire drama framed within the suddenly prison-like limitations of the Gémioncourt farmyard and its buildings. The interior of the barn filled quickly with the smell of piss and shit, with the stink of foetid eggs that parched the throat, while Liberté's ears were assailed by the continuous rattle of ramrods in musket barrels; by the distorted sounds like ripping linen sheets as the French infantry units attacked the place with volley fire; by the louder volleys, returned by the Dutchmen holding the orchards just beyond the walls; by the hailstone storm of their bullets pummelling against the wall's exterior; by the gasps and groans as the deadly lead balls whined with either luck or precision, through the narrow embrasures and found fleshy targets; by the screams of those already wounded but for whom the initial numbness of nervous shock had now turned to merciless agony and torment;

by the incongruous and discordant competition between a Dutch regimental band and the incessant *TAN-tra-tran, TAN-tra-tran* of an Imperial drum corps beating out the Quick March, the *Pas de Charge*; and then by the attacking cannon battery picking up the song of war at the chorus once again, heralding the start of another verse. All those other sounds that ran together, formed the verse's separate lines against a changing rainbow-prism of colour: the rise and fall of green or blue tunic sleeves as muskets were loaded and rammed afresh; the stark whiteness of teeth that gaped at her where lip and cheek had been carried away from a Fusilier's jaw; the bubbling scarlet foam that frothed from the face of a fallen Jäger as he guzzled on his own blood; the spark and flash of primer in frizzen pan. There was a taste to close-quarter combat too. An iron taste that settled on the tongue, spread there thick as grease by the released essences of flowing blood, of over-heated weaponry, of pounding shot or shell.

A recollection of the woman who had tried to kill her in Charleroi flashed through Liberté's mind. *What an irony*, she thought. *Somebody wanted me dead. Somebody from among my own. It must be. But who? Fouché himself? Somebody else? And what does it matter? Here I am, about to be blown apart by French cannon. Or maybe I survive this, just so that Wellesley and his spy-master can have me shot. Well, a pox on them all!*

The Dutch militia officer was doing his job well, forcing his way through the acrid, drifting smoke from one end of the barn to the other, shouting encouragement to his mixed command, urging them to hold firm, patting a shoulder here, exchanging a familiarity there. But, despite his apparent *sang-froid*, she saw him glance with increasing frequency out through the open doors and obliquely up the yard to the gate, where the fighting was now hand-to-hand. Short sections of wall joined each side of the gateway to the adjacent buildings, each wall much less than two fathoms high so that, on the inside, carts had been rolled forward, partly to help barricade the gate itself, partly to provide firing steps for the defenders. But space allowed no more than a half-dozen soldiers on either of the walls and those men fell, one by one, at regular intervals, new soldiers coming forward to take the posts of the fallen, clambering over the sprawling bodies of the dead, often impeded by others helping to shift the wounded across the cobbles, to receive whatever makeshift medical attention might be available to them. And, with some unwritten mathematical certainty, as the death count and confusion mounted within, so too increased the frequency with which a French shako would appear above the parapet, muskets firing on those inside, or thrusting with bayonet, until these faces too were bloodied and mutilated, fell back in their turn, to be replaced by comrades of their own. It was almost a fluid and visual accompaniment to that song of war, the alternate piston rise and fall, rise and fall of defenders and attackers, punctuated more and more often as the French managed to get somebody onto the wall's coping stones, where they would also die, or live long enough to jump down into the yard only to be stabbed or hacked or clubbed into oblivion. Yet even this suicidal activity had an arithmetic beat of its own, each attacker surviving a second or two longer than his predecessor, until there were two of them inside at the same time, fighting for their lives. Then a third. And a fourth. Then a to-and-fro tussle to lift the drop bar and allow friends to enter, or to force it back into the strike bracket and deny that access to the enemy, while the timbers themselves screamed and splintered with the thud of French axes wielded by regimental Sappers determined on simply breaking the damned thing to smithereens from outside.

Suddenly, there was no more room for firing or lunging, and men began throttling their enemies, gouging out eyes with their fingernails, biting each other's arms, or legs, or faces. The animal business of men at war. And it was time for the Dutch militia officer to make a decision. Or two. He drew his sword for the first time, barked orders that called forth each second man from his post and hurried them out of the haze-filled interior to form a slender firing line. But those at the farthest end were incapable of hearing anything, so the fellow stalked in their direction, shouting as he went, until he came abreast of the upright beam against which Liberté had been sitting. As he passed, she slipped to her knees, held up her bound wrists towards him.

'*Alstublieft*,' she said. Please. Her only word of Dutch. She had even managed to generate a tear that now trickled a dirty track down her cheek. He paused briefly, his face grim, impassive, before he moved on, resuming his task, until he had grabbed the attention of the last man, shouted his orders and turned back, passed Liberté for a second time, now ignoring her entirely. But she did not care. She had expected nothing from him, was more concerned with the stragglers hurrying to follow him into the yard. The very last of them, in fact. He was young, wearing the green tunic of a Jäger, stumbling over his own feet and struggling to fit the bayonet to his musket, gripping the socket but cursing to himself as he consistently failed to fit the gun's foresight into the blade's corresponding L-shaped slot. He dropped it, of course, exactly as she had willed him to do.

'*Alstublieft*,' she repeated, and he stopped. She had selected him carefully, listed him earlier among those who had displayed some pity on his face, perhaps in response to her bruised features, rather than the lascivious stare of several others – those, she had assumed, who viewed her as they might have hungered for one of the pox-ridden *horizontales* to be found in the bawdy houses of Brussels or Charleroi.

The soldier crouched to pick up the bayonet but his gaze fixed to her own, and she extended the rope-tied wrists again, her eyes imploring, lost and afraid. She was probably twice his age, not quite old enough to be his mother perhaps but…

'*Alstublieft*,' she murmured, and managed to stretch her fingers far enough to touch the pale hairs on the back of his hand. The shock that passed between them was palpable, and he recoiled as though stung. Yet it was enough for her, enough to grant her access to the soldier's soul and inner thoughts, enough to show her a domestic scene as though she was present herself. The young man at his own kitchen table; a much older woman, presumably his real mother, stirring a cook-pot; a second woman, not his wife, though nursing a small infant, and most likely a sister; and a name, prominent among the soldier's thoughts. Saskia. *The sister?* she wondered. *Or the babe?* Though it did not really matter.

'Saskia,' Liberté whispered the name to him. 'Saskia?' And, from the very edge of her vision, to the right, she saw that the militia officer's firing line was fully engaged, emptying volleys into the Frenchmen crowding through the now demolished gate.

The young soldier was talking urgently to her in unintelligible Dutch, though she caught the name *Saskia* often enough. So she repeated it too, held up the bunched fists, the cord tying them together, elbows bent and pressing against her breasts so that, when she struck, it came with the force of a sabre thrust, straight to the bridge of his nose and so fast that his eyes still showed the confusion of hearing the familiar name, rather than any shock from the blow. It was sharp enough that it set him, first, on his arse and, second, onto his back, one hand coming up to his eyes. And in that second she had picked up the bayonet, grasped its socket, two-handed, straddled his hips and forced seventeen inches of triangular English-forged steel up beneath the Dutchie's ribs.

Chapter Fifteen

Friday 16th June 1815, 2.30pm

Liberté Dumont had learned the fingersmith's art in Egypt, at Fouché's recommendation. 'The very place,' he had told her, before she shipped overseas from Toulon. Thirteen ships of the line; fourteen frigates; four hundred transports. And they had slipped the entire fleet under the nose of that fool, Nelson, without a shot fired. He had caught up with them at Aboukir Bay, of course, destroyed many of the Emperor's warships, but by then the campaign was well under way. And in Cairo she had found the Circassian Mameluke, Amjad, who had taught her to fashion and use torsion wrenches and a variety of picks that would open any lock she had ever encountered. He had acquired a beautiful set for her, and she had kept them ever since, until the Thénardiers had stolen them, of course. But Amjad had taught her other things besides. To cut all manner of shams, retrieving, fool-taking, executing the mace cove and the fawney drop. To fork pockets, whether it was sack diving or drawing wipes. And to employ every inventive manner of escape in the unlikely and shameful event that such questionable activities might lead to any form of apprehension or imprisonment. But it still took her almost fifteen perilous minutes to manipulate the wrist knots that bound her. She had contemplated using the bayonet's edge but knew that to be a risky business. And besides, it was still wedged firmly within the Dutchman's lungs and heart. So she had scampered back into the darkest corner of the barn, watched while the enemy militia officer, realising the impossibility of his position, expertly fought a rear-guard action to extricate his men from the farmyard and out through the shattered gate.

Only a few of the Jägers remained in the house itself, now stolidly besieged by the French infantry exchanging fire with them from whatever cover they could find. But the barn was entirely overlooked, no longer holding any strategic importance to either side. And, as she soaked the ropes in a trough's stinking dregs, created still more slack, slowly began to loosen the bonds, to insinuate her right hand painfully through the narrow loop, Liberté idly wondered whether the Dutch officer had yet realised he had lost his prisoner. *Well*, she thought, *he has better things to occupy him now. And so have I.*

She rubbed at her liberated wrists, edged to the barn's wide open doorway, peered through the sun-pierced drifting haze and spotted a French infantry sub-lieutenant, impossibly young, ten paces away, sheltering with three of his men behind the wheels of a seed drill, or similar contraption. He directed their assault on the house, pinning the occupants with one squad while advancing a second to reach the relative shelter against the walls.

'Lieutenant!' she yelled. Then again, louder, until he turned his head. In fact, she had managed to turn several heads. She watched surprise and a dash of annoyance change to laughter, the creased concentration of engagement switch to the welcome release of raucous banter, the brief fraternity of a shared light interlude rolled back to restoration of the sub-lieutenant's authority. And though the troops resumed their fire on the farmhouse, she saw them frequently look towards the place of her partial concealment while a sergeant was dispatched, ducking and weaving, to the barn.

'Lieutenant Brissart's compliments, miss,' panted the sergeant, crouching beside her, 'but he wants to know what you're doing here. You from the farm?' He punctuated the question, syllable by syllable, pointing his finger first at Liberté, then at the straw-strewn floor, in case she might be a Walloon-speaker, her French lacking.

'Do I look like a farm girl, Sergeant?' she snapped and, for the second time that day, she unfastened the ties at her shirt neck, displayed the Legion of Honour's ribbon and medal. 'You recognise this?' said Liberté.

The fellow looked from the medal to her cavalry-pattern breeches.

'Now where did you find that pretty bauble?' he said.

'Funnily enough,' she replied, 'I *found* it in the palm of the Emperor's hand. After Brienne. Were *you* at Brienne, by any chance, Sergeant?'

He looked deeply into her eyes, his own half-closed, as though squinting at something far in the distance. Then he nodded. And she knew from the slow drawl that he was briefly living the moment afresh.

'I was there, miss,' he said. 'Yes. And what should I tell the Lieutenant?'

'Tell him I need a uniform of some sort, and to find it without the risk of being shot as a scavenger. Tell him I have business to complete. Tell him it's for Minister Fouché. And tell him that if he helps me in this task, I shall make sure the Emperor himself will hear of it.'

He digested all this, his grey-stubbled jaw working side to side as though he chewed on the words. Then he grinned.

'This is a rare day, to be sure,' grinned the sergeant. 'I'll tell him.' He turned, still squatting, looked around the doorway's heavy frame. He glanced over at the dead Dutchman, then back at Liberté, whistled softly. 'And me, miss?' he said. 'You'll mention me too?'

Young Lieutenant Brissart felt so comfortable with his occupation of the Gémioncourt farm that he allowed his sergeant to accompany Liberté in her quest, by way of an escort. It had all been absurdly simple, even without Fouché's letter. His name, it seemed, still functioned as fully as a talisman. But she was determined to retrieve it. And that meant finding the Thénardiers, as well as her mule and other possessions. There was little doubt that they would not be far behind the army, waiting for whatever additional pickings they might plunder once this battle was over. So she would need to stick around. But perhaps get back to her regiment too. Report to Colonel Planzeau, wherever the Second Dragoons might now be, though she did not fancy her chances of surviving here for very long unless she was more suitably dressed and equipped. Anything would suffice for the time being and, to make a start, the sergeant persuaded one of his wounded men to part with his jacket. The fellow was a little larger than Liberté, but the thing fitted well enough: faded imperial blue with the epaulettes and collar of this unit's *voltigeur* Skirmisher company that had once been vibrant yellow but were now rinsed to the shade of wet hay. She picked up a piece of the cord also, the same that had bound her hands, and used it to tie up her hair, bunched it at the nape of her neck.

'Let's see what the Dutchies have to offer,' she said, nodding towards the gate and, without waiting to see whether the sergeant followed, she ran, bent almost double, from the barn to a water butt, from water butt to hay wain, and hay wain to the smashed gate, with musket balls whistling in just about every direction, while her clogs tapped a counterpoint tattoo on the cobbles. She pressed herself against the outer wall, heard the sergeant reach her side.

'These bloody clogs have got to go,' she said, as she surveyed the scene, or as much as could be observed for the smoke. To her right ran the brook, the Gémioncourt stream, flowing through its wandering channel and lined with alder, the occasional oak, so that the trees on the farthest bank gave cover to the French skirmish line that had now formed there, stretching away and just ahead of the infantry columns coming to a halt behind them. To the skirmishers' left flank, but beyond the road and barely visible above the intervening shoulder-high wheat, the shakos and muskets of many more of the Emperor's men. And in the space between, Line Lancers, crashing through the crops in pursuit of the Dutch retreat.

'They've got some balls, those Dutchies,' said the sergeant, watching as the erstwhile defenders of the farm fell back in good order, keeping the Lancers at bay, heading north towards a slight rise and then crossing the road towards the wood, towards another of Thin William's battalions. They were supported too, by the arrival of a squadron of Dutch-Belgian horsemen – Light Dragoons, Liberté thought, judging by their green tunics – that had wheeled into view behind the militia. She was not sure where they had come from, but it was obvious that they were blown, either from an over-long march or the heat. Or, most likely, from both. Yet they trotted forward all the same, bits and bridles dripping with flecks of spittle, heaving flanks slick with sweat, and placed themselves between the fugitives and their pursuers, causing the Lancers to swing about, return to their lines.

'The lads aren't even bothering to form square,' she said. And nor were they, the French infantry maintaining their formations, despite the enemy cavalry's proximity. 'Not much use bringing up horse,' Liberté continued, 'unless you can work them into a charge.'

'That's you is it, miss?' said the sergeant. 'One of the horse boys? I start calling you Trooper, maybe? Or an officer? That's it. You're some sort of officer. No?'

'Try Dumont, Sergeant. That will do just fine. I never even made corporal.'

'Well,' he said, 'Dumont it is. And those horse boys may be no use to themselves, but they might just be what *you* need.'

They watched as the enemy horsemen, taking fire from the closest section of the French positions, also urged their mounts' heads about, but swinging away from the road on a track that would bring them close to the stream before turning towards their own guns.

'And that bugger,' said the sergeant, moving closer to the brook's margent, tapping his musket barrel in the general direction of the enemy horsemen, 'he's about your size, don't you reckon?'

She followed every movement of his musket barrel as his right hand gripped around the small stock and lifted the weapon. So that, for a moment, it stood precisely before the mid-line of his body, his left little finger brushing the feather spring while his glance fell quickly to the frizzen's pan-steel, checking the priming. The right thumb came sharply to the head of the cock, pulling it back fully before the sergeant allowed the muzzle to sink forward and down. His left hand flipped along the wooden stock, as far as the Charleville's tailing pipe, and he pressed the butt into his right shoulder, fore-finger on the trigger and his eye lining along the steel barrel to the forward sight. Liberté could see his target now, a wounded Dutchie, who had already lost his bell-topped shako and was slowed almost to a stop on his weary horse.

The sergeant's finger tightened on the trigger and squeezed, making it look smooth and easy, though she knew from experience that the mechanism of the Charleville required a fair amount of pressure and considerable discipline, particularly under fire, to avoid dipping or twisting the muzzle and remain absolutely still. There was a spark and smoke from the frizzen, the small flame that licked through the vent hole, the almost simultaneous report, flash and the eruption of more smoke from the barrel's end. Then the enemy horseman's sabre froze for a moment, the grip slipping from his fingers so that it dangled and swung useless from the wrist-strap, while the man's chin slumped to his chest, as if he had suddenly fallen asleep. He slipped sideways and the horse walked forward a few paces, turned a half-circle in response to the pressure on its reins, while its rider continued to slide from his saddle and crashed to the ground, legs twisted, left foot still in the stirrup. The beast's head came up and it snorted, shaking its mane, before dragging the cavalryman three steps more, to a patch of grazing grass alongside the stream.

'Nice shot,' she said, and set off at a run, scrambled down the bank, splashed through the thigh-deep water, sheltered against the trunk of an alder while the rest of the Dutchmen retired.

'Be quick!' shouted the sergeant, wading across behind her.

Liberté slowed deliberately as she approached the horse, though she thought it unlikely that the pale chestnut mare would bolt. The beast may be spent, lacking beauty but it seemed otherwise strong in character, like one of those that the Cossacks so frequently employed. She knew very well that the best reward for many agitated animals was simply to leave them alone, but this one craved company, so she set her right hand gently on the mare's neck, offered a bunched left fist to its nostrils for the mare to smell, whispering and blowing over her knuckles.

'There, beauty,' she murmured, then moved slowly down the beast's flank until she could lift the cavalryman's foot from its stirrup. 'Would you take the reins, sergeant?' said Liberté. He complied, though gingerly, keeping his distance from the creature.

'Good horse,' he said, while Liberté freed the lower buttons on each leg of the dead man's overalls, pulled loose the spurs, then his Hessian boots, tried them for size herself. They were a little loose, but better than the clogs, and she quickly unbuckled the straps that held the sabretache to the sword belt, tossed it aside, but unfastened the snake-clasp of the belt itself, pulled it from beneath the Dutchie's body, relieved him of the sabre too, then fastened the black leather around her own waist, wearing it over the uniform coat, while the noise of battle shifted to a different and more intense level.

'Look!' she said. 'Bloody cannons.'

The ground ahead of them rose to that narrow spur alongside the road, where still more Dutchmen were unlimbering a pair of light horse artillery pieces.

'Take this thing, for pity's sake,' snapped the sergeant, holding out the reins. 'I'd rather be standing here bare-arse naked than with an empty gun.'

'That's not a pretty thought,' she grinned, and took the black leather reins just as a bullet ripped into the trampled grass beneath the mare, causing the animal to side-step nervously. *She'll be steady enough when she's rested*, thought Liberté, *but I need to get her out of here first, find the Regiment.* There would be little chance of her reaching the horse lines and her own Lucette, of course, yet her priority now was to re-join the Second. The sergeant was busy with his own drill, had taken a paper cartridge from the dark-tanned leather ammunition box at his hip, bitten off the tip of the powder compartment and primed the frizzen afresh, all of which reminded Liberté that she could not rely on the sabre alone.

'Come on, beautiful,' she whispered to the mare, turned the horse and, twisting the reins once about her arm, hearing the rattle of the sergeant's iron ramrod, she knelt to relieve the dead Dutchman of his carbine and its strap, the fellow's own cartridge-box too. She checked that the carbine was loaded, glanced to the hill as she slung each of the pipe-clayed belts across her own left shoulder, saw the two enemy artillery pieces now ready for action.

'Looks like it might get hot again,' the sergeant laughed. 'I'd better get back to the Lieutenant. The young fool's lost without me to look after him.' But he waited for her, all the same, as she led the horse down and back across the stream.

Liberté pulled the reins gently to make contact with the horse's mouth, set her foot in the left stirrup, holding the carbine against the black-dyed sheepskin of the saddle bow, gripped the cantle and swung herself up with practised ease.

'And I've got my own business to settle,' she told him, as she snapped the carbine's shoulder sling swivel to the weapon's bar-rings, set the butt against her thigh, holding the gun upwards and ready for use rather than setting the thing in its muzzle bucket. The firing at the farm had now died away completely while, all the way from here to the wood, it had intensified, volley exchanged for volley, the French artillery busy somewhere to the rear, but their efforts evident from the howitzer shells that exploded above the Dutch-Belgian lines. 'Anyway,' she said, 'I'm off.'

'Hey, Dumont,' said the sergeant. He lifted a hand, waved it in front of his bristled cheek. 'Underneath those bruises of yours, all the shit on your face...'

'If you're going to play the line about me being a handsome woman, Sergeant,' she replied, 'I'll use this bloody sabre and give your own ugly kisser a few extra creases to remember me by.' *By the Host*, she thought, *how many times have I had this conversation!* But there was something in the sergeant's honest and open regard that gave her pause. It had been a long time, a very long time, since she had found any man that interested her beyond the need for a quick bedding or two. And she normally found sufficient satisfaction simply from reading her Diderot or Laclos. Yet this fellow was looking at her again with that same far-seeing appraisal he had exercised when he first came to her side, in the barn. So she rubbed a sleeve across her forehead, as though to rub away some of the filth, offered him her most alluring smile. 'There,' she said. 'That better?'

'Nah,' he laughed, 'you looked better when you were covered in crap.'

'Bastard,' Liberté snarled, though unable to prevent a half-smile flickering across her lips. She pulled the reins to turn the horse's head and dug her heels to get the beast moving. 'But I know where you are, Sergeant. I'll be back!'

It was a half-hour and two horses later before Liberté Dumont returned to the Gémioncourt farm. She had not succeeded in locating her own regiment but, in that fruitless search, a dozen frustrated enquiries, she had come up with the 6th Regiment of Horse Chasseurs and determined to temporarily abandon the quest, to throw in her lot with these fellows. Specifically, she had approached one of the squadron captains who, it transpired, had heard of her exploits at Brienne, so did not trouble her with the normal foolish questions but suggested

– though she needed no persuasion in this regard – that she may be more at risk from her own side than from the enemy by roaming the field in this way. And he was right. It might pose one set of dangers to be here as a lone woman in civilian dress, but quite another to attempt leaving it in uniform. So she had been provided with a fresh mount and taken a position in the second rank of the Third Squadron's 7th Company.

Yet when they moved forward, came within sight of the farm again, she was shocked to see that, while it still stood behind the French lines, the fighting around its fringes must have remained savage. And the Chasseurs' charge, when it came – with all the certainty that the Dutchies would break and run – actually threw them straight into the teeth of a perfectly timed point-blank volley, and grape-shot from the two artillery pieces, that devastated the regiment's First Squadron and threw the rest into chaos. They had re-grouped, swept forward for a second time but with an identical result, and this time, Liberté's horse was shot from beneath her. A minor miracle that she suffered little hurt either from the fall or the pounding hooves around her. By the time she had limped back, found another mount, the Brigade's two Line Lancer regiments had been advanced, made a charge of their own and, incredibly, also been repulsed. It was ignominious, but the Dutchies fell back, finally, only when several French infantry battalions marched up on the right, drums thundering and cries of 'Long live the Emperor!' The threat to the Dutch flank, their disciplined retreat, allowed Liberté's squadron, the Line Lancers too, to take up a new position at the Gémioncourt stream. And in that way did she come back to the farm.

It was peaceful there. Too peaceful. And she needed no arcane talent to know the nature of the silence that shrouded the place. It was a silence that stunk of lilies and incense, of mildewed tombstones. Yet she sought leave, all the same, to break ranks, and when it was granted, trotted back to the farm's approach road, picked her way carefully between the cairns of green and blue at the gateway, swatting aside the shimmering fly-swarm that rose and fell and droned around the yard.

No, she thought, *I was wrong. Our Lady be praised!* For, on the farther side of the cobbles, gathered around the threshold to the farmhouse where she had been interviewed by Thin Prince Willem van Oranje-Nassau, were the Frenchmen who had held this place – as the Dutch-Belgians had done before them – against the bayonet onslaught of their enemies in a last stand defence of the two-storey house. She scanned their tired faces, sure that she would see the grizzled sergeant in their midst, and she was therefore shocked to encounter his penetrating gaze before she was even halfway across the intervening shambles. Seeming to have a question almost formed on his lips, he peered at her from the near side of another low mound, a tangle of dark-sleeved arms, sleeves with cuffs of red and piped in white wool, splayed fingers that clawed towards eternity, grey or tan trouser legs, bared shins and waxen features, bloodless like the sergeant's. His face remained untroubled, but his torso and limbs were riddled with bullets, ripped cloth and puncture wounds, a bayonet and its attached musket still hanging from his ribs where he sat, his fallen foes around him and, at his back, as though the sergeant had gone down looking after him, even as his final act, was the mangled corpse of young Sub-Lieutenant Brissart.

Liberté thought briefly about continuing to the survivors, certain that they, at least, would know the sergeant's name. But she was already struggling with some absurd sense of loss, so she bit him off from her thoughts, turned the horse about and clattered back to the road.

Those bloody Dutch militiamen were back on the farther side of the farm. *What was this now?* thought Liberté. *The third time?* Attack and counter-attack. Thirsty work and not a canteen-mistress to be found. She reached down, patted the horse's shoulder, and startled a spray of sweat droplets from its hide.

'We could both do with a drink, couldn't we?' she whispered into the beast's mane while a shimmering mere of welcoming water laughed at her, just away to the left, where the Gémioncourt brook ended its eastward descent at the lake. Between lake and farm, six battalions of French infantry had formed square, come to a halt, as enemy cavalry moved ahead of them – the same green-coated Dutch Light Dragoons and sky-blue Hussars from earlier. And if they had seemed spent then, the intervening endless engagements could not have done much to revive them. Yet they seemed to have discovered some second wind. It was not unusual, of course. She had been there herself. Just when you thought you were finished, your last ounce of energy exhausted, there would be a collective rush of blood to the morale and strength of the squadron, the entire regiment, and all the weariness would ebb away again. For a while.

Sometimes it could be attributed simply to the sudden presence of a single individual, and she had seen Bonaparte pull the trick often enough. *But how can a sodomite like Thin William also manage it?* She almost laughed. Unthinkable. Yet there he was, easily distinguished by his gold-braid and black pelisse, standing in his stirrups and driving forward still more of his militia down the highway, waving the plumed hat around his head, his column's drums hammering and the men yelling as they advanced towards the far side of the French battalions – battalions that were pinned in square by the proximity of the Dutch cavalry and, thus, a dense and easy target for their militiamen. *And there*, she thought. *That will have put some iron back into them as well.* For, beyond the French squares, beyond the Dutch militia column, beyond their slow-moving cavalry brigade, beyond the fields of gold, on the higher terrain around the white cluster of Quatre Bras, and closer, along the Namur road, there were the first streaks of scarlet. The English. And a new sound. Bagpipes. Not the pastoral melody of the Breton *veuze*, but the barbarian wail of Wellesley's wild Scotsmen.

Through the smoke and the chaos, she saw Thin William's column begin deploying into line, and a cloud of green-coated Jägers appeared from the flanks, formed a skirmish line ahead of the advancing companies. There was a galloper, an Aide from Ney's command post, she assumed. Trumpet calls, and she felt the horse tense between her knees. In truth, she felt somewhat exposed, for the troopers around her all had the benefit of a rolled riding coat wrapped tight over one shoulder, tied at the opposite waist so that it gave some protection to chest and back from sabre slash. But there was no time to worry about that now, for the Lancers to their left were already wheeling, orders stretching them out, squadron by squadron, troop by troop, as they moved off along the northern edge of the stream so they might pass behind their own battalions.

'Sixth Chasseurs...' Their turn now. Liberté straightened in the saddle. And then the overlapping commands as each of the regiment's squadrons, each component company, received their own instruction, repeated by the trumpets.

'Third Squadron will move to the left...'

They took their place in the column with precision, six riders abreast, along the rear of the squares, a swing to the right, to the northwest, between the battalions and the farmhouse. More commands.

'Seventh Company...SWORDS!'

Every trooper's right hand reached over his bridle arm, grasped the sword grip and twisted until the guard faced the rear before drawing forth the first few inches of steel, before completing the movement, bringing the blade across to the Carry. There was the practised contact of inner leg against saddle flap beneath the sheepskin shabraque; the heightened smell of sweat and leather; the jolting chime and creak of harness rhythms; the furnace blast of sunshine on Liberté's shoulders and in her nostrils the hot odour of ripening summer crops singled out from the stink; the buzz of flies around the horse's flickering ears; the muted background rip and crackle, the rumbling restlessness of the day; and the smoke-hazed ballet as, simultaneously, the French infantry battalions, suddenly secure in the protection of Piré's cavalry, began to slide from square back to line, while the Dutch column commenced exactly the reverse manoeuvre. But they had left it too late.

Thin William should have seen it coming! She laughed as, on the rising ground to the front, and over the shakos of the Chasseurs, she snatched occasional glimpses of the Line Lancers, the brass of their black-crested helmets flashing like watch beacons, the red and white pennons dipping as they took and skewered the first of the disordered Dutch Jägers. The rest was just a crimson mess. The wired grip of this light sabre felt fragile in her fist, the curve of the thing at odds with the long straight edge that she would normally wield – as much bludgeon as blade. But this was a good butcher's tool, she had to admit afterwards when, reining sharply to a halt among the crawling, shapeless remains of the militiamen, she wiped a sleeve across the blood and brains that had splashed in her eyes.

Trumpet again. Shouted orders useless now in this deafening confusion.

But the Recall, clear enough, and she looked around for the rest of the Sixth, though the Division was mingled all together, spread mostly along the slight ridge where, earlier, there had been Dutch artillery pieces and where, now, lay only the charnel house remains of their gunners and a ragged band of prisoners. Yet the Division was within five hundred paces of Quatre Bras itself, and even closer to the beech wood's edge, just to their left across the highway.

Ahead of them, everything was tumult: half of the surviving blue-coated militiamen streaming back towards the hamlet, packs and weapons thrown on the road, while the rest, perhaps a hundred of them, being harangued by Thin William. *And there*, she thought, *by Rebecque too*. But they could be urged to no more than an orderly yet still broken retreat towards the formations in their rear. Another intact Dutch-Belgian battalion, this side of the wood. Some companies of green-jacket Nassauers closer to the Quatre Bras farm and along the Namur road. Then, pushing up behind, the English regiments while, to the right, the Dutch cavalry from earlier, still holding their position.

Time to finish this! she thought, happily, as her brief respite came to an equally abrupt end. The call to yet another charge and they were off, Lancers, Chasseurs and Liberté Dumont in her patchwork uniform, down the farther side of the slope. She could taste the dismay on the faces of the Dutchmen below them, almost heard Thin William's cry of fear and fury as he gave up all effort to rally his men any further and set spurs to his horse's flanks. But he also had delayed too long. Trooper Dumont knew it and had, she felt, a score to settle. *Each Dutchmen worth ten of our own*, she remembered. *Is that what you think, young sodomite? And what was your promise to me? That I should pay the appropriate price?*

They were gaining on him and the group of Aides at his tail.

'Run, you bastard!' she screamed, though he could never have heard her. Yet she kept her arm perfectly straight, the Guard position, the sabre extended, diagonally across her body, the tip raised slightly so that it might protect both her own body and her mount's head.

She was coming up fast on her prey, peered ahead to find Thin William, saw him overtaken by a Lancer who grabbed the Prince's bridle, veered left, forced him to stop. *Now!* She planned to finish him. Yet her way was suddenly barred. Rebecque, appearing from nowhere, his hand raised flat, as though instructing her to halt. And men from that fresh battalion of Dutch-Belgians came running across the Brussels road, an abbatis of bayonets rapidly formed, from which her horse shied, reared, spun while she, in turn, fought to retain her seat, maintain control, remembering to stay loose, to settle the beast back into a controlled run. A Chasseur's mount was down beside her, on its knees and sliding into the swelling enemy ranks that opened briefly, closed again around the rider, stabbed him repeatedly to death. And although it seemed at first that the Lancer who had captured Thin William might succeed in dragging away his prisoner, he too was quickly surrounded, the Prince yelling his own name, time and time again, while his men dragged the Lancer to the ground.

Just one more push, Liberté thought. She could see it, feel it. One more push from the Division and they would scatter these Dutchies for the last time and, once through them, they could break the English too while they were still attempting to form their lines. But Piré's regiments were falling back and she knew that she had no choice except to follow them. So with disdain, she turned her back on the Dutchmen, ignored the musket balls whistling past her ears, allowed her horse no more than a nonchalant walk to her own lines. She took one last glance over her shoulder, just in time to see Thin William's moment of triumphant relief. For the Prince had thrown open his black pelisse, seized the broad blue ribbon of whatever chivalric Order he wore across his chest, jerked it free along with the glittering, enamelled and many-pointed star to which it was attached, and tossed the thing theatrically to an ensign bearing the white and green-wreathed colours of the battalion that had rescued him. She could not hear the words he shouted, but his face was illuminated with laughter and the palpable beam of deliverance.

Chapter Sixteen

Friday 16th June 1815, 5.00pm

'At last!' muttered Marianne Tambour, as the Middle Guard's Fourth Regiment of Foot Grenadiers began to form its column. It had been a frustrating couple of hours.

The attack had begun against the several hamlets away down the undulating amber fields to the left, and along the stretch of stream that pushed out towards the French line. The closest and largest of these settlements was St. Amand, with its church and neighbouring château plainly visible among gardens and orchards. A band had struck up *The Victory Song*, the Eagles going forward in force, an entire infantry corps, sweltering in the greatcoats that were still easier to wear than to carry. And the villages had almost been taken. Lost again. Then taken once more. As they should have been, in Marianne's humble opinion, given that the Prussos seemed to have no more than a brigade to defend them. But they had well-placed and plentiful artillery up on the low hills so that even at this distance, Marianne had felt the ground shake beneath her feet from their bombardment, the noise almost unbearable. To add insult to injury, the buggers had launched an attack of their own, virtually captured the ground afresh until, finally, a stalemate had ensued and each side fallen almost silent.

The story had been virtually the same ahead of the Guard's position, where the stream swung away from them again, towards the north-east, and splitting the larger village of Ligny, its tall spire a veritable magnet drawing one French column after another until, finally, it seemed that the place must be taken. Yet that also had resulted in a further Prussian counter-attack, their troops pushing down from the slopes behind to check the French advance and stall the entire battle, though it was hard to believe that anybody could still be alive in that place, which was wreathed entirely in smoke and flame, raging with the screams of those still burning alive in its ruins.

'Listen!' said Suzanne Prairial. 'Like an echo.'

She was right. In that brief moment of respite, in front of Fleurus, they could hear the sounds of another engagement, away to the west. *Ney and the Left Wing*, thought Marianne. *And maybe Hawk-face too*. But the word was that Ney should be marching here, to help destroy the Prussians once and for all.

'Do I march with you and the column, Maman?' demanded Florisette.

'You have to help Prairial look after the baby,' Marianne told the girl, a sharper response than she had intended.

There was usually somebody among their baggage train to keep an eye on Poppy, and it was normally safe enough, though there was always the possibility that the train might be taken. It had happened at Vitoria, had it not? And with considerable slaughter of the non-combatants. Yet there was no chance of that today, she was certain.

'I reckon she'd rather be with Onion and the other kids, wouldn't you. Poppy?' said the mulatta. 'Me and the babe will be fine.'

'She'll stay away from Argonne *and* her brood,' snapped Marianne, 'if she knows what's good for her.' And she grabbed Poppy's ear, twisted it hard. 'You hear, girl?'

Florisette squealed but her face was set with defiance. Her mother's daughter.

'I hope the Prussos get you!' hissed the child.

Marianne laughed.

'You and that bitch Argonne, both! Anyway, there's the cart to tend and the goats to be fed.'

The girl had a soft spot for the stupid creatures, had given them names. Grognard and Giselle. Slept with them most nights. 'And then you can decide which of them can get its gizzard slit tonight. The lads will want to celebrate with a good goat stew. They always pay well after a fight.' She saw Poppy turn her head away.

By the Host, thought Marianne, *she needs to be toughened up. Too soft by half.*

'You think Argonne set you up?' said Suzanne Prairial, rocking the cradle that hung from the pony's saddle frame. 'With the hen?'

'Is the Grand Turk a Mahometan?' Marianne replied. 'Of course she set me up.'

And tomorrow, or the next day, she fumed, *they'll drag me in front of a drumhead court. Then I'll be right in the shit.* For there were two certainties. First, that she could not point the finger at Catherine Argonne even if she had any evidence. There was a certain honour, after all, between the women of the Eagles. And anyway, the woman had been around the Battalion a long time. She had a lot of friends in too many places. So the second certainty was that Marianne could not avoid battalion punishment. She could appeal to Vicquot's better nature, of course, remind him about the favours he owed her. The way she had cared for Letort, maybe. But she knew that when it came down to disciplinary issues Captain Vicquot *had* no better nature.

'Well,' said Prairial, 'there's nothing that can be done until the battle's over. And look, the wagon of the Ankou.'

It was the Emperor's dormeuse, being whipped away to the rear.

'You Bretons and your superstitions.' Marianne shook her head.

'The Ankou?' said Poppy.

'Death,' replied Marianne. 'The Reaper.'

*

Marianne had the same problem as Fronsac and his mates but, while they chose to wear the distinctive blue greatcoats of the Guard rather than carry them, she decided to roll the russet jacket and sling it through the shoulder straps of her haversack. She thanked the stars that she had no heavy backpack to deal with, just this canvas satchel she had taken from the cart, filling it with the supplies she thought she might need. A couple of extra water bottles too, of course. The brandy cask, naturally. And the Battalion's drummers called them to the Ready, the Grenadiers rising as one man among the stalks of broken rye, adjusting bearskins, shakos and forage caps.

'Here,' said one of the rear-rankers. 'You want to finish this?' He offered her the clay pipe that he had only recently lit. 'Shame to waste a good smoke.'

She agreed with him, promised to find him later, to return the pipe, maybe an ounce of tobacco besides.

'Yes,' he said. 'Later.' Then he turned from her, began checking the sling on his Charleville.

The regiments of the Young Guard were already on the move, their bands playing and the men bellowing salutes to the Shaveling as they passed him at the mill. He was back on his white horse again, waving them forward, hat in one hand, a gleaming goblet in the other, raising it to them exactly as he had toasted Marianne at Beaumont.

'Thank Christ he's back,' said one of the men just ahead of her. 'Things have got so much better since his holiday on Elba. All last winter I was cold and hungry. Now I'm just fucking hungry.' It was an old joke, but the fellows around him laughed anyway, as the Middle Guard itself was stood ready. Closed Column of March, by Platoon. Ready to advance up the highway, with the Emperor's Big Brothers, the iron breast-plated Cuirassiers forming up away to the right, their huge horses snorting, manes tossing as they sensed the same charged atmosphere that animated their riders.

It could be a lonely place at times, here at the arse end of the Battalion with not even the cart or Cocotte for company. But that was Tambour's allotted position and she would stick with it. She could, she supposed, always move along to the place, seven files away, where Bufanda was flirting with the men closest to her. But she could not be bothered with the *manola* and, on a day such as this, among the steaming press of the Empire's greatest warriors, it was hard to feel alone. And victory must surely be in the air for, apart from toasting that part of his army that surrounded him, the Shaveling and his entourage now raised their glasses more and more often towards the west, the direction from which reinforcements were expected.

'Hey,' she shouted. 'How many Prussos does it take to tile a roof?'

'Depends how thin we slice 'em!' called back the closest platoons, and somebody turned around to thump her playfully in the shoulder.

A single voice, lifting high, somewhere ahead. Then the drum commands, washing back towards her in overlapping waves from unit to unit, the curling wisps of dust raised as the column's head moved off, the first breeze of the day carrying its whiff of rancid sweat and unwashed wool. The Fourth Regiment's Second Battalion picking up the step at last, and a song to keep them going. *Cadet Rousselle*, of course. What else? The Battalion's favourite, except that, in their own version, the bailiff did not have three houses, three dogs, three boys, and the rest. No, in this version he had three balls, three dicks, or whatever other bawdy bits the platoon poets had been able to devise.

She finished the smoke, knocked the hot dottle from the bowl into the palm of her hand, dropped it onto the road and crushed it beneath her heel before tucking the pipe into the band of her bonnet. Yet they had travelled no more than two hundred paces before gallopers came thundering along the lines and, within moments, the entire advance had halted.

'Hang about,' somebody shouted, 'Drouot's just realised he's set off without his sextant. Silly bugger always gets us lost without it!'

Drouot had recently found himself in charge of the Guard when their regular commander, Mortier, had complained that his sciatica put him out of action. But Marianne knew that despite their banter, the lads had respect for Drouot. Twenty years' service under his belt. A fair bit of that at sea with the marines and, most famously, at the naval battle fought against the English at Trafalgar.

'Nah,' said somebody else, 'the Shaveling's decided it's not safe for us out there. He worries about us, you know?'

And so it went on until, company by company, they were required to About Turn, while a new ripple of rumours whispered its way along the ranks.

'Another bloody general gone over to the other side, I bet.'

'Ney's been beaten by the English.'

'Listen, you can't hear anything from over there now. It must be true.'

'Ney's dead, they reckon.'

'We've been sold out.'

'Bloody generals. Worse than the aristos.'

'The Shaveling should shoot the bleedin' lot of them.'

For, whoever else might be to blame for their ills, to the Old Grumblers of the Guard, their Emperor was beyond reproach.

Among them all, Marianne reminded herself, *he is the one who never puts himself before our need to defeat the enemies of France*. The enemies of the Revolution. She might hate him for having stalled the Revolution's forward march, but she loved him with a passion that knew no bounds for not having hurled it into reverse. *Not like this*, she thought, as they themselves reversed back towards Fleurus and she had to stand aside while the Battalion passed by so she could pick up her place at the rear once again. There were a few hurried words with Fronsac when the Fourth Company came alongside, then more gallopers as the columns approached the mill once more, back to their starting positions. A halt. More rumour. Until Sergeant Flambert wandered through their ranks, spoke to each *peloton*.

'Steady boys. No more gossip now, if you please. Just a change of plan. No, Ney's still alive and kicking. Giving the Goddams a bad time, so I'm told. But there's some activity to the rear and nobody seems to know who the buggers are. Probably just reinforcements. They'll find out soon enough though. And the boys over there need some help. So, there it is, lads. Any more moans, groans, beefs or bones?'

Annoying bastard, thought Marianne, as Flambert thumbed over his shoulder to the north-west, to the extreme left of the French attack positions, and she could now see that two large formations were breaking away to march in that very direction – the whole of the Young Guard's Division and two regiments, she thought, of the Old Guard's Foot Chasseurs. There was too much smoke to make out their destination, but she knew that if anything was needed to stiffen the nerve of the units away over there, it would be the appearance of the Shaveling's Immortals.

'There go the Big Brothers too!' somebody cried, and she turned to see squadron after squadron of those heavy cavalrymen trotting away past the baggage train. 'They'll soon find out if some bugger's trying to sneak up on us.'

But the panic seemed to be over, for the Battalion had orders of its own.

'Never mind what I told you before,' said Marianne, 'you can march with me after all.'

'But Maman,' Poppy replied, 'what about Prairial and the babe?'

The panic might be past but there was still no real word about whether the forces to their rear were friend or foe. It was a tough call but, on balance, Marianne believed her daughter would be safer with the re-organised column than here with the baggage. It was a smaller column, only the Third and Fourth Regiments of Grenadiers, but that must simply mean that their new task, whatever it might be, could not be too onerous.

'Don't argue with me, Florisette,' she snapped. 'You wanted to march with me, didn't you?'

'Not if you're going to kill Grognard or Giselle!'

Those damned goats again.

'Fine,' said Marianne, 'the goats get a stay of execution.' Poppy grinned. 'For today.'

'And tomorrow too?' wheedled her daughter.

'Agreed. For tomorrow too. But after that…'

She stopped, as the sides of the world began to collapse around her, forming that familiar tunnel in which sounds and events spun and dizzied, the tunnel from which all her premonitions emanated so that, suddenly, she could no longer see *any* future beyond the morrow.

'After that?' said Poppy, from somewhere far distant.

'What are you doing, woman?' It was Catherine Argonne, hobbling towards her from among the wagons, though Marianne was struggling to focus her vision on her. 'You should leave the child here, Tambour. Safer here.'

'Safer?' Marianne snarled. 'With you, bitch? And what scheme will you hatch against me next?'

'Hatch against you?' Argonne was forced to grip her crutch just that bit tighter to prevent a sudden explosion of mirth from overbalancing her. 'Hatch? You're talking about the speckled hen? That's priceless.' She struggled hard to regain her composure.

'Get back to your brood, Catherine,' said Marianne. 'We don't need you here.' At least her head was clearing, though she still struggled to understand why Argonne was silently mouthing the word *brood* over and over again, as though that was amusing too.

'I never laid any scheme against you,' said Argonne at last, before another bout of laughter shook her. 'And I'm telling you the truth, madam. I got the bird in good faith from one of the lads in the Second, just like I told you. The peace offering seemed like a good idea at the time. But that wasn't entirely my own, I must confess. No, it was Bufanda who put the thought in my head. A fine one, it seemed at the time. Until I went back and quizzed the lad from the Second some more. I asked him who'd told him the bird was bad luck. It seems he'd been having his fortune told. The cards read. And a bit more besides, so far as I could gather.'

'Cards?' Marianne's brain was now functioning more fully again. 'Bufanda?'

'You can never trust a *manola*. And certainly not a *manola gitana*. Seems she put the idea in *his* head. That I might take it off his hands. And she, in turn...'

'I get the picture,' said Marianne. There was indeed, at one level, a sense of collective honour among the army's women, almost a thieves' code, to protect the sisterhood as a whole. And yet, within that, she never ceased to be amazed at the petty jealousies, which inspired so many acts of seemingly random mischief and mayhem. 'But Poppy still comes with me,' she hissed. For, if there was no future beyond tomorrow, what did it matter?

Florisette skipped along happily enough at her side, the tips of slender fingers gripped in Marianne's hand. The child had insisted on carrying another spare water bottle and seemed oblivious to the dust that clouded around them, matted her straight hair, turned it a richer shade of red, and clogged in the snot at her upper lip, complaining only when her mother squashed the little pug nose by attempting to wipe the thing on her shirt sleeve.

If I survived on all those bloody fields with Maman Cholet, thought Marianne, *I'm sure Poppy can survive them too. For now, at least.*

The war must be won soon, surely. The sooner the better. The girl might survive, but she deserved a better life than this. And Marianne's earlier premonition was fading fast now, as her premonitions always did. But this one faded faster than most, superseded by thoughts of Bufanda. She recalled the mark-up she had added to the Spanish woman's share of the supplies that Poppy and Prairial had brought her. Had she worked out that she had been fleeced? So, tip for tap? For a good cat, a good rat? A debt laid and dues repaid? She turned to look at the *manola*, away there on the far side of the column, caught Bufanda staring back at her, smiling, as though she might be thinking of similar sayings in her own tongue. Cocky bitch!

The band was playing. *The Departure Song*, the men singing along with their own inimitable lyrics again, to the rhythm of the Jingling Johnnies that chimed clear even above the artillery bombardments and the rending rattle of musketry.

'Why are they shooting at the flames, Maman?' said Florisette.

For so it seemed from here. Ligny village coming up on their left, beyond the batteries of French Horse Artillery, gunners' portfires applied to one piece after another for a rolling salvo in which, by the time the last gun was fired, the first had been sponged and loaded ready to begin again. Shot after shot after shot against the Prussos' cannons up there on the smoke-shrouded slopes beyond, while the enemy shells, for their part, seemed directed only at the conflagration below. And it was not only the Prussian cannons, but the French skirmishers and infantry battalions also, that poured volley upon volley into the well-spread bonfire. A considerably larger village than she had realised. Almost a small town. And there was that church spire, still visible as the drifting black billows parted from time to time.

'Not at the flames,' Marianne murmured, for she could see now that there were small figures dancing in the fires. Or so they appeared to her. Dark stick men with no real form, though they still ran from here to there, pointed their muskets in seemingly random directions, stabbed them at unseen targets, rising and falling, then arising on occasion once more, all set against and within the licking luminosity of a funeral pyre.

Burned and blackened faces at the roadside too now, uniforms still smoking and the sweet, sickly scent of roasted flesh to mask the more normal sights and smells of the dead and dying.

There can be no place on earth so desolate, so close to a living hell, she thought, *as a battle's dressing station.*

Ambulances came in with routine regularity, on two wheels or four, the corresponding numbers of wounded inside. Returned empty to fetch more of the infinite numbers available to fill them again, or trundling past for evacuation of more complex cases to the hospital camps or lodgings established back in Fleurus. For the army's surgeons, its medical officers, its companies of brown-coated military orderlies, were drilled as hard as any infantry corps in the prescribed regulation for the care of casualties. They owed it all to Saviour Larrey who, twenty years before, as the army's Surgeon-in-Chief, had carried the revolutionary principle to the battlefield. And the Shaveling himself be praised that he had fostered and encouraged the thing. Always start with the most dangerously damaged, regardless of rank, Larrey had demanded. Well, that was the theory. Though she had never known it breached through intent but only ever because, regardless of the drill, no system on earth could ever truly cope with chaos like this. Still, there were Larrey's ambulances, and the semblance of a system for getting the wounded to succour, or succour to the wounded.

'Water!' somebody croaked at them from the rows of crumpled bundles, and Poppy's fingers slipped from Marianne's grip as the girl flourished the flask she carried. She was gone before Marianne could stop her, ran to the man's side as he coughed up another gob of lung blood, his eyes red-rimmed and showing starkly within features that were otherwise entirely smoke-stained.

'You hurt bad, mister?' Poppy asked him as she twisted the stopper from the water bottle.

'Just need to catch my breath,' muttered the soldier. 'Then I'll be fine.'

Marianne knelt alongside her daughter.

'We can catch up with the boys later,' she said. Her duty lay with her own Battalion, she knew that. But perhaps they could spare a few moments here. So she knelt at the next man in the line, while an orderly tried to ask the fellow's name, the place that he came from. But he was beyond answering and, truly, no longer even a man at all. Thus she turned to see how her daughter was faring.

'He won't drink water, Maman,' Poppy complained.

'Against my religion,' wheezed the soldier.

'You should know that all religions are a lie,' said Marianne.

'I'd rather smoke that pipe.' He lifted a filth-rimed finger from within his rags, pointed at Marianne's bonnet. 'And a decent plug of the dark stuff to go with it.'

He coughed again, then gasped for breath.

'It wouldn't help that cough, I think,' Marianne scolded him.

'Christ's Hooks, no,' he replied. 'Bad for my health, you reckon?'

'Is he hurt bad, Maman?'

'Not so bad,' said the soldier. 'But it will do, child. I just need to get my breath. Then I suppose they'll send me back.' He moved his head slightly towards the village. 'In there.'

Marianne looked at the faded tan greatcoat wrapped about him, the spreading dark stain that soaked its front and side, and she saw Poppy staring at it too.

'Do you have a daughter, mister?' the girl asked him.

'Three,' he whispered, his breath coming in short, desperate bursts. 'As soon as I've rested a bit, I'll tell you about them.' Another racking cough, a trickle of blood from his nostril.

'I bet you love them all very much,' said Florisette, and she stayed with him until he died, while Marianne moved slowly among the others close at hand, delving in the knapsack for a linen bandage, or the vinegar bottle, or her contusion-wash of *eau de vie* and ammoniac – but careful not to exhaust the precious supplies that her own boys might so soon need. And when Poppy joined her, the girl said not a word about the passing she had just witnessed and shared, quietly appearing at her mother's side, expertly pressing together the edges of a dangerous gash while Marianne used her suture hook and silk thread to close the thing. *Perhaps*, thought Marianne, *she is already tough enough, after all.*

Her patient was an old scar-face who barely winced as the steel and stitching passed through skin and nerves.

'It's like the whole battalion just melts in a foundry,' he told them, his face clenched with pride. 'You've seen molten metal, girlie? When it flows into ingot moulds? Well, it's the same. Slow. White hot. But we gets there in the end. To that sodding church. And the town square. Never seen anything like it. Biggest brawl in history, in that square. Then we ends up in the bone yard. Fights them for every gravestone. We even brings up two of the Shaveling's Little Daughters. Just four-pounders. But, Jesu, that grapeshot makes a mess at that range. Sorry, girlie, but that's the way of it. There's all sorts dead in there, too. Majors. Colonels. Generals. The lot!'

'Did we save that one, Maman?'

'Yes, we saved him, I think. But we need to get back to the Battalion now. They'll think we've deserted.'

The girl fell in alongside her again as they hurried up the highway, dodging through all the coming and going of conflict's turbulent traffic until, after a long silence, Florisette finally spoke again.

'Maman,' she said, 'if Papa Fronsac and Marle, or Trinquart and Uncle Muhler, or any of them… Well, if they really need a goat stew tonight, you can take Giselle. Or Grognard. Both, maybe. But you won't make them pay for it, will you?'

Marianne ignored the question, stared straight forward to the column ahead, to the first awakening groans and angry stirrings as the battle roused itself even there on the furthest right flank. They had saved at least one life, she and the girl, brought succour to many others that might also achieve salvation as a result. But her daughter would never remember them. It was only the ones you could not save that stayed with you. Like the fellow with the three daughters. And they not only stayed with you. They helped shape you too.

In the end, there had been little for the Battalion to do there. Marianne and Poppy caught up with the formation about a thousand paces further on, as it moved into Column of Companies while, at the same time, advancing alongside the Third. To Tongrenelle. The far right of the French positions. Yet, by the time they reached the place, there were no Prussians left, their units having fallen back to the north and east, and to the château, so they halted briefly on the far side while regiments of line infantry took occupation of the deserted village.

'What now?' she asked, as they waited for their next orders.

'Hey, Tambour,' said one of the Grenadiers, the same who had shared his smoke with her earlier. 'You got my pipe?'

'I lost it,' she lied, remembering that it had still been clenched between the teeth of that lung-shot soldier when he died. *You see?* she thought. *There's no escaping them.* 'I'll get you a fresh one,' she told him, 'when we're back with the carts.'

But he was not listening to her, stared over her shoulder with the same hungry stupidity as the other men around him, much as they always did when Juanita Bufanda was flashing her wares in the vicinity.

'They did not really need us, after all,' said the Spanish woman, as though she felt the need to make conversation.

'We only ever go where we're needed, don't we, Maman?' said Poppy. It was true enough, for the very presence of the Guard had already made a visible difference here without even the need to fire a shot.

'And we'll be wanted there next, I think,' said Marianne, nodding back towards Ligny village, where the stalemate seemed interminable. 'Though not all of us may be wanted equally.' She set her lips tight, raised an eyebrow in Bufanda's direction.

'In the sisterhood, Tambour,' the *manola* replied, 'we are all equal, are we not? Tomorrow might be different, of course. If there is a court. A trial. They tell me you are charged with looting. A speckled hen, of all things. I could read the cards for you. Or the lines on your hand. Tell you how it might all end?'

Marianne was tempted to ask the obvious question, but she already knew that Bufanda might have a dozen different reasons for implicating her. In any case, the Spaniard was unlikely to make any form of confession, and merely to beg for a reason was a terrible weakness. Yet she felt Poppy tense at her side, as the mood between the two women became heavy and acrid.

'Stay close to me, girl,' Marianne told her daughter. 'Hold my apron and *keep* holding it.' Florisette clutched a corner of the black say-cloth in her small fist. 'And you!' Marianne turned to Bufanda. 'If you don't stay out of my face, there'll be no need of cards to predict what's coming *your* way, lady.'

She saw Bufanda lift both hands to the sides of her face, the fingers held flat and straight, the thumb beneath wagging like a chattering tongue.

'Harsh words, *nena*,' she said. 'But you'll be in no place to make threats if you lose the commission.'

There it was again. That resentment about her commission.

'Is that what this is about, Bufanda? About Lomballe? The commission?'

Marianne cursed herself. *Dammit*, she thought. *Didn't I decide not to ask the reason why?*

'You think I had something to do with the speckled hen?' Bufanda laughed. 'That's what you mean, *nena*?'

'Tante Argonne told us all about it,' chimed Florisette. 'She says you are a wicked bitch.'

Juanita Bufanda laughed again.

'Ah, little one,' she said, 'you will go far. Very far, I think.'

The *manola* slipped away among the ranks, began plying her own wares within two of the Battalion's companies and leaving Marianne to provide refreshments in the others, though business was far from brisk. There was a direct link, she always calculated, between the amount of blood shed and the volume of rotgut sold. But today she was more concerned with Bufanda's words. *What did she mean?* she thought. *About Poppy going far?* She had no idea. But she knew this. That the words had closed that tunnel of premonition around her all over again.

The Recall had been drummed quickly, the march reversed, skirting Tongrenelle now to regain the Fleurus road as quickly as possible. The sun was still up, though lowering in the west, while the sky itself had begun to darken with towering imperial blue anvils, roiling bases of deepest grey. Their arrival was heralded by the blare of Prussian trumpets too. Or it seemed that way until the flankers, Marianne too, and her daughter, Florisette, turned to see cavalry at their rear, Prussos crossing the bridge behind Tongrenelle in force.

By Marat! thought Marianne. *Caught here in the open.*

'Shall we form square, Maman?' Poppy shouted, and it seemed suddenly absurd that a child so young should be so familiar with such routines. Yet Marianne had the illusion that the Battalion had taken her daughter's question as instruction, for she heard no other command before sections of the Second and Third Companies were wheeling to left and right respectively, forming the defensive square's two sides, while the Fourth, Fronsac's company, halted briefly, the second section moving up alongside the first, then moved forward to fill the remaining face, executed a tidy enough About Turn, but opening a narrow gap, quickly closed again, through which Marianne herded her daughter, to the protective safety of the hollow interior, where the Battalion's drummers were gathered and the esteemed staff took post. Major Boyer, of course. His two Adjutant-Captains and a couple of Adjutant-Lieutenants. The unit's Paymaster – important, that one, a good man to keep alive. Their own Assistant Surgeon and his team of orderlies. The Eagle-bearer and his party. The Major's Aide. And the Drum Major.

'I bet the bloody Prussos thought we were retreating,' said Fronsac.

His platoon held the position that was normal for them in a square, and a square was the best place to be if you had to fight against cavalry. And there were swarms of the bastards. All of them Lancers. All in long coats of Prussian blue, like Cossacks. But some with oilskin-covered shakos, the rest wearing the tall, square-topped headgear that the Poles called a *czapka*.

No laughing matter either, these Lancers. *Uhlans*, the German States and Austrians called them, and if the lads let them get close enough, they could use those long stickers to spear men like they were wild pigs, drag them squealing from the ranks, open gaps, a breach in the square's dyke wall through which the horsemen might pour and then, like the French had done to the Prusso squares beyond Gilly, all would be lost.

'Dog-dog!' Poppy was calling, strutting up and down behind her father's squad. 'Best in the Battalion. Get it while we've got it. Two sous a shot.'

'Here,' shouted Catherine Argonne's husband. 'There's a lad in the front row needs a cup. A bit of liquid courage, I reckon.'

'The boys in the front row can settle up later,' Marianne told him, filling a cup from her cask and handing it over the intervening shoulders. 'And no sipping. Pass it forward.'

'That's not fair,' yelled old Muhler in his heavy German accent. 'They already got the best seats.'

The front rank was kneeling, musket butts dug firmly among the trampled crop stalks, barrels braced tight in their grip to present a *cheval-de-frise* of bayonets from which any sensible horse would shy away, while the second and third ranks would try to keep up a steady fire.

'Never mind the bloody Prussos,' Sergeant Flambert bellowed. 'Just take down those sodding horses.'

A cavalryman without his mount was no more use than a eunuch in a harem, Marianne knew. And if she got close to any of them, there was still the little *salvavirgo* in her bodice.

'Dog-dog!' Florisette sang again. 'Lovely croaker. Fine for the Forlorn Hope!'

Where the hell has she heard that one? Marianne wondered, remembering how Maman Cholet had used the same phrase to ply her trade. Meanwhile, the square filled with stinking smoke, like rotten eggs, and the ripping volleys ran from one face to another, all around the square, a sure sign that the horsemen were now weaving their patterns about all four sides, this Battalion cut off from each of the others as surely as a rock awash at high tide. And then the very fabric of the rock itself seemed suddenly to fall apart.

She saw the *Uhlan* turn his horse straight at the square, absurdly tall, high above the intervening bearskins, bi-corns, shakos and forage caps of Fronsac's section, and his lance levelled, the white over black pennon flapping around the brown shaft, the iron point gleaming almost gold. There were clods of earth flung up above the fellow's head, the mount's hooves shaking the ground even against the rest of the din and chaos until, at the exact moment when he must surely impale himself on the waiting bayonets, the rider gave a guttural scream, a war cry, that launched his beast up and over the heads of the front rank. Muskets came up, fired, fired again, one lead ball after another slapping into the horse's stretched belly, blood spraying down onto the faces below, men ducking and covering their heads as the lance point came down, took the Basque, Pons, in the chest, pierced him so that the pennon itself all but disappeared within, left a small white and black swallow-tail like a medal ribbon fluttering from his lapel. And then the horse came down too. In a sickening crash and crack of snapping bone, the animal fell squarely on Senent, turned his face to pulp and then slid forward on shattered knees like a runaway cart, with only a wide-eyed Poppy in its path and old Muhler racing alongside the dying horse as its neck extended, lower lip and chin ploughing a furrow through the corn stalks.

Marianne was running too, screaming her daughter's name, but too far away to reach her, and seeing Florisette frozen, like a rabbit caught at night in the glare of a lanthorn.

Pons had gripped the lance shaft with both hands, was staggering backwards, not a big man but strong as an ox. Strong enough to pull the rider from his saddle, where other men of the platoon, Abnet, Cazajus, Bloc and Corporal Poncet buried their bayonets in the Prusso, or beat his brains out with their musket butts.

While Muhler – wonderful Württemberger Muhler – had jumped clear across the horse's head, snatched up her daughter and thrown them both clear.

Chapter Seventeen

Friday 16th June 1815, 5.30pm

Liberté could still not entirely believe that Thin William had escaped. It was absurd. Her squadron was resting its horses on the rise just north of Gémioncourt while the rest of Piré's light cavalry, the Lancer regiments, continued the pursuit of Prince Willem's battalions back and back, towards Quatre Bras, almost as far as the Namur highway.

'Now we must have the bastards,' she murmured.

The crossroads presented a scene of total chaos, with Wellesley's troops moving up in force but mingled with those still in retreat and, away on the right, columns of French infantry marching obliquely from the lake for what must surely be the final assault on the English positions.

'They've more lives than a black cat,' replied a trooper of the 6th Chasseurs at her side. 'Look.'

The Lancers' charge had been wild and valiant, but they were now scattered across a wide front and, as Liberté watched, she saw the very road itself erupt like a volcano, a devastating volley from an enemy she could not even see. Yet the magma they spewed forth was enough to turn the horsemen and, as they wheeled and fell back, their attackers came after them through the smoke. Green-jacketed Nassauers and kilted Scotsmen. But they did not follow for long, and quickly returned to their refuge, which was formed, Liberté now realised, by the road passing through a long defile, the highway sunken within, and edged by high banks.

At the same time, the Dutch cavalry that Piré's men had so recently put to flight were now reformed and advancing once more to the attack, heading straight for the French assault columns, away over there on the right.

Silly bastards, she thought. *Do they think we're just going to sit here and watch them?*

'Sixth Horse Chasseurs will advance in line,' came the command. Threes right wheel. MARCH!'

Her right leg applied an ounce more pressure to the horse's flank and she squeezed back gently on the right rein. Ahead of them, the fields were now patterned by swathes of mystic glyphs, etched by the passage of a half-day's advances and retreats. But the crops between the Dutch horsemen and the French columns were still virgin yellow, unbroken except where the two forces closed, one upon the other. The infantry's leading battalions, almost without slowing their pace, were forming square but still maintaining their line of march, while the Dutch were moving equally smoothly into echelon.

'Sixth Horse Chasseurs will prepare to trot... Trot MARCH!'

The horse responded to the extra pressure of her legs, her backside briefly deeper in the saddle, until she picked up the rhythm of the mare's natural impulsion. *They haven't seen us*, thought Liberté, and hoped that it would remain so, that they would take the Dutchies in flank.

'The regiment will draw swords... Draw SWORDS!'

Sabres scraped from scabbards, the old hands doing so carefully to avoid blunting the edge too much, and the squadron came up with their enemies not only in the flank but also slightly from the rear, following the contours of the ground, their path broken by low walls and hedges that lined a narrow lane running towards a smaller beech copse. There was no longer any possibility of hearing the regimental orders now. The trumpets sounded only at the last possible moment, to both bring the Chasseurs to the charge and also wreak havoc and panic among their foes. For the blow fell precisely at the moment when the French squares blasted apart the Dutchies' leading ranks.

Three of the Chasseurs' horses went down, one after another, as though they were synchronised skittles, and then those nearest to Liberté finally realised their peril, began swerving left and right, without proper direction, slamming into each other. Tensed legs, slapping scabbards, dragged curb bits, each created their own confusion, conveyed panic and contradictory messages to the mounts, spilling riders from saddles, horses going down. The sun-scarlet faces of enemy troopers closest to Liberté were no more than a couple of fathoms away now, trying to swing about, to meet the danger, fixed in fury or in fear. There was an impact as her horse's chest caught the rump of another, and her own legs straightened, reflexive, as she sought to avoid the crush, to sweep her blade from the Guard position, straight-armed, to cut diagonally across one of those Dutch faces from top left to bottom right, to open it like a ripe melon. And then the blur of blood, screaming men and screeching horses, the green-coated Dutch-Belgian Light Dragoons only distinguishable from the green-coated Horse Chasseurs by a flash of dye-shade at collar or cuff, a style and texture of horse furniture – details that, in the chaos of battle, became anything *but* distinguishing. And there was this too: a thing that cut through the red haze of Liberté Dumont's battle frenzy. That the troopers exchanged howled insults, back and forth, yet always in French, a graphic reminder that, until the intervention of the bloody Prussos and English, many of these had been Belgian comrades of the Eagles, possibly serving in the same units. But the Chasseurs swept them away all the same, cut and hacked them down, chased their tails all the way back to the Namur road again.

They drew rein just in time to see those French-screaming Belgians, in their green French-style tunics and shakos, welcomed home to the lines of their new English allies. It was horribly predictable. Those same Scotsmen that Liberté had seen taking shelter in their sunken road, came scrambling once more up its banks, formed a solid bare-shanked line along its edge, presented their muskets with admirable precision, and fired into the Dutch-Belgians at point-blank range.

I wonder, she thought, *whether it ever occurred to any of them to consider why "enemy" cavalry would approach so close without showing any of the normal signs of attack.*

'Those Scotsmen minced more of them than we managed to do,' laughed a trooper at her side as the squadron trotted back to its ridge.

Just below her, new enemy forces had been thrown into the fray, and these were not English either.

'Brunswickers,' said a trooper. 'I've seen them before, at Salamanca, when I was with the 13th.'

Liberté supposed that you could not really mistake them, black broadcloth uniforms, their commander an old fellow in a dark braided coat and soft cap, walking his horse up and down their lines, casually smoking his pipe regardless of the shells exploding above them. Four battalions, so far as she could make out, stretched across the road ahead and over to the left so far as the edge of the large wood.

There was heavy artillery fire to the right also now, where the French columns were on the march again, from the lake and angled towards Quatre Bras, and confronted now by a more organised defence. She could count most of the enemy battalions over there, however, only by their regimental colours, hanging limp in the torpid afternoon air above the cereal crops that concealed the ensigns bearing them. Indeed, the rye was so tall that it hid the whole downhill charge, which hit the leading French troops.

Together with her fellow-troopers Liberté watched its progress through a strange sense of distortion, the flags fluttering with a sudden forward movement and a rippling wave that surged across the crop-heads, the whole length of a large field, until a ragged line of more wild Scots burst into the open with barbaric war cries, threw themselves upon the French skirmishers, drove through them and slammed at bayonet point into the companies beyond, hurling them back. But the Scotsmen were quickly raked by French canister, and Piré's cavalry was ordered forward yet again.

'Easy pickings!' yelled Liberté as they moved up, seeing more redcoats, English battalions now, smearing scarlet across the landscape ahead. But it was the Scots who took the first counter-strike, caught by Piré's Lancers before they had properly formed square, and Liberté's troop charged past the rear of their ruin and smashed into a redcoat formation that seemed to fragment even as they struck, to break down into small knots of frightened fusiliers who fought like demons for their very lives, unable to escape, afraid to retreat.

The Chasseurs charged up and swept around one group, eight Englishmen, knee-deep in broken rye stems, a young officer in their midst who tried to keep some order, arranging his men so that, by turns, four of them would prod ferociously, blindly, with their bayonets to keep the horsemen at bay, while the other four loaded and fired their muskets. The boy lieutenant yelled his instructions with authority, though Liberté could see that tears were running down his cheeks. He was the first to die, too, when Liberté reached for the carbine that hung at her side from its shoulder sling, cocked the gun and put a ball through one of his crying eyes. Others followed her example, taking down a couple more of the Englishmen until the survivors began to run and were hacked to death in the brief pursuit.

They cantered on, almost a leisure ride, a sabre practice, losing hardly a man of their own, only slowing when enemy horsemen appeared to their front, and Liberté was convinced that the Recall would be sounded. But she was wrong, and the trumpets blared out the notes of another charge, rousing them to the gallop, yelling and whooping like fools as the last dregs of the Dutch-Belgian cavalry, failing to offer even a token resistance this time, turned and fled. And there, in the middle of them, abandoned by all but his closest Aides, was Wellesley himself.

Our Lady be praised! thought Liberté. *We can finish this thing now.* The speedy end to France's troubles was in sight. A better end than the quick defeat, or the bluff hand of *poque* on which Fouché had wagered all their stakes. A victory that would establish Bonaparte's manifest destiny for all time.

'Wellesley!' she screamed, and others of the troop picked up this new battle song.

'Is it him? Is it the devil?' cried a Lancer.

'Yes,' Liberté shouted. 'Wellesley. Kill the pig!'

She pointed her sabre, kept it aimed at Wellesley's back, a signpost for the others to follow, as the Duke, weaving a frantic path between his fleeing soldiers, approached the Namur road.

And how wonderful, she laughed to herself, *if he is now shot down by his own men, like the Belgians before him.*

For the same Scotsmen were up, out of their sunken road again, muskets and bayonets pointing in every direction, but Wellesley screeching at them. She could hear him, though not understand his words. Yet the Scotsmen must have understood well enough, since a group of them, kilts flying and arses bared, leapt back down into the defile at the very moment the English Duke set his mount, a lathered chestnut stallion, to the jump, hurdling the raised bank and, she guessed, the soldiers sheltering below. But he had gone, the moment lost. And it was not long before the Scots recovered themselves, began firing into

Piré's huntsmen, who were now at last being recalled.

She could have wept with frustration. Twice in one afternoon. The enemy's commanders under her blade, and on both occasions they had escaped her. Liberté's own turn now to make a getaway, to stay low, to weave an irregular path along the redcoat lines, lead bullets whistling around her until, when she was almost clear of them, she came to the point at which the last of the English battalions formed a junction with the Black Brunswickers, the ridge and salvation ahead of her. She registered that the redcoats' cuffs and collars were pale yellow, not significant in itself and simply one of those absurd details that stayed with you in the middle of chaos. And most of their fire was going wide or high, as though they had been caught with their pants down by the sudden appearance of French cavalry so close to their front. But one of them, at least, had some presence of mind, for she saw him break from the end of the line, run forward to seize her bridle. The fellow's arm came up as she pulled the horse's head around to the left, and she saw the sergeant's English-style chevrons clearly. He had her curb chain in one hand, his musket and bayonet poised like a spear in the other, and about to strike. Yet she parried easily, retrieved, brought the blade up and would have finished him. Until she looked into his face. There was a moment's nausea that she had to fight down, to haul the bridle free, while she saw again those images of a walled town all ablaze, Marianne Tambour's nightmare renewed, and this fellow with the rotten teeth, the livid birth mark, the size and shape of a cauliflower on his right cheek.

This same English sergeant. Who as she hesitated, ducked away and out of her reach.

She wondered whether she might have been mistaken, though she knew enough to understand the ways of fate, the roads upon which life set each of us, and the manner of one road's crossing with another once the destinies were linked. And there could be no doubt that her own track had become entwined with that of Marianne Tambour, and hence through Tambour to this English defiler. She should have killed him, of course. Yet he had avoided her sabre as effectively as Thin William and Wellesley before him. It was a cursed day. The English should, by all the logic of warfare, now be destroyed. Yet here they remained, battered but still in force. At a glance, now in greater numbers than Ney had at his own disposal.

There was only one consolation. For Ney had now brought up what must surely be the last of his reserves. Liberté could see them, perhaps fifteen hundred paces to the rear, towards Frasnes, formed on both sides of the highway south. They were paraded beyond the Gémioncourt farm, and also beyond Ney's uncommitted infantry battalions that stood in line, or in column, and stretched from highway to Bossu Wood. Lancer pennons that undoubtedly belonged to the Imperial Guard's Light Division, and the gleam of sunlight on breastplates. Cuirassiers. Baron l'Héritier's brigades. They must be, for there were no more Cuirassiers attached to this left wing. Ney's only heavy cavalry. But if the Cuirassiers were there, then so must be her own regiment, since the 2nd and 7th Dragoons formed their own brigade as part of the Baron's 11th Cavalry Division. She could not make them out clearly from this distance, but she knew they must be there. So she sought leave in turn from her corporal, the troop's sergeant, the company's sergeant major and lieutenant, then the squadron's captain, to fall out and re-join her proper unit. Permission granted, somewhat reluctantly, though with a requirement that she should leave the horse behind with the farrier and his remounts. Some banter, therefore, from the ranks about abandoning them just when things were getting interesting. Yet she was soon foot-slogging down the road, wishing she had chosen a pair of boots with more walking comfort about them. *By Christ's Hooks*, she thought, *it's a good job I'm not with the infantry*.

She made a strange sight, she knew, in her hotchpotch of clothing and equipment, but not excessively so, for regulation uniform had become a thing of the past long since within much of the Emperor's army. On the other hand, Liberté was a cavalry trooper, higher standards expected, and she hoped that the regiment's baggage might be close enough to let her collect her own kit. But she attracted some strange stares from the Cuirassiers when she came up with them, the leading squadrons resting their mounts and those at the rear so relaxed that many had been allowed to off-saddle. Horse tails whisked at the air, manes were shaken and ears twitched, all to flick away the flies that bothered them, while their riders flapped ochre gauntlet fingers through swarms of smaller summer evening gnats biting at any exposed flesh.

'Hey, Guignol,' shouted a trooper, 'where did you get the rags?'

'Not from you, that's for sure, Madelon,' she called back, 'with your tin tits!' Mourguet's puppet would have been proud of her wit, she thought. And even Bonaparte, they said, was a devotee of the Guignol shows that had been all the rage these past few years. 'And have you no canteen-mistress in this godforsaken regiment?'

The trooper laughed, pointed back down their line, where she found the woman, a real fop, wearing a red braided hussar tunic, a grenadier's shako perched jauntily on her head. But the face was badly pocked, the woman's mouth scarred as though she had been sabre-cut. Liberté bought two shots of rotgut from her all the same, barely felt the first go down yet savoured every drop of the second. She thought about Tambour again, of course, wondered briefly how she was faring; wondered once more at the twist of either fortune or purpose that had brought them together; wondered how she would ever explain to the knife-woman that the English sergeant had been under her own blade yet escaped; wondered whether the Empire's diamonds remained safe within Bonaparte's dormeuse; wondered about the remnants of her family in Arcachon; and wondered where those bloody Thénardiers and her belongings might be. Yet her musings did not flow in such an ordered manner as did the dog-dog trickling down her throat. No, these were like a brandy cask smashed upon the ground, its contents splashing chaotically in all directions at once.

She handed back the cup, then marched on until she found Squadron I of her own regiment, also off-saddled. The familiar green coats and collars, red lapels, cuffs and turnbacks, helmets laid to one side, the men smoking, as though they were a hundred leagues from any danger, soaking up the sun in their nine-man Sections; two Sections in each Sub-Division; two of these to each Division; two Divisions to a Company; two Companies for every Squadron; four Squadrons to the Regiment. Beyond them, her own Squadron II, where she was recognised more often by the men of the 2nd Company.

'Hey, Dumont, you lost something?' There was little that inspired scorn so much as the sight of a trooper deprived of the facility to ride.

Or, 'Look boys, the gentleman volunteer's back and she's joined the clod-hoppers!'

Far more familiar faces as she reached the 6th Company.

'Where in the name of Christ have you been, Dumont?' screamed Sergeant-Major Lamy.

'The Colonel's been looking for you, Trooper,' said Lieutenant Henry. 'Report to him at once.'

'Good to have you back, Dumont,' sneered Divisional Sergeant Fournier. 'Enjoy your leave?'

'Well, if it's not the prodigal!' said her Sub-Division's Corporal Mayer.

'You know where the Colonel is, Corp?' Liberté asked him.

'He went that a-way,' Mayer replied, pointing back in the direction of Frasnes, another low hill twenty *toises* distant, where the senior staff had gathered to survey the progress, or otherwise, of the battle.

Sergeant-Major Lamy came trotting up behind her.

'Didn't you hear the Lieutenant tell you the Colonel wants a cosy little chat, Dumont?' he bellowed. 'Or are you too busy just now?'

'Like this?' she said, glancing from her filthy attire to the staff officers.

'Well at least it's a bloody uniform,' hissed Lamy. 'Of sorts. I suppose I should be thankful for small mercies.'

'And over there?'

'What?' said the Sergeant Major. 'You shy all of a sudden, Trooper? Oh, but I forgot. You're the one who's had dinner with the Shaveling, aren't you? So I guess the company of a mere Marshal of France is a bit beneath you, eh?'

'I thought it was the Colonel who...' she began.

'He's with old Copper-top, isn't he! Well? What are you waiting for?'

'Nothing at all, Sergeant-Major.' She snapped briefly to attention and made her way through the remaining dozen of her Sub-Division, including those from the First Section, with whom she normally rode.

'Leaving us again so soon, Liberté?' said Suchet. 'Thought I was going to lose my Chosen Man promotion for a while just then.'

Within the Regiment, and despite her service, her Legion of Honour, the only step she had ever received was her allocation as the Section's Chosen Man, the fellow who would pick up Corporal Mayer's duties if anything happened to him during a scrap. It was like she always said, her superiors were never quite comfortable about having her around.

'Looks like you can keep it a while longer,' laughed Liberté. 'But don't let it go to your head, Suchet.' It took her only a few minutes to cover the twenty *toises* to the hill, skirting around the scattered taunts from Squadrons III and IV and, as she climbed the slope, an Aide rode forward to intercept her. 'Trooper Dumont to see Colonel Planzeau, sir,' she said. The Aide looked around, uncertain, until he caught the Colonel's eye, there among the senior officers surrounding the unmistakeable figure of Michel Ney, Marshal of France, Duke of Elchingen, Prince of Moscow and, in Bonaparte's own famous words, the Bravest of the Brave. But to the men of the army, he was simply Copper-top. Or Redhead. Yet the cooper's boy from Saarlouis did not look his best this afternoon. His usually florid face was spectral pale, his hand clenched around his brow as though he had suffered a wound there.

'Who gave the order?' he was shouting, though every word seemed to cause him further pain. 'And do not tell me again, Delcambre, that it was the Emperor. Because I don't believe you. Not a word of it. The Emperor could not seriously expect me to take the crossroads without d'Erlon's Corps. And he expects me not only to smash Wellesley but then also to fall upon the Prussians at St. Amand.'

'I can only tell you, sir,' said a dust-covered Delcambre, 'that those were the orders received by the Count and hand-written by the Emperor himself. That he was to turn about and march on Ligny.'

'Delivered by whose hand, General?' Ney insisted.

'The hand of La Bédoyère, sir,' said Delcambre. Liberté had met him, at the Legion of Honour dinner in March, at the Tuileries. As it happened, she had met Ney there too, though he would not remember. And, in truth, she felt no affinity for the Marshal. He had an impressive and well-deserved reputation for his bravery but, like most men of power, he wore the self-protective aura that, with time, became impenetrable even to those closest to them, as though this borrowed personality eventually devoured them from the inside and dominated them. 'I saw him myself,' Delcambre added.

Liberté moved discreetly to Colonel Planzeau's side, trying her best to avoid being noticed until she stood at her commanding officer's stirrup.

'Ah,' said Planzeau, 'and about time!' He walked his horse forward alongside another of Ney's Aides, a striking fellow in scarlet dolman and matching shako. 'Apologies, Colonel,' he saluted, 'but the trooper I mentioned to you... Might I be excused a moment?'

'Of course, Colonel,' said the Aide, 'but you should stand ready to receive instructions, I think. His Grace, the Marshal Prince, is likely to need your messenger very soon.'

'Messenger, sir?' Liberté said, as quietly as possible, when they were a little way down the slope again.

'You have that document?' Planzeau asked her, the words slurred somewhat by his Provençal accent. 'The one from Fouché?'

'Lost in the fighting, I'm afraid, Colonel,' she lied.

'Yes, you look like you've taken a beating.' He shifted the left arm in its silk sling, as Liberté touched her own cheek. It must be a pretty mess of bruising now, she supposed, though the throbbing had long subsided. But it was still enough to keep that prick Thénardier always in mind.

'I think,' she said, 'that for all the bruises, I still look better than our good Marshal Prince.'

'Redhead?' Planzeau looked quickly up at Ney. 'His lodging last night boasted a very fine cellar, they tell me. It all rather delayed things this morning, of course. Now, if we'd had Davout in command...'

'And this messenger business?' she thought it best to rescue him from a potential breach of tact.

'You completed your business on behalf of the Minister of Police, I take it? Or should I not ask?'

'Completed, sir. Though perhaps not quite in the way that Minister Fouché intended.'

'The devil, you say!'

'And this message, Colonel?'

'He's talking about sending more gallopers to d'Erlon.'

'To countermand the Emperor's orders?' She must have sounded incredulous, remembered the way that Rebecque had ignored Wellesley's instructions earlier in the day, without which there would have *been* no battle here, and Ney would by now have controlled the whole area. And with d'Erlon's Corps of twenty thousand men at his disposal, he might still do so. But unpicking Bonaparte's imperial commands was another thing entirely, regardless of the outcome.

'The Marshal, it seems,' murmured Planzeau, 'is not convinced that they *are* the Emperor's orders.'

Ney's lucky to even have a command, thought Liberté. For the whole world knew that it was only months since Ney, hearing of the Emperor's escape from Elba, had promised Fat Louis that he would bring Bonaparte back to Paris in an iron cage.

'But I'm hardly Aide-de-Camp material, Colonel,' she said.

'No,' Planzeau replied. 'No, Dumont, you are not. But he wants a fire-mark. An insurance against deception in the normal channels. A trusted man, as Heymes put it to me.'

'Heymes, sir?'

'The fellow all in red. Ney's principal Aide.'

And, like a scarlet Satan when his name is mentioned, Colonel Heymes was suddenly at their side.

'Is this your man, Colonel?' he said, his turn now to sound incredulous. 'Fouché's spy?'

'Trooper Dumont received the Legion of Honour very recently, sir,' said Planzeau, almost an apology. 'She's a gentleman volunteer with a faultless record both within the Regiment and as, er...'

'An Agent of the Imperial Crown, sir?' suggested Liberté.

'An Agent of the Minister of Police,' smiled Heymes, 'is not always precisely the same as an Agent of the Imperial Crown, Trooper.'

Well, she thought, *I can't argue with him on that point.*

'And where will I deliver the Marshal Prince's dispatch, sir?' said Liberté.

'One thing at a time, Trooper,' Heymes told her. 'You said that there were documents, Colonel Planzeau. From Minister Fouché?'

'Trooper Dumont has been engaged in the fighting for some time, sir,' said Planzeau. 'Independent from the Regiment, it seems. So she no longer has the authority documents, though I can vouch for them. I saw them only yesterday.'

'Independent action?' Heymes smiled. 'Your own regiment not exciting enough for you, Dumont? Well, never mind. When the Marshal Prince has finished writing his note, you will deliver it to Count d'Erlon. Nobody else, you understand?' He reached into his sabretache, drew out a tattered map, held it against the sheepskin that covered his saddle holsters. 'Let me see,' he continued. 'Here. General Delcambre will act as the official courier. He says d'Erlon was coming up the road from Charleroi when he received the Emperor's order. North of Gosselies. He'll have turned right. Along the old Roman road to Liège. You see it? You'll deliver Marshal Ney's second note to d'Erlon there. Find him somewhere along this stretch. This side of Wagnelée. And how hard can it be, on a straight road, to find a Corps of twenty thousand men? Even for a woman.'

Chapter Eighteen

Friday 16th June 1815, 6.00pm

Colonel Planzeau gave her leave to make a brief halt at Frasnes, even instructed one of his Aides to take her there, so that she might collect her own uniform and kit from the Quartermaster, and Lucette from the horse lines, though there was no time for emotional reunions. But the big dappled grey Percheron nuzzled at her affectionately enough while Liberté stroked her elbows and knees, her gaskins and hocks. They were sound enough, and the mare was in decent condition, the greasy heel entirely cured.

She had led Lucette away from the lines and stopped outside an inn on the southern edge of Frasnes, the mare licking noisily at a water trough, Liberté sitting on the stone corner to replace those uncomfortable Hessian boots with her own knee-length heavy cavalry pattern and cotton stockings, though she retained the buttoned Dutch overalls, since they were better than her own. The yard was otherwise deserted, though there was a considerable noise coming from the customers within. Colonel Heymes had impressed upon her the need for haste, and Planzeau had been particularly anxious that she should reach d'Erlon, if possible, ahead of the official galloper. So she was surprised when Lieutenant Henry came trotting up to the inn.

'There you are, Dumont,' he said, pleasantly enough. 'I didn't expect to catch you so soon.'

'Change of orders, Lieutenant?' she said, giving the second boot a final heave into place. The familiar contours of the worn leather felt good.

'You might say so,' he replied. She did not know him very well, for he had transferred to the Squadron, to her 6th Company, only at the start of the campaign, just before her summons to meet Fouché, so she had never formed an opinion of him.

'What now?' she said. 'Copper-top decided to forget about d'Erlon? Keep all the glory for himself?'

'Oh, I'm certain he'll manage just fine. He was sending in the fresh Divisions when I left. Jamin and Gauthier.' It made sense, for she had already picked up the deeper bass and intensity to the volleys and salvos. 'No,' the Lieutenant smiled at her, 'the Colonel's decided he needs you for yet another duty, it seems.'

Liberté noted the casual way he sat his horse, forearm resting on the pommel, his right-hand fingers toying with the wolf's-tooth cloth that edged the saddle's sheepskin cover.

'So no Wagnelée?' She was disappointed, in truth, for the new orders had presented her with a chance to catch up with Tambour, share her news about the English sergeant. There were the Thénardiers to settle with, but they were the least of her problems just now.

'No Wagnelée,' said Lieutenant Henry. 'But the Colonel's keen to find out how your previous orders were carried out. He should have asked earlier, I suppose. Come on, let's get moving.'

She was checking Lucette's girth, almost ready to mount.

'Previous orders, sir?' she said.

'Yes,' the Lieutenant replied. 'Documents to deliver. Wasn't that it?'

His horse side-stepped to the right, away from her, and when she looked up, her foot in the stirrup, she saw that the sheepskin was now folded back on the shoulder away from her.

He's cleared the pistol holster, she thought, and tensed as the danger signs began to assail her.

'Documents to deliver, sir? Is that what Colonel Planzeau told you?'

'Ah,' he smiled. 'I've been indiscreet. Or are you going to tell me he never asked you the details? That you never told him?' The pistol came up smoothly, a Year XIII model, a Saint Étienne. 'That's a shame. I was looking forward to some intelligent conversation. For a while, at least.' The pistol was levelled at her, a steady and well-practised aim, the weapon already cocked, too close for him to miss, nowhere for her to hide, and the musketoon that replaced her borrowed Hussar carbine safely strapped and booted on Lucette's other flank, along with her helmet. 'Then I suppose I must pass on the message here, Dumont.'

'Message?' Lucette nudged her, snorted quietly.

'From Minister Fouché, of course. I take it you *did* deliver his documents?'

'And if I didn't?'

'Then I assume the Minister would consider your usefulness outlived in either event.'

She laughed, despite herself, stroked Lucette's shoulder.

'And I just adore a woman who can smile in the face of adversity,' he said.

'I was just thinking that I gave up the Imperial bounty to answer Minister Fouché's summons,' she replied. 'And he promised to compensate me. In gold. How will I get paid now?'

'Forgive me for being blunt, Dumont, but that's not something you need to worry about any more.' But she knew he was wrong. This was like any other blusterer's threat. The fellow who *truly* meant to murder you simply got on with the job. In that sense, the assassin in Charleroi was so much better than this braggart. That woman had just moved in for the kill, and if Tambour had not been there... Well, at least she now knew for certain that the attempts on her life were Fouché's call. And she knew also that this bastard's weakness, his delay, his prattle while he tried to steel his nerve, would be his undoing. He opened his stupid mouth once more. 'Anyway, that's...'

The inn's door crashed open and it seemed as though a wall of sound burst forth that drowned out even the background cannons, a woman's shrieking voice, a confused babble of curses, heaving bodies, and that rogue Thénardier came stumbling onto the cobbles, his woman with her swaddled brat just behind, and seemingly engaged in a tug-of-war over some disputed garment. The Lieutenant's eye was drawn inevitably to them and it was the only chance that Liberté needed.

She sprang straight for his halter, forced the horse's head around, away from her, followed as its knees and forearms came up, the hooves scrabbling, sparking on the stones. Liberté hoped that the flailing legs would not catch her, heard the pistol's report loud in her right ear and the splintering whine as the ball ricocheted off the yard, the sulphur smell of the discharge stinging her nostrils. A reload was impossible but she could not hold back a yell of pain as Lieutenant Henry hurled the gun at her, the brass butt plate bouncing off her shoulder bone as she yanked at the halter, twisted and heaved on the bit, deliberately hurting the beast and hating herself for it, but knowing that she had no choice. From the corner of her eye, she could see the Lieutenant struggling with the nearer side of the sheepskin, fighting to bare the other holster, a second pistol.

They went round in a half-circle, so that Liberté, still scribing the arc by pushing the horse before her, could see the astonished way that Thénardier regarded her. His arms pinioned by some apron-clad giant from the inn.

'Holy Jesu,' he wheezed, his eyes wide, the air almost squeezed from his lungs, 'it can't be!'

Liberté could not see his wife any more, but the woman was presumably in the middle of a separate mêlée, just alongside the door. Yet her immediate concern was this bastard, and she could feel herself tiring. She twisted the bit again, pushed it upwards as far as she was able, saw the horse's back legs collapse, its buttocks hit the ground, and Lieutenant Henry half-fall, half-spring from the saddle, his arm reaching across for his sword. She released the harness, and she prayed.

The cavalryman's worst nightmare was a blunted blade, and each time it was drawn from a metal scabbard served only to dull or chip the edge a little more. Like many others, Liberté tried to keep her scabbard well maintained, oil-soaked. Her only problem was that she had not tested it since collecting the sword from her Quartermaster.

Lieutenant Henry's own sword was already in his hand, and she felt vulnerable without the helmet that he wore, and she did not.

'Fouché tells me you're something of a sword-sharp,' he said. *More blather,* she thought. *That's good.* She slipped her fingers inside the knuckle guard, wrapped them around the wired leather grip, prayed again, and eased the blade, breathed a sigh of relief as it shifted. And she looked into his eyes, searched for the fear within, knew it was there, even though he hid it well.

'You should have used the pistol when you had the chance,' she said, pulled free the metre-long blade with its twin grooves, its spear-sharpened point. She balanced it, sighted along the flat upper edge with its familiar arsenal marks, while the Lieutenant's horse heaved itself to its feet, limped to the trough. 'And now what?' she asked him. These were hardly duelling blades, after all. There was no subtle slash and parry for a Dragoon, the heavy sabre either wielded straight as a lance, or hacking like a bludgeon. A butcher's cleaver, she always thought, this backsword, as opposed to the light cavalry sabre's flensing knife.

Lieutenant Henry had dropped his guard, allowed the heavy steel tip to touch a cobblestone, and he looked down upon it, drew an imaginary circle on the ground.

'Now?' he said, as though he had not previously considered what might happen next. But he knew well enough. Of course he did. And though she could no longer see his face, she knew the move was coming long before his left side flexed, his right leg came forward, bringing all his weight with it so that the sword arm swung wide and fast, its edge keening through the air, sluicing towards her neck. But she was already retreating, her right foot leading each backward step and the left stamping to catch up with it, her sword held in the hanging guard, hilt at the level of her eye, upper body bent forward and the point aiming diagonally down at the Lieutenant's thighs. Her left hand was stretched in front of her, the palm open, flat, so that this arm might smack aside any thrust to that flank, and she wished she had her gauntlets.

Lieutenant Henry's blade swept down through empty space and, as it passed in front of her, Liberté followed with an inside half-hanger that pushed his sword further out of harm's way, carried him off-balance. And it left her in a perfect position to continue the movement, bring her own sabre back to the guard and advance in a fast half-pass that would bring her up on his now exposed right side.

She thrust. And she swore.

'Shit!' cried Liberté, as the Lieutenant's boots slipped on the cobbles, her sharpened point failed to pierce him, and his legs fouled her own, brought her down heavily.

She rolled, came up on one knee with her blade at the *Quinte*, the Fifth Guard, across her face, her head and shoulders pushing to the left by pure instinct as her enemy's thrust passed within a whisker of her right ear.

'Bastard!' she swore. He was faster than she had thought, but she slammed her sword against the mid-section of his steel, a true cross, exposed his side once again, yet chose not to waste further precious time on recovering for a riposte. Instead, she shifted her weight, sprang at him, grabbed with her free hand for the brass fitting at the front of his helmet crest that held the black brush pompom, while keeping up the sabre's pressure, sliding it down the length of Lieutenant Henry's own blade until their knuckle guards jarred together.

Not in the manual, she thought, *but what the hell!*

Liberté heaved on the fitting, pulling the helmet towards her, forcing his head almost between her knees and then, releasing the pressure on Henry's sabre, she brought the heavy pommel tang of her own sword down hard on his neck. He made a small blowing noise, dropped like a wet sack, so that she stood over him, reached to pick up her enemy's weapon, sent it skittering across the cobbles. The fellow moaned gently as she turned him over, spat in his face. She should kill him, but something stayed her hand. Instead, she reached into his coat, found his purse there. Fouché owed her a small fortune and here there were no more than seventy francs. Three gold Napoléons, a few loose coins, a small handful of sous, all of which she tucked into a pocket of her uniform coat.

Lieutenant Henry groaned, opened his eyes, fingers clawing instantly for the sword that was now far out of reach, but Liberté strode forward stood on his outstretched wrist until he shouted with the pain.

'You spoke of messages?' she snarled.

'Fouché will have you hunted down like a dog,' he replied.

'I have no doubt he will try again. But you're already the second. Has he got nobody better in his pay?'

'The second?' He sounded truly surprised and she laughed, treading harder on his wrist. 'Anyway,' Lieutenant Henry winced, 'he has *you* in his pay does he not.'

'Not any more, I think. And it's me will be doing the hunting now. He still owes me fourteen hundred francs, less this pittance you were carrying. You can deliver *that* message now, Lieutenant.'

'You intend to free me?'

'You sound surprised,' Liberté replied. 'So what are you thinking? That Fouché will send you back to finish me? But that's because you don't have the full message yet.'

His eyes widened as she put all her weight on the right foot that trapped his wrist. He rolled onto his side, tried to grab her boot, but her other heel was already stamping, stamping, stamping, until she had crushed his sword hand and fingers to a bloody and permanent pulp.

'I don't particularly care what you do with the creature later,' Liberté told the innkeeper, 'but I will have my property first.'

'It was all for the babe, lady,' Thénardier's wife mewled and the child itself howled. The woman was even more ugly and scabrous than Liberté remembered. 'For my Little Mare. Poor Éponine. Not been able to give her the teat for days. And the other one…' Her wretched face fell as she shook herself free from those who still restrained her, settled filthy fingers on the swollen lump of her womb.

'I fear I may be losing this precious gift with which Our Lady has blessed us.'

'And that fellow outside?' said the giant. He seemed even bigger now that he was confined within the strictures of the hostelry's interior, where he held Thénardier himself by the throat, up against a wooden pillar, while wiping the free hand repeatedly on his apron, as though his contact with the rogue may have smeared him with some noxious substance. 'What if his mates find him and think we've done for 'im?' He nodded his head towards the north, the more muted sounds of battle. 'What if they think we're all like those bloody murdering *manolos*? What if there's reprisals?'

'This bitch tried to steal my coat,' snarled a man, grasping the woman's arm afresh and causing the baby to wail still louder.

'My dear wife was taken by a moment's weakness, gentlemen,' said Thénardier, and was instantly seized by another violent bout of coughing, his sallow skin slicked with feverish sweat. 'To buy food for our sweet infant, medication for this honest but ailing veteran of the Twenty-Seventh Line.'

'It was the Ninth Light last time we met, was it not?' Liberté laughed at him, and Thénardier shrugged. She turned on the man who was still pulling on the woman's arm. 'And be careful how you handle her,' snarled Liberté. 'Whatever else she might have done, she's still heavy with child. Did you never have a mother, you pig?'

'Oh, Our Lady bless you!' Thénardier's wife beamed at her through blackened teeth, while the baby screamed.

'And what about the reprisals?' the innkeeper said again.

'There'll be no reprisals,' said Liberté. 'That scoundrel was a spy.' She thought it was unnecessary to be more specific. 'Besides, the bastard's not even dead. Not quite anyway. He'll be scuttling back to his paymasters by now. The Regiment will have him down as a deserter, or another turncoat, before the day's out. And I, gentlemen, am an agent of the Crown. As I shall show you when I get my possessions back from this thief.'

'Should string the bugger up,' shouted another customer. 'Tried to sell us tobacco and pipes. Prices were daylight robbery too. And all the time this slut of his was forking our purses. Got them back, heaven be praised. But should be strung up, all the same.'

'Lord, help me to be pure!' said Thénardier. 'But not just yet. Not while I have these infant mouths to feed.'

'This rogue is fond of quoting Saint Augustine, I find,' Liberté told the crowd. 'But who would you string up? The babe with them?' It was meant to play to whatever sensibilities these Belgians might have, although, from the way they scowled at the howling infant, she would not have liked to put the thing to a vote. 'The tobacco and pipes he was trying to sell you were mine also,' she pressed on. 'You can share them, if you like. No charge. And you take back anything they've stolen from you. But he's got my purse and my credentials.'

They turned Thénardier upside down, held him by his Hessian boots and shook him until his own teeth rattled and those he had collected from the dead spilled like divination bones cast upon the floor. Yet little else emerged from his deep pockets except Fouché's crumpled document and a set of lock-picks, both of which Liberté naturally snatched up as her own.

'What about the mule?' said the innkeeper. 'They came in with a mule. It's tied up in the old stable.'

'The mule's mine too,' Liberté replied, though most in the crowd took the claim with a pinch of salt. 'And they won't have left anything valuable out there. Not these two. So you can have the mule for your troubles. And maybe we should just check that this poor mite is comfortable before we send them on their way.' She turned to Thénardier's wife. 'What did you say the child is called?' she said, as gently as she was able above the babe's shrieking, its mouth so wide it could have swallowed the moon. 'Éponine? Was that it?'

'Let them go?' cried several of the inn's customers. 'We should string the buggers up. Hand them over to the Prefect at least. For justice.'

'Yes, lady,' said the woman. Then she looked down at Liberté's uniform. 'Sir...' she stammered. 'Éponine it is.'

'Then perhaps you would let me hold her a moment?'

'Oh, she frets something shocking when she's not swaddled to her mother.'

'Could she truly fret any more than this?' said Liberté. There seemed to be little wrong with the child's lungs at least. 'Now loosen those swaddling rags or I shall do it for you.' She recovered the purse, as she knew she would, though she had not expected it to be still quite so intact nor, on the other hand, quite so damp and stinking of baby piss. But she pocketed the thing and turned to the innkeeper. 'And since you can make a tidy profit from the sale of my mule, what about a shot of brandy for the road?'

'Gladly,' the giant replied. 'But these two? You surely cannot mean to set them free? There's justice to be done, as we say.'

'Justice?' said Liberté, an image of Police Minister Fouché flashing through her mind. 'Isn't it justice enough that the woman is saddled for life with a worthless creature like this one?' She poked Thénardier in the chest. Then she swung back towards the rogue's wife, gripped the side of her toad's head, the grime-greased red hair, looked deep into her eyes. 'And besides,' she said, 'I can write this slut's fate for you, if you wish. She will die in prison soon enough, this one. Lost and alone. And all but one of her children gone before her.'

Madame Thénardier's eyes opened wide, as though she had been hexed. And then the fear seemed to change as the woman realised that, worse than any curse, the certain and unavoidable track of her future had just been foretold.

'No!' she whimpered. 'Which one?' And, for the first time, the child Éponine fell silent. 'Which one will survive?'

Stepping back, Liberté bent to set her hand on a three-legged stool, as though to steady herself. 'And as for justice,' she said, seeing that Thénardier himself was still looking at her with that same defiant criminality which had marked him out at their first meeting, 'this will have to serve.' She hefted the stool and, before he could do anything about it, she had slammed the solid oak frame against the side of his face with all the force of her sword arm.

Chapter Nineteen

Friday 16th June 1815, 7.00pm

The rotgut fortified Liberté Dumont as she rode south from Frasnes, clay pipe clamped between teeth that naturally adjusted their bite on its stem to match Lucette's steady trot. *Some time*, she thought, *I will buy myself one with a fine seafoam-stone carved bowl. And an amber mouthpiece. Like those the generals smoke.* But then she wondered whether, if her station in life changed, if her dreams became anything approaching reality, she might have to give up the tobacco entirely. Well, there would be no sunlit uplands unless she could find a way to recover the debt Fouché owed her. A debt, she now calculated, at sixty-seven gold Napoléons.

There were the orders from Colonel Planzeau to fulfil too, of course. But the more she thought about them, the more absurd they seemed. The battle she had so recently left, sounded still more intense now. Yet it also appeared to be strangely closer, as though it ebbed towards Frasnes, rather than flowed, as it should, in the direction of Quatre Bras. Similarly, from her left and front, came the renewed thunder of the Emperor's Grand Battery. One or other of the two engagements should be resolved by now, should it not? Yet the evening lengthened, just a couple of hours before full dark, and it took no more than a simple mathematick to weigh the result, at this late stage, of turning d'Erlon's Corps about yet again, of having his twenty thousand march permanently *between* battlefields rather than arriving to deliver a *coup de grâce* at one or the other. And there was filthy work afoot. Fouché's agents out in force. So what if more of them were whispering in Ney's ear, urging them to this foolishness? Yet more effort to deliberately undermine the Emperor. More vested interest in the betrayal of France. To prevent the decisive blow they needed.

What was it Fouché said? She tried to remember. The fortunes to be made if the war was prolonged. In all the countries of Europe. And therefore a patriotic duty to thwart the profiteering of the bankers and their like. Fouché's plan. Not authorised by the Emperor. Yet the conundrum. That Bonaparte, had he known, might still have endorsed the strategy. That he might relish the thought of a speedy end to the conflict. Honourable defeat. But the Minister of Police had then hinted that his documents for Wellesley might be more than they seemed, and she had allowed herself to be beguiled, to swallow the pretence that

Fouché was running a double bluff, that the possibility of encirclement would be enough to drive the Englishman back to the coast.

Yes, she thought. *Beguiled*. That was the word. For the more simple explanation was that Fouché's documents were precisely that which they seemed to be. A straightforward betrayal. And one that would ingratiate the Minister with those he hoped would be the eventual victors. So how much more likely was it that this foolish game with d'Erlon's Corps, this back and forth insanity, was simply one more deliberate duplicity to deny France her victory?

Liberté's shadow pointed like a signpost to her left, stretching towards the precise area where, she suspected, she would find d'Erlon himself. And she was suddenly happy to let fate lend a hand in her dilemma. If Delcambre was there before her, the column halted, or even already reversed, then she would deliver the message entrusted to her, the message that would be redundant in any event. And, afterwards, she would allow the path to take her wherever it might. If not, well, she may simply leave Count d'Erlon to go his own merry way too. After all, if the Emperor had ordered him to march east, who the hell was Ney to countermand that instruction?

She reached another inn, where a rutted lane branched off eastwards and, from her recollection of the journey north the day before, probably half a league from the old Roman road, the Brunehaut Causeway, which ran all the way from Amiens to Cologne. There were labourers here, clearing ditches around the field edges, folk gathered around the inn. But she had no need to ask them about the 1st Army Corps, for the signs of its passing were scraped wide across the landscape, the yellow crops flattened in two great swathes, one on each side of the lane, and the track itself with all the appearance of being recently ploughed, the surface churned by baggage and artillery wheels regardless of how hard the sun may have baked it. Further south, towards the Causeway, there was more dust, lots of it, and she guessed that this would be the tail-end of d'Erlon's units. But the main body had turned here and, if so, she was sure that Count d'Erlon himself must be with them.

The scandalised, rolling terrain took Liberté past farms and orchards, scattered dwellings, hamlets and a chapel from which every trace of Christian decoration had been carefully carved away, until she reached a rise, a substantial wood cresting the horizon to her left, a substantial village ahead to her right – Villers Perwin, if she remembered correctly – and there, beyond it, the rear of a column: a dark and stationary stain upon the land. The fates, it seemed, had decided. Delcambre must have arrived before her and, if so, there was no reason to deliver the dispatch she carried for d'Erlon, but neither was there any purpose in failing to do so.

She rode slowly through the lines, an infantry division whose battalions wheeled and marched, their forward progress arrested and turned about, like pieces on a chequer board, slowly preparing to retrace their steps against the angry hornet-hive grumble with which they grudgingly fulfilled each manoeuvre.

And besides, she thought, *old Planzeau gave me no clear orders about what to do after I've handed the note to d'Erlon.* She fancied that, had the ground been a little higher, or once she reached the Corps commanders, she might be able to see the very place where Bonaparte was fighting the Prussos, with Tambour among his Imperial Guardsmen.

There were cavalry brigades here too, occupying a plateau where there was another chapel, a large farm, just north-east of Villers Perwin, but they did not seem destined for the return march to Frasnes, for they were moving south, a fluid sea of green jackets, Horse Chasseurs, Light Line Lancers and Hussars. *Left to protect d'Erlon's flanks,* she imagined, and she dismounted, unslung her canteen. The big Percheron turned its head, nudged her with its white-whiskered muzzle, the pink wetness of its nostrils, until Liberté tickled the horse's ear, causing the beast to lift its dappled neck, open its mouth wide so she might let it drink, tipping the bottle and pouring water down the animal's throat.

'Well, old girl,' she murmured. 'No turning back now, I suppose. Deliver the dispatch. Then we make our own rules, eh? Over there somewhere.' She looked to the east, where the sky already seemed to be darkening. And she knew it was more than simply the smoke clouds still rising from Bonaparte's battle. She sensed connections there. Something that drew her. Mixed images of her mother's fate; of a hosted table cabaret on the Rue de Grenelle; of Fouché's treachery; of Nostredame's Boar and Leopard Quatrain; of the State diamonds in the Emperor's dormeuse; of Marianne Tambour's English sergeant; of Tambour herself; and of something new. A taste of livid fear. Tambour in danger. Or, more properly, Tambour's daughter, the one she called Poppy.

'They were good men,' said Fronsac, as the Battalion marched steadily towards a gathering gloom that even the flames of Ligny village could not diminish. 'That's another score to settle with these bloody Prussos.'

Marianne had been able to help neither Senent, crushed by the *Uhlan's* horse, nor the Basque, Pons, who had wheezed away the last of his life while his lung-blood bubbled about the lance shaft and pennon.

'Well, they're with God now,' said the Württemberger, Muhler.

'I may owe you for my daughter's life, Muhler,' Marianne sneered at him, 'but that doesn't mean I need to listen to all that old nonsense.'

The blackness rolled towards them, as sheet lightning licked the undersides of those simmering clouds and raindrops began to slap against the parched ground. The Prussian Lancers had been chased off and the Regiment had completed its return journey without further incident. But no sooner had they reached their initial assembly point than the Imperial Guard had been formed afresh and marched back into action.

'It's funny,' said Fronsac. 'You'd think we wouldn't be able to tell the thunder from the drums and guns.'

And he was right, of course. They were like instruments in the regimental band, so that you heard the whole, but each separate bassoon and serpent too, within the overall refrain. It was the drums that dominated, for they were the closest, but there was a rolling barrage taking place as well, from the great batteries to their rear, and the guns nearer St. Amand, a cross-fire concentrated on the already devastated ruins of Ligny. And while the storm gathered over the village, the six battalions of the 2nd, 3rd and 4th Grenadiers lowered their bayonets and marched towards the hamlet's south-western boundary, with the bearskins of the 1st Grenadiers and 1st Foot Chasseurs away to the left, in their own battalion columns, advancing at half-distance. A hell of a sight! On each side. Beyond them, the heavy cavalry, and the artillery reserve while, between, on a long mound of raised earth, the Emperor himself.

'No quarter!' yelled each unit as they passed him.

'I wasn't afraid, Maman, was I?' said Florisette.

'No, girl,' replied her mother. 'A proper little soldier.'

But Marianne had noted the way that Poppy now clung to her mother's apron, had not let go, nor said more than a couple of words since Muhler delivered her from danger.

And now I'm dragging her into another pile of shit, she thought. Yet her daughter's narrow escape made the point that here, at least, there was a whole platoon to watch the girl, whereas back with the baggage, there was nobody but bloody one-legged Catherine Argonne. Marianne's hand strayed involuntarily to the brandy cask, the concealed cache of Napoléons that might eventually grow enough to buy them a new life.

'Look,' cried old Cazajus, 'a Republican Wedding!'

And some of the others laughed as they passed two of the recent dead, one French, one Prussian, here at the edge of the first houses, locked in an eternal embrace, each of them bayonet-stabbed over and over again by those, presumably, who had fought in the same skirmish.

Marianne liked Cazajus, still the fanatic, bred in the bone, another who would follow Bonaparte to the ends of the earth and yet damn him with every living breath for betraying the Cause. The veteran had told them stories often enough. About the punishments they had inflicted on the Whites, on the counter-revolutionaries, twenty years back. No quick guillotine for those bastards, he would say, and brag about how they had taken husband and wife, a marriage of traitors, bound them together and tossed them into the river to drown in conjugal bliss. The Republican Wedding.

'Hey, show some respect!' shouted Fronsac, his thumb pushed up the bulbous nose. 'That boy died for France, didn't he?'

He had changed since his time on the hulks: was more touchy, had lost his sense of humour. And Marianne knew that those who could not laugh at these horrors were likely to be driven mad by them. She glanced to the right, could not see the 1st Grenadiers any more for the columns of line infantry attacking in the centre, and for the smoke, for the flame. It was a journey into hell. The drum call commands. Corporal Poncet's bellowing voice carrying across *Peloton* A.

'Word's come down the line,' he cried. 'The first man to take a prisoner gets shot!'

Battle fury: the Battalion beast's bayonet horns and head lowered; Marianne clinging to its tail; the ground throbbing with the rhythmic tramp of boots. The band striking up *The Departure Song* while the rampant creature raged through the western outskirts of Ligny and simply swatted aside each and every vestige of resistance. It blustered over bridge and brook, the scent of blood in its nostrils, and their boot-nails now muted for they could not advance without walking upon a solid carpet of the dead as they were drawn ever onwards to that church spire, which itself waded in a wash of gore.

And if our Battalion is truly a beast, thought Marianne, *then we are that sacrificial creature, a feast on the hoof, led in the procession of a real marriage ceremony.* She had attended many of them in the days after the Church had been cast down. *Just like this*, she remembered. Except that here the thrown rice was a shower of acrid ash; the almonds tossed to children were lumps of cindered masonry; the white ribbons used to line the wedding route were the pipe-clayed cross-belts of the crippled and dead; the orange blossoms of fertility were the scorching sparks and flying flames of blazing Belgium; and the silk canopy to protect bride and groom from descending malice was the lowering shrouded sky. *Yes*, she thought, *we are the feast.*

On they went, stepping over the first of the Battalion's fallen now, a fellow shot in the thigh and dragging himself over the rolling corpses, away from the column, pale and retching. Marianne recognised him vaguely. From the Third Company, she thought. A friend of Juanita Bufanda's man, Corporal Cluny.

'Something hit me,' he murmured, as she unslung the brandy cask.

'It happens,' she said, then looked down at Florisette. 'Let go now,' she told her daughter, pointing at the man's bearskin, 'and help him take off that bee-hive.' Marianne helped the Grenadier sit, took the *salvavirgo* from her bodice and sliced open the cotton fabric of his breeches, cut all the way around the trouser, caused him to yell, the colour to drain still further from his face. Not much blood from the wound though. Normal. And the ball seemed to have passed right through, the skin blackened around the edges of the entry hole, more ripped and ragged where the bullet had emerged.

'Will they take the leg?' the fellow winced, while Poppy finished removing the fur bonnet.

'I doubt it would be any use to them,' said Marianne, pouring a cup of dog-dog, handing it to the girl so she could feed it to him drop by drop. Then she reached into her haversack, found a roll of linen charpie. 'But it needs cleaning. So you get a choice. You'll need a second shot of my rotgut. You can either have it inside, or I use it to scour the wound. Your choice.'

'If I drink it?'

'The wound will go bad. Green-stink. Then they'll cut off the leg. If you're lucky.'

'How much for the second shot?'

'You can pay me once you're up and running again.'

'Better clean it up then, I suppose,' said the soldier. 'Shame to waste good brandy though. And I hate to be in your debt, Tambour.'

The Prussos faltered in their final defiance at Ligny's further edge. It was almost dark and yet Marianne could see more of the moment than was normal for any battle in which she had been engaged. For a breeze had blown up to drive the thunderclouds and the sheeting rain, carrying much of the smoke to the army's rear. And there was something else. Hardly a gun fired these past twenty minutes. It had all been bayonet work, the enemy constantly pushed back but always at the closest quarters. Until a few heartbeats ago when the Battalion had halted to reform its ranks. Only an instant, but enough for a narrow gap to open between them and the Prussian infantrymen to their immediate front.

Marianne could hear the band, away to the left somewhere, sporadic firing and 'Long live the Emperor!' to her right, while the anvil chorus of the breast-plated Cuirassiers hammered and beat, time and again, into the enemy's flank. But ahead, stretched among the hedges and enclosure walls, on ground that sloped up towards a mill, were the Prussians. They seemed solid enough, but Marianne's practised eye could see their doom, and when the Battalion's drums picked up the Advance once more, she was close enough to look inside the soul of her foes. It was not a charge. The Guard did not charge. It was beneath them. In fact, they had learned to advance as slowly as possible. Nothing so destroys the will of your enemy than the mindless determination of your attack, the realisation that, no matter how they might outnumber you, those advancing towards them are unstoppable.

It's why we make so much bloody noise, she thought, *so that, even when the buggers can't see us for the filth, they can hear us coming for them.*

'Long live the Emperor!'

The Prussian line trembled briefly, then broke, some men scattering up the hill while the best of them formed squares and fell back more steadily. And the whole glorious French line spread from west to east, climbed after them in the gathering dark, halting often to reform so that, with each stop, Marianne was able to turn a fancy franc or two, the brandy flowing free and her brave Grenadiers happy to pay for it. Their own casualties were light but the Prussos' wounded lay scattered everywhere.

'Can we help them too, Maman?' said Poppy.

'They're Prussos...' she began, but the stupid girl was already kneeling alongside one of them, a boy who seemed little older that Florisette herself, but raving, his guts spilled upon the grass.

'Oh, dammit!' Marianne moaned, as another of them gripped her ankle, sobbing wildly, begging for water, she guessed.

Poppy's boy had fallen silent, dead, and she had moved on to another casualty, a crawling fellow, whining and dragging his right leg. There were trumpets, a blur of enemy *Uhlans* angling across the hillside, just as they had done during the Battalion's withdrawal from Tongrenelle a couple of hours earlier. But this time there was no French square formed. There was no need. For, while it may have been a wild charge, it was shapeless, and the Regiment's muskets came up to meet them, a single shattering volley that sounded as though it was ripping the very ground apart.

The Battalion advanced again, climbing over the carcasses of dead and dying horses, their ditched riders, the Grenadiers using cold steel to dispatch them. Except the old fellow who had become Florisette's latest patient.

'No!' the girl screamed, spreading her arms wide to protect the man and his companion, a younger fellow, kneeling, his shirtsleeves dripping wet. Marianne could scarcely believe the age of the older one. *He must be nearly eighty*, she thought. *Bloody old fool!* And he was trapped by his fallen mount, covered by his companion's coat. But the men respected Poppy, laughed at her.

'Remember,' said Corporal Poncet, patting her on the head, 'whatever you do, don't take the old goat prisoner, else the Shaveling will have you shot, girl.'

They were still moving steadily up the hill. Winning at last, surely. Yet it was hard to tell, for jets of flame split the darkness. Musketry and cannon fire, seemingly from all over the hillside and from almost every direction. Marianne felt dizzied by it and, from the gloom, another squadron of enemy cavalry emerged. Dragoons. More Lancers. She had kept a careful eye on Poppy, but now she turned her head for a moment. No more than a moment. The Battalion's muskets were levelled once more. Another volley. The dirty stench-cloud wafted around her but, when it cleared, the Prussian horsemen had disappeared.

And so had her daughter.

Chapter Twenty

Friday 16th June 1815, 11.30pm

They searched the hillside until exhaustion overtook them, those men from *Peloton* A, Second Section of the Fourth Company. And others too from the Battalion, slipping away from the line against the specific instruction of their senior officers. Yet even Captain Vicquot joined the quest, with Sergeant Flambert holding a lanthorn for him.

'I don't think there'll be any night attack,' he said, as though he needed an excuse to be there. 'And never fear, Tambour, we'll find her.'

But Marianne was not so sure. About either point. For while the firing had undoubtedly diminished, almost ceased entirely, there were still occasional outbursts of musketry all around. The sound of horses too, in significant numbers. So their Battalion, which like each of the Guard's foot units had been bivouacked along the line of the crest beyond Ligny, formed into square, three ranks to each side of the formation, fires forbidden, and the ranks rotated so that those innermost were able to rest, while the others remained standing at arms.

'I hate it,' she murmured, 'when it's like this.' She was thinking about the many other times it had been thus, a battle over but without any real sense of victory achieved. In fact, no real sense of whether you had won or lost at all. The enemy killed, driven from the field, but no elation. Simply that weary dread that the buggers would come back again for another round.

'Chin up,' Vicquot replied. 'She'll be here somewhere.'

Yet, in her heart, Marianne knew that this was not true either. She no longer had any sense of her daughter's proximity, could not tell whether she still lived, but understood perfectly that, if so, Poppy was no longer in this place. But she could not say so and plodded relentlessly along with the others, wiping the rain from her eyes, shivering with the damp, climbing over and around the groaning wounded, shouting the password, 'Arles!' whenever challenged by sentries, hurling insults or worse at the scavenging wraiths that haunted the field, hearing a horse approach through the blackness.

'Who goes?' yelled Sergeant Flambert, his own musket and those of others swinging towards the noise. 'What password?'

Silence.

'Shaveling,' said the rider, and a dozen hammers ratcheted to full-cock.

'Wait!' cried the voice. 'In the Emperor's name, I am a friend.'

The tone was deep, but not deep enough to disguise that it belonged to a woman. A voice that Marianne recognised.

'Unless I'm much mistaken, Sergeant,' she said, 'I think our new arrival is Trooper Dumont, 2nd Dragoons.'

'A woman...?' said Captain Vicquot.

'A gentleman volunteer,' said Liberté Dumont. 'And a comrade-in-arms. Is that you, Tambour?' She walked the horse within the meagre beam of the lanthorn's light, bent low over the phantom-grey neck of her mount and squinted through the murk.

'She'll turn up in the morning,' said Fronsac, as they sheltered in the lee of a low wall. 'That girl's got more lives than a farmyard hen.'

It was an unhappy reference, the threat of Battalion Punishment still hanging over Marianne's head on top of this present terror. Long past midnight now, and not a sign of their daughter.

'She's your daughter too, old fool,' she snapped. 'The only child we have left.'

'Is that my fault?' he shouted.

'What then? Mine?'

'I didn't say so. And by Christ's Nails, what makes you think the Prussos have taken her?'

From the corner of her eye, Marianne saw Liberté Dumont lift her head, stare at him.

'We both know it, soldier,' muttered the woman. She was wrapped in a drenched riding cape and crouched at Marianne's side.

'Some women's witchcraft?' Fronsac sneered. 'I'm telling you, you're talking shit. Come sun-up you'll find the girl back with old Argonne, curled up with those damned goats. Anyway, we need to get back to the Battalion. Who knows? She may be there before us.'

'You go,' said Marianne. 'Dumont and me, we're going after her.'

'Oh, good plan,' said her husband. 'Two women. On their own. To do what? Walk into the middle of the Prussos' army? You don't even know where they've gone.'

'They've gone north,' Dumont told him. 'That's the way most of them have headed.'

'Bollocks!' said Fronsac. 'Anybody in their right mind would know that they'll run for the Rhine. Specially after today's pasting. So what will you do, follow them all the way back to Berlin?'

'Whatever else the Prussos might be,' said Dumont, 'they're not runners. And I'd wager that we've not hurt them as much as we think. No, they need somewhere to rally. Somewhere easy to find. Somewhere that's on all the maps. Like Wavre. The obvious place.'

'And suppose you're right?' Fronsac stood, shook himself like a wet dog, so that the raindrops flicked from his greatcoat and away, like fireflies, into the dark. 'How in Marat's name do you hope to find her? Might as well look for a darning needle in a meadow.'

Marianne stood too, wished that she had a greatcoat of her own instead of just the old russet jacket. 'You've already said it,' she replied. 'Women's witchcraft.'

'He has a good point,' Trooper Dumont told her. 'Your man. He's right. We may be convinced that the Prussos have taken her. But why would they?'

But Marianne did not dare to think. There had already been too many waking nightmares, so she simply carried on stripping the dead Prussian of his waxcloth-covered shako, his long frock coat.

'Not the best fit,' she said, pulling on the coat over her own jacket. 'But near enough.'

'This will be my third change of uniform in the past few hours,' said the hawk-faced Dragoon. 'Must try not to get caught in these though.' She was fastening the chin scales on a similar piece of headgear.

'You think we'll get through their lines like this?' Marianne was unsure.

'It's our best chance,' said Dumont. 'Two Lancers, one horse. Lucette can carry us both. We'll take one of their pig-stickers for the sake of appearances. If we take it slowly, I doubt anybody will stop us.'

'And if they do?' said Marianne. 'You know any Prussian, or whatever it is those bastards speak?'

'Low German,' replied Dumont. 'I'm fluent.' But Marianne suspected this was a lie. 'And next time we stop, we'll tie a bandage around your face,' Hawk-face continued. 'That way it won't seem strange if you just mumble. If we'd had time, we could have collected that old mule of yours, carried on with your normal disguise. You're good at it. And there must be plenty of Belgians tailing them for trade.'

Not for the first time, Marianne wondered if the woman might not be slightly touched, though she was right in this respect, that it would have been easier to work their way into the Prussian lines with a few sacks of merchandise than dressed up like common idiots. Still, she had the brandy cask with her, simply because she could not have entrusted it to Fronsac.

But who knows? she thought. *It might be handy, even if only to keep this bloody chill out of our bones.*

Yet, once mounted – Marianne perched behind the Dragoon – they fell into silence, partly to avoid enemy ears from picking up their French, and partly because it would have been incongruous to do otherwise. For an army in retreat does not waste its breath on chatter or idle gossip, and the relative stillness was shattered only by an occasional curlew's call, or the solitary shout of some lost soul searching for his unit, or the clatter and jangle of horses close at hand – these to be avoided at all cost, of course, against the chance that they might also be *Uhlans*.

Yet one group could be heard so uncomfortably close that they had no choice but to stop. Dumont blew gently in the big grey's ear, keeping the beast quiet while the Prussians trotted like darker spectres out from the already lightless rain-soaked night.

This bloody horse must show up like a beacon, Marianne decided, as the enemy horsemen drew nearer.

'Play dead,' murmured Hawk-face, and she slumped forward against the grey's neck, arms hanging down, limp and lifeless on either side.

There'll be no need for play-acting, thought Marianne, *if those buggers catch us dressed in this kit*. And she followed Dumont's example, collapsing across the woman's back, shako askew and her hands also dangling. Her nose was pressed into the wet German wool, while the horse played out its own small but admirable part in the drama by lowering its head, cropping the roadside grass and ambling along as though it was entirely free to do so.

Marianne heard them come still closer, swishing through tall grass or crops away to the right, their mounts snorting and the riders talking to each other in that guttural tongue they used, but quietly, almost in whispers. A question. Then an answer, she imagined, until they halted, one of them coming forward alone, the sound of its hooves changing as the animal plodded up from the softer ground of the field and onto the harder surface of this rutted lane.

'*Hallo?*' said a voice, and Marianne felt Dumont's spine stiffen. She sensed, rather than saw, that the woman had something in her left hand, the side away from the Prussian.

God's Hooks, she thought, *please tell me she's not going to try and fight them!*

'*Hallo*,' the Prussian said again. '*Wie geht's, meine Freunde?*'

Dumont's horse moved a little further. The Prussian followed, so close now that Marianne could feel his mount's breath on her leg. And then there was a hand on her back. It was so unexpected that she almost flinched, but any movement she might have made was masked by the horse plodding onwards again.

'*Sie sind tot*,' said the Prussian. There was a command, the fellow riding off again, then the whole troop of them moving past until, at last, they were gone.

Marianne's heart was pumping so hard she could scarcely believe the soldier had not noticed.

'What did he say?' she asked, straightening herself and setting the shako back in position.

'He told them we were dead,' replied Dumont, and despite the darkness, Marianne caught sight of the woman lifting a corner of the sheepskin shabraque to set a heavy pistol back in its holster. But she was relieved, at least, that Dumont did indeed seem to have a grasp of their language. Hawk-face turned to her, patted her leg, and Marianne recoiled slightly. It was the other thing about the woman. Pussy-fisters were common enough, and good luck to them, she usually said. There were plenty of stories. Women who were that way inclined, joining the army, pretending to be men. And the men themselves, of course. She heard them coupling at night often enough. It was just the way life went. The other thing about the Revolution too. All those old laws about sodomites and pussy-fisters, all gone now. But it was not for her. She just hoped that Dumont did not have the wrong idea.

'You sure that's what he said?' Marianne asked.

'Well, obviously!' said Dumont.

'Tell me again what happened before she was taken,' Dumont asked her when they were forced to shelter beneath a tree during a particularly nasty downpour, and Marianne repeated the story, pouring out her own guilt with every sentence. Poppy's care for the Prussos. The old fool wrapped in his young friend's coat. She had turned her head for a moment. Only a moment.

'And you?' she said. It was one of the rare moments in her life when she felt the need for idle chatter. Something to quell the shaking in her legs that she knew was more than just the cold and damp. 'Anybody else tried to slice you?' Marianne recalled the woman's delusions.

'Quite a few,' Dumont replied. 'That's been a bitch of a fight over there. Dutchies first. Then those sodding English. And I've got news for you, by the way. But that's not what you mean, is it, Tambour? You mean our mutual master, I think. The Emperor's beloved Minister of Police, eh? Well, I could tell the Shaveling a thing or two about that bugger. Or do you already know?'

Here we go again, thought Marianne. *Mad as a hatter, like I said.* But there was still that possibility that Hawk-face might, after all, be some sort of imperial agent. She certainly seemed to come and go as she pleased. And Marianne needed help now. An ally. More than ever before.

'You still got that magic letter?' she asked. 'The safe conduct from Fouché?'

'Now I have,' Dumont laughed. 'Bloody Thénardier.'

The reference was entirely lost on Marianne.

'You think we'll find her?' she said, fighting down an urge to be sick. 'Safe, I mean?' She was certain that Poppy had been taken but her ability to think clearly about why that might be was clouded by images of Maman Cholet, of Saint-Sébastien, of frightful possibilities. Terror gnawed at her innards, tightened her belly.

'Of course we'll find her. And don't worry. She'll be safe.' But something in Dumont's tone made her certainty less than convincing. 'You'll see. Just think about how she'll fling herself at you. Her own Maman come to free her.'

'The child dotes on her father, not me,' said Marianne. I have no purpose in her life except to feed her. Or darn her clothes.'

'She put up a spirited enough defence of you back in Charleroi, when the Gendarmes tried to take you.'

'She was probably thinking about her next meal.'

'You should stop punishing yourself,' Hawk-face told her.

'What? You think all that nonsense about dreams and visions means you can see inside my soul?'

'It's just not unusual,' said Dumont. 'When you've already lost two children, they say it's sometimes hard to get close to anybody else. Fear of the possible pain, of losing that one too.'

Who the hell does she think she is? Marianne fumed, but she was too exhausted to say so. Weary to the bone.

'You asked me yesterday if I'd ever seen a battle,' she said.

'It was a stupid question. Just look at you. You may be afraid for Poppy, afraid of losing her, but apart from that, fear's something you've never known.'

'That's not what I meant,' snapped Marianne. 'I was going to ask you a similar question. Have you ever had kids?'

'You know I haven't. But that doesn't mean I don't understand what it is to lose somebody precious.' Marianne listened as Dumont briefly told the story of her mother's disappearance.

The same day I was born, thought Marianne.

'Well, everybody loses a mother,' she said. It was a harsher comment than she intended. 'But losing a child, lady. You've never known grief until you lose a child. Believe me.'

'I believe you,' said Dumont. 'But look, the rain's easing. We'd better move on. God alone knows how far they will have taken her.'

The woman climbed to her feet, rubbed at an aching back, untethered the horse.

'Wait,' said Marianne. 'You said you had news. Something about the English?'

Dumont turned to her, hesitated.

'I've seen him,' she said, at last. 'Your English sergeant. The fellow with the purple face.'

'Another dream?' Marianne murmured.

'Not this time,' said Dumont. 'He's over there.' She pointed over her shoulder. 'At Quatre Bras.'

They must have travelled a league from Ligny, maybe a little less, Marianne's mind a turmoil of emotions. Could it be true? The same English sergeant so close? But mainly frightful images of Florisette. Still a couple of leagues south of Wavre, Dumont reckoned. Yet they seemed to have found a fair gathering of Prussians. Not their final rallying point, since units were still being directed onwards, up the road. But a hamlet, and all ablaze despite this middling hour of night, with lanthorns, torches, lit windows, a line of braziers. A picquet that would be difficult to penetrate and, beyond, units of infantry standing to-arms just as Marianne's own Battalion had been when she left it.

'Now what?' she said, but Hawk-face was already telling her to dismount, urging the grey mare off the road, where she took a linen shirt from her saddle pouch, ripped away a sleeve and wound it around Marianne's face, smearing it with mud for effect.

'Here,' the woman told her. 'All you have to do is moan like a German. Can you do that?'

'I can feel her,' said Marianne. A tremor of excitement had coursed through her as soon as they came in sight of the village. 'She's close.' There was a stream running through a thicket where Dumont hid the horse among bushes of redcurrants.

'I feel it too,' said the woman, and she took Marianne's arm, draped it around her own neck. 'Let me take your weight. Limp a bit. And for pity's sake keep that bloody cask between us. You might as well be carrying one of the Emperor's Eagles as that red, white and blue.' But as the *tonnelet* pressed against her, the woman jerked away, startled. "What the hell have you got in there?' she said.

'Just my rot-gut,' Marianne lied, thinking of her little cache of treasure, the gold Napoléons that, she determined, would buy a new life for Florisette if she could ever get her back again.

'My arse!' said Dumont, pressing herself once more against the cask. 'But we'll talk about this later. First, let's find the girl.'

They hobbled together out of the thicket and through a stand of alder trees, emerging close to a sprawling farm that swarmed with activity, black figures coming and going like ants. There was a strong guard too.

'*Halt! Wer da?*'

'*Kameraden!*' shouted Dumont.

She sounded confident enough, though Marianne had the sinking feeling that she had heard the Dutchies in her Battalion use the same word. *Well*, she thought, *they're probably much the same, Dutch and that Low German.*

'*Was hast du gesagt?*' shouted the guard. '*Wer da?*'

'*Kameraden*,' Dumont repeated as they carried on limping towards him, Hawk-face dragging the lance behind her for effect.

'*Gott im Himmel*,' the Guard complained. He sounded exasperated, as though the steady trickle of incoherent fugitives was becoming a real trial. '*Da drüben!*' he said, and pointed down the paved street, waving them past.

There was a church, its graveyard serving as a dressing station, wounded men gathered around an ancient tree, but nobody paid them any heed as they moved past, joined a thin trickle of others moving in the same direction, the thoroughfare lined on each side by Prussian soldiers sitting against the walls of each scattered hovel, sitting anywhere they were able, huddled together and trying to snatch some sleep. The two women stepped over the outstretched legs, gave up any pretence of their own limping dramatics until Hawk-face tugged at Marianne's sleeve and dragged her down a side alley that led back into fields on the left. Hardly deserted, but there was certainly less sprawling humanity here than on the main street and, at the path's end, a tiny chapel, entirely deserted.

'We've got this wrong?' said Marianne, the full weight of despondency pressing upon her already crushed shoulders. 'She's not here, after all.'

'I'm not sure any more,' Dumont replied. 'Sometimes, the closer you get...'

'I'd have known if she was back there. And there's only a few houses left.'

'Well,' said Hawk-face, 'we'll check those soon enough. But let's have a shot of that brandy first.' The woman shivered. The rain had stopped now but it was still cold. Or perhaps it just felt so after the sweltering heat of the day. 'And you can tell me what you've really got in that precious cask. I don't mean the gold you've doubtless got stashed in there either. Something else. What is it?'

'You're talking shit,' Marianne told her, pouring a cup of dog-dog for them to share. 'But we need to get one thing straight. I don't care what you think but I'm nobody's agent. I'm canteen-mistress to the Battalion. Nothing more. No disguises. Nothing. That bitch I cut in Charleroi, she was after *me*, not you. Understand? She saw your jacket and bonnet in the crowd, thought they were mine.'

It was still too dark to see Dumont properly, yet Marianne guessed that the woman might still not believe her. But she heard her chuckle quietly.

'You think I'm some mad loon,' Hawk-face murmured. 'Is that it? One too many battlefields, maybe?'

'Mad?' said Marianne. 'Did I say so?'

No, she thought, *not out loud. But it's gone through my mind a few times. All that crap about dreams and second sight. Well, just look at us. Stuck here in the middle of the Prussos' bloody army. Not a sign of Poppy. Fronsac's probably right. She'll be back with the lads somewhere.* But the visions of her daughter's imminent danger refused to be so readily set aside.

'Well,' said Dumont, 'mad or not, I know this much. That there's more than one thing that draws you and me to this godforsaken place. More than one thing that binds us together too. And the sun will be up soon, Tambour. We'd better get moving.'

The woman led the way back to the road and the north end of the village, where even the few stragglers had now disappeared. The dwellings here were even more sparse, progressively more dismal, until they finally came to the end, a solitary cottage that stood watch over some baggage wagons, a carriage and the flat open fields that disappeared from view into the oblivion beyond. Yet this partially derelict pile attracted almost as much activity as the large farm at the hamlet's opposite boundary. And, despite herself, Marianne experienced again that sharp scent of the familiar that she had felt upon their arrival at the village. A living connection to her daughter.

'Why here, of all places?' she said.

'Makes us both mad then,' replied Dumont. 'All we've got to do now is work out how to get inside.'

Marianne began to shrug off the Prussian frockcoat, folded the thing and slung it over the *tonnelet*, making sure it covered the Battalion's inscription that she had painted so carefully just a couple of days earlier.

'Easy,' she said, shaking a little, nervous yet straightening her own russet jacket. 'Just keep watch and tell me how the Prussos say "brandy".'

Chapter Twenty-One

Saturday 17th June 1815, 3.00am

The place stank. It was fugged with smoke, reeked of blood and shit, but all its essences wrapped up in the distinctive sweet-sour smell of rhubarb. So strong she could taste it, bitter, on her tongue. A sordid little house, a single room, with only a brace of candle stubs to flicker shadows against a flaking whitewashed wall to Marianne's right, from which the moans and murmured pleading of wounded souls rebounded and mingled with the hushed but insistent debate of four staff officers, haggling around a heap of filthy straw against the opposite wall.

But where...? she wondered.

One of the officers turned to face her as Marianne entered. He looked puzzled.

'Schnapps!' she cried, holding up the cup as though it were perfectly normal to be plying her trade an hour before first light.

She had all their attention now, and they moved apart slightly so that she could see the man around whom they had gathered, an old man, thinning white hair, a thick moustache. He was wrapped in a dark blue coat rather than a blanket. An old man with blazing eyes, crazed, trapped in some dreadful delirium. And, though it barely seemed possible, she recognised him, had seen him only hours before. That suicidal charge by the Prussian cavalry while the Battalion was clearing the slopes beyond Ligny brook.

God's Hooks, she thought, *the old fool that Poppy protected.*

She remembered her daughter as she had last seen her, arms outstretched and begging for the old fellow's life, confused the image with this different Poppy that she saw now, before her, balled up in the corner, beyond the old man's head, her eyes wide with fear, filled with tears.

For a moment that seemed, to Marianne, to last forever, the world stopped, fell silent.

I should have waited, she thought, *until they slept. Something. Anything.* Yet she knew that it was too late.

And then the silence was brutally shattered.

'*Ja!*' shouted the old man. '*Schnapps. Schnapps.*'

The officers turned frowning faces to him and Marianne seized the chance to catch her daughter's frightened eye, to lift a finger to her lips. The girl nodded, wiped a hand across tear-stained cheeks, and Marianne thought the gesture had otherwise gone unnoticed until she realised that she was being observed by one of the casualties near her feet. The man was perhaps forty, his features milk-pale, sunken, shrunken, and he was covered by a grey cloak that was now soaking up blood from the bandages wrapped about his amputated left wrist. For a moment, she thought he would cry out, but he quickly pursed his lips and looked away, just as one of the staff officers turned to her, beckoned her forward.

'*Komm her,*' she heard him say, though the rest of his commands were lost on her. Yet she took them as an instruction to approach the old man, realised that the heavy odour of rhubarb emanated from him, as well as strong fumes of gin, she thought. Garlic too. She sometimes used garlic and rhubarb herself, to rub into bruises, assumed that they may have done the same with this fellow. Yet who was he? Staff officers naturally meant somebody important. A Prussian general then, which would explain his age also. And she began to wonder. It was common knowledge that the Prussos' commander, Blücher, was a decrepit old goat. But surely this could not be he.

'*Schnapps!*' he shouted again, and Marianne knelt close to him, tried to avoid glancing too often at her daughter, held the cup under the cask's spigot and filled it with brandy.

He must already be pissed as arseholes, she thought, noticing the huge and empty champagne bottle that rolled from the straw as he lifted himself on one elbow to receive the rot-gut.

'*Meine Kinder,*' he shouted into her face, lifted the cup in a toast to the wounded men around him, swung it left and right, most of the brandy slopping onto the flagstones. Then he craned his neck so that he could see Florisette, and his eyes dampened. '*Und mein Liebchen,*' he sobbed. '*Mein liebe Tochter.*' He dropped the cup and, while it clattered on the floor, he stretched out his hand towards the girl's foot.

'No,' Poppy screamed, curling herself even tighter into the corner. It was too much.

A red mist filled Marianne's eyes, so great that she sprang forward. She would grab the girl and run. And she still had the *salvavirgo* in her bodice, would use the thing if she must. But strong arms gripped her, pinioned her. One of those bloody staff officers. She kicked, felt her clogs connect with his shin, though he did not release her and, in the struggle, she felt the frockcoat dragged from the brandy cask. Shouts of German anger as the hated tricolour appeared in their midst. More than anger. Alarm. And they hauled her away from the old man's makeshift bed.

'*Was gibst?*' he cried. '*Ein Elefant. Ein Elefant.*'

Elephant? thought Marianne. *Did he say elephant?* She was sure he had said so, wondered if she might, after all, be dreaming all this.

Somebody drew a sword, and with curses and exclamations the stricken soldiers bestirred themselves as though they were all one.

'Maman,' yelled Poppy, and Marianne saw her daughter restrained by another of the Prussians.

'*Assassine*!' bellowed the fellow who was still holding her. He screamed it into her ear, almost deafened her, his breath stinking of foetid meat. '*Spion*.'

The words he shouted were unmistakeable. *If only I could reach the knife*, she thought, *I'd give him spy and assassin, both*. But she could barely breathe, let alone wield a knife.

There was more yelling, the whole hovel filled with it. Yet Marianne thought she caught some words of familiar French cutting through the harsh German. Again, louder this time. A man's voice. Strange accent. But French all the same.

'Are...you...her...mother?'

'Yes,' she roared. 'Yes.'

She was able to turn her head only marginally, but enough to see that the French-speaker was the same bag of bones with the amputated left hand, struggling to sit up, shifting himself within the grey riding cloak that fell partially aside to reveal a mud-streaked scarlet jacket beneath. He was calling out in apparently fluent German now until, finally, she was released from the Prussian's grip, though forced back at sword-point against the door frame.

'What do you do here?' said the bag of bones, an English pig, she thought.

'A better question,' she replied. 'What is my *daughter* doing here.'

'You have come from Ligny?'

'Is that Blücher, General?'

'I am not a general.'

'But Blücher?'

'Yes. Field Marshal Count von Blücher. They think you are a spy. An assassin.'

Marianne laughed.

'If I'd known, I would have killed the old bastard and *then* taken my daughter.'

The Prussians began to shout again, jerking their heads, certain to be asking what she had said. But the Englishman – she was certain now that he was English – paused a moment before answering them, and though she did not understand much of it, she distinctly heard the word 'Mama.'

'*Mein liebe Tochter*,' Blücher called again.

'What did he call her?' said Marianne.

'The Field Marshal has not been himself,' said the Englishman, 'since his fall. He thinks the girl is his daughter. Or sometimes an angel sent to him on the battlefield. That she came to save him.'

'Tell him he's welcome to her,' she said, 'for the right price. And you? The hand?'

'A gift from your Emperor,' he replied. 'A cannon ball.'

She nodded.

'You were with the Prussos? When they charged the Guard?'

'Yes.'

'I was with my Battalion when they brought the old fool down. I turned my head, and my daughter was gone. Why did he take her?'

'He would not leave without her. We had no choice.'

'*Ein Elefant*,' shouted Blücher. '*Ein Elefant*.' And two of the staff officers tried to settle him back on the straw, their tone as soothing as total subservience would allow.

'And he seems to imagine,' said the Englishman, 'that there is also an elephant in the room.'

'An elephant,' Marianne murmured. 'So this is what they send against us.'

'*Ich stinke*,' Blücher said, and he yawned amiably.

A Prussian spoke quietly to the Englishman.

'He says,' the bag of bones told her, 'that the Field Marshal will sleep soon. And then they will give you...' He could not find the word in French. 'They will help you get back to Ligny.'

'And the Field Marshal himself?' said Marianne. 'What did *he* have to say?'

The Englishman must have been in great pain, seemed near to collapse, but he still managed the ghost of a smile.

'He says... well, he says that he stinks.'

Marianne sneered. 'What's he talking about, the garlic and rhubarb, or his generalship?'

'You can't win,' said the Englishman. 'You know that, don't you?'

Marianne's tongue twitched with the desire to retort, her heart heaving with pride for her nation, trust in the leadership of the Shaveling, a love for him, and she would have spat in the Englishman's eye, asked him whether he seriously thought this broken remnant with its demented Field Marshal could possibly still be a threat to France. Or whether Wellesley's rag-tag army might fare any better. But she feared that any outburst may cause these buggers to reconsider their position, alert them to the possible danger of releasing her to carry back word of the Prussians' whereabouts, their strength – and their evident weakness. So she bit that treacherous tongue and held it until Blücher finally dozed and she was outside in the darkness once more, mounted on a donkey procured from the village, Poppy huddled before her, saying nothing, her slight body shivering in her mother's arms. Marianne kept imagining that Hawk-face would appear at any moment, ruin the whole thing by some act of lunacy, but there was no sign of the woman. Yet one of the Prussian staff officers was here, stiff and formal, with a little speech, before he clicked his heels together and bowed to her.

'He apologises,' the Englishman translated in his hesitant French, 'on behalf of His Majesty, King Frederick William. And he salutes your courage.'

'You might ask him,' snapped Marianne, unable to constrain herself any longer, 'what would have happened to my daughter if I had not come for her.'

'Perhaps better to leave things as they are,' replied the Englishman. 'He also says that this soldier will escort you back to Ligny. To your outposts at least. They're close to here.'

The man holding the donkey's rope looked as though he would not find his way safely even to the next house.

'Here?' she said.

'They tell me the place is called Mellery.'

'And no recompense?' she said. 'Not for the theft of my daughter? Not even for the rot-gut that the old goat wasted? Well then, a couple more debts for the tally. And leave things as they are? I don't think so. Give us a day, General, two at the most, and we'll settle all our accounts.'

Liberté Dumont was a person who believed in contingency plans. Yet, as Tambour disappeared inside that last hovel of the hamlet, she realised that they had not discussed any of the eventualities. It was the problem of action in the middle of the night. Invariably misguided. Never do before dawn, she always said, what will last until daylight. Something to do with the aether, she thought. For there was no doubt that the respective worlds of men and the spirits were closer, more aligned, during the hours of deepest darkness.

Well, she thought, *I'll simply settle down and wait to see what happens.*

But she wished she had brought a pistol or two as well as the sabre and this useless bloody lance. She let the thing drop into a ditch on the far side of the road, scrambled down after it, cursing to herself that there was no dry patch to be found. It was hard to imagine what must be happening inside the cottage, yet Liberté was now certain that the girl was here, that Tambour was reunited with her daughter, though the precise circumstances remained something of a mystery. Minutes passed, until the silence was broken by a commotion. A girl's scream.

Poppy, she thought. *It must be.*

Raised voices. Shouts of anger. Liberté leapt out of the ditch, sabre rattling from its scabbard as she raced for the closed door. But she stopped at the threshold, her hand on the wooden latch. The shouting continued. And she did not understand a thing. Not really. In truth, she possessed a couple of words of German. Some Dutch. Enough to get by. But this was an unholy row worthy of Babel's Tower, cut through only by Tambour's own unmistakeable tone, urgent yet not especially afraid. And there was another voice. Louder. More strident. She thought that she caught the word 'Elephant.' Though that was absurd. Yet, regardless, within moments, the commotion died away. Conversations continued, but no obvious crisis. Except, of course, that Tambour and her daughter were still inside.

Have faith, thought Liberté, allowing her inner senses to provide reassurance; remind her that if there was danger, she would certainly know about it. So she would continue to wait, see how the situation developed. But she could not stay here, and the ditch did little to entice her back across the road. Anyway, some siren song, like that which keens to a diviner, turned her attention towards the open ground to the north, beyond the hamlet, where she could just distinguish the dark outline of wagons, carts, a carriage or two.

No harm in having a look, she told herself. *To pass the time.*

She crept through the blackness, followed the house wall and then the shallow furrows of an abandoned, weed-filled vegetable patch.

There must be a guard, Liberté knew. *If there's anything in those wagons at all, there must be a guard.*

She inched forward, covered the intervening couple of *arpents*, could make out no movement, had almost decided that she must be wrong, then picked up the distinct sound of snoring ahead. The sword was still in her right hand, the left clutching its scabbard so that it might not betray her. She crept on, drawn by the noise, though knowing this was not the refrain that had initially tempted her in this direction. But the snoring man was indeed a guard. Or should have been, if the fellow had not taken advantage of the wagon's shelter to lay down his head.

The sleep of the dead, she thought and, fittingly, gave him a wide berth. For something else whispered to her, soothed her, drenched her with drowsiness. Hardly surprising. When had she last slept properly? She found that she could not remember, collapsed against the wheel of a closed carriage, felt the incision as her spirit began to free itself from physical constraint, floated just a fathom above the recumbent form of her body, held there briefly before the inevitable journey into slumber that followed. Visions of Tambour and Florisette. Images of her mother. Images of death. The uplifting promise of good fortune. The solid feel of the carriage against which she was resting. Something calling to her from within.

Then Liberté felt her spirit snap home, a sickening jolt that brought her back to consciousness. She cursed herself, had no idea how long the experience had lasted, no real idea whether she had truly travelled the aether or whether she had simply slept. But she believed it to be the former, and it must have lasted some little while for there were streaks of light in the eastern sky, a drum call away across the village, the first straggle of Prussian soldiers limping north again, and that lazy guard finally aroused from his repose.

The fellow crawled from under the axle tree, cursed as he banged his head on one of the wagon's frame railings, dragged his musket and shako behind him. He yawned and stretched, looked at Liberté, cocked his head to one side, then the other, as though he could not quite focus, or quite understand what he saw. The man yelled at her. German, of course. Some question, to which she responded with a guttural and incoherent snarl, shrugged herself deeper within the uniform coat, folded her arms and pretended to doze again. She sensed him standing there for an interminable minute, and then the tread of his boots moving away as he began a circuit of the increasingly visible wagon park.

Liberté spared a thought for Tambour, wondered how she was faring, but she needed to work fast, before the Prussian came back. She reached into a frockcoat pocket and took out the hide wrapping in which her recovered lock-picks were rolled. A quick check to make sure she was reasonably sheltered from prying eyes on the road and her hand was on the carriage door. She peered inside. A tangle of travel chests, basket-weave hampers, some bolts of cloth, forage sacks. And only that one negligent guard to protect them. It was a sign, she thought, of two things. First, that this Prussian army must be exhausted indeed if it was past caring about looters within its own ranks. But the other side of the coin? That the looters must themselves be weary beyond endurance if they could not even muster the strength to snatch prizes on their own doorstep. There was an old adage, that an army without the will to loot has no more stomach for the fight. And the second thing? That their dead and their valuables must lie so thick along the Ligny Brook that the normal night-prowlers and scavengers had richer pickings than these to occupy them still.

She shifted some of the baggage, lifted a few lids, but paid scant regard to the dress uniform gold braid, a silver-wired sabretache, the potted caviar, quail's eggs, preserved fruits and fine wines, but she happily picked up a tobacco jar, decorated in blue and white. And then she thought about Fouché's instructions, the Emperor's dormeuse, the diamonds beneath the seat. This particular carriage was a more modest model, of course, but it was worth checking. So she climbed up on the folding step and began to shift every item until she had cleared the upholstered rear cushion, set her fingers under its edge, and heaved it free to expose the compartment beneath, the iron strongbox that it concealed.

Out on the road, artillery pieces could be heard, though hardly seen, and Liberté climbed fully inside the vehicle, gripped each of the chest's forged side beckets, the bare metal pulsating cold against her fingers, and she employed all her strength to lift it, balance it on the seat's edge, while she climbed out and then dragged it behind her. The box was not particularly large, but its solid weight slammed it to the carriage floor with the noise of a four-pounder cannon, and from there it clanged against the folding step with a report louder than a musket shot. She swore, ducked down instinctively, certain that the guard – the whole hamlet, in fact – must have heard. But there was nothing, and she thanked the Fates for the tramp of boots, the steady clop of hooves, that now laboured along the lane in the grey light of dawn.

The strongbox was impressive, a pair of vertical hasps secured with padlocks through their staples, and a false escutcheon key hole on the chest's face, the real lock hidden beneath a sliding panel disguised as part of the central hinge bracket.

So, she thought, *padlocks first.*

And she deftly applied the slender tension wrench to the activating lever, felt for its direction of turn and held it there before sliding the correct pick into place above it and manipulating the two wards until the lock springs surrendered to her completely, each in turn. The main mechanism presented more of a trial, however, and she was forced to employ every trick that the Circassian Mameluke, Amjad, had impressed upon her. It was a sensitive little beast, each of the double-action tumblers requiring the torque to be eased or sharpened uniquely until the bolt could be moved. Yet at last the lid lifted, although Liberté was thwarted once more. The strongbox was virtually empty. Some personal papers, an ornate campaign *nécessaire*, a matching mahogany brass-bound writing box. An absurd amount of security for such a trivial treasure. Perhaps she had missed something. The front seat perhaps? She crouched down, checking underneath the carriage for more hiding places. Then glancing back at the chest, finally she spotted the obvious: it was considerably deeper on the outside than she recalled from the interior dimensions.

Silly cow, she thought to herself, *you must be getting old*. She started looking for the additional concealed lock or catch that she knew would open the false bottom – and found it, in the form of two raised rivets which, when pulled simultaneously, released the spring-loaded base. And there they lay, swaddled in a blanket, shrouded in shadow, the smell of their leather still fresh. A clutch of money bags. She poured some of the coins into her palm, peered at them. Silver thalers. The normal mish-mash of different weights and sizes that you could expect from the German States. There would be a real mix here. From Bavaria, Hesse, Saxony. A dozen others, as well as Prussia itself. Not much, but better than nothing, the silver value a decent supplement to the eight gold Napoléons and twenty loose francs that she already carried.

Chapter Twenty-Two

Saturday 17th June 1815, 4.30am

The whole place had sprung to life, though in that bizarre way of defeated armies, and Liberté Dumont marvelled at the resilience of these Prussians, meeting the morning with all the enthusiasm that might have been expected from the victors rather than the vanquished.

She hid herself, the tobacco jar and the money bags in some bushes within safe watching distance of that cottage which she had seen Tambour enter less than two hours earlier, and she became increasingly agitated as the evacuation of the dwelling proceeded, wagons arriving one after the other, to be loaded with the wounded occupants, few of them capable of even walking. The routine was broken only when a two-wheeled gig reined to a halt and several preening officers helped an especially enfeebled fellow to climb into the back, where they settled him among filled sacks to soften his journey, though he raved terribly as they travelled up the road.

It took a while for the cart to disappear too, since that road was becoming increasingly busy, the fields on each side as well, the Prussians moving once more towards Wavre and, whether their units were company strength, or even straggling sections of platoons, most of the buggers were singing.

They're not done, she realised, *not by a long chalk.*

And where was Tambour? The girl, Poppy? Nobody had emerged from the hovel for a while, and she began to fear the worst, so that, after as much time had elapsed as she could endure, Liberté slipped around the corner, backed to the doorway and risked a glance inside.

Empty. She was certain that Tambour had not been evacuated with the rest. But had she escaped? It seemed unlikely that she could have been released, but there was no sign. *What happened while I slept?* thought Liberté, cursing under her breath. *Well*, she decided, *no point in sitting here all morning.*

She needed to reach the copse where Lucette was tethered, prayed that the horse had not been discovered. Yet a direct route back through the village was now impossible, such was the press of Prussian uniforms pushing between the huts and houses. It would need a wide sweep either to east or west if she were to avoid them. West, she determined, sauntering across the road when there was a decent break in the traffic, with all the nonchalance she could muster then following the narrow lane to the tiny chapel where she had rested earlier with Tambour. She almost expected to find mother and daughter waiting for her there, but it was deserted still.

Liberté decided to discard the frockcoat here, the Prussian shako too, knowing that she would now be more at risk from her own French patrols than from the Prussians. She tucked her valuables into overall pockets and was soon tramping along the edge of a field, the purses and Dutch jar clutched like babes in her arms and the dream-thin crepuscular sunlight piercing the clouds and scratching at the back of her linen shirt. Black crows circled, called like lost shades, strutted across the damp-scented soil, and the first flies rose to greet the day.

Away to the left was a patch of woodland and she angled that way, checking that she could still see the spire of the hamlet's church, happy that she would be able to keep it on that side, until it aligned with the climbing sun, before swinging south of the place to pick up Lucette. She thought briefly about avoiding the woodland for the easier terrain and open ground but, in the end, she settled on a straight cut between the boughs of beech and birch. And, in this incautious way, Liberté walked almost straight onto the tines of a pitchfork.

She would have reached for the sabre, but she was encumbered by the bags. In any case, some sharp-witted scoundrel had beaten her to it, slipped from behind one of the trunks and was pulling the blade free, while a third fellow thrust the maw of an antique blunderbuss in her face.

Scavengers, she thought. *Just my bloody luck!* They would have her gold and silver at the drop of a hat too. *After all that!* She almost laughed. Almost. For it was certain that they would not settle simply for the treasure she carried. They would want her too, probably kill her in the process. Not quickly either. But she would give them a run for their money.

'You know, boys,' she said, 'that nothing comes free. And, in my case, not even cheap.'

'French?' said pitchfork. He seemed surprised, looked her up and down, from her face to the cavalry overalls and scabbard.

'Sharp claws too,' she smiled, stared straight into his badly crossed eyes until he was forced to avert his own gaze and she could turn to the blunderbuss. 'And if you keep shaking like that, the damned thing's likely to do your friends more harm than me.'

'What you got?' said Blunderbuss. 'Food is it?'

'Only for the soul,' Liberté replied, to the man's consternation. On second thoughts, she realised, these men seemed more like farmers than looters, though in poor condition, even for farmers.

'A woman,' said the fellow who had taken her sword, and he looked down at the blade.

Well, she thought, *full marks for observation*.

'A soldier of France, my friend,' she replied, now feeling more confident that she could survive this encounter, and beginning to understand why the village was so devoid of citizens. 'You're from the hamlet, over there?'

'Soldier of France?' snarled pitchfork, and he prodded her once more with the tines. 'Pig shit! What's a woman doing dressed up like that? She's some sort of spy. For the Prussos.'

'If you don't get that thing out of my belly, I'll take my sword back from your friend and carve you into a dozen pieces,' said Liberté. It was a casual remark, but it caused the man to back away a step or two.

'Just bloody try it,' quaked Blunderbuss.

There was a woman's voice from deeper within the undergrowth.

'Jeannot, put that down, you fool.' An emaciated crone blustered from the bushes, hitching frayed skirts and apron, clucking like a farmyard hen. She was followed by two younger women, hollow-eyed and ragged. 'Put it down, damn your eyes.' The blunderbuss was lowered. Pitchfork moved back still further.

'You're from the village?' Liberté repeated.

'What's that to you?' said the crone.

'The Prussians are pulling out,' said Liberté, and she recalled all those other villagers she had seen over the past twenty years, in more countries than she cared to recall. Those whose homes had been plundered and pillaged by one side or the other, the citizens tortured, ravaged or dead. Those that had taken to the road with their meagre possessions, in an endless pitiful stream, pushed one way then the other, depending on the whim of the winds of war. Those who had tried to hide themselves away, sometimes with success, sometimes without. And Liberté heaved herself free from a mire of memories, wishing at that moment that she could drink Tambour's *tonnelet* dry.

'For how long though?' pitchfork said to her. 'They've picked us clean twice already this year, churned up the fields again just after sowing, then trampled what's left of the crops two days ago.'

Yes, thought Liberté, *there are all those too. The ones who simply starve to death in the winters after we've passed through.*

'They won't be back,' she said. 'The Emperor's got them on the run now. You'll be free of them forever. Part of France again.'

She felt a fool even as the words left her lips.

'You think that will put food on our tables, lady?' said the crone. 'But come.' And she flapped her bone-thin fingers at Liberté, beckoning her to follow as she hobbled deeper into the trees.

The rest of the villagers, thirty of them, were settled in a fern-filled depression through which a dirty stream bubbled and spat. Their priest was here too, though he seemed soon destined to depart this life, a sickly old fellow tended by a young girl. Liberté thought at first that it was Tambour's daughter but when the child turned, she realised the features were different, though one grime-faced urchin looked pretty much like any other. Yet they had a fire, and a black pot of watery porridge simmering above it, so she set down the small leather bags, took the stubby clay pipe from her pocket and prised open the jar.

'Smoke?' she offered the old woman when she had lit the tobacco. *Sweet*, she thought, as she savoured the fragrance, passed the pipe around.

'They'll be coming after them then?' said the crone. 'The Frenchies, I mean. After the Prussos?'

'Do you not think of yourself as French then?' said Liberté.

'Are we? I don't bloody know any more. French, Dutch, Belgian, Netherlanders, French again. Who gives a sod? Mellery's our home.'

'The village? That's Mellery?'

'Whenever some bugger's not fighting over it,' the old woman replied. 'But it's never for us, eh? The fighting. Never for us. And meanwhile we just starve. Those slops in the pot are just about all we're left with.'

Liberté remembered Fouché's words, his lecture about the private fortunes being made from the government bonds and annuities of the warring nations, the returns on all their subsidy loans; the profits of the arms dealers, the victuallers, the horse-breeders, the clothiers, the boot-makers, the wagon builders; their collective influence on cabinet members, ministers, ambassadors, and monarchs themselves to perpetuate the conflict for their own ends. While the people starved.

'Is there nowhere to buy food?'

'With what?' said the crone. 'In Charleroi perhaps. But with what would we buy food?'

Watching the woman sucking the smoke into her shrunken cheeks, Liberté passed the pipe again, then drew her purse from the band of her overalls. Eight gold Napoléons, twenty loose francs. Pitiful. So she added the bags she had so recently acquired. The Prussian silver thalers. She made a small pile of it all, pushed the pile towards the crone's hands. If she was ever going to open that cabaret on the rue de Grenelles, she would just have to find some other way to do it.

'This time it's for you,' said Liberté. 'This time.'

The Prussian soldier escorted the donkey, Marianne and Florisette only so far as the next village, beyond the woodland where Hawk-face had left her horse, past the sculptured lakes that looked as though they may once have belonged to a monastery, through a succession of half-inhabited hamlets.

What happened to her? she wondered. *Taken by the Prussos?*

She hoped not, though it was possible. But the woman remained a mystery to her. She recalled the way Dumont had set a hand upon her leg, that peculiar sensation. Far from revulsion. Something pleasant. Warming. Though not the obvious thing. Hawk-face was a different kettle of fish entirely. And when Marianne turned for a final backward glance after they left their reluctant escort, she almost expected to see the woman riding up behind on that big Percheron grey. Yet all she saw was the stupid Prusso. The fool even raised his hand to wave at her. By Marat's ghost, he had hardly stopped prattling from the moment they left Mellery. Question after question, though she understood not a word. But he did not seem to mind. That look in his eye that men always possessed. Incapable of believing themselves anything but irresistible. No matter how old, nor how ugly. All the same though, for the most part she loved them for it. Men were such simpletons. And this Prussian had gestured expansively to her that she should keep the donkey, shooed her southwards.

Florisette slept in her arms and Marianne dozed too, past the endless open fields and scattered dwellings, her head jerking occasionally awake, reminding her to check that the sun still lifted to her left, or lit the lines of cloud that, ominously, were also the darkling shade of Prussian blue. And each time she woke, there seemed to be more and more of the enemy's casualties strewn along her route so that, by the time they reached the next village – it could have been Mellery's mirror image – the dead and dying were thick upon the ground. Those that were able stared at them with pitiful eyes.

We must look, thought Marianne, *like one of those church pictures I saw all over the place in Spain. Virgin and Child on a Donkey.*

She shook her daughter awake.

'Look, girl,' she said. 'More of those Prussos that you like to help so much.'

'You said you would sell me,' Poppy whined, 'to that smelly old man.'

'Only if the price was right,' replied her mother.

There were French patrols here. Groups of Line Lancers, the army's eyes and ears, picking their way through the human debris. These Lancers stared at her too, but nobody spoke. Not even a bird singing. Not a single citizen of this place evident either.

'They're beautiful, Maman,' said Poppy. She stretched and rubbed her eyes with tiny fists.

'The Lancers?'

'No. Them.' She pointed a finger towards the nearest group of Prussians. All living, yet horribly disfigured, one with his jaw shot away, tongue lolling on his throat and white teeth exposed where lips should have been, another with brains showing through a hole in the upper side of his skull. He had been scalped, perhaps by a sabre slash. Every manner of horror.

'Beautiful?' said Marianne. She normally succeeded in shutting out the worst of the images when she was tending wounds. It was a mistake to dwell on the damage that could be done so easily to human flesh.

'I mean, the way they are,' said Poppy. 'Doesn't it hurt? When those things happen to you?'

Marianne thought about General Letort.

'There is something in men,' she said, 'that seems to stop them feeling it so badly. As though the worse their pain, the better they can endure it.'

'And is that not a beautiful thing?'

'I suppose, in a way,' said Marianne, 'that beautiful is one way to describe it. But not all men are like that. A lot of them though. Something in their blood.'

'Men like to make war,' Poppy yawned.

'For many men it's easier than being at peace.'

Yes, she thought, *the girl's right. There is something magnificent about their silent suffering*. She was sure they'd had this conversation before, but could not recall where. She held her daughter closer, a rare moment of shared intimacy. Hawk-face had worked it out. The terrifying thought of losing Poppy as she had lost the other two, that intolerable grief, was too much to contemplate, and it somehow kept them apart. But what else could she do? She inhabited this mad world of blood and death because that was where fate had set her down. All those battlefields. Too many of them. Yet she sensed that the greatest of them still lay ahead of her, that whatever carnage she may have witnessed in the past, it would pale alongside the carnage still to come.

We must escape, she thought, *before it kills us both*.

The donkey took them no further than that village – Marbisoux, Poppy discovered – and refused to take one step further south, so they were forced to turn the beast loose and undertake the last stage of their journey on foot. And they found the Battalion exactly where Marianne had left it, formed astride that ridge above Ligny Brook, the mood somewhat morose, but a few cook fires at least now burning. Yet, apart from this, there seemed to be little sign of activity. Some of the baggage had caught up, however, and it did not take long before Marianne identified the Fourth Company's location by the presence of her own cart, the canteen tent erected, after a fashion, alongside and the pony, Cocotte, grazing the grass at the road's edge.

'There,' she pointed. 'Your damned goats.'

Poppy let go of Marianne's skirt and raced off to embrace the animals but was intercepted by Catherine Argonne, who had come hobbling up on her crutch. The girl ran to her, flung her arms wide as Argonne took the child to her ample bosom, tears upon her cheeks.

That child couldn't care if I should live or die, thought Marianne. *Probably a good thing too. It doesn't pay to get too close to anybody. Except Argonne maybe. That bitch is one of life's survivors, for all her scheming ways.*

'You brought her back,' shouted Argonne. 'Our Lady be praised. Everybody thought...'

Her cries disturbed the strange peace that reigned over the bivouac area, soldiers beginning to roll from their blankets to find out what the commotion was all about. There had evidently been no Diana beaten this morning and the disturbance to the men's respite was plainly resented. Here on the ridge, at least. Although below them, around the windmills, through the morning mists of

Ligny's streets, there were Gendarmes herding groups of citizens. They must have found them hiding in the surrounding woodlands and now they were being put to work digging pits for the dead. The inevitable scavengers too, picking over a thousand corpses.

Other things were disturbed as well. The mewling cry of Prairial's child off to the right where Marianne could see the second canteen tent, Juanita Bufanda's place.

Now what's Prairial doing over there? she wondered.

The waking soldiers looked generally in poor shape.

'Heavy night, Cazajus?' she shouted. She had missed out on a fair profit last night, she knew. There was always brisk trade in the aftermath of a fight, and especially when some of the boys had been lost. So Bufanda must have cleaned up. Marianne wished she could have trusted Fronsac to look after the business, but he could not really be trusted with anything very much. She would be lucky if he had not helped himself and the lads to the last of her brandy.

'We put a few away for Pons and Senent, that's all,' said Cazajus, but he gave her no other greeting and looked away quickly, snotting on the ground, first one nostril, then the other. In truth, several the platoon members also ignored her. She had expected at least some acknowledgement of her return, perhaps not a hero's welcome, but some recognition that she had brought the girl back safely. After all, they each thought a lot of the child, did they not? But, damn it all, this felt like the cold shoulder. It was confirmed when Abnet, one of the more fastidious fellows, stripped to the waist and washing his armpits from a bucket where he knelt, suddenly plunged his head into the water rather than speak with her. She stood like a fool, turning this way and that for any sign of Fronsac, saw Catherine Argonne leading Poppy away to her own bivouac, where the other children were gathering firewood. And then, finally, Marianne picked up the pig-like staccato of Fronsac's snoring. Inside the tent, naturally. Probably sleeping off the previous night's excess. It made a fine accompaniment to the *tra-ta-tra* of the Diana as the drummers belatedly began to beat the Battalion awake and Sergeant Flambert scurried towards her.

'Ah, Tambour,' he cried, 'we've been looking for you. Orders from Captain Vicquot. There's a Council meeting at ten. You're to be there. That business with the stolen hen. Special hearing. Where the hell have you been anyway?'

Did he truly not know? There was a biting riposte forming on the edge of her tongue, but he had already gone, his message delivered in obvious haste and without even one of his normal homilies.

'Any moans, groans, beefs or bones, Sergeant?' she murmured, though he was now beyond earshot. She was accustomed to the routine of the Battalion that pulsed on, regardless of location and circumstance. It was therefore no surprise that, this being Saturday, the Administrative Council should be holding its normal meeting to deal with the men's allowances; to determine any necessary purchase requisitions; to consider or submit any exceptional propositions for the Central Committees for Organisation, Health or Honour and Reward. It was usual too for them to hear all charges relating to breach of regulation, to determine Battalion punishment, or to refer more serious cases to the Special Courts, the army's Military Tribunal. But the dubious theft of one speckled hen? It was absurd. She had not given the bird a further thought since that conversation with Argonne, the woman's claim that, in truth, Juanita Bufanda had put the idea into the head of some impressionable and superstitious fellow that he might gift the hen to Catherine. Marianne had not bothered to consider whether she even believed Argonne's story. Vicquot may have threatened a Battalion Court of Justice, the Administrative Council's judgement on the theft, though she had not believed for one moment that they would waste time on this. And today, of all days? Their boys still to be buried? Not for the first time, she felt as though life, the entire world, was in conspiracy against her.

Yet the drums still hammered, and she could hear the choking sound that Fronsac always made when he was rudely awoken, his snoring bitten short in a way that might make the casual observer fear for his life, such was the violence of the noise, the abruptness with which his airways were throttled to silence.

'Christ alive. My head!' he groaned from within the tent.

She was about to pull back the flap when she imagined she heard some other sound. It carried to her like the whine of a child. Or perhaps…

Drawing back the canvas, Marianne peered into the dim interior, began to discern Fronsac's shirt, pale against that gloom; her husband himself, sitting among his blankets, nursing his head. While, at his side, something stirred. That moaning again. Soft and satisfied. The twin amber moons of a naked arse that instantly recalled the rest of Catherine Argonne's words.

'You can never trust a *manola*,' she had said. 'And certainly not a *manola gitana*.'

Chapter Twenty-Three

Saturday 17th June 1815, 7.00am

Marianne moved with all the grace and fury of a wounded she-wolf, ducked below the flap, slipped the *salvavirgo* from her bodice with one hand and gripped Bufanda's ankle with the other, strength multiplied by her rage so that she hauled the woman – naked, kicking, screeching, dragging clothes behind her like a lifeline – out into the morning before the *manola* had any real chance to understand what was happening to her. But the Spaniard at least managed to roll onto her back, fangs showing as she saw that her assailant was Tambour, that wicked little blade of hers flashing back and forth between them.

'Marianne,' shouted Fronsac, stumbling behind them in nothing but his shirt, 'you have come back!'

She dropped the woman's ankle and swung her arm all in one smooth manoeuvre that smashed the backhand of her fist into the side of his ugly nose and sent him sprawling on his buttocks.

'*Puta Madre*,' yelled Bufanda, trying to scramble away. But Marianne jumped on her back, pinned her to the ground, one knee pressing into each of the *manola*'s sides. She grabbed a handful of the coarse black hair, dragging back the head to stretch her throat for the knife. Yet, even as she reached around to slit the bitch, a kick in the ribs tumbled her sideways. She landed heavily on her own brandy cask, the knife flying from her hand, but her other fingers still gripping Bufanda's head.

'You've come back to us,' Fronsac shouted once more, nursing his nose, blood dribbling between his fingers. He was limping now too, from the kicking he had given her. 'Marat be praised!'

Men began to gather, a circle to form, as the Spanish woman twisted until she could sink her teeth deep into Marianne's arm. The pain was exquisite, forced her to let go of Bufanda's hair, though she did not do so before delivering a vicious slap to the *manola*'s cheek.

'Dirty whore,' said Marianne, while the men began to shout odds, wager bets on the outcome, laughing all the while as various parts of Juanita Bufanda's filthy anatomy were exposed in unusual positions.

Marianne looked around for the *salvavirgo*, spotted it near the edge of the thickening perimeter ring of onlookers and went after it on all fours, only to see it booted away by some fellow who, she imagined, must have bet against her. Even worse, as she glanced back, she realised that Bufanda's attempts to keep a grip on the clothing owed nothing to modesty and everything to the presence of her own blade hidden in the recesses of her skirt. She was trying to untangle the thing – until it, too, was kicked away, skirt and knife together sailing into the air, falling into the crowd.

'Keep it fair, girls,' shouted Fronsac, and he winked at Marianne as though he had done her a favour in putting the knife beyond Bufanda's reach. The two women circled each other, both crouched low and seeking an opening.

'Of course I came back,' Marianne spat at him. 'My business is here.'

Bufanda sprang at her and they both went down, rolling in the damp grass as the singing began. Marianne caught the *manola*'s fingers before they could dig into her eyes, rolled once more to bring herself on top of the Spaniard.

By the Host, I hate that bloody song, she thought, as the first chorus was reached.

'*Ron, Plon, Plon, the Drum Beats On*,' the soldiers sang. Or at least her supporters did so, screaming out her name even louder than the other lyrics every time the word *tambour* occurred.

The two women scratched and gouged and bit while the famous Drum Major was celebrated in song one more time, went about his customary exploits, boasted about the size of his big baguette, raped the young virgin of Pomerania yet again, made all the normal soldierly excuses for his deeds until even Bufanda's supporters had forgotten their partisan preferences and were chanting out the lines, clapping time with their hands. Marianne wanted desperately to stop, both the fight and the singing. She felt defiled herself every time she heard it, could not help thinking of the girls she had seen ravaged in Spain and elsewhere, by her own side and by the English too. And she thought of Maman Cholet, the way she had died. But more than anything, she thought of Florisette. Her attention wandered, just enough for the *manola* to get a foot in her stomach, heave her backwards so that she crashed between the singing soldiers. Bufanda was coming after her and Marianne moved deeper into the crowd, her fingers making a chance contact with the *salvavirgo* so that she took the hilt in her hand, kept scuttling back until there was room to stand, the knife hidden partially behind her until the Spanish bitch was almost upon her. Marianne's left hand caught the woman around the throat, stopped her in her tracks, while the right swept around in an arc that would plunge the short steel fatally under Bufanda's ribs and into her heart.

But the blade never found its mark, for a cavalry gauntlet gripped Marianne's wrist, halted its forward drive while, over her other shoulder, a second gloved fist landed such a blow on Bufanda's forehead that it felled her like a pole-axed ox.

Marianne had to be hauled bodily from the fray while Hawk-face shouted instructions for Bufanda to be carried away and the Grenadiers responded with every profanity they could invent about horse-boys in general and, in particular, about that variety of woman to which they thought the Dragoon must belong.

'Why not call it a drawn game?' shouted Dumont to those who specifically complained that, with the contest unfinished, their wagers remained unresolved.

'Why not call it the Game of Flats?' one of them replied, and his fellows laughed, made those gestures with their fists that had only one meaning.

'I'm going to finish the whore,' cried Marianne, the crimson mist of her fury unabated. 'And who the hell are *you* to interfere?' She struggled to free herself from Liberté Dumont's arms as she was forced towards her canteen tent. 'I'll kill the Spanish bitch then cut off *his* balls,' she stretched an accusing and judicial finger at Fronsac as he hobbled along beside them.

'Marianne,' he said, 'it was just a mistake. It means nothing. And we had to give Pons and Senent a proper send-off, didn't we?'

'I didn't realise that customs had changed so much,' she snarled. 'In the old days we just used to have a few drinks for the lads that fell, not...' She waved her hand towards his bare shanks. 'Not... *that*, you filthy pig!'

Hawk-face glared at him. 'You were having that woman,' she snorted, 'while your wife was risking her life to rescue your daughter?'

'He was about as much use as you,' Marianne said, while Dumont released her just inside the tent. 'Where the hell did you get to?'

'I found a small fortune,' Dumont told her, though she made it sound less than good news.

'And you found the little one,' Fronsac said to his wife. 'We knew you'd be fine.' He rummaged for his trousers, separating them from Juanita Bufanda's apron.

'And where was that whore's so-called husband while you were banging her?' sneered Marianne. 'That's always supposing you managed it?'

'Cluny doesn't care so long as Bufanda makes a few sous along the way,' Fronsac shrugged. 'And I managed just fine.'

'You paid for *that*?' Marianne ached intensely, felt that she was being devoured from the inside. Betrayed, of course, though her relationship with Fronsac owed more to their long association than to any true affection. She had borne his children, three of them, and shared the rigours of his campaigns. Yet, after Maman Cholet's death she could not have made her own way, she believed, without him. That counted for a lot. But he had been no use to her when their other two had died and this was not the first time with other women. It was the army, after all. *Ron, plon, plon, the drum beats on.* She pulled herself free, at last, from Dumont's embrace, though the woman still gripped her wrist. 'And you,' she said to her, 'your bloody stupid visions. They couldn't even warn me about this? Or that I'd walk back into the lines and straight into a Battalion Court of Justice? I was better off with that crazy Prusso.' She wanted to weep, but would not do so for the benefit of these two.

'In the cottage at Mellery?' said Dumont, releasing her wrist.

'The bastard that took my little Poppy?' Fronsac asked.

'The old fool thought she was his own daughter.' Marianne ignored her husband, directed her answer to Hawk-face. After all, she had at least been there. 'That bugger Blücher. Can you believe it? We'd shot him off his horse in that last charge they made against us. He was right there, within spitting distance. And our stupid daughter protected him. So he took her.'

'Blücher?' said Dumont. 'You mean *that* Blücher?'

'How many can there be?'

'It was him, inside the cottage? Raving?'

'The same.'

Hawk-face almost doubled up with laughter.

'Oh, that's beyond price,' she said. 'All three of them. Thin William of Oranje. Wellesley. And Blücher too. Each of them under our blades, Tambour. Yours or mine. All in one day. Yet we managed to finish not a single one of them. Can the Fates ever have played a more wicked trick? Ever have been so warped?

Marianne sat alone, a little way down the hillside, in a light and smoke-stained drizzle, to smoke her pipe and lick her wounds. She did so literally with the bite marks that Bufanda had left upon her arm, the skin broken and, she thought, likely to become infected from that pox-ridden whore. She lifted the side of her shirt too, dabbed a touch of dog-dog to the badly bruised ribs, caught the rank smell of her own unwashed flesh upon the linen.

Later, she decided. *I'll get the clean shirt from the cart later.*

For the present there were the remaining injuries, those to her soul. But they were at least eased a little by the tobacco, and she clenched the clay stem tight in the corner of her mouth, puffed hard on the pipe's comforts. Her mind raced with too many images, flitting from one anger to another but, as always, she drew some comfort from the presence of the *tonnelet* and her horde of meagre treasure. She glanced around, checked that she was unobserved, then stood the cask on its end, slid a finger into the two small rings that passed for additional cup hooks, and turned the whole face anti-clockwise until it came loose. The cloth pressed inside hid both her purse and Maman Cholet's locket and, as usual, the familiar feel of the slender gold chain brought her solace. She ran the tip of her thumb over the engraved 'C' of the locket itself and wondered, not for the first time, at the tale that might lie behind her adopted mother's possession of this fine trinket. Cholet had never spoken of the thing, even when pressed by Marianne as an inquisitive child, yet it had been more fun to use her imagination, and especially when the blood ran, or the nights were split by screams or drunken debauchery. So she had invented a string of lovers for a younger Cholet, each more handsome, more exotic than the last, a series of amorous adventures in which Cholet had been gifted with the locket as a pledge of undying love only to leave the luckless suitor with a shattered heart.

'So that's where you keep all your ill-gotten gains.'

Marianne almost jumped out of her skin, closed her fist around the locket, furious with herself that she had not heard Hawk-face approach.

'How do you do it?' she said. 'Clodding around in those bloody big boots and never more noise than a cat. It's not natural.'

Dumont looked down the hill, then left and right along the mile after mile of meandering tree line that marked the path of Ligny Brook, punctuated at so many regular points by the villages still burning and billowing; by the groups of returning citizens frantically trying to salvage whatever might be possible of their possessions. Marianne took advantage of the moment to push the locket back into the cloth padding and replace the face of the cask.

'They say the Prussos lost twenty thousand down there,' said Dumont.

'And our boys?' Marianne replied. 'Only half that number. We did well, eh?'

Ten thousand too many, she knew. But that was the price. For getting their enemies away from France's sacred borders. Everybody understood. Or did they? *What about those villagers?* she wondered. She supposed that, whenever somebody got around to it, there might be soup provided for them later. That was the usual thing. *But then what? We'll march away and leave them wondering whether they were better off with the Prussos.* Oh, she knew, either the Mayor or somebody else would eventually submit a demand for reparation. And the Shaveling or his staff would consider the demand. But all these sacrifices seemed to merit a more conclusive outcome. *We should have pursued them.* Yet when she looked around at the weary hollow eyes near to her, it was obvious why so many Prussians had escaped. All those she had seen near Mellery. And tomorrow, or the next day, there would be another instalment to be paid. Yet their foes must pay a price too, and if that price could be made high enough...

'You said something about a Battalion Court of Justice?' said Dumont.

'They say I was a party to looting. In Fleurus. A speckled hen.'

'Needless to say, you would never stoop to such a thing.'

'I've taken my share in the past,' said Marianne.

'We all have.' Dumont shrugged.

'But for a speckled hen, who could be bothered? I had it from Catherine Argonne.'

'The woman with the crutch?'

'The same. And she claims she had it from a Grenadier.'

'A hearing, though? For that?' said Dumont. 'And where's the hen now?'

'You know the army,' Marianne replied. 'Regulations are regulations. Good thing, too, says I. But the hen? I gave it back.'

'Hardly a flogging offence then?'

'No,' said Marianne, 'but there's the commission at stake. Or worse. Without the business, how the hell will I ever get my girl out of this?'

'Not through your husband, I suppose.' The point did not even merit a response. 'So how much have you got hidden away in there?' Dumont nodded towards the *tonnelet*. 'And what was the little bauble you stuffed away so quickly when my back was turned?'

'Why don't you have one of your stupid visions?' Marianne sneered, behind her saw Poppy running through the men, and at the same time a great roar began to swell all around them.

'Look, Maman, look!' cried her daughter, as the sections, companies, battalions took to their feet in a wave that spread and rolled across the hillside.

'Long live the Emperor,' they began to chant, as the familiar Arab grey pranced towards them, the Shaveling in his campaign dress, the old greatcoat and cocked hat, a stark contrast to the blue, the gold braid, the tossing plumes of the staff officers in his entourage. And it seemed to Marianne that as Bonaparte swept that famous black felt bicorn from side to side, he visibly wafted away the weariness that hung about the whole army.

'He is friend and father to each and every one of us,' murmured Liberté Dumont.

No, thought Marianne, *I am mistaken. He does not dispel our fatigue, he soaks it up*. She had rarely seen him look so exhausted, and she tried to count the hours. How long since they left Paris? *When was it?* Before dawn on the Twelfth. *Five days and nights. Is that all?* A string of battles. Marches. *We've barely rested. And, as always, the Shaveling will have rested least of all.* The whole of France to govern, from the saddle or from his dormeuse, beside the campaign itself, while Wellesley and Blücher, she concluded, would have been stuffing their faces at Belgium's expense.

She lifted Poppy so the girl might see him better, and her daughter squealed with delight, pushing herself still higher and peering between the raised arms, through the tossed shakos and forage caps.

'Hey, Majesty,' shouted a sergeant of Foot Chasseurs, the parade ground bellow carrying above the general clamour, 'how's the boy?'

Bonaparte caught the question, side-stepped the small white stallion closer to the man.

'My Little Eaglet?' said the Shaveling. 'Safe and well. With his mother, as you would expect. But once we've settled with the Prussians and the English, I need to arrange a visit with my Austrian in-laws. Perhaps you would all care to come with me? A reunion, of sorts.' The response was almost deafening, and Marianne's heart went out to the man. *Yes*, she wanted to scream with the others, *we'll come with you and bring back your son!* As she had just done with her own child. It was an outrage. Another insult against France. That the young Prince Imperial, Bonaparte's four-year old son, King of Rome, Prince of Parma, should have been spirited away by his Austrian mother, to live at the court of her father, the Emperor of Austria. More than a year since Bonaparte had seen the boy, and an army of one hundred thousand Austrians, possibly more, gathered on the Upper Rhine to block their reunion. The Shaveling cupped a hand to his ear. 'What's that?' he yelled. 'You'll join me in Vienna?' There were tears on grizzled faces again, but their devotion seemed to lift the tiredness from him also. 'Very well,' he went on. 'First the English, then the Austrians. The Little Eaglet will be Emperor after me one day, you know?'

But that was almost too much to think about. France without the greatest of all Frenchmen? *Never again*, Marianne promised herself. The period of his exile on Elba had felt like a lifetime.

'Long live the Emperor!' she howled as he came alongside them, Poppy still in her arms. Bonaparte looked at her, a smile of recognition, then at the girl and, finally, at Dumont. At this proximity, Marianne could see just how deeply the weariness was etched into his sallow skin. He tugged on his reins, slapped the arm of the man beside him, a fellow attired in the exotic livery of a Mameluke Guard.

'Look at this, Saint-Denis,' said the Emperor. 'If the devil cast his net, eh?' Louis Étienne Saint-Denis was no Mameluke at all, naturally, merely the Shaveling's personal body servant and elevated to that position, adopting the name Ali, when the former post-holder, Roustam – genuinely a Mameluke – had deserted his master the previous year. 'Do you have any of that excellent rot-gut left, canteen-mistress?' said the Emperor. 'And is it still over-priced for officers?'

She set her daughter on the ground and, while Bonaparte stretched down to tousle the girl's greasy hair, Marianne shakily poured another cup of brandy for him. So the Shaveling remembered her. She looked around for Fronsac, her faithless husband, who had mocked her story of meeting the Emperor at Beaumont. She could not see him. She scanned the press of men for Captain Vicquot, or any member of the Battalion's Administrative Council, who might now tremble at the thought of prosecuting a personal acquaintance of the Commander-in-Chief. Or Catherine Argonne, who may now finally accept her significance. Or that whore, Bufanda. But she saw nobody and was stabbed with disappointment. Yet, at her side, a small girl tugged at Marianne's nankeen trousers.

'Maman,' mouthed Poppy, 'the Emperor knows you!' And there was such wonder, such respect painted on the upturned tear-stained face that Marianne could have wept too.

'Today, Sire,' she said, 'for you there is no price at all. It is the least I can do to thank you for our victories.'

'This?' he replied, looking around the field. 'It's nothing. Merely a beginning. We need to settle with the English. They fear us, did you know? The way that the will of our people is exercised through their Emperor. A free people, we French. But can you imagine the English ever being free? Free of their bankers? Their merchant masters?' He swallowed the dog-dog as the rain began to fall heavily again. 'And you, Dumont,' he said, his gaze passing over Marianne to rest on Hawk-face. 'What are *you* doing here? Some mischief of Fouché's?' He turned to Marianne once more as the Imperial Guardsmen pressed in upon them.

'You know this woman, canteen-mistress? This gentleman volunteer, Liberté Dumont?'

'I know her, Shaveling,' Marianne replied, though she found herself looking at Hawk-face with precisely the same expression that Florisette had worn only a moment earlier.

He might have remembered me by my trade, she thought, *but this woman he knows by name.*

'And I see you're back in uniform, Dumont. But why here? Are the Second Dragoons not with Ney, Soult?'

Soult thrust out his jutting cleft chin. Soult the turncoat. Soult that nobody in the ranks trusted.

'Indeed, Sire,' the Chief of Staff replied. 'And Ney must be in Brussels by now.'

'I fear not, sir,' said Liberté Dumont. 'I left the battle just before dark. With dispatches. Marshal Ney was still before Quatre Bras when I left.'

The little colour that remained in Bonaparte's face drained quickly away and Marianne saw a small vein twitch in the side of his jaw.

'When did we last hear from him, Soult?'

'Sire,' said his Chief of Staff, 'I doubt we should set much store by the word of this... this *trooper*.'

'I asked you a question, Soult.'

The rest of the entourage tried to edge their mounts away from the two men, to distance themselves a little, but the press of soldiers around them prevented any escape from the Emperor's cold fury.

'Perhaps, Sire,' said Soult, with as much dignity as he could still muster, 'we might assess the situation in a more private...'

Bonaparte erupted at last.

'I tell you this, Soult,' he shouted, 'that I would trust these honest soldiers of France, these soldiers of liberty, before I would trust the mercenary interests of a single general. A single one.' He turned the head of the white stallion and waved an imperial arm so that the men before him opened a path for his passage, like the Red Sea opening before Moses. Yet he regarded Hawk-face one last time. 'And you, Dumont, back to your regiment. Tell your Colonel that I shall have need of him soon. You can help me drive those meddling Englishmen into the sea. I shall do it myself if Ney cannot do it for me.'

Chapter Twenty-Four

Saturday 17th June 1815, 10.00am

'When will they call you?' Hawk-face asked her.

'After the rest of their business is done,' Marianne replied. 'I had hoped you might speak for me. An agent of Minister Fouché. And a confidante of the Emperor, no less.'

'Hardly that. I've met him a few times, nothing more. As you have also, Tambour, so it seems?'

'I served him brandy at Beaumont. He drank a toast to my health. Proudest moment of my life. But he doesn't know my name.'

'Perhaps one day he will.'

The Imperial Guard's battalions and squadrons were forming for the march, though no specific orders had yet been issued to them. But word had spread fast. If the Shaveling were heading to Quatre Bras, the Guard would not be far behind him. So Marianne had packed away the canteen, loaded the cart and harnessed the pony, Cocotte. No sign of Fronsac, naturally, so she had made her way here to the tent where the Administrative Council was meeting. She crouched in the lee of the cart against the worst of the downpour, where Hawk-face had found her, tethered her own mount to the wheel's rim and settled down beside her.

'Tell me about this fortune you found,' said Marianne, by way of a distraction from her worries.

'Ach, you know the way it is with fortunes. The easier gained, the sooner lost.'

'It's gone?'

'Gone,' said Dumont. 'So we'll need to find a fresh one.'

'We?'

'Without you, Tambour, I would never have found the last one. Something caused that old fool Blücher to steal your daughter. Something else gave you the faith to follow and me to take you there. We make a good team. Like...' She paused, as though changing her mind about what she had been going to say. 'Of course, if we earn some gold we'll need somewhere safe to hoard it. And it seems you have a gift for hiding things. Might I?' Hawk-face pointed at the *tonnelet*.

'Help yourself,' said Marianne. 'But go easy. I'm down to my last two bottles, and precious little chance of finding more between here and the English.'

'I only want...' Dumont stretched out her fingers and touched the cask, the false rear face. But she recoiled as though it seared her skin. 'When I get back, Tambour, there are things we must talk about.'

'You're a great one for promising to chat, lady,' said Marianne, 'but I may not be around when you get back.'

Her spirits rose when she saw there were at least a couple of familiar faces on the Council's Court of Justice. Captain Vicquot, of course, one of the five administrative officers who would act as her judges – hardly a friend yet no stranger either. Then her old comrade, Henri Marle, one of the twelve chosen rankers, three from each company, who today would serve as her jurors. Marle was probably Fronsac's closest friend after old Argonne, but he had a reputation for fairness and Marianne liked him. In addition, there were another five or six that she could name, regular customers.

The presiding officer, Major Thiébault, explained the procedures to her and, with few preliminaries, Captain Vicquot was called upon to read the charges – aiding and abetting an act of unlawful looting, and receiving stolen goods for personal gain – and then to report the facts as he knew them. She was pleased that this task fell to Vicquot for, while the bastard would do her no favours, at least he was her own company captain, and only occasionally could she fault the impartiality of his account. He described the old couple who had reported the theft to him in Fleurus. Yes, he confirmed, they had seen the perpetrators and following an inquisition about the style and facing colours of their uniforms, could identify them as Grenadiers. So far as facial details were concerned, they could have been almost anybody. The victims were, however, more positive in regard to the stolen property – namely, one speckled hen. Vicquot strayed from his simple account merely to describe the bird as 'a fine specimen' and Marianne briefly considered challenging his competence to make such a distinction, yet chose in the end to let it pass. But she did raise one objection.

'Forgive me, Captain,' she interrupted, and rose from her bench. She looked over at Major Thiébault who nodded his agreement that she might speak. 'You say that the couple identified the bird. Can you recall their exact words?'

'Do you now wish to deny that it was the same hen they had lost?' said Vicquot.

'I neither confirmed nor denied in the first place, sir. I merely admitted that I had been given a hen in good faith and that, if the old couple had lost one, they were welcome to my own bird.'

'You returned their stolen goods to them?' asked the Major.

'I gave them the hen that had been gifted to me, Your Honour.'

'Yet you refused to tell me who had bestowed this gift,' said Vicquot.

Yes, she thought, *honour among the Battalion's women. What sort of fool are you, Tambour?* She recalled Argonne's hilarity when she had confronted the woman about it; the claim that a couple of fellows had given it to her in turn, the suggestion – planted by Bufanda, so she had alleged – that Catherine might use it as a peace offering with Marianne. But it did not really matter and as the hearing droned on, she began to wonder whether loss of her commission would be such a disaster after all. She paid scant attention to the rest of the proceedings and had concluded that the case was already lost, when there was a disturbance outside the tent. She turned to see a couple of Grenadiers backing through the flap. They were dripping rain and carrying a litter between them while still arguing with the sentries.

'What is this?' demanded the Major.

'Important witness, Your Honour,' said one of the men.

'This had better be good,' Thiébault told him. 'And relevant to this case?'

The Grenadier nodded, and the Major gave him leave to proceed. The litter was duly set down alongside Marianne and she was able to see that it was the same soldier she had treated during the advance through Ligny, the Third Company man, thigh-shot, friend of Corporal Cluny. She recalled that he had accepted a second cup of rotgut from her to clean the wound and prevent the green-stink. Only thirteen or fourteen hours had passed, but she could see that he would, on reflection, have derived more benefit from drinking the stuff. The smell was very bad and his fever already high.

'Name?' said Major Thiébault.

'Vincent,' murmured the soldier. 'Third Company, First Section, *Peloton* B.'

'And your business here?'

'It was me, Your Honour.'

'You?'

'What stole the hen, sir.'

'You admit the theft.'

'Yes, sir.'

'And were there others involved?'

'Yes, Your Honour. My mate, Mondrillon, too.'

'And where's he?'

'Dead, sir. In the churchyard at Ligny.'

'Anybody else?'

Vincent hesitated.

'Yes, sir,' he said. 'The canteen-mistress.'

Bloody lying wretch, thought Marianne, and began to relish thoughts of the agonies he would endure before the green-stink and fever finished him.

'She asked you to steal the bird?'

'Yes, Your Honour.'

'And this is the woman here, alongside you. Is that correct?'

Vincent struggled on the litter, tried without success to lift himself.

'Christ no, sir,' he said. 'Not Tambour, Your Honour. The other one. That Spanish whore, Bufanda.'

*

Regulations demanded that a new hearing should be convened to consider the case against the *manola*, that she should be afforded the chance to speak in her own defence, that any punishment should be declared in the Orders of the Day. But Major Thiébault seemed somewhat tired with the process and the woman was hauled summarily before judges and jurors within no more than a few minutes and a decision made that she would be subject to Battalion punishment rather than the case referred to a higher authority. Marianne would never be certain whether Vincent had testified through some sense of natural justice or because, as she suspected, Bufanda's man, Corporal Cluny, had perhaps not been so tolerant of his wife's whoring as Fronsac had supposed. Yet, in any case, Marianne bitterly regretted her moment of ill-will against the dying man and wished she could now do something to aid him. But she knew it was a hopeless case and thought, once again, how she had always been shaped by those she could not save. And so she found herself in company with Catherine Argonne, Suzanne Prairial and the assembled children, to watch as Bufanda's head was ceremonially and brutally shaved until her scalp bled, she was stripped naked, set upon a broken-down nag and whipped from the camp.

'Not your fault,' said Catherine Argonne, as Bufanda ran that ignominious gauntlet, the men of the Battalion jeering on each side, or singing that damned song again. *Ron, plon, plon, the drum beats on.*

'It's the war's fault,' said Marianne. 'Everything is.' She thought of Cholet. 'But she didn't deserve that. Nobody does.'

'You would have killed her,' said Argonne.

'But it would have been clean, and in the heat of the moment,' Marianne replied.

'What do you think will happen to Bufanda's commission?' said Suzanne Prairial, the baby clasped against her shoulder.

It was a timely question, for Bufanda herself had just symbolically disappeared from view, over the crest of a small rise, and the Battalion's soldiers began to break up into smaller groups, to drift away laughing.

'You could put in a bid for it,' said Argonne. 'It might be the making of you.'

'Unless Bufanda comes after you with a knife, of course,' Marianne sneered. 'Then you'll find out who your friends are.'

'Are you *never* going to let that Lomballe business go?' said Catherine Argonne. 'She was my friend, Tambour. What did you expect? That you'd waltz along, take her commission when the poor cow was at her lowest, and everybody would love you for it?'

'I don't think the Dragoon Lady should get the commission,' Florisette piped at them. 'I don't like her.'

'And me, you little wretch,' Argonne gave the girl a playful smack on the backside with the tip of her crutch, 'do you not like *me* any more either?'

Poppy laughed at her.

'You're my favourite,' she said. 'Apart from Onion. And Mami, of course.'

'Me?' said Marianne. She was shocked. 'One of your favourites?'

'You know the Emperor,' the girl told her, boastful, as though that was sufficient justification.

'They're all the same these days,' said Argonne. 'Our kids have become mercenaries. When did that happen?'

'Would your friend, the Dragoon, really want the commission,' Prairial asked Marianne.

'That lady has some very strange ideas,' Marianne told her, 'but holding a canteen commission isn't one of them. No, girl, you should put in for it while you've got the chance. You can't fail.'

But she felt a fraud, wanted to scream at the Breton mulatta that she should do anything *but* take the commission, that she should take her baby and run, get out of the army before it was too late.

'At least the Dragoon Lady won't mind,' said Marianne to her daughter. 'You and me, we may have met the Shaveling, but the Dragoon Lady knows him like a brother. You should not be so hard on her. I think she's a friend too.'

But this was too much even for an eight-year old to swallow.

'Maman,' she scolded. 'Like a brother? It's a very bad thing to tell lies.'

There had been all the usual complaints and grumbles about waiting around, about the various changed orders they had received since she returned to the bivouac area, four hours earlier. But Marianne had not complained. She had used the time well, taking Cocotte and Florisette the half-league to the village of Marbais which, she calculated correctly, due to its position north and west of the battlefield, may still have some useful supplies that she could purchase. A dozen bottles of brandy and several ounces of tobacco were her reward. And no sooner had she come back to the ridge than she turned a pretty profit. The men were bored and restless, so good customers for her wares. Then there was a visit from Captain Vicquot. He made no mention of the hearing, and why should he? Duty was duty. But he made a point of paying back the loan he had secured from her with the normal interest, naturally. He was also directed by the Council, he said, to offer her the purchase of Juanita Bufanda's stock, an offer that Marianne declined.

'She would have bought that stuff with the money from her own business. I may hate the bitch, but I won't steal from her.'

Yet she had no such qualms about inflating the price she charged him for a pinch of tobacco, and she smiled now, counting out her coins once more, sheltering under the cart with Poppy beside her as they waited for the 6th Corps to pass by and the Guard to begin its own march.

'How much do we have, Mami?' said the girl. 'And what's it for?'

Nineteen gold Napoléons still, plus thirty loose francs and the small change now. Not nearly enough.

'That's my business,' said Marianne, but she put her arm around the child and they peered out together as Lobau's Line and Light battalions trudged past in their greatcoats, flanked by Horse Chasseurs and Lancers, and interspersed with artillery batteries.

'It looks like a lot of gold,' said the girl.

'Well, you keep your mouth shut about it, or see what you get.'

'Grouchy?' said Marle, as they trudged west towards Nivelles. 'What the hell does he know about commanding infantry?'

'At least he's still with us,' said Firenzo. 'What's happened to all the others? That's a better question. The Shaveling used to have his pick of Marshals. Play them all to their strengths. So many we couldn't keep count of them. And now what have we got left? Five. Five!'

'And the best of those?' grumbled Trinquart. 'Davout left behind in Paris. Suchet messing around on the Swiss border. It's a piss poor bunch we've been left with.'

'You're being too hard on them,' said Argonne. 'They have a bugger of a job finding lodgings for themselves.'

'And for us, too,' said Daubanne. 'Wonder where we'll end up tonight?'

'Somewhere decent, I reckon,' said Cazajus. 'After all, there's two less of us to worry about now.'

'It's a fact,' Agide laughed, 'Pons and Senent will at least be warm and dry tonight.'

'Well,' said Muhler, the hero who had lifted Florisette from the path of that Prussian *Uhlan*, 'they'll certainly be dry. Not so warm though, lads.'

Fronsac had been notably quiet throughout the march so far, shunned by most of the other men in the platoon, so it was a surprise when he spoke.

'It's bloody stupid,' he said, 'sending off Grouchy with the whole Right Wing to find the Prussos when a few Chasseurs could have done just as well.'

But nobody picked up his observation. Some had simply shunned him since the Bufanda incident. It was one thing that he had bedded her, quite another that he was now guilty by association with the woman who had tried to play such a filthy trick on Tambour – and implicated Argonne's crippled wife in the bargain. But others were stilled by the first evidence of that other battle, fought while they and the rest of the army's central columns had been otherwise engaged at Fleurus and Ligny. Quatre Bras, that was the name of the place, was it not? And here were its signposts. The wanderers, they called them. Always the same, after any major battle. Those who had left their wits among the carnage and who, for the most part, would never recover them. Those whose brains were now permanently scrambled by the fearful noise or the sights to which no man or woman should ever truly be exposed. They ambled aimlessly in all directions, out from the point of impact, heedless of their surroundings, like human shrapnel, like mad folk escaped in hundreds from some huge lunatic asylum. The Grenadiers laughed at them, naturally; made a modest entertainment, a competition, by trying to identify their nationality or regiment from the clothing still worn by those who had not stripped themselves naked. Dutch and Belgian. English and French.

'Why is nobody talking to Papi?' said Florisette almost incidentally, standing to get a better look at them. She balanced precariously on the cart among the sodden sacks and canvas bundles, rain dripping from the end of her pug nose, one hand on Prairial's shoulder. They were towing the mulatta's own cart behind them, as usual.

'Because he is a pig,' said Marianne. 'And the boys know it.'

'Don't you like him now?'

'Don't ask stupid questions,' Marianne replied. 'And stop staring at those men. You'll fall if you're not careful.'

'When will the rain stop?' said Suzanne Prairial. Or, at least, that was the question that Marianne *thought* she asked, for the girl had taken to rambling entirely in Breton for the past half-hour. She did not look good, and nor did the baby, but neither did anybody else.

'Anyway,' Marianne said to her daughter and ignoring the mulatta, 'what's all this about the Dragoon Lady? Why don't you like her?'

'She frightens me. It's like... looking at a shadow.'

'And since when have you been frightened of shadows, girl?'

'No, Maman. It's like looking at *your* shadow.'

The approach to the hamlet was marked by more of the wanderers, of course, but also by those that Marianne called the half-lives, the wounded that were beyond help yet incapable of death. They were always a problem, for they might survive weeks, months, before they finally succumbed. Many of these from their own army would make the long, cruel journey back to Paris and the Invalides, be succoured there, stench-ridden, then simply slip away one night into oblivion without any rhyme or reason.

Yet the approach was marked in a different way too. The Nivelles road was a well-constructed highway, paved, wide enough for eight men to walk abreast, for a couple of carts to pass each other and, here at least, flanked by a verge of compacted sand so that those a-horse might make comfortable and unimpeded progress. They had come over a slight rise, the downpour easing slightly, with woodland and a lake away to their left, and the hamlet straight ahead. But the fields between, which should have been tall with crops at this season, seemed as if they had already been harvested. For the most part, only stubble remained even though, in parts, curving slender hedges of head-high wheat and rye still separated one section of the flattened stalks from another. Thus could the lines of advance and retreat, of attacking column and defensive square clearly be seen, and from those reaping grounds the dead were being threshed, some with tender respect, others dragged by hooks through their heels, but all destined for the pits already dug around the village perimeter.

Despite the presence of scavengers, there was still the everyday debris as well, almost a carpet of forage caps and cartridge pouches, belts and badges, papers and playing cards, linen and love letters. Everything scented with sulphur and smoke, of course. And the sickly stink of incense as a couple of priests sauntered casually around the open graves, swinging their censors as more bodies were mingled and mulched with powdered lime, and nothing to smooth the paths of eternity but the mumbled nonsense of an intercession for the fallen in place of Extreme Unction.

The Battalion halted alongside one of the pits, the crossroads for which the hamlet was named visible ahead of them but made unattainable by the units that blocked the way. The fields to the north were little better either, clogged with regiments trying to detour around the village simply to be caught on open ground that was quickly turning to quagmire. So the men delved in knapsacks, rummaged for their dried rations, found many of them soaked and inedible, turned to Marianne for any preserved sausage or morsel of cheese that she might be prepared to sell, a shot of dog-dog to drive away the bone-numbing dampness.

'It's supposed to be bloody June,' complained Trinquart, chewing on a tough strip of cured ham.

'Stop whining,' Marianne told him. 'You could still be in Spain with your balls burning off.'

She left Poppy and Prairial to look after any more customers and picked her way through the ranks until she reached the orchards of a large farm that occupied the nearer right-hand side of the settlement, its white perimeter walls pocked by musket balls and splashed dark crimson. The wounded sat huddled in a continuous line along the wall's foot, the half-lives of each combatant army, their nationalities, the reasons for their former animosities, now strangely unimportant.

Among them, Marianne spotted a familiar face, Bloom, who had served with them in the 22nd, though initially with reluctance. An Alsace Jew, he had lost everything with the Emperor's Decrees that were supposed to help assimilate his race into the rest of the nation. After all, was it not the Shaveling who had saved the Jews of Ancona, who had brought them rights, re-opened their synagogues in just about every country that had come under French influence? But the Decrees of seven years earlier, designed to attack usury, had imposed terrible restrictions and financial penalties on the majority of honest Jews, and Bloom had been among them. Angry and bitter, he had joined the army in the following year, but his faith in the Emperor had been restored when, over the intervening years, most Departments of France were encouraged to abandon the worst clauses of the law and equal rights were restored to Jewish folk. Bloom had taken the opportunity to apply for promotion to the Guard, as Fronsac had done, but found himself, instead, transferred to a Cuirassier regiment.

'Tambour,' he whispered, his neck and cheeks a sickly shade of green, 'what kept you so long, woman?'

'What a stupid bloody question,' she snapped. 'Want me to loosen that lobster pot?'

He nodded weakly and she began unfastening the leather straps and shoulder plates that secured him within the breastplate. There was a hole through its lower centre, just like a belly button. Gut-shot, though he showed no pain, did not even wince when she eased the chest-piece away from the blue uniform coat beneath. No blood, a sure sign that he was filling up inside. She resisted the temptation to offer him brandy or water, and he did not ask for any.

'We couldn't shift them,' he said. 'Can you believe it? They just kept coming. The Roast Beefs. We should have wiped them out earlier. Too late, too late.' A tear ran down his cheeks. 'We were charging them in the dark. Couldn't shift them. In the end they must have outnumbered us two to one.'

'You've been here since last night?'

He nodded.

'They started pulling out a while back. A few hours, I suppose. I've lost track. Just their cavalry left. But they ran like rabbits when the Shaveling turned up.'

'You saw him?'

'He came up that road like a knife through butter. Chased them off towards Brussels. But they'll stand, Tambour. They'll stand. And it won't be good for us. I know it. Now, you must do something for me.'

'You're not going to ask me for a loan?'

'Now that things are back in order, I could offer *you* one,' he said.

'That's tempting. I wouldn't have to worry about the payments for long, would I?'

Bloom smiled weakly.

'I like you, Tambour. I've been waiting for you. Can you stay for a few more minutes?'

Waiting for me? she thought. *Poor bugger's raving.* But she had a sudden recollection of something about predetermined fates, and a shiver tickled her spine.

'Fine,' said Marianne. 'I've got nothing better to do. Will your God look after you, Bloom?'

'I've made my peace with Him. I've had nothing better to do than recite the *Viduy*. But I think the Lord God of my fathers may be tired of me now. I should try not to vex Him.' He chanted a few lines in Hebrew, and murmured in French – the same words, she assumed. 'Master of the Universe, may it be

Your will that my passing be in peace.' He drew in a difficult breath. 'Now, say Amen for me, Tambour.'

'Amen,' she murmured, and instantly saw his eyes flash with their last ever laughter.

'We'll make a believer of you yet,' he whispered.

'Bloody Jews,' she replied.

She held his hand as he slipped away, then went off to find the Battalion again, carrying Bloom's news with her. The English in retreat towards Brussels and the Emperor pressing hard upon their heels. And his Imperial Guard eventually managed to follow behind, turning north on the main highway. Marianne thought briefly of showing Fronsac the place where Bloom was now lying dead against the wall but, by the time they got there, he had already been hauled away.

'Well, that's it then,' said Trinquart. 'Tomorrow, I reckon. Sort out the English. How funny if it was the same place we caught up with the Austrians and the Dutchies that other time. Twenty-one bloody years ago. To come full circle. And I still can't remember the name. What did Senent say it was called?'

But Marianne Tambour remembered. She had never forgotten. And it still made the hair stand on the back of her neck whenever she thought of it. *Vaterlô*, in the Walloons' tongue. The "wet clearing". Waterloo.

Chapter Twenty-Five

Saturday 17th June 1815, 4.00pm

'You think this war is being fought for your personal amusement?' Colonel Planzeau had raged at Liberté Dumont when she rejoined her Regiment. Ironically, she had found them near the Gémioncourt farm where she had spent so much of the previous day's fighting, and the carnage on the battlefield seemed far worse than she recalled. They said that each side had lost four thousand, dead and wounded, and the mass graves all around bore sombre witness to those figures. But she had been correct, and Ney had still not taken Quatre Bras. And with the sheeting rain, the Marshal seemed to be making little attempt to force the outcome even now.

'Yes, Colonel,' she had replied, to his further interrogation, 'I do realise that it was eighteen hours ago.' And she went on to explain that having delivered the dispatch to Count d'Erlon, she had then been required to ride on to Fleurus, to find the Emperor on d'Erlon's behalf and take him a note that explained why d'Erlon's Corps was now turning back to Frasnes and Quatre Bras. It was all nonsense, of course, but she doubted that the Colonel would bother to check. It was, after all, a plausible enough story.

'And Lieutenant Henry,' Planzeau had said, 'did you, by any chance, come across the fellow on your travels?' She had feigned surprise, denied any knowledge of his whereabouts, secretly hoped that the bastard was lying in a ditch somewhere and suffering all the agonies of hell with that crushed hand. 'Well,' the Colonel had continued, 'I just hope it's not another desertion. Imagine the shame on the Regiment.'

There had been some explanation required concerning the length of time it had taken her to get back, even allowing for the sojourn to Fleurus and Ligny, but Planzeau did not press the point and especially when she broke the news to him that the Emperor had mentioned him by name – well, almost.

'The Emperor told me personally, sir,' she had informed him, 'to say that he should have need of you soon. That you would help him drive these meddling Englishmen into the sea.'

She had therefore been particularly relieved when, at around an hour after noon, the Emperor had indeed arrived, energised the entire stalemate by gathering together his cavalry service squadrons, mostly the Guard's Lancers and Horse Chasseurs, along with six guns of the Guard's Horse Artillery, and thundered off at their head to Quatre Bras, only to find that the main body of the English and Dutch-Belgians had long since left the place and were in full flight north towards Brussels. But they had left their own cavalry behind, to cover their retreat and, after a pursuit that had lasted these past two hours, it was these that stood now at bay before the French for the sixth or seventh time on this miserably wet afternoon.

Liberté felt guilty still that she had not stayed to help Tambour in the Court of Justice hearing, though doubted the woman was in any danger. but she would have to worry about that later, for there was a distinct change in the nature of the chase. Until now, each time those swirling columns of red or blue Englishmen had tried to turn for the attack, the French artillery had deployed like lightning, threatening to pour case shot into their squadrons, with the Emperor always at the fore, always among the guns, as she remembered him at Toulon, stirring them to ever more frenzied activity.

'Fire, fire,' he would yell at the gunners. 'Can't you see those are the English?'

But the Goddams had not given them that chance for some time and now the chase was running to its end, the terrain before them, for the first time, giving the English horsemen a tactical advantage.

They must have reconnoitred the place well during their ride south, thought Liberté, *and ridden like hell to have got themselves through so quickly.*

The ground dipped below her position to a cluster of houses, then the bridge over a sluggish green river, the Dyle, she ascertained. Beyond the bridge, more houses lined the road, which swung away to the right before curving sharply again through Genappe's centre, the town square discernible at this distance by its church tower. In fact, the whole district seemed exceptionally blessed with such architectural features: steeples pointing to the grey heavens wherever there was a clump of trees or any sign of habitation anywhere in that tumbling landscape. But it was also largely enclosed by higher ground. True, there were fields on each side, but Liberté's overall impression was that Genappe formed an oblique defile, with the Brussels highway emerging from its northern perimeter to rise and rise again to those surrounding hills and trees.

Along that road, less than a kilometre distant, beyond the town, were the dark smudges that could only be the English cavalry squadrons, with the heights occupied by further units and their artillery, still limbered and angling like a line of ants running across the hillside.

The Emperor's cannons, however, were already in action, Bonaparte himself directing their fire from the back of his small white Arab stallion, which danced proudly among the olive-green twin trails of the gun carriages, mud-splashed as high as its withers. The gunners seemed clumsy in their capes and oilskin-covered busbies, but they worked like demons as they tended touch holes, sponged and wormed the barrels, fed the charges and canisters, rammed them home to the breech, spiked powder bags through the vents, sighted and adjusted the lay with elevation screw or trail spike and, finally, applied port fire and slow-match to quill fuses so that the muzzles gushed flame and thundered backwards, one after the other, over and over again. Yet their targets were distorted by the filthy weather and Liberté guessed that few shots found their mark.

And then the first howitzer shell came screeching from the enemy guns that were now, themselves, in action. They had some advantage too, having halted on higher ground along that ridge opposite, as well as from the evidently greater weight of their roundshot. Nine-pounders she calculated as the balls began bouncing up the rise whenever they touched drier earth, skipping and whistling above the cannoneers. And it took no more than a few minutes before the second cannon in the French line erupted in a direct hit.

Gunners, skewered by shards of wood, iron or bronze, reeled back, faces shattered, limbs smashed. The Emperor, still among them, had barely flinched, though all French troopers within sight of the incident must have collectively convulsed, choked with terror until he emerged again unscathed from the smoke. His staff officers crowded to him, naturally, tried to seize his bridle, haul the stallion bodily from danger. Bonaparte's enraged voice carried clear across the slope, ordering them to leave him be. Yet, for all his admonitions the effect of the hit was plain, the French fire slackening significantly while, in the distance, it seemed to signal an advance by the English horsemen.

French units were beginning to emerge from the north end of Genappe too. Scouting squadrons, Liberté imagined, thinking she caught the flutter of lance pennons. The 2nd Line Lancers, somebody said. Probably only a guess, but if so, those she had already seen in action many times, often enough in past battles, distinctive in their green tunics and brass helmets.

But what the hell are they thinking? Liberté wondered while, all around her, old hands in the green ranks of her squadron pointed fingers, shook their helmeted heads and mumbled about stupidity.

Yes, said somebody else, the 2nd. Sent in to check out the town. And it seemed that the leading troops, the unit's scouts, had passed through without problem and were now in open ground, perhaps looking around for their comrades, yet finding themselves alone. And it was awful luck, or perhaps clever leadership, that the English cavalry had been so close, already commenced the charge that caught the Lancers like an avalanche, buried them and trampled them before breaking around the town's houses.

Bonaparte was still with his five remaining six-pounders, and Liberté was convinced that at any moment he would leap from the horse and seize port fire or trail spike for himself. This was the man she had first seen in action twenty-two years earlier, and she loved him as much now as she had then, when he had taken Toulon back from those Royalist enemies of the Revolution and their friends, the English. She loved his luck, as much as anything else. Or whatever detail of his personality protected him. And here it was evident again now, with the arrival of a fresh Horse Artillery troop, six more guns appearing from absolutely nowhere yet, without any instruction and in their captain's instantaneous assessment, wheeling around, just to Liberté's right, so that the new cannons would bear easily upon the enemy. They were in action within a few minutes, trail transoms lifted clear of limber pintles and the teams led to the rear, while still more friendly horsemen arrived: the covered czapkas, the blue or red tunics of the Guard's Lancers, barely visible beneath capes and redingotes; a squadron of Cuirassiers, similarly protected from the rain; some troops of Horse Chasseurs, but at the head of this new column, a regiment of their own Hussars, these wearing the braided green pelisse of the Fighting 7th, part of the legendary Hellish Brigade and led, she saw, by the dashing figure of the Hussars' colonel, Marbot, whom she had last seen at Leipzig. They formed alongside Liberté's Dragoons while Marbot himself was greeted by the Emperor like a long-lost brother.

Down in the town a mêlée was developing, the rending crackle of carbines echoing in the streets as cavalrymen formed skirmish parties or fought house to house. Their positions became obscured by smoke, but Liberté could discern where they were from the firing, which increased in intensity closer to her and diminished to an intermittent pop-pop-pop further away, while the shot from the newly arrived gun troop was now falling with regular accuracy among those dwellings where the English had taken cover, so that tiles and stonework were soon blasting in every direction.

Trumpets called the English horsemen to retire, while a canteen-mistress of Liberté's own regiment came plodding through the ranks on her donkey, the shaft of an open parasol strapped to her back, as was her custom, to keep rain or sun from the elegant Spanish shako she had picked up before the rout at Vitoria.

'Want a shot?' the woman asked, and Liberté said yes, before remembering that she had given every last sou to the old girl in Mellery.

Why did I do that? she wondered. It seemed foolish and sentimental to her now.

'Am I good for one on account?' she said.

But the tight-fisted bitch was no Marianne Tambour.

'Not for the likes of you, my lovely,' sneered the woman, sheer contempt in her eyes. And Liberté considered, not for the first time, whether Tambour might also share that opinion of her. Men in the army, for the most part, took her at face value. But the women? She had heard the various names they gave her for the past twenty years and they bothered her little, though she did not understand them. After all, the canteen-mistresses, the laundresses and the rest might all pretend that they were in the ranks through duty to a husband, or a wicked twist of circumstance. Yet, in truth? Most of them were as much in love with the risk, the adventure, the escape from the humdrum, the heightened sense of living, as the footsloggers and the horse-boys, Liberté among them.

But what about Tambour? she thought. She was convinced that she knew now why they had been brought together. *Imagine taking her for one of Fouché's agents!*

She laughed, and the trooper at her side glanced in her direction.

'You're right,' he said, evidently mistaking her amusement for irony. 'It's a bloody mess, and going to get worse.'

The Lancers – she was certain now that they were, indeed, the 2nd – had reformed north of the town and charged up the slope to reach the Englishmen who had stung them so badly, and an untidy running fight was taking place, men and horses everywhere, in twos and threes, all across the hillside. It was almost tiresome to watch.

But I need to be sure, she thought, *about Tambour.* She remembered how close she had been to touching the thing. The *tonnelet.* Yet now she was unsure whether she would ever see the woman again.

'It just got worse,' she said to the trooper, and stretched the finger of her gauntlet to the opposite slopes where the Red Lancers still played the game of tip and run with the enemy horsemen while, above them, the English second line began to spread, thick and dark, down the incline. They began at a walk, slow and deliberate, while, from the French lines, trumpeters desperately tried to recall their men, to warn them of their danger.

'Fools,' said the trooper. 'Are they deaf?'

They were indeed, and blinded too, even when the English broke into a trot, gathering momentum as those already engaged broke away and sped diagonally uphill, leaving the Lancers momentarily confused and alone. And if the earlier attack on their scouts had been like an avalanche, this second onslaught was more like a landslide that sent them tumbling and crashing back towards Genappe or away to the east.

Marbot may have held no seniority among the various colonels who had arrived with their cavalry regiments at Genappe, but following a flurry of courier activity and a hastily convened meeting with the Emperor, word swiftly rippled through the ranks that they all now constituted a disparate Brigade of Light and Heavy, Guard and Line, and all under Marbot's command. He had wasted no time, either, in bringing them to decisive action, each squadron receiving its orders and taking its place in the growing column that moved fast, by fours, down the road, across the narrow Dyle bridge and up into the town itself. Here the column had divided, the leading units turning down the streets to the left, out to the fields beyond, but the remainder – the Second Dragoons included – continued to climb into the main square and towards the chaotic sounds of conflict. And the mess, at close quarters, seemed even worse than it had done from the hill.

To Liberté it felt like Brienne all over again although, at Brienne, there had been the flames to contend with, rather than this bloody rain. But here too, the squadron arrived between the houses lining a straight section of the Brussels road at a crossroads, where they burst out into an open space, the market square, a red-brick inn to their immediate right, the street going straight ahead for a short distance before forking around each side of a grey stone château, and the right fork curving away past the church that stood on the square's north-east corner. The square itself presented an awful scene, the Lancers, many of them on foot, being pressed back by rearing, kicking dock-tailed horses of English Lifeguards, the Lancers in their crested helmets and cloaked for the most part against the downpour, but some of them still sporting their scarlet tunics, though these were largely spattered with mud. It was a hacking and slashing contest, with an occasional crack of carbine where somebody managed to keep their powder dry long enough to get off a shot. The trumpets were blasting out the Dismount, the tune's notes immediately conjuring words to the little ditty that was drilled into every recruit until they could hear it in their sleep. *Feet on the ground, cavalryman! Feet on the ground, quick as you can!* Sixty Regulation Fanfares in total, and the three dozen troopers of the 6th Company knew them all, better than they knew their mother's names. They dismounted as though they were one.

'Dumont,' yelled Sergeant Tranchante, 'take your Section and get working on a barricade. Here. I don't want those buggers getting any further than here. See what you can find at the inn. Move it! The rest of you, inside by twos and start picking off those Roast Beef Bastards!'

The square heaved and crawled with the dead and dying, a real butcher's yard, but the English were pulling back, the Lancers too dazed and broken to follow them. But there was no such respite for the Second Dragoons. Trumpets again. The Mount, as Tranchante bawled at the Company to get itself moving, and the horse-holders came running back with the mounts for Liberté's nine-man Section. Muskets were slung back in their saddle buckets, and they swung easily into the saddle, her three files taking up their places as the Regiment formed along the side of the church, and the chase began again through the northern streets of Genappe and well beyond, to a substantial farm where the Dragoons found themselves once more on open ground.

Ahead of them, and off to the left, the rest of Marbot's hotchpotch Brigade – his own 7th Hussars, the Polish Lancers, the Horse Chasseurs, the Cuirassiers – were wheeling across the fields and, with luck, might catch the retreating Lifeguards in flank, though the mud was now so thick that both sides – except those lucky enough to be on the road – were slowed to little more than a walk.

What now? Liberté wondered, as the Regiment came to a halt. It would leave old Planzeau with something of a quandary. The normal thing would be to form by squadrons in line, or in echelon, try to take the Lifeguards from the rear. But on the open ground they would never reach them, and an attack in column, like this, would be suicide, expose them to a flank attack of their own. And, indeed, even as she thought it, here came the English Hussars and Light Dragoons, down the slopes to their right, covering their comrades' retreat. Unaccountably, she recalled her father's tale of how he had been wounded at Yorktown, helping the Americans win their own independence from the English tyrants. He had been a proud man. Major Dumont of the Saintonge Regiment. Then Deputy to the Estates General. But broken by the unexplained loss of his wife, Liberté's mother. *Well*, she decided, *I will bring him news after this campaign, be it good or bad.*

The Walk sounded. Then the Right Wheel, which angled them towards the enemy Hussars. The Draw Sabres, quickly followed by the Trot, though uphill, in the mud, there was little difference to their actual pace. But they picked up the step when they reached some drier ground, a plateau, where the Colonel ordered the Charge to be sounded. Sabres were extended, straight and true, to the Guard position, as they thundered from canter to full gallop, headlong into the leading English ranks. They too were at the Charge, both sides almost impossible to control, spreading apart, leaving the slowest behind, or bunching together. Two screaming hordes.

Mother of Christ, thought Liberté. It was unusual for her Regiment to be so disordered. They were famed for the coolness of their advances, usually so disciplined. And she knew that the vast majority of such crazy charges simply failed, broke up before they made contact with the enemy. Yet here, both sides seemed equally frantic. And it was a strange thing, this business of heavy cavalry against light horse. Not for the first time, Liberté felt that surge of power when she realised the height and weight advantage she enjoyed over these invaders. Yet she suddenly found herself well ahead of her Division, alone, one of the Hussars swinging towards her, stretched along the neck of a silver-dappled chestnut, its flying mane half-concealing his face, the cords and red busby bag flapping in the wind created by his headlong dash.

She waited until the last possible moment, until the Englishman's outstretched arm betrayed the direction of his intended slash, then she touched Lucette lightly with thigh and bit, swung her neatly across the Hussar's front and hacked down to the left, at the side of his head. He saw it coming, of course, tried to bend himself away from the cleaving blow, but that simply meant she took him in the ribs. There was a frightful crunch of shattering bone, a sucking sound, the stink of horse sweat and saddle leather, the chestnut's scream as it stumbled, the background blur of hooves, and smudges of splashed colour – blues, and reds, and greens – while Liberté recovered the blade in a backward circle, over and into the defensive Guard again.

An Englishman swept past to her right, another to the left, and she was through the first wave, risking a glance over her shoulder to see the rest of her Section still behind, but catching up fast so that they ran into the enemy's second line almost in a wedge. She saw Falco's powerful black stallion ram straight into a much smaller Hussar piebald, crashing it sideways and down, while Falco himself swiped at the rider's face as the fellow tried to jump clear.

He would have done better to go down with his horse, she thought, as a fountain of gore spurted from the Englishman's neck.

Through the second wave, and nothing beyond, so they reined in, Liberté dragging harder on Lucette's mouth than she had intended.

'Easy, girl,' she said. 'Easy.'

But the Percheron, forgiving as always, tossed her head and snorted spittle as the rest of the Division came through. Trumpets, and the Company's troopers finding their places, more or less, Sergeant Tranchante haranguing them for their earlier lack of order.

'This time stick together,' he bawled. 'It's not some Goddam's fancy ball. What the hell were you doing? Dancing with the bastards? Take them down. Take them down.'

And they were on the move again, steadier now, the line holding head by head, sabres extended in a single line of steel, as though they were all one.

By Our Lady's Tits, thought Liberté, *was there ever anything to beat this?*

She found the Englishman after that second pass. They had, indeed, taken down many of the Goddams, just as Sergeant Tranchante had required. Yet this one was still mounted, left behind and dazed, nursing an injured sword arm, blood dripping from his fingers. From his braiding he was plainly an officer, a captain in all likelihood, and he made a weak attempt at lifting his sabre towards her as Liberté approached. She flicked her own straight edge against his curved blade and knocked the sword from his hand so that it dangled from the wrist strap, useless in his surrender. And she noticed, for the first time, the insignia on the side of his portmanteau where it showed beneath the rear of the sheepskin saddle cover. Roman numerals. VII. These were the English Seventh Hussars then? While, on the other side of the field, Marbot's *French* Seventh Hussars were engaged with their own struggle.

'What shall I do with this one, Sarge?' she shouted.

'Cut the bugger's throat for all I care,' said Tranchante, then thought better of it. 'No, wait. Is that one of their officers? Right, take him back into town. Somebody'll know what to do with him. And hey, Dumont, try to get back to us some time tonight maybe?'

As it happened, she needed no direction since, back at the square, one of the buildings had a cluster of other Englishmen waiting outside under the watchful eyes of the Emperor's Guard Chasseurs, but each of the prisoners seemed seriously wounded and none of them held any significant rank.

'This one an officer?' asked the Corporal of the Guard, and when Liberté made some riposte she was ordered to take the Roast Beef upstairs. The place smelled of freshly tanned leather, a belt-maker's workshop and store, with his produce hanging from racks and, lined around the walls, the rolling razors, straight edges, skivers, hole punches and bevellers of his trade. The first floor contained two meagre rooms, the craftsman's living quarters, but these were empty and stunk of stale food. Yet the second narrow staircase – no more than a ladder really – led to an upper storey and Liberté could hear voices up there. She prodded the fellow, ignored his incoherent mumblings, urged him upwards and followed him, until she could see that this loft opened onto the rain-swept street, a hoist rigged at the open window and, on the floor beneath, a stack of hides that gave off a pungent odour. But it was the voice behind her that turned Liberté's head. A voice speaking in English. Two other enemy officers already here. One, a Light Dragoon. The other, a Hussar – the same as the man she had brought in – yet neither of these looked as though they had long to live. And their inquisitor? Marianne knew him at once. General Charles de Flahaut, the Emperor's Aide-de-Camp, rumoured to be both the bastard son of Talleyrand and lover to Bonaparte's stepdaughter, Hortense. At thirty, he was acknowledged as a brilliant intelligence officer; hated Fouché with a vengeance.

But Flahaut's flamboyant crimson tunic and breeches were in stark contrast to the room's other occupant. Seated, his grey riding coat dripping wet, sparse black hair also slicked with rainwater as he held the corner of his cocked hat, slapped the felt against the side of his riding boots. It was Bonaparte himself.

'Ah, my gentleman volunteer,' he said. 'I should have known. Tell me, Dumont, have you brought this fellow for me, or is he reserved for the Minister of Police?'

'Minister Fouché's English is somewhat lacking, Sire. I'm sure he wouldn't mind me gifting this one to yourself and Colonel Flahaut. Good evening, Colonel.'

'Look at these Goddams, Dumont,' said Flahaut. They had first met at the dinner to celebrate General Bonaparte's success in the 1800 referendum that had placed all the powers of government in his hands as First Consul. Liberté had made a name for herself in the Egyptian and Syrian campaigns and had returned, as part of the guard for those treasures not stolen by the English, to find that she had become something of a curiosity in fashionable society. There were those who said that Charles de Flahaut was only there due to the influence of Talleyrand. There were those that said it had been Liberté Dumont who had inspired him to first join the army just afterwards. There were those who said many things about the young Charles and the older woman, Dumont. Not all of them true. 'Are these the same Englishman who led us such a dance in Spain?' he said. 'The same that our Minister of Police keeps telling us we should fear so much?'

'Never mind that, Flahaut,' said the Emperor. 'They are officers, English or otherwise, and should be treated with the respect they deserve. Treated well. What were you thinking, to haul them all the way up here when they can barely stand? And me too. Did you not say that the prisoners would be useful? Have a cot rigged to that hoist, will you? Lower them down safely and make sure Larrey's fellows take a look at them.'

'And this one, Sire?' said Flahaut, pointing to the Hussar captain, Liberté's prize.

'Tell him to sit. Have some cheese and wine sent up. We'll question him when you're done.'

Flahaut spoke to the Englishman, but the Hussar seemed confused, looked with disbelief at Bonaparte, clutched the wounded arm. 'Yes, sit,' Bonaparte said to him and then, loudly, deliberately, flapping his hand downwards like a beating wing. 'SIT!'

To everybody's surprise, the man responded in passable but heavily accented French.

'Is it possible,' he said, 'for somebody to look at my arm? I should hate to lose it.'

'Well, Flahaut,' said Bonaparte, 'it seems we shall not need your excellent translation services after all. But send up a surgeon straight away, will you?'

Colonel Flahaut disappeared down the ladder and Liberté suddenly realised the responsibility upon her shoulders.

'Sire,' she said, 'should I also call for your guardsmen?'

'Whatever for?' said the Emperor. 'I hardly think these two gentlemen pose any threat.' He gestured at the prisoners questioned earlier. 'And I assume that Captain… it *is* Captain, is it not?'

'Elphinstone, sir,' replied the Englishman.

'That Captain Elphinstone,' he said the name slowly and carefully, 'will have given his parole?'

'I have, sir. And an Englishman's word…'

'Yes, yes, Elphinstone,' Bonaparte waved impatiently, 'we have the same protocol in France, you know? Honour is not the preserve of the English. But will you answer me a question, Captain? Tell me a little more about Wellesley's cavalry. What is its strength, would you say?'

'I fear I cannot do so, sir,' Elphinstone seemed almost smug. 'It would be a breach of my *own* honour. I am happy to divulge my unit, the Seventh Hussars. But for the rest of the Duke's forces – the Duke of *Wellington*, sir…'

'You think I am an imbecile, Elphinstone?' Bonaparte did not raise his voice but it had gathered an icy edge like the trailing side of a foul weather front. 'I am not talking numbers, Captain. I could give you a lesson in that regard. Down to the last squadron. Including your own. And is it not a strange thing, Dumont, that we should have *two* Seventh Hussars, the English and our own, facing each other in the same fight. Has Marbot realised, do you think?'

'I'm sure he has, Sire,' Liberté replied, and Bonaparte nodded.

'Yes, I'm sure too. But I was asking your opinion as a professional soldier, Captain Elphinstone. To tell me the quality that makes your English cavalry so good.' He turned to Liberté again. 'Wellesley does not deserve them, Dumont. Do you know that? Fine horsemen. And not just from hunting foxes, I think. I shall ask him when he is beaten. I have never met him, Dumont, but I look forward to the pleasure.'

'You won't be disappointed, Sire,' she replied, and wished that she had bitten her tongue. But Bonaparte seemed not to have noticed the comment.

'Well, Captain Elphinstone,' he said, 'you must at least know your Duke's intentions. And we will find out soon enough, shall we not? Will he fall all the way back to Brussels, do you think?"

But Elphinstone would not be drawn or did not know, and Liberté supposed that it mattered little. In any case, the place was all activity again, a couple of Chasseur Sappers begging permission to enter and bringing with them a stretcher that they rigged to the hoist then began the evacuation of the two Englishmen. They were followed almost immediately by a surgeon and medical orderly, who set about the task of stripping Elphinstone's wet pelisse, the dolman beneath, and revealing the three separate slashes to his arm that gushed blood as soon as the pressure of the double woollen sleeves was released.

'And you, Sire?' Liberté said quietly, 'do you think Wellesley will stand?'

'Well, my dear,' Bonaparte whispered, 'unless I miss my guess, you may be in a better position to answer that than me. Or am I mistaken? Was there not some hint earlier that while I have not met the Duke, *you* may have done so?'

I should have known, she thought, filled anew with love and admiration, *he misses little*. 'Yesterday, Sire,' she replied. 'At Quatre Bras.'

'You stormed the place alone, I suppose. Captured Wellesley briefly, but could not keep him prisoner because Ney, with the entire Left Wing at his disposal, was unable to support you.'

'Almost, Sire,' she said. 'Though it was myself who was the prisoner, I fear.'

Flahaut reappeared at the top of the ladder.

'The English are still running north, Sire,' he said. 'Our leading squadrons following them close. But we've had word there may be somewhere that might serve you for the night.'

'Not that thieves' den where Wellesley spent last evening, I hope?' said the Emperor, then turned to Liberté. 'An inn. Just around the corner. Called "The King of Spain". Nerve of the fellow, eh?' Trooper Dumont smiled.

'No, Sire,' said Flahaut. 'A large farm. Some way along the road, but more suitable to your needs. "The Pebble", it's called.'

'Good,' said Bonaparte. 'I'll take a look at the place. It cannot be worse than this leather loft.' He turned to Elphinstone. 'Bid you good fortune, Captain. I hope that you don't lose your arm. And perhaps when we meet next, you can tell me more about the fighting qualities of your horsemen.'

'You're too kind, sir,' said Elphinstone, 'though I expect that I shall not be a prisoner too long.'

'Ah, that's the spirit, Captain, the eternal optimism of the English,' said Bonaparte. 'But you, Dumont, I think we need to finish our little chat. I'll have Flahaut write an order for you. You can meet me later. At this farm. The Pebble.'

Our little chat? she thought, and trembled, cursed herself for letting her tongue run away with itself. That quip about Wellesley. And now? An interrogation by the Emperor himself to look forward to? How would she tell him about the task Fouché had set her? Worse, what in the name of hell would she tell him about Berthier and that fall from the window?

Chapter Twenty-Six

Saturday 17th June 1815, 8.00pm

'That is a filthy habit, Dumont,' said the Emperor. 'Do you know? And will you not take some wine?'

Liberté glanced at the clay pipe she had lit from the meagre fire in the Shaveling's hearth. It was likely to be the last warmth she might feel for some time, for the weather outside was now even worse. How long since the rain began? Ten hours? Eleven? And she wondered what had become of the family that must have been recently turned out of the place, presumably with all its furniture, since there were few homely comforts in evidence throughout the farmhouse.

'I fear that I'm too old to break the habit now, Sire,' she replied. 'As for the wine, it's a kind offer but I fear it may have to wait until the Regiment finds whatever cosy nook we're going to occupy for the night.'

'Once Kellerman brings up the rest of your Corps, you'll be heading back to Genappe. I've just issued the orders.' There were three secretaries packed into the small bedchamber, each sitting at his own portable table to take down the Emperor's commands or correspondence while, in the next room, Flahaut was busy with several other dispatches. There was a constant procession, too, in the hallway beyond, of senior officers – Soult included – up and down the stairs to the first floor. Bonaparte glanced through the window, where the companies of his First Regiment of Foot Chasseurs were marching in, to bivouac in the orchards and garden. 'It's getting dark early. But still enough light to chase Wellesley a little further. Keep him on the run. Now, tell me about him, but make it quick. We need to be back on the road.'

She omitted all mention of her mission, not from dishonesty but for both the sake of brevity and because she was convinced it would neither be of surprise nor interest. So she reported only that she had been knocked unconscious near Frasnes, drew to his attention the remains of the bruising and abrasions on her cheek, left Thénardier from the story entirely, and confirmed that she had been taken to Quatre Bras for questioning. She mentioned Rebecque, the arrival of Wellesley, described his physical attributes, his likeness to an image she had seen of Augustus Caesar – this made the Emperor snort with derision – and told about the arrival of Grant, the Duke's Head of Intelligence. Bonaparte was familiar with the fellow's activities, naturally.

'And did he mention Fouché at all?' The Emperor's hollow, red-rimmed eyes peered deep into her soul.

'He assumed from the outset that I was a spy, one of the Minister's agents, Sire, and asked me whether I knew that Minister Fouché had already made overtures to him on your behalf. Something about the possibility of a Regency. Your son to be recognised as Emperor when he comes of age.'

'I would have given it all to Berthier,' Bonaparte whispered, 'to see my son one day on the throne.'

'It would have been unthinkable, Sire. France without you to lead us.'

The merest nudge, she recalled. *I simply gave that old man the merest nudge. And down he went into the street. Four storeys.*

'Well,' he said, 'it was not to be. The fates were against us. Poor Berthier,' he went on. 'But these odds.' He raised a hand to his forehead, squeezed as though he was in terrible pain. 'There are those who think me a maniac. To keep fighting so many foes.'

'The army does not think so, Sire.'

He grimaced, though not in response to her comment, she thought. For he reached down, bent his knees and yanked at the crotch of his breeches, eased them away from his buttocks.

'So many hours in the saddle, Dumont. And me with piles. Or some damned thing. Ask a dozen saw-bones what ails a man and you'll get a dozen different answers. But they all agree on one thing. They tell me I must suffer one of their damned treatments later. Well, I know what it is that aches my guts so. It's that our enemies have never left us any choice. About whether to fight or not. When you fight, you may not always win. But if you do not fight, you will surely lose. And did you manage to conclude anything about the Duke's intentions, my dear trooper?'

'It may have been simply for my benefit, Sire, since they had so clearly decided that I was a spy. But Wellesley was convinced that Marshal Ney would continue to sit on his hands. His words, Sire, not my own. That this would give the English a chance to retire, to trap us between themselves and whatever was left of Blücher's Prussians. They intend to stand, Sire. And somewhere near, I think.'

The Emperor had promised to hear the rest of her tale, the story of her remarkable escape, perhaps later, but Liberté thought it unlikely they would meet again very soon. In any case, she also knew that she would not have the stomach to tell him how, her escape apart, she had almost won the war single-handed, within an ace of cutting Wellesley down during his flight from the subsequent French attack. But, for now, she was back with the Regiment, reinforced by yet greater numbers of their own cavalry.

There had been more skirmishing; enemy cannon fire taking its toll among some of the other units, then a storm of those absurd screeching rockets that the English favoured so much. But that had all served no other purpose than to allow Wellesley's horsemen to fall back. And now this miserable pursuit began. Liberté doubted whether, had Bonaparte himself not been at their head, they would have bothered. But even the Emperor looked in a sorry state, that famous cocked hat so drenched that the flaps had collapsed, were draped absurdly around his shoulders. Three times the charge was sounded, and three times they found themselves floundering in mud that sucked at the legs of their mounts. She could not recall a more infuriating half-league, the English permanently within musket shot yet her weapon useless, like everyone else's, and not a chance of closing the narrow tract of ground that separated them to get within sabre reach.

Indeed, at one stage, the Goddams were turning in their saddles to shout insults at them. But they soon gave up that entertainment and both forces, the English rear-guard and the French van, each wrapped in coats and riding cloaks, heads bent against the rain, slogged on across the desolate terrain beyond the Pebble Farm at the slowest walk Liberté had ever known. More lightning. And each forked flash illuminated their filth, the blackness that was beginning to envelop every one of them. Coal blackness. For the road had been paved here long before, to help with the carrying of coal from the mass of local mines, through the villages to the factory towns of Belgium and beyond. A century or more of endless coal wagons had spread the mineral's grit thick and deep within the surrounding soil.

'Filthy muck,' said Bertine, wiping splashes of the stuff from his face. 'We'll never be rid of it. Why do they bother mining? They could have just harvested it like salt.'

'Don't mention salt,' Falco snarled. 'Can anybody remember when we last ate? Christ, my belly's sticking to my ribs. What I wouldn't give now to hear them sound the Soup.'

'I think I'm too tired to eat anyway,' said Liberté, though 'tired' seemed such an inadequate word. Like 'defenestration' had once been for Fouché. But she was right. Soldiers did not tire, as somebody might do when they had read for too long, or stuffed their stomachs too much, or taken one cup too many of wine or brandy. They became fatigued to the point of emptiness, drained away to nothing, a void in which they continued to function, though only like the living dead. And that was precisely how she felt.

The highway flattened, straightened, stretched past another farm, then another, the French squadrons in two broad columns, one on either side of the road in a way that dogged the steps of the enemy before them, until they arrived at a low ridge, stopped alongside yet a fourth crop of farm buildings that also served as an inn. And, as the squadrons stopped, miraculously, so did the rain. A small cheer went up, and Liberté peered into the grey twilight. The ground dipped ahead of them, a shallow valley filled with crops rising to another ridge beyond. To their left, nearing the farther side, the dark smudge that marked the tail-end of the

English cavalry, some French Horse still on their heels, intermittent cannon fire.

'Are they there, d'you reckon?' said Falco, at her side. 'The English?'

'We'll soon find out,' she said, as the Emperor sent out riders, began to assemble all the available Horse Artillery batteries now at his disposal and deploy them along the rise. But it was slow progress. God's Hooks, it was slow, the gunners having to manhandle the cannons through the quagmire.

What the hell will happen, she wondered, *when we're trying to get the big sisters in place?*

Yet the line of cannons grew steadily longer while more and more cavalrymen came up to form behind them.

So, are they there, or are they not? It was hard to believe that, if the English were on the other side of the valley, they could have resisted such a tempting target.

'They're still on the move then,' said Bertine, drawing the same conclusion. 'Running for Brussels.'

But as he spoke, a single gun fired through the gloom, a shot that accurately struck the Cuirassier regiment on the Dragoons' right flank.

'One gun?' said Falco. 'So it's just the rear-guard again.'

It was like a curse. For the opposing slope suddenly erupted in a sheet of flame that was followed, seconds later, by the salvo's rolling thunder. The entire English artillery train, surely. The French guns answered, each leaping backwards on its twin-trailed carriage as it spat and roared, stinging smoke and sulphurous stench adding to the already gathering gloom. And, once again, as earlier before Genappe, they almost lost the Emperor, a roundshot scattering his entourage in confusion.

I should have told him, Liberté said to herself. *About Fouché's plan. About old Berthier.* She was fifteen again. That day of Revolution when her mother had disappeared. Her wicked secret. About the boy. So that when Maman failed to return, Liberté had blamed herself. The guilt of the Catholic. Prayed to Our Lady, promised never to do it again, promised to confess herself, if only her mother could be sent back to them. But she had sinned with the boy once more only days later and, naturally, her mother never had returned. And it was the same here. She should have made her confession to Bonaparte while she had the chance, had failed to do so, and now look what had happened. Liberté closed her eyes tight, prayed to something, anything, that if the Emperor lived, she would make amends, tell him of her transgression.

'Long live the Emperor!' the cry went up, and Liberté felt that flood of relief when she opened her eyes and spotted the white Arab stallion and its rider, safe and well.

'Not just the rear-guard then,' said Falco.

'What's that behind them?' Bertine peered into the distance.

'If I remember right,' said Liberté, 'there's a decent-sized forest between here and Brussels, isn't there?'

'Soignes,' Falco replied.

'The Roast Beefs are going to fight with a forest at their back?' laughed Bertine. 'Are they crazy?'

The cannon fire was easing as the daylight finally failed, and when the trumpets of the Second eventually sounded, it was not the call to Soup, nor even the Fodder for poor Lucette, but the series of ditties that formed them back into Column of Fours, swung them out of the line as the first infantry companies came in, those poor sods who would spend the night here in this godforsaken place, while the Dragoons plodded back through yet more coal-slimed mud alongside the road to Genappe, back past the Pebble Farm where the Emperor would spend whatever part of the night might be allowed him, back past the bivouacs of his Imperial Guard Grenadiers. Liberté was almost asleep in her saddle, but she came awake briefly, when she heard them singing.

'*Ron, plon, plon, the drum beats on,*' they chanted, and she wondered where, in all this chaos, she might have found Marianne Tambour, the answers to her questions too.

The rain had stopped and that intrepid Sergeant Flambert had taken advantage of the lull to light a lanthorn. He held it aloft at the place where, just as the few bright stars of Genappe's windows came into tantalising sight below them, a lane ran off to the right into pitch blackness.

'This way, my boys,' he called to them. 'This way. We need to keep the highway clear for the Shaveling's Beautiful Daughters. Come on, keep moving. This way.'

But it was not easy to keep moving in this filthy stuff. It was oily, stunk like the pits of hell. Coal, they reckoned.

Coal, thought Marianne. *Imagine having a sack of coal. A grate to start a fire.*

She had lost her clogs an hour before, sucked from her feet by that cloying quagmire, and half the Platoon seemed to be in the same predicament, their boots lost.

'Come on,' she said. 'Push!' And she heaved on the wheel spokes of the cart, while Florisette tugged on the pony's reins. Fronsac, Marle and Argonne had their backs to the cart's tail and Suzanne Prairial attempted to help them. But the mulatta's face was now so pale that it shed almost as much light as Flambert's lanthorn, fading away fast behind them as he directed the rest of the Fourth Company. Prairial's own dolly was still trailing behind the cart and now transporting Argonne's wife, Catherine, for whom the mud had become an impossible challenge. And the pony, Cocotte, was still carrying Prairial's infant, in his gimballed crib, of course.

By the Host, Marianne said to herself, *what a sight we must make.*

Every tortuous turn of the wheels churned up clods of mud, and every step accumulated more of the muck like lead weights on their trouser legs, or the footwear of those still lucky enough to be shod.

'Does this count as looting too?' shouted Fronsac. 'If we steal all the soil from one place and drop it off some place else?'

The track led them down to the banks of a river, a fording place, where they stumbled about in the darkness and were halted, half way across, by a *peloton* of the Guard's Foot Chasseurs, completely lost and coming in the opposite direction.

'Glabais,' one of them said, 'we're looking for Glabais.'

'Well, us too,' said Marle. 'And what d'you think we are, you silly sods? Bloody guides.'

A scuffle broke out, a lot of pushing and shoving, until Sergeant Flambert caught up with them, cursing each of them for a troublesome fool.

'Fools?' said Fronsac. 'It's not our fault we're all pissing around in the dark. Some idiot of a general, as usual. Treasonous buggers, the lot of them.'

'Oh, stow it,' said Marianne. 'Tomorrow we settle with the English, one way or the other. So stop whining.'

What was she going to do with him? He had worn the same hangdog expression all day, suffering the stony recriminations of his fellows in A Platoon with all the fortitude of a martyr, as though he was somehow the injured party in all this, rather than Marianne herself. Indeed, she had begun to feel guilty about it all, then filled with self-loathing for being so gullible.

'Well, it's true,' he complained. 'They're all the same. Even bloody Vicquot. You think he's out here in this swamp? I don't think so. He'll be in some fancy house now, warming his socks by a fire while his servants cook his dinner.'

'Does he *have* a servant?' Marianne asked, as they heaved the cart once more, cleared the river.

'That's splitting hairs,' said Fronsac. 'And what do I care whether we fight the English tomorrow or not?'

'What about the way they treated you on the hulks, Papi?' said Florisette. 'What about that? And the way they killed Maman Cholet?'

'He's out there somewhere,' said Marianne. 'That bastard with the purple face.'

'You can't know that,' said Fronsac.

Yes, I can, she thought. And she *was* sure. Because Liberté Dumont had told her so. Because there was something about Dumont that she had come to trust. More than just Dumont. She could almost see a trail, a sequence of connections. That strange gift of far-seeing, though she could not quite fathom the end. But she patted the *tonnelet* that held her treasure and Maman Cholet's locket.

'If Marianne thinks he's out there,' said Catherine Argonne from Prairial's dog-cart, 'that's good enough for me.'

Not sure I can cope with this new-found companionship, Marianne thought. She had agreed to the Argonnes standing as Poppy's Protectors mainly due to Fronsac's fondness for his friend, but she had never really expected the couple to ever be called upon to fulfil their vows. Yet now, with perhaps the greatest fight of their lives before them? Perhaps it was best to keep things sweet.

'Will you help me cut the bastard's balls off, Catherine?' she shouted.

'If I can catch him, I'll cut him,' laughed Argonne. 'But I doubt I'd be much use to you with this.' She tapped the stump of her leg with the crutch.

'Then put on the peg,' Marianne told her.

'I can't,' Argonne replied. 'I need to keep it safe. It's the only pension I've got. Did nobody tell you?'

'I told her,' said Prairial. She was barely audible. 'I told Marianne about the peg-leg.' It was a sad little statement, spoken to nobody in particular, like a mad woman's rambling.

'There'll be pensions for us all after this one,' said Marianne. 'We beat the English, settle with that purple-faced bugger, and then there'll be peace again. We'll pick up the Revolution where we left off. Women like us, Catherine. All the recognition we deserve. You'll see. The Shaveling will put it all right again.'

She glanced around in the darkness as they pushed their way through a hedge, but nobody picked up her comment. All too busy, she decided, pulling aside those damned branches. And then there was a hamlet to negotiate. Deserted, naturally, and no pickings left after all those who had gone before them. Two more streams, and they struggled into a ploughed field, Sergeant Flambert there, alongside them, and the rain coming down once more.

'This is it, lads,' he told them. 'Welcome to Glabais.'

Fronsac peered all around in the blackness.

'Glabais?' he said. 'What, this field's got a name?'

Flambert waved towards the field's invisible farther side.

'It's over there somewhere,' he replied. 'Now, let's get settled down. Any moans, groans, beefs or bones?'

'Bastard!' somebody shouted.

'Well,' said Marle, 'we've no wood and no straw. It's piddling down with rain. And nobody knows where the rations are. Apart from that, everything's bloody wonderful, Sarge.'

'Look at it this way,' said Flambert. 'You've got this nice ploughed field. It'll be like a feather bed. You'll just sink into it and sleep like babes. And if you turn over in the night, the rain will wash all that shit off the dirty side. You'll look like proper soldiers for the Roast Beefs in the morning.'

'You'll be telling us next,' said Argonne, 'that we should think ourselves lucky we're not a Line Regiment.'

'That's right,' said Marianne. 'Nothing's too good for the Shaveling's brave boys.'

And that's true, of course, she thought. *We've been spoiled. Not used to anything like this since we left the 22nd.*

'Fine bloody promotion this was,' Fronsac complained. 'And where's Vicquot anyway? Not out in the rain, I'll bet.'

'*Captain* Vicquot,' said Flambert, 'will, I'm sure, be taking care of his proper duties. And anyway, Fronsac, you're getting the extra pay, aren't you? What more d'you want? Now get yourselves sorted out.'

They struggled to get the small canteen tent erected, though the rain defied every effort to light a fire.

'What am I going to do with this now?' called Muhler, holding up a rabbit that, somehow, he had acquired during the day.' But there were no sensible suggestions so he flung the thing away, heard it splash somewhere in a puddle.'

Some of the older hands managed to rig their own shelters, using the same techniques they had employed before Fleurus to cope with a blazing sun, but that only triggered another bout of miserable nostalgia. And more grumbling, of course, mainly about the officers. Until, from the darkness, they heard a horse and rider slopping through the sludge, Captain Vicquot with a couple of sacks hanging from his saddle. He was coughing, looked sickly, but tossed the bags down to Marianne.

'Here,' he said, 'I've been out foraging. Not that there's much around. But there's some stale bread. And three cooked hams. A bit of cheese too. Hardly enough to feed the whole Company, Tambour, but see what you can do, eh?'

'No fishes to go with the loaves?' she sneered.

'Afraid not,' he replied. 'But all the water you could ever want, if you'd care to turn some of it to wine.'

'I wish I'd taken up that offer to buy Bufanda's stock now,' she said.

'Where the hell do you think half of this stuff came from?' Vicquot replied. 'Cost me a fair few francs though. I'll need another loan to pay it all off.'

'Well, you needn't come to me for one,' she told him. 'Not after dragging me through that nonsense over the hen.'

She did her best, all the same. Unloaded the last of her own supplies, added them to the food that Vicquot had brought in, and tried to separate the provender into roughly equal rations to feed the whole Company. It was pathetically little and some of the men had simply fallen asleep, exhausted, without eating even a morsel. The food was small comfort to those still awake, but comfort all the same.

And comfort seemed to be her main concern, as she surrendered the canteen tent – to Poppy, naturally; to Catherine Argonne too, who nestled herself against the girl; to Suzanne Prairial, raving constantly now in her Breton tongue; and to Prairial's baby, that Marianne had tried to fortify with a spot of brandy mixed with his milk, but who had now given up even the attempt to mewl.

Comfort, she thought. *I bet Hawk-face is sitting pretty though. Those horse-boys always know how to look after themselves.* But she missed the woman, wondered where she might be at this moment. Almost midnight, she guessed.

'Just a bit of comfort,' whispered Fronsac, as he crouched beside her under the cart. 'That's all it was, Cabbage. With Bufanda. You were gone and I needed some comfort.'

'Don't call me that, you fool,' she hissed. 'I'm not your bloody Cabbage. And gone? What d'you mean, gone? I was out there, surrounded by sodding Prussos, trying to fetch back our daughter. *Your* daughter. You couldn't keep it inside your breeches for even that long. So guess what? I suppose I'll now have that Spanish bitch chasing after me with a knife, the same as Lomballe did.'

'You'll soon be as famous as Dupont,' he said. 'Or Fournier.'

Wonderful, she thought. *They're famous right enough.* The two officers had become something of a legend. Dupont had simply delivered a message to Fournier, who had taken offence at its content. So he blamed the messenger, challenged him to a duel. The result had been inconclusive, so another had been arranged. And another. Thirty of the damned things in total, over nineteen years and the affair only settled around the time of Leipzig.

'Is that what I've got to look forward to?' she said, but, in truth, she missed hearing news of their latest scraps. Soldiers had become zealous supporters, partisans, for one man or the other, Dupont or Fournier Clubs springing up in every regiment, wagers laid.

'Well, you've got a reputation of your own now,' he said. 'It makes me proud.'

She felt him edge closer.

'I felt sorry for the woman,' she said, 'when they shaved her head like that.'

'You're right,' he murmured, 'she didn't deserve that.'

'Of course she deserved it,' Marianne snarled. 'But I still felt sorry for her.'

'You're a good woman, Tambour. The best.'

'And what now?' she said. 'You expect some comfort from me too?'

He moved closer still, and she felt his hand touch her nankeen trousers.

'Big fight tomorrow,' Fronsac whispered. 'You never know what might happen.'

'You've got some bloody nerve,' she said. 'And here? Slopping around in the mud like a pair of pigs?'

'Well...' he began, and slipped his hand inside the soaked russet jacket, up under her shirt, then pulled back when his fingers came in contact with the hilt of the little dagger. *Christ's Teeth*, she thought, *what am I doing? But he's not the only one who needs some comfort tonight.* And at least she could not see his ugly nose and blotched, liverish skin in the dark. 'Well, you never know,' he went on, 'we could always start another little one.'

She could have laughed. As if she would bring another babe into this madness. *And how little he knows me*, she thought. *After all this time, he's never worked out that I don't bleed on campaign. No bleed, no babes. Men are such sodding idiots.*

Chapter Twenty-Seven

Sunday 18th June 1815, 4.00am

She awoke and had no idea where she might be, but her face was buried in Lucette's coarse mane and the familiar scent of the Percheron's still damp pelt was heavy in her nostrils.

Wounded, thought Liberté. *I must have been wounded.* How? At Genappe? At Quatre Bras? Or something to do with that assassin of Fouché's. Or Thénardier. *No, none of those*, she recalled. Just the damned weather. The wound to her pride. For she had always believed herself capable of sleeping anywhere, so long as there was time to do so. From the deserts of Syria to the frozen forests of the east. Yet last night it had been beyond her, the most miserable, the longest of her campaigning life.

She lifted her head, the heavy helmet still fastened under her chin and the crest's black horsehair tail clinging, cold, damp and itchy, to her neck. There were shafts of light beginning to pierce the greyness, the rain slackening to a light drizzle. Looking along the line of picketed horses, she saw that she was not alone. Others had followed her example and, unable to sleep anywhere on the ground, had bare-backed, stretched themselves out along the necks of the mounts, wrapped themselves in their cloaks, and snatched whatever rest might be possible. Liberté, arms and legs dangling, felt Lucette shifting beneath her, the Percheron twisting its neck to nuzzle at the gauntleted fingers that lay against her shoulder, and then lick them.

'I know, beauty,' said Liberté. 'We'll get you fed soon.'

She eased herself upright, looked around at the miserable sight before her. The Regiment had been allocated its bivouac site and picket lines on precisely the same plateau where, yesterday evening, they had fought the English Hussars. It was just another reason for the disturbed night, the low moaning of those too badly wounded to move but not yet ready to die.

'I've never understood it, have you?' said Falco. He was a couple of horses away but also trying to straighten himself after the ordeal of the past hours.

She knew what he meant. It was a familiar topic.

'I have not,' she replied. 'We take all that care to shoot the horses. Put them out of their misery, isn't that what we say? Then we leave these poor buggers writhing around until they die like dogs.'

'Don't let that happen to me, will you?' he said.

'Nothing's going to happen to you, Falco,' Liberté replied. 'You're too bad to die young.'

'It's not the dying that bothers me,' said the trooper. 'It's the bit beforehand.'

The Reveille was sounded an hour later.

Did you ever know that whore from Nancy...?

Liberté wondered how many thousands of cavalrymen were roused from their rest each morning with the unconscious association in their brains that instantly linked that much-maligned town with the indelible concept of prostitution.

The morning brightened perceptibly, the drizzle abating some more and, while she folded the oilskin with which she had tried to protect her saddle and tack, the trumpets called the infirm and the malingerer to Sick Parade.

And there will be a few of those today, she thought.

At Fodder, she unstrapped both the sack that held the last of her oats and also the netting bag with its wet straw, and left Lucette feeding while she went down to the stream and fetched water, for her own wash and to quench the Percheron's thirst.

The notes of the Soup invited troopers to dine next, but most of the rations were ruined and their supply wagons had not appeared. Besides, that witch of a canteen-mistress, with her bad breath and manners, her fancy Spanish shako, was also either cleaned out of merchandise or holding on to her goods until she could squeeze up the prices later. So Sergeant Tranchante, sweet man, sent some of them off to forage in the local villages.

'Not worth bothering with Genappe,' she told the rest of the detail and, at the same time, off to the east a church bell began to peal. They could see the steeple's tip above some trees. 'First call to early Mass,' she said. 'Come on, let's try there.'

They followed a likely track and soon found themselves in a single street of houses in a shallow dip, a stream running along its bottom. The street crossed this rivulet at a fording place and headed south, but another cobbled road led Liberté and her party uphill to more dwellings, mostly thatched cottages, their line broken in the centre where the road curved by a white stone church, itself surrounded by a graveyard, this too on sloping ground. Above and beyond the church, a large farm and, between farm and church, standing in the thoroughfare, a priest with hands thrust inside his cassock.

'Parishioners all still in their beds, Father?' said Bertine.

'Good morning to you, my sons.' He paused, confusion followed by contempt on his pinched features as he noticed Liberté. 'Have you come to confess your sins then?'

The troopers all looked at her too.

'What?' said Falco. You think...? With Dumont?' He roared with laughter. 'This one's more chaste than the Holy Virgin. Her only sins are all matters of omission, Father. The Chosen Man for our little Section, but she doesn't feed us well. That's why we're here.'

'You'll find nothing in Plancenoit, if it's looting you're about.' But he cast an anxious backward glance at his church.

'You needn't worry about us, Father,' Liberté told him. 'We're just looking for food. Although we'll maybe be back for the altar wine if we can't find anything better.'

'Ah, more of Bonaparte's heretics,' said the priest. 'But you're wasting your time. The village folk are all gone, taken everything with them. Fled yesterday when they knew you were coming to liberate them.'

'Not all heretics, Father,' said Liberté. 'And, if you've no congregation here, you'll find plenty who'd appreciate your blessing, maybe even a full Mass, just over yonder.' She pointed away to the northwest, where she knew their battle lines would form.

Well, it's true, she thought. *Most of the lads still like to hedge their bets when it comes to mortality.* Perfectly reasonable, given the nature of their business though, for herself, she mostly shared the Shaveling's belief – as Fouché had reminded her – that all religions owe their origins to man, not God. But if she was forced to pick one, she would most likely have settled with the Mahometans. At least it was less absurd than the nonsense spouted by priests like this one.

'And would your Emperor welcome the Word of the Lord among his men?' He stressed the final word.

'Why not?' said Falco. 'In France we have three Church Feasts every year again now. Three: Ascension Day; All Saints, and... oh, bugger, what's the third? I can never remember.'

The others laughed.

'Take no notice of him, Father,' he's just a fool,' said Liberté, reflecting that it had been an accommodation Bonaparte had famously reached with the Church of Rome in his efforts to put an end to the anti-revolutionary antics of black-robes like this one. And the Church had swallowed it all with good grace and considerable relief, its wealth protected, allowing the Shaveling to write his own Imperial Catechism, confirming that Bonaparte himself was "raised up by God." The hypocrisy of it all brought a sneer to Liberté's lips, which she quickly masked with a friendly smile.

'Well,' said the priest, 'I would be lacking in my duty if I did not offer the sacraments to honest believers.'

'That's the style, Father,' said Bertine. 'You can get about the Lord's work, and we'll look after our own. With a bit of luck, you can then settle down to a nice peaceful day. We'll try not to disturb your Sunday too much.'

*

They returned to the bivouac area as the Mass bells rang for the third and final time – seven o' the clock, Marianne assumed – while, ahead, some clown was blowing the Douse Fires.

'That's what I like,' said Bertine, 'a regimental trumpeter with a sense of humour.'

They had not passed a single cook pot in action all the way back, simply more huddles of tired men chewing miserably on their reserve rations. But the patrol had done reasonably well. Some negligent villagers of Plancenoit had made a poor fist of hiding their store of root vegetables, and there was more cheese as well, at the inn. A decent haul of wine bottles there too. And another of the foraging details had done even better, fetched back some meat that might be slightly on the turn yet would suffice for a soup. There was bread too.

'We've just had orders,' Sergeant Tranchante told them, as they rode in. 'We're to be ready for the march by nine. That gives us two hours to rustle up some food and get cleaned up.'

'Soup?' said Liberté. 'We've just heard Fires Out.'

'Ignore that,' said Tranchante. 'Some of the boys have gathered a bit of dried firewood, so we're laughing.' There was a small stack of house furniture piled up behind him.

'And did you say something about cleaning up, Sarge?' said Falco.

'That's right. The Shaveling wants us all ship-shape before we hit the road. Need to show the Goddams what a proper army looks like. But not you, Dumont. You'll have to get yourself sorted later. You're wanted at Headquarters.'

'Hey,' said Bertine, 'give him our regards, won't you?'

At the Pebble Farm, the Emperor was just eating breakfast, but General Flahaut instructed Liberté to wait in the room already occupied by several Aides. For lack of a chair, she squeezed through them and stood alongside the open doorway to the adjoining chamber where she had met the Shaveling last night. The secretaries were gone now, but the campaign cot and strewn bedding remained. Flahaut seemed content for her to stay there even though, from beyond the bedchamber, she could hear the imperial entourage digesting the day's news as loudly and readily as their bacon. Ney blustered, recognisable by that Germanic Lorraine accent of his, that Wellesley was now in full retreat, but Bonaparte believed not a word. Yet he sent for Flahaut, all the same, issued an order that Count d'Erlon should check out the situation. And while Flahaut arranged his notes and couriers, Liberté picked up Soult's voice too, nervous, hoping that Ney was correct, that the English would run rather than show that dangerous resolve he had seen in them at first-hand. And he dared suggest that it may have been a mistake to dispatch so many men with Grouchy's Right Wing when the bulk of those 33,000 men might have been better utilised here, to deal with Wellesley. The Shaveling dismissed this too, insisted that the English were bad soldiers, ineffectually led, easily defeated. Somebody else tabled a report of troop movement away to the east, far to the east. The Prussians, it was suggested And another story, from the waiter at an inn back in Genappe. Wellesley ate there on the previous day, had been boasting openly of making a stand before the Forest of Soignes and holding there until Blücher came to support them. But how could this be, she heard the Emperor insist, when the Prussians had been so badly beaten at Fleurus, at Ligny? It would take Blücher two days at least to bring his defeated forces here. And, in any case, Grouchy and the entire Right Wing, those same 33,000 men, stood between this place and the Prussians.

'Well,' Bonaparte said to her when the breakfast was over and his senior officers, the Marshals of France, his brother Jérôme, were dispatched to their duties, not even the secretaries present, 'you heard all that?'

'I did, Sire,' she replied. 'And might I comment?'

'I would value your opinion, as I always have, Trooper Dumont,' he said. 'But I only have a few moments. I must go and see for myself whether this nonsense of Ney's has any substance. About Wellesley still retreating. And there is something I need from you.'

'Then I must say that I fought the English in Spain. Their skirted Scotsmen too. Give them a position to defend, Sire, and they are the very devil.'

'I know that,' said Bonaparte. 'But today my generals need fire in their bellies, not the truth.'

'And the Prussians, Sire. I saw them on Friday night, moving through Mellery. They looked far from finished, and still close to our flanks.'

'That too, my dear, I understand. But they cannot get here in time to save Wellesley. One swift hammer blow against the English and France will be free of them. Forever, I hope. Now, tell me the truth of this errand upon which Fouché sent you. It was to meet Wellesley himself, was it not?' So she told him. All of it. Felt the confession lift the weight from her shoulders. 'It might have worked too,' he said when she had finished. 'Reveal my campaign plans to buy the Duke's confidence. It hardly mattered, after all. They were barely secret, and my plans are never rigid in any case. How could they be? Then frighten him with the risk that he would be cut off from the sea. They say that God moves in mysterious ways, Dumont. But God could take a lesson or two from Joseph Fouché.'

'There's something else too, Sire,' she said. 'About Marshal Berthier.'

He held up a hand to stop her.

'Whatever it was,' he said, 'it is not worth the telling now. In any case, I have my own mission for you.'

'Anything, Sire,' she said. 'But it will not take me from today's reckoning, I trust?'

'No, my dear, it will not. We need every one of you today. And I wish we had more. Soult may be right about sending Grouchy off with so many of our best. A fraction would have sufficed to keep Blücher off our backs. But we will prevail, all the same. You understand that, Dumont? We *will* prevail. But if things go badly in some way that I cannot foresee, there is this…' He went to his personal writing box, lifted the lid and produced an envelope bearing the imperial seal. It was addressed to *Napoléon François Charles Joseph Bonaparte, Prince Imperial of France, King of Rome, Prince of Parma.* Liberté knew that, by that disgraceful treaty of the previous year, following the Emperor's abdication, these were mostly titles that had been stripped from the boy. 'For my son,' he said. 'Though I need you to find some way of getting it to this man.' He turned the envelope over, showed her a penciled name with which she was unfamiliar. 'He is a trusted member of my wife's suite. You should find him at the Schönbrunn.'

'But, Sire…' She was filled with dread, a hollow pit in her guts that was far more than the lack of soup. Liberté, like many others in France, had felt bereaved when he divorced the Empress Josephine, five years earlier. But they needed an heir to the throne and she had been unable to deliver him a son. Of course, everybody knew there must be another story behind the official line, yet it was all so sudden, his second marriage, to Marie-Louise of Austria, taking place just three months later and, within a year, the birth of the boy.

How much we all wished, she recalled, *that it had been Josephine who had given him the son.*

'It is nothing, Dumont. But we go into battle today. And every good soldier should be prepared, do you not think? I have been plagued with absurd dreams. Nothing, I expect… Still,' Bonaparte remembered himself, 'when all goes well, as I expect, you may give the thing back to me. Now, Fouché paid you for the mission, I assume?'

'You may recall, Sire, that my further secondment to the Minister of Police's service meant that I was not able to take the imperial bounty. Minister Fouché therefore promised that I would receive the equivalent, fifteen hundred francs, from his own hand.'

'And you received it?'

'Simply a down payment. Five gold Napoléons, Sire.'

'You expect to receive the rest?'

She paused.

'I do not, Sire.'

She had paused too long, made him suspicious.

'I thought as much. Fouché didn't expect you to live long enough for the balance to be collected, I imagine.' Liberté said nothing. 'Flahaut,' the Emperor called and, when the General entered, he ordered Trooper Dumont to be paid the outstanding seventy coins. Flahaut was surprised, but naturally did not argue. 'No, wait,' said Bonaparte, 'I have a better idea. Pay her in stones, Flahaut. Easier to carry. But weigh them carefully.'

'Sire, I had not expected…' Liberté tried to say. Stones? Her mind went instantly to the diamonds that Fouché had told her were hidden in the dormeuse.

What an irony if she should now be paid from this cache. And all the world suddenly seemed focused on the unforeseen. The Emperor's letter to his boy. Fouché's concern for those same diamonds. '*If there is a threat of danger to the Emperor's dormeuse,*' he had said, '*you will liberate the diamonds and return them to me.*'

'It is France's debt to you, Dumont. And the task that I've given you, well, I cannot promise to pay for that also. The stones must suffice. Now look, the wind is coming up and the rain has gone off, at last. As always, it will be the Grand Battery that wins for us today, as soon as the ground dries and we can manoeuvre the guns. This wind will help, don't you think? By the time I've checked that Wellesley still stands…' Yet he must have seen the uncertainty on her face. 'What, something else?'

She hesitated, wanted to tell him how much they loved him. But it seemed inadequate, infantile.

'We are all with you, Sire,' she said. 'All France stands at your side today.'

He nodded, turned away towards the window.

'Yes, yes.' His voice sounded strange. 'Now, about our business. Unless…?

'There is one thing more, Sire. Might I have leave to visit the Fourth Regiment of Grenadiers? There is somebody there…'

He spun around.

'Well,' he said, 'you still have some form of safeguard from Fouché, I imagine?'

'I do, Sire.'

'Then use it, Trooper Dumont, with my blessing. But what is this? You've found a lover, at last?'

'No, Sire, a friend. You'll remember her perhaps? The canteen-mistress of the Second Battalion. We were together, when you rode through the lines on the morning after Ligny. You asked her if she knew me.'

And yes, he remembered the woman, the one with the over-priced brandy.

They buried Suzanne Prairial just before the appointed hour for the Battalion to hit the road. Marianne laid the babe beside her in the shallow grave and said her silent farewells while the mulatta's husband, the First Company's Josef Wybicki, shovelled mud over them both, mumbled prayers in Polish, and planted a crude wooden cross that refused to stand upright in the manure-soaked sludge.

Marianne had been awoken in the middle of the night by the Breton girl's weak sobbing, freed herself from Fronsac's snoring embrace, and crawled into the canteen tent to find the infant already dead and his mother not far from joining him. The mulatta rambled for another hour, cursed her mother for sending for her, for succumbing to the fever, for bequeathing her like a family heirloom to the Pole. In between, she fell into a child's voice, spoke only in Breton. And then she simply drifted away. Prairial had been with the army for no more than two years and, by Marianne's calculation, she was little more than eighteen years old.

Yet she felt vaguely vexed, as though the girl and her child had both somehow wasted her precious time. All that effort with the birthing.

'Not many of us left,' whispered Catherine Argonne.

Hardly worth an answer, but she pulled Florisette closer to her, looked around the grave at the others gathered here. At those few men from the First and Fourth Companies who had bothered to attend. At Marle, and Argonne's husband. At Fronsac and Cazajus. And at the strange Italian boy with the beautiful eyes who had arrived just after the Diana had been played. He was a boy indeed, but wearing the ill-fitting uniform of the 4th Hussars, dark blue dolman and badly slung red pelisse, each with yellow braiding.

'If you please,' he had said to her, while she was preparing the dead for their final rest, 'do you know where I might find my regiment?'

Catherine Argonne had teased him about whether he was strong enough to wield the sabre that he carried, suggested he might do better with a gun. And then his sorry tale had begun to unfold. His own possessions stolen from him by a sallow-faced rogue in Hessian boots and with a pregnant wife, a small child too. Somewhere back near Frasnes. The boy had bought the uniform because he wanted to fight. For France. He was Italian, he had told them. Fabrizio. And he owed the Emperor for their freedom from the Austrians. Twenty-one years old, he had said. The lying little sod.

Wybicki still struggled to mount the wooden cross, carved with Prairial's name and that of the child.

Too tiny, thought Marianne, *to be buried with such a man's name, Josef.*

But at least they made a presentable sight now. The Shaveling had decreed that they should eat and then clean themselves, so the entire Battalion had taken up the task with enthusiasm, for the idea of fighting caked in their own filth was unthinkable, a serious slight upon the honour of France. So mud had been scraped patiently from campaign trousers, from tunics, from their blue summer greatcoats, from knapsacks, and from whatever headgear had been issued to them, whether it was shako or bearskin, or simple forage cap. Spit served as polish for cartridge pouch, bayonet sheath and cross-belts. Weapons were cleaned, serviced and readied. And that left only the shoes. Most of the men carried one or more spares, along with replacement soles and a stock of hobnails. But it took Marianne a while to find somebody with a small pair that she could use to replace her lost clogs. Yet shoes only came in three sizes, and even these smalls had to be packed with straw before they were almost comfortable.

'I'll be crippled by the end of the day,' she said.

'It's the strange thing about feet,' the Italian boy replied. 'They're different shapes, left and right. But shoes are all one shape. Boots the same. Just imagine how much better they'd be if they were made to fit each foot.'

Marianne shook her head in disbelief.

'Can you imagine what that would cost?' she said. 'Different shoes for left and right? And you're not really twenty-one, are you? Admit it. You can't be a day over seventeen.'

His face flushed.

'How did you know?' he asked her.

'And you're here because there's some little girl back home that you want to impress. Brave Fabrizio, soldier of fortune. But you're more likely to get yourself killed, boy, if you're not careful. Just look at that broken old nag you're riding. Some peasant's horse, only fit for the knacker's yard. It'll fail you at the first shot!'

''Leave the boy alone, Marianne,' said Catherine Argonne. 'He's come all this way to save us from the English, after all.' And, as she spoke, the drums beat the Assembly.

Platoons fell in by Sections, Sections formed Companies, Companies extended into Battalion Column, while Marianne unlashed Suzanne Prairial's small dog-cart, refused all help, hauled and sweated the thing through the mud and left it like a monument, a marker, for the mulatta's final resting place. It was the least she could do to atone for feeling vexed earlier. Then she harnessed the pony, Cocotte, set Poppy and Catherine Argonne on her own cart.

'Come on then,' she said to the Italian, 'you'd best stick with us for a while.' There were hoof beats, and she looked up to see the familiar grey that belonged to Hawk-face riding up the flank of the column. 'Ah,' she pointed, 'now here's somebody who can tell you all about horseflesh.'

Chapter Twenty-Eight

Sunday 18th June 1815, 9.30am

'I don't think I've ever seen anything quite like it,' said Liberté.

They had reached a rise in the largely flat and slightly undulating countryside, a rise that might serve as a vantage point, and demanded that she should climb upon the cart to tell them what she could discern. But even those of their small and mournful party, without the benefit of a Dragoon's practised eye, nor the additional height afforded by the tumbril, could not fail to be caught up in the general magnificence and precision of it all. This army beast was as far removed from the miserable, scattered and mud-soaked rabble of the night before than anything Liberté could imagine. True, they were very far from the polished brilliance of parade dress, yet the orders had arrived thick and fast, Aides-de-Camps swarming in every direction with the schedule that set each unit in motion at the allotted time and in the correct position within its column. Bonaparte's genius writ large upon the golden page of the Belgian plain. Bands played and, above the sweat and leather smells of regiments on the march, there was that wonderful summer morning scent of wheat fields after rain, swallows and swifts darting and diving around their heads.

'How many columns?' asked the one-legged woman, Argonne, trying to lift herself from the mostly empty sacks on which she was perched. She was having difficulty seeing very much herself for the constant passage of their own Guard battalions on every side.

'Eleven, I think,' Liberté called down, though it was hard to tell. Such an expanse of terrain, and the columns sometimes seemed to merge or multiply. In any case, each column itself was formed by two or three different parallel serpents, and those columns divided into two phases. 'The front line's mostly in place. Light Horse over on the far left.' She could tell Lights from Heavies simply by their motion. 'Then an Infantry Corps.' She turned, so that she could look due north. 'Another Infantry Corps ahead of us. More Light Horse off to the right.'

'Can you see the 4th Hussars?' shouted the strange young Italian in the ill-fitting dark blue and scarlet, whose fur busby kept falling over his eyes. Tambour seemed to have adopted him as some form of mascot, though where she had found the lad, Liberté did not yet know. But he was clearly no cavalryman, though he kept up a perpetual stream of boyish blather about horses and swords. Liberté would have ignored him, but it was a good question. *4th Hussars?* she wondered, then realised that she knew the answer after all. The only Hussars with the main army were those she had already seen, at Genappe. Marbot's Fighting 7th. And the rest...? She made a great play of turning to the east, stretching herself on the tips of her toes, cupping her hands above her eyes to keep out the glare of that watery sun.

'Ah, yes,' she said. 'I have them now. 4th Hussars, you say? Four leagues away. No, five, more likely.'

'Four leagues?' said the lad. 'Can you really...?'

'She's taking the piss,' Tambour told him, then looked up at Liberté. 'Are the 4th with Grouchy?'

'Yes, I think so. Anyway, what does it matter? If that boy's with the 4th then I'm a Dutchman.'

'Never mind all that,' said Argonne. 'Is the second line in place yet?'

'Second line still coming up behind,' she replied, and felt a surge of pride when she recognised the Heavies of the Third Cavalry Corps, though she could not make out her own unit. But the sunlight glistening on the breastplates of Kellerman's Cuirassiers was unmistakable. 'Heavy Cavalry on the left. Then another Infantry Corps. Light Horse here again, just off to the right. Then the other Cuirassier Corps.' This would be Milhaud's men, she calculated.

Liberté did not bother to describe the eleventh column, their own, coming up at the rear, for they were parked in the very middle of it, although even here the Imperial Guard was divided into its component parts: their own Heavy Cavalry on the left flank, two dozen battalions of Foot and their artillery batteries in the centre, and the mounted Chasseurs with the Guard Lancers off to their right and rear.

'I can't see anything but legs,' shouted the child, Florisette.

'Well, that won't do,' Liberté told her. 'It's not every day you get a sight like this one. She crouched down, stretched out her arms to take the girl up. 'What's the matter?' she said. 'You're not afraid of me, are you?' The kid came forward reluctantly, but Liberté lifted her easily, held her as high as she was able, pressing Poppy against the green wool of her jacket's shoulder. 'There,' she whispered, 'what about that? Seventy-five thousand soldiers, all as neat as you like. Every one of them in the exact place and time that the Emperor has decreed.'

'He knows Maman,' said the girl. She seemed shy, unusually so for an army brat. 'The Emperor.'

'Yes,' Liberté replied. 'He does,'

Marianne remembered what Poppy had said about Hawk-face, about how the Dragoon Lady frightened the child. Like looking at a shadow, she had said. *No, like looking at* my *shadow*, she corrected herself.

She was mounted once more behind the woman on that big grey of hers. All very mysterious. The chat she had mentioned. They needed to have it now, apparently. Somewhere private.

'Where are we heading?' said Marianne. 'What's all the mystery about?

But the woman did not reply, simply set the horse to a brisk trot that shook every bone in Tambour's body, as though this were answer and punishment, both.

'Hang on!' shouted the Dragoon, but Marianne had already done so. Plodding about on Cocotte was one thing, but she was no rider.

They skirted one large farm, around which the leading troops of the Imperial Guard – the Young Guard's eight battalions of *Tirailleurs* and *Voltigeurs* – were coming to a halt, and the couple soon closed upon a second. At least, it looked like a farm but, on inspection, it more closely resembled an inn. There was a coterie of generals here, along with their Aides and attendants, but no sign of the Shaveling. Yet at least Hawk-face had slowed Lucette to a less uncomfortable walk once more, as she rode the horse past the building's west-facing façade, its stone walls, its doors, windows, and red-tiled roof.

'This is the place,' said Dumont. 'I was here last night. Look, the English.' She pointed across the shallow valley ahead of them and, sure enough, there were dark scarlet smudges over there, within cannon shot. 'Your purple-faced sergeant's somewhere among them.'

Marianne felt a shiver of fear, then swelling anger as she thought of him, but Hawk-face had already turned the horse along the building's northern wall. There were no doors and no windows on this side. Just a sign written in large black letters.

'*The Hotel of the Beautiful Alliance*?' said Marianne. The name implied more than a formal union, of course. There was friendship hidden in its meaning too. Intimacy. 'That what you think we've got, lady?'

'We'll see,' said the woman, turning another corner. There was a barn here, a patchwork wall of stone and brick topped by a thatch, and through the open sections they could see the inn's yard, and a well, complete with a slated pyramid-shaped roof. A narrow track led eastwards to another collection of buildings, more barns, some derelict sheds, a few pigsties, the whole bunch surrounded by stunted apple trees displaying the first miniature fruits of their future bitter crop. 'This will do,' said the Dragoon. 'Get down.' It was something less than an order, and just as well, for Marianne Tambour did not take kindly to orders. But the woman's tone had something of Maman Cholet's ways about it, something of authority, but protection too.

Dumont tethered her mount to a broken branch and squatted in the long, still damp grass, set her back against the gnarled trunk and unfastened the chinstrap, eased the helmet from her head.

'Better?' said Marianne, over the noise of tramping feet, shouted commands and bandsmen, just a stone's throw on the other side of their hideaway.

'Better if we could share a pipe,' said the Dragoon, and she looked around, as though seeking the possibility of a flame.

'I took my first pipe the day some fellow first took me,' Marianne told her, then thought about Fronsac and last night. 'The weed still gets better with every smoke,' she went on, 'but the other sours at every rut.'

'Then we'll just have to make do with that rotgut of yours. The Shaveling tells me it's over-priced though.'

'Only to officers,' Marianne laughed, proud that they must have discussed her and that the Shaveling remembered. Yet she was wondering again what this was all about, as she unslung the *tonnelet*, removed two of the small metal cups from their hooks. And she caught Hawk-face's hungry gaze follow the cask's every movement. Something far more than a simple craving for the liquor.

'The staler the life, the sweeter the brandy. Isn't that what they reckon?' said Dumont, but in that way of people who are simply making chatter, avoiding the big issue.

'Why don't you just gob it up and spit it out? Whatever it is you want to say.'

The woman lifted the tails of her green coat with their red linings turned back, delved into the waistband of her overalls, drew out a tiny silk purse.

'Know what this is worth?' she said, shaking the thing but producing only a slight scratching within, not the solid sound of honest gold.

'More than a sow's ear, I suspect.'

'How large a sack would we need for seventy gold Napoléons?'

'Not huge,' said Marianne. But she tried to imagine her attempts at forcing such a volume of coins into the back of her cask.

'Too big to fit in that,' said Hawk-face, and pointed at the *tonnelet*. 'I need you to keep these for me. In there, if you please.' She jabbed her finger at the cask again, for emphasis.

Marianne knew there was more to come, but she opened the hidden compartment anyway, as furtively as she was able, masking the mechanism as a child embraces its precious food when the bowl has been empty for days. Then she snatched the small purse, rubbed the hard contents between her fingers, knew them for what they were.

'Bonaparte's diamonds,' she said. 'Is this all he's got?'

The Dragoon laughed at her.

'Like I told you, there's a whole tea case full of them. A fortune. France's fortune. But these? You must guard them. All the same, you see how I trust you, Tambour. You have my diamonds. These are my tokens to you.' She waved a hand towards the back of the inn. 'A token of our beautiful alliance. Now, what about something in return?'

I knew it, thought Marianne, though she had no idea what this crazy woman might want from her. She had met all sorts in her time. In the army.

On campaign. Through the villages, towns and cities of all Europe. Hard women, some of them. Whores of a dozen different varieties. Pussy-fisters. Peach-eaters. Thieves and cardsharps. Child-slavers. But this one simply did not fit the images.

'What is it?' she said. 'I don't go in for any weird stuff. And, as for your bloody tokens, what the hell d'you think they're worth to me? A fistful of diamonds that I'd never be able to fence in a month of Sundays. You can have them back, if you like. Here!' And she flung the silk purse at Hawk-face, who caught it neatly, left-handed while the horse, Lucette, lowered its face, brought its muzzle up sharply, smacked it against the side of Marianne's face, knocking her bonnet all askew.

'She hates raised voices,' said the woman. 'Fine in battle. Will ride through hell. But not good when the lads fall out with each other.'

Marianne took off the bonnet completely, tied it around the shoulder strap of the cask.

'I apologise to the horse,' she said. 'But I mean it. About the tokens.'

Dumont was tossing the purse of diamonds up and down on her palm.

'You know,' she said, 'it took a long time for me to swallow the fact that the woman in Charleroi was really trying to kill you, and not me. But I can see it now. It must have been an easy mistake for her to make. Just her bad luck that I'd chosen a jacket and bonnet like your own. But that wasn't the only thing that fooled her, was it?' *Here she goes again*, thought Marianne, but her instincts were pricking at her. Something like danger. Close. 'Show me what you keep hidden,' Hawk-face said to her.

The *tonnelet* was still in Marianne's lap, and she turned it slowly, lifted out the sacking with her own savings, and then the piece of oiled paper that held Maman Cholet's locket.

'This?' she dangled it from its slender chain, so that the gold caught the sunlight as it spun.

Marianne was cautious of the locket at night, had made the mistake of falling asleep sometimes with it clasped in her hand, and had always drifted straight to that awful nightmare of Saint-Sébastien. The woman at her side seemed to read her fear.

'No, Marianne,' she said. 'Today, we hold it together. I think there's maybe a journey we have to make. That's what I need from you. Make that journey by my side?'

'I think I'm happy where I am,' Marianne told her, though she knew it was not true. There was always an empty place inside her. And happy here, when all she dreamed about was the chance to take Poppy and run?

'Don't be afraid,' Hawk-face said. 'I knew it after Mellery. Remember, I said that we made a good team? But it was more than that.' She tossed the silk purse back to Marianne, stretched out her fingers so they framed the locket that still flashed golden as it turned, slowing. 'We need to hold it together. Yet only if you're ready.'

Marianne jerked the chain, the precious thing spirallinging up through the air, landing on her own palm, the engraved letter 'C' facing upwards.

'Heads,' she said. 'You win.' She extended her hand slowly towards the Dragoon, open as an offering, and she felt the woman's flesh make charged contact with her own, their fists closing together.

Another ocean of time and space to cross, a tunnel of blackness, their hands clasped about the locket as the two women spun together through the aether. Their union illuminated for Marianne those things that Liberté had already seen. The Paris apartment. An image of a girl, aged about fifteen. The girl's mother and the unborn child. The mother's concern for her husband. The storm outside that was the source of that concern. Paris in turmoil.

'No, my dear,' the mother said, 'you must stay and care for the little ones. I have to find your father.'

'But Maman,' the girl replied, 'the baby!'

Yet the mother left the apartment anyway, out onto the street, away from the sounds of cannon fire in the stifling summer's heat. She cradled her swollen belly, trying to keep to her own shaded side of the road. An enormous stone and marble fountain. Expensive mansions. A ragged group of men, women and children, hauling a field piece, pushing an ammunition cart.

'To the Saint-Antoine!' they yelled. 'To the Bastille!'

In response to her questions, they confirmed that the Invalides was still held, and that was good since she believed the Invalides had been her husband's intended destination. She pressed on, the crowd growing thicker, more raucous, until she finally reached the building's moated boundary, where citizens of the Revolution were trying to free an enormous siege gun, the wheel of which had become firmly jammed around a gateway bollard. A horseman cavorted back and forth.

'No,' he yelled. 'Use the handspikes. The handspikes!'

The woman moved on, tried to cross the bridge, until that fool of a horseman side-stepped his mount towards her. It loomed up, until she could see nothing but its coarse pelt, the smell of the creature filling her nostrils. She tried to avoid its skittering, fearsome hooves. And as she moved away, her own shoe caught on the lower step of the gatehouse. She fell badly, head smacking against the paved road, shrieking with an intolerable pain that jolted through her whole body.

Marianne Tambour and Liberté Dumont shared the mother's agony and terror, watching together from some place that was both inside the scene and beyond it. They heard the woman's rending screams, saw the blood spread across her skirts. The horseman gave her one dismissive glance and rode away.

'Help me!' moaned the woman, though the crowd had the siege gun on the move now. Yet one of them, another woman, wearing a soldier's old uniform jacket, left the cannon and her comrades, came back across the bridge to stand with hands on hips, staring down at her. In fact, she seemed to be staring, too, at Liberté and Marianne, as though she could see them. And Marianne recognised her, of course, so that Liberté was also finally able to know her also. It was Maman Cholet.

A man ran to join her, Cholet's husband – though Marianne barely remembered him – and together they carried the woman across the cobbles to the gates of the Veterans' Hospital, calling for help themselves until, at last, a couple of medical orderlies in filthy aprons appeared. There were corridors. Stairs. A maze of rooms. Sunshine filtering through shuttered windows and lighting up a million motes of dust. And a chamber that stunk, even in its visionary form, of death, of gore-stained timber tables and leather straps where they worked upon the pregnant woman until, at last, there was no more work to be done.

She lay with one alabaster arm hanging rigid from the wooden board, her head lolled to one side, wretched and drained, blue around the eyes and lips, unrecognisable, her life ended, though even now, the crimson essence of that life still pumped weakly from the opened lower torso and orifices of her body, trickled in gobbets to supplement the slippery mess already gathered about the table legs.

And that life's blood still coated the babe, the arms of Maman Cholet who held the tiny thing, while her husband shook his head in answer to whatever questions he was asked, went to look once more at the dead woman's face, noticed the gold chain and locket that still hung there, tangled in the sweat-matted hair. He unfastened the thing, held it up to the light, at the very moment when Marianne and Liberté began to release their grip on each other's fingers so that they, too, could examine the pretty plaything with the engraved letter 'C' and were hurled backwards through the sable darkness of the ethereal tunnel, leaving them each drained and bereft by the apple trees behind the Hotel of the Beautiful Alliance.

'Your mother's name...?' said Marianne.

'It was Claire,' replied Liberté Dumont.

Chapter Twenty-Nine

Sunday 18th June 1815, 10.30am

If they wept, then none of their tears seemed sprung from the wells of newfound sisterhood, for each hid them from the other as though they were ashamed. They said nothing, and Marianne's only emotion, as she climbed inelegantly up behind the Percheron's saddle one more, was a sense of her own grime-encrusted inadequacy. She recalled two things most vividly. First, the elegance of that Paris apartment where, had history been different, she may have been raised – and knew she would never have been worthy of the place. And, second, the image of that woman dead and ugly within the butchers' shambles.

'What would they have done with her?' she said, as the horse walked back around the outside of the inn. 'Afterwards, I mean.'

'The Invalides has its own cemetery, does it not?' Liberté replied. 'I think my... *our* father searched even there at some point. From desperation. But many of the graves were unmarked and I think, now, that he would not have searched too hard. There were others who disappeared that day, for one purpose or another. He could not accept even the possibility that she might be dead, after all. He made enquiries time and again at the hospital though.'

To Marianne's ear, there was a hint of accusation in her voice.

'Maman Cholet told me she tried many times to find out. About... how I came to be there.'

'She can't have tried too hard. And Father had handbills posted up all around the area.'

The word *Father* hit Marianne like a hammer, and she felt those bloody tears begin to choke her again.

'He's still alive?' she said. There was a thrill of excitement here, the first she had felt. Easier, perhaps, to deal with the concept of a surviving father.

'Just about,' said Liberté, her voice losing its hard edge for the first time. 'Though greatly enfeebled now. I swore I would bring him good news from this campaign. But I'm not sure that I can bear to tell him any of this.'

Any of this? thought Marianne. *No, I suppose not. Bad enough to tell the old fellow the manner of his wife's end, without the grief of this other detail. 'Oh, but good news, Papi. I've found the long-lost bitch who caused her death.'*

'Will you tell me about him?' she said.

'Perhaps later. I still don't understand why your woman, Cholet, did not have the locket investigated. Father had it made at the jeweller's just along the street. A short spit from the Invalides itself.'

'Perhaps she did not think of it.'

'Perhaps she was too busy thieving the thing. And stealing babies too, of course.'

Marianne's anger rose in her gorge, but she swallowed it fast. It was fair game, she thought. But she still kept faith with Maman Cholet's kindness, could not allow that part of her to be destroyed. *You cannot live twenty-five years as one thing, then suddenly find that you are another, and that all which embraced you for those years was suddenly a sham. Yet so much of me is collapsing inside*, she thought. *Like a building suddenly stripped of its keystones and lintels.* But the one thing she could not evade was the thought that the Cholets had known and never told her the truth, not even when she was a woman grown. Had lied about finding her on the drum. Had made a travesty even of her name. How could that be? Though she knew this was an answer that would always be hidden from her, that no amount of delving into dreams would ever divulge.

'When did you know?' she asked. The words came out like an angry accusation. It was all very well for this woman to interrogate her about Maman Cholet's motivations, but what about her own? If she had been so sure…

'Don't bark at me, girl,' Hawk-face snapped back at her, 'or you can walk back to your bloody battalion.'

'*Show some respect for your sister,*' Marianne heard a voice inside her head, an echo of something that might have been.

'We're too much alike, I suppose,' she said. It was her best attempt at diplomacy. 'Lomballe, for instance. In Charleroi. As you said, it wasn't just the clothes that confused her.'

'And the way you handled that knife, Marianne. I couldn't have done it better myself.'

Has she ever called me Marianne before? She tried to recall.

'I was *taught* how to fight,' she said, and remembered those *gitanos* who had shown her the best techniques. No fancy frills, just straight to the kill.

'You need a gift for it first,' said the Dragoon. 'Natural talent. We've both got it.'

From where? Marianne wondered. *From this father I've never known? From others? Still further back?* Their conjured spectres began to crowd in upon her.

'And this other gift,' she said. 'Or curse, whichever it is. The far-seeing and the dream-travel. That too?'

'I think Maman may have had it,' Dumont replied, and the word pounced upon Marianne like a cat taking its mouse. She found herself shaking free of the Cholets, trying to replace that woman, who was all the mother she had ever known, with some new image. But not that dead face she had seen on the surgeon's wooden slab.

'Do you have no likeness of her?' she asked.

'Father has one. I'll show it to you. When we've done with all this.'

The Dragoon set the horse to a trot once more, but she did not invite her to hold tight this time. Yet Marianne wrapped her arms around the uniform coat all the same, felt her sister's warmth for the first time.

'When?' she shouted over Liberté's shoulder, felt the wind against her face, her hair streaming out behind.

'Once we've been back to the rue de Grenelle. There's a cabaret that I mean to run there. We'll pool our money. But I know nothing about business. That's where you and the girl come in. After that, we'll go to Arcachon. See Papa.'

Marianne chewed on that thought all the way back to her lines, savouring its flavours. And then something else struck her. She knew that she had become Marianne some time after the Revolution itself. Cholet had told her so. The name had become the Republic's symbol by then. The song, *Marianne's Cure*, one of its hymns. And then that image of Liberty upon the barricades. Marianne.

'Do you know if...' She had to struggle with the word. 'If Maman ever intended a name? For me, I mean.'

'No. But Father might know. Why?'

Between the columns of soldiers marching towards her, the head of the Fourth Grenadier Regiment's Second Battalion, she could see her cart now, Florisette at the reins.

'No reason,' she replied. 'Marianne is a good name. But you mentioned the girl.' She realised that Liberté was not listening, was gazing away to the right where, at some distance, another Dragoon seemed to be watching her in turn.

'I'm sorry,' Liberté murmured. 'You were saying? About the girl?'

'She says you frighten her. That looking at you is like seeing *my* shadow.'

'Sharp girl!' said Liberté. 'It runs in her veins too then. How will she take to me as her new auntie, d'you think?'

'Well, you'll need to get rid of that bloody uniform for a start.'

They embraced briefly, for the first time, as her sister's battalion began to wheel into position with the rest of the Middle Guard, behind those *Tirailleur* and *Voltigeur* regiments, a kilometre south of the Beautiful Alliance and slightly north of another farm on a gentle ridge.

'Look after everything,' said Liberté. 'Stay safe. And...' She leaned from her saddle so she might more easily whisper in Marianne's ear, 'get rid of the stupid Italian boy. He may be pretty, sister, but he's a liability.'

She saw Marianne glance at the lad.

'I think he may be worth a few francs first,' she replied. 'And we need all we can get, don't we?'

'You see?' said Liberté, straightening herself once more. 'I told you. We need somebody with a business head like yours.' She looked around for the girl, saw her sitting on the cart's tail, swinging her grubby little legs. 'Hey, brat!' she called. 'Are you afraid of me?'

Florisette screwed up her face, made that gesture with forearm and fingers that unequivocally told the Dragoon what she could do with herself.

That's my girl, Liberté smiled. *Just like your mother. I might have known. Cats don't make dogs. You'll do, child.* And she laughed, long and loud, as she touched gentle heels to Lucette's flanks, tickled the left rein, clicked her tongue to put them back on the road home to her Squadron. But she took her time with the return journey, careful to look as though she was dozing, chin on her chest, allowing Lucette to pick her own way through those units still threading to the front lines, ignoring the jeers of the marching, swearing, singing footsloggers, but watching surreptitiously, through eyes only half closed, for any further sign of that murderous bugger, Lieutenant Henry.

Oh yes, she thought, *it was him, right enough.* And she had given herself away, distracted by Marianne's questions, allowed him to see that she had spotted him. In truth, she had been shocked by the matter-of-fact way Bonaparte had simply assumed that Fouché would want her dead. She had calculated that, with a favourable outcome today, and given Henry's attempt on her life already failed, the Minister would forget all about her, be happy with the fact that she had received no payment beyond the five gold Napoléons. But now she saw that this was a foolish belief, that it was not in Fouché's nature to abandon a course once he was set upon it. And how much more risk to her if the outcome was, indeed, something else. Inconceivable, yet even the Shaveling must have considered it. Why else was she now carrying the letter to his son? *So, conclusion*, she thought. *One way or the other I shall never be free of Fouché. It might have bought me more time if I'd killed Henry but not much. And after Henry it would simply be another. Then another. And you know what it is that makes you such a target, Dumont? It's your own conceit. Your damned celebrity. All those meetings with the Emperor. Dinner at the Tuileries. Liberté Dumont, the gentleman volunteer. The most famous Dragoon trooper in France. Very clever! Well...*

Yet she saw no more of Fouché's assassin, began to convince herself that she might just have been wrong. Only a glimpse, when all was said and done.

And what about Marianne? she wondered. *Was I too hard on the girl? She can barely be blamed for being born that way.* Liberté even found it difficult to be too resentful about the woman, Cholet. *She may have told the truth, I suppose. About trying to find out.* Yet there were so many reasons why she may have chosen to keep the child. *Afterwards*, she supposed, *with her man gone, it would have been too easy to persuade herself that the invented story was the real one. And, Christ's Teeth, those few years saw so many tragedies.* She remembered afresh the purge of her father's own Girondin moderates, the thousands butchered in Lyons, and the countless victims of the Terror, executed by the National Razor – not just the aristos, the priests and the anti-revolutionaries, but the vast majority who were simply peasants, often wrongly accused of everyday crimes. Fingered like witches. Jealous and malicious neighbours. Even family members. *Particularly* by family members.

Our little tragedy is barely worth a swallow of soup in comparison. The big thing is to get out of all this, build my own family afresh. New life. New identity perhaps. And she felt a thrill of excitement now at this thought of her new sister. So evidently her sister too, she realised. *Almost like looking in a mirror.*

It was relatively simple to find the Regiment, for they were stationed with their right flank obliquely to the left of the main Brussels highway, along with the rest of Kellerman's Corps.

'You likely to grace us with your presence for an hour or two now, Dumont?' said Sergeant Tranchante when she took her place within the troop. 'If so, I'll give the Shaveling a shout and say you've shown us the thumbs up. I'm sure he's just waiting for you to give him the go ahead.'

'You passed on our regards, I hope?' said Falco.

'I told him,' she said, 'that if he wanted the men of my Section to follow his orders, he'd better have them written in big letters and explained very slowly.'

'Bitch!' spat Bertine.

'*Chosen* bitch to you, worm,' she replied, then stood in her stirrups so she might better see how their position stood. They were out on the left flank, of course, these Heavies of Kellerman's. There was another Dragoon regiment, the Seventh, immediately to their right, two regiments of Cuirassiers behind them. Two regiments of Carabiniers – very distinctive in their white coats, breastplates of burnished bronze and scarlet helmet crests – stood to their left and, behind those, two more of Cuirassiers. To the right of Kellerman's Corps, blocks of foot in column and, ahead, the battalions of Line and Light Infantry that made up the foremost legions of their host, solid long walls of blue jackets, grey or tan summer overcoats, black shakos.

Liberté knew that, in front of those battalions, the ground slipped away into a shallow valley but she could not see it clearly from here, only a small wood, or substantial orchard, that hid at its rear a large walled house, a chateau, standing almost due west of the inn. She had seen it earlier, despite its expansive poplar perimeter, from the Beautiful Alliance. Yet past the nearer, eastern edge of the trees, she was able to make out that the valley rose again to that other ridge, the twin of this which their own army occupied, but angling somewhat northward, where units of Wellesley's redcoats could still be observed at their manoeuvres. The very centre of that other ridge was sliced by the same main highway from Charleroi to Brussels, near which Liberté was now mounted. And just across from the Beautiful Alliance, yet another farm, its roof tiles gleaming in the gathering sunshine. Those parts of the valley that she could see from here were yellow with wheat and rye, and she knew from her earlier journey with

Marianne that the entire plain was rich in these tall crops. Indeed, they grew all around her here too.

They grew like the cheering. Liberté felt it first. Almost before she heard it. For it rose like an onshore breeze. Stirred the cereal heads. Trembled through the still damp ground before battering against her ears in great waves. All the bands of the Infantry Corps to their right. The *Veillons au salut de l'Empire* striking up. That old Anthem of Liberty. The Revolution's hymn. And a thousand hats were thrown in the air, the words picked up all across that mighty martial sea.

> '*Let us protect the life-blood of Empire,*
> *Let us maintain the rights we have won.*'

Liberté loved the song, roared out verse after verse until her throat hurt.

'Long live the Emperor!' other soldiers yelled. Light glittered on naked steel. Bayonets punched the air, like spear points. Some image of ancient armies. Like the warriors of Jeanne d'Arc. And among them at the gallop, the Shaveling's white Arab stallion. All the glory of the Emperor's gold-braided entourage following behind. Heads turned. They craned their necks to catch the merest glimpse of him. And the power of his presence swept through the ranks. A tangible thing, like a voltaic charge, jolted and stunned their senses. Standards and fanions waved. Drummers beat their tattoos. Cries of praise, respect and adulation for Bonaparte. They rippled from unit to unit. For the values that, to each of them, he represented. The gains of the Revolution. And then he was surging ahead of Marianne's own Corps. Men slapped each other's arms or backs, mouths wide, bellowing in ecstasy. So, when she turned to smile at her fellows, she saw tears streaming down those ugly faces, realised at the same time that her own cheeks were wet with emotion too. The second time in one morning.

Chapter Thirty

Sunday 18th June 1815, 11.45am

There was precious little fanfare to celebrate the opening round. Something of a disappointment, Liberté considered. Yet it was often thus, after all the theatre and spectacle of the Emperor's Reviews. A flourish of couriers. Then simply the drummers of the battalions ahead. On the far left The *Pas de Charge*, At the Quick. They seemed to sink into the ground. Over the rim. Down into the valley. One after another, until only a bare space was left behind them. The ghost of their singing and their *TAN-tra-tran, TAN-tra-tran* drifting back, muted by the slope down which they had descended.

Diversion, thought Liberté. *It must be.*

'Think they'll fall for it?' said Falco.

'Doesn't look much like a real flank attack, does it?' she replied. 'What's that we've sent? A Division? Wellesley won't be fooled. It never tricked him in Spain. Not likely to trick him here either.'

Over on the extreme left, and forward of them, stood Piré's Light Cavalry – the boys that Liberté had joined after her escape from Gémioncourt Farm, the lads who had carved up the Dutch-Belgian horsemen, almost taken down the English Duke. And though the Lancers and mounted Chasseurs held their position, their artillery batteries galloped forward and vanished also.

'That'll sting them a bit though,' said Bertine and, soon after, they heard against the first rip and crackle of musketry the cannons go into action.

'Shouldn't take them long to clear out those trees.' Falco was picking at his teeth, looking bored. 'And hey, you missed soup.'

Liberté lacked the heart to tell him she had dined perfectly well from the Emperor's breakfast scraps.

'Oh, the trees should be easy enough,' she agreed. 'But just behind those trees,' she pointed at them, 'is a bloody big house. Solid as a fortress. I just hope somebody's told them.'

There was nothing they could do, and now simply the waiting. So her thoughts turned to business issues once more. To the little place she had seen on the rue de Grenelle last winter. Ideal for the sort of cabaret she envisaged. The rent standing then at just over one hundred francs per year. She had calculated her other overheads at a similar amount. Living accommodation should be no problem, for her family still held the abandoned apartment further along the same street. It would be a tight squeeze, with Marianne and the girl... *But what about her man?* she suddenly thought. Liberté had not even considered that complication. And, from what she had witnessed, the man Fronsac might be a problem. Yet, regardless of all that, the diamonds gave her an investment that should see them clear for, say, the next five years. By that time, she hoped, they might have established themselves, perhaps even made some small profit.

'Look, here they come.' Falco's voice intruded on her dream.

She could see guns moving along the English ridge above the trees. They seemed in no hurry. Perhaps that was the mud too. Yet, within minutes, a veritable duel was taking place.

'Shooting at each other?' said Bertine.

'Well, who else would they be shooting at?' Falco sneered. But it was a fair question, for shell and shot, on the occasions that it could be seen, seemed to all be arching over the top of the orchards, rather than falling among the respective forces within them.

A galloper raced through the lines, made directly for Kellerman's command group and, moments later, the Lieutenant General's own messengers were in action, orders rippling down through the normal communication channels – Corps Commander to Divisions, Divisions to Brigades, Brigades to Regiments – and Liberté could feel that familiar frisson. They all did. She could see it on their faces. The thing that held all of them in thrall.

'Come on,' said Bertine, his teeth gritted tight. 'Send us to see those bastards off. We could be up there before the Goddams even know we're on the way. Come on!'

There it is, she thought. *The reason for all this. Fighting for our homes? For the pay? For France? For the Shaveling? For each other? For hatred of the English? A bit of all those, maybe. Even if we know that some of those things might be deceptions. But mainly? It's because we can't bloody do without it. It's got more of a hold on us than the rotgut brandy.*

Yet it was not their turn. The chain of orders spiralled no further than regimental level. Shoulders slumped and slackened as only their own horse batteries spurred and whipped their way forward over the cloying ground. Each cannon with its six-horse limber. Every limbered gun followed by its pair of long ammunition caissons. And the mounted gunners cantering alongside, yelling encouragement to their teams and drivers.

'We'd have ridden straight into those buggers if we were making for the guns,' said Liberté, and she nodded to the ridge again, where solid blocks of the enemy, mainly green-coated Germans or Nassauers, could be seen scurrying down past their artillery to hurl themselves into the fray below.

'Dumont!' shouted Sergeant Tranchante, trotting along behind the Company. 'Don't the Emperor's orders apply to you no more?' *Bloody sergeants*, she thought. *Why can't they just say what they mean?* And she knew that she must have looked either stupid or insolent. 'Your uniform, Trooper,' he went on. 'You were supposed to get cleaned up.' She looked down at the inky mud that smeared her green jacket, the red-lined lapels turned back to form the tunic's front, the grey buttoned overalls where they showed above her knee-high filth-streaked boots, and every part of Lucette up to the mare's forearms and gaskins. The trumpets blew the Dismount. *Feet on the ground, cavalry man! Feet on the ground, quick as you can!* 'Right lads,' said the sergeant. 'Looks like we'll be here a while. Rest your weary nags. Smoke if you've got it! And Dumont...'

'Yes, Sarge,' she said. 'I'll deal with it right now.'

Up front, drums were beating again. More infantry vanishing down that forward slope, sucked towards the line of trees, the tops of which were now obscured by smoke.

Diversion? she thought. *This is turning into a real meat shredder.*

Fronsac's Platoon grumbled as they always did. About pensions. About pay. About lack of promotion. About the officers. About the generals who commanded the officers. About the constant failure of the supply lines. About the lack of sleep. About such-and-such, crippled at one battle or another, and now relying on charity and handouts at the Veterans' Hospital. About the disgrace of a society that sent them out to fight and then treated them like dirt. About the way things had been back in the old days – whenever that might have been.

'Don't listen to them, Fabrizio,' Marianne told the boy. 'They wouldn't have it any other way.'

The Italian lad still looked shocked.

'Do we not fight for the glory of France?' he berated them, though they only laughed in his face. 'But the Emperor,' he said. 'That review. I've never seen anything like it. One minute you can hardly keep awake. The next you're all cheering and singing like loons.'

'That was just for the benefit of the English,' said Marle. 'Nice piece of theatre.'

But there were many who still showed tear streaks through the grime of their cheeks.

'If you hang around long enough,' said Marianne, 'you'll see for yourself whether that was theatre or not. These silly sods will be falling over each other, lining up to die for him before the end of the afternoon.'

'That's different,' said Fronsac. 'He's our Little Shaveling. He's our man.'

'Why does the Emperor look old and fat?' said Poppy, and a dozen pairs of angry eyes fastened upon her. 'Anyway, I'm hungry.'

It takes a child sometimes, thought Marianne, *to see what all the rest of us ignore.* For she had herself observed that, while the Emperor's Review might have been glorious, the Shaveling himself had looked pale, tired, while so many of the soldiers, even here within the Imperial Guard, remained shoeless, lacking their normal spark.

'Hungry?' she said. 'Then it's the goats for supper, my girl.' There was a cheer of support from the men around her. But Poppy looked wounded, went off to find the creatures, and Marianne wondered how and when – even *if* – she should break the news to her daughter, even to Fronsac, about this strange turn of events with Hawk-face. But now, with the woman no longer at her side, she had begun to doubt whether it was even real. Could she even be sure that they had shared the same vision? Or dream. How was it possible? What had it been, exactly? She would have to accept that the Dragoon's mother may indeed have been called Claire. Yet could she be so certain that the locket was the same? It was twenty-five years, after all. And people could deceive themselves pretty well over such a span of time. Anyway, did it matter? If Dumont wanted to adopt her as a long-lost sister, what was wrong with playing along? Yet there was no denying the similarity of their features.

She saw herself serving restoratives – *restaurants* – or *bouillons*, lamb in white sauce, decent wine, in a respectable eating house. Dumont's cabaret. Paris, of course. The rich and famous coming to dine there. Poppy taking orders, waiting on tables, learning to cook. Fronsac washing plates out in the yard. '*Take it or leave it*,' she would say to him. '*But if you want to keep that fine roof over your head, to get your regular ration of brandy every day, you'd better make those dishes shine, mister.*'

'When will we see some action?' said Fabrizio.

'Can you not hear it, boy?' sneered Cazajus. He cupped a hand to his ear, turned it towards the front and left, from where the sounds of gunfire had been swelling now for a half-hour. 'How much action do you want? Our boys are bleeding over there.'

'There'll be nothing much until the Shaveling gets his Beautiful Daughters sorted out,' said Marianne. 'We never get going properly until he's happy with the big guns. You want to see?'

'I'd rather eat first,' said the Italian. 'I'm hungry too. Have you got anything I can buy?'

'Depends how much you've got,' Marianne replied. *This should be interesting*, she thought.

The boy delved inside the barrelled sash around his waist, took out a purse and held up a gold Napoléon.

'Will this buy me something?' he said.

'Not very much,' Marianne lied, saw Poppy at the corner of the cart, biting her lip. 'Let me see…' She rummaged among the bits and pieces left in her sacks. A small cut of cured ham. The end of a cheese. Curl of garlic sausage. A cob of black bread. 'What about that? Fair exchange?'

'I think so,' he said, but he sounded doubtful, looked around at the grinning faces of Catherine Argonne and the Grenadiers. 'I've not quite got the hang of the money yet.'

'You bloody fool,' said Marianne, hand in her pocket for all the loose change she had garnered during the day so far. 'Have you got no less?' For there was just less than twelve francs there, and she had no desire to open up the *tonnelet*. 'What I've given you comes to one franc and ten sous. So I owe you eighteen and a half francs in change. But I've only got twelve here.'

'Owe me the rest,' said Fabrizio. 'There's no rush.'

'And never flash your purse like that,' said Catherine Argonne. 'Never! You're lucky that Tambour's so honest. Some of these buggers would loot their own mothers.'

Marianne felt herself weaken, choke back her emotions at the recollection of the pale corpse that had given birth to her, the only image of motherhood she could now summon.

'Catherine's right,' she said. 'If you survive today at all, you're still likely to be robbed blind if you're not careful. And, for Marat's sake, buy a better horse if you're so flush. There'll be plenty for sale later. But no more than ten francs. You understand? Not even if they tell you it's a magic horse, like Bayard. You heard of Bayard?'

Fabrizio nodded.

'Got it,' he said. 'And the Emperor's Beautiful Daughters. Can I see them?'

'Take the lad,' said Catherine. 'I'll watch things here.'

'Will you ride with me?' said Fabrizio.

'On that sag-backed mare?' Marianne replied. 'I'd rather walk.'

But they had taken no more than a few steps, Marianne holding the Italian lad's stirrup leather, when the troops all around them began to part. The Shaveling and his generals riding back down the road from the front lines, his head bowed, the weary face almost invisible within the collar of his grey riding coat. She wanted to offer him another shot of brandy, thought better of it. Yet she lingered long enough to see his Aides set up a map table for the Emperor on that same mound, opposite the Rosomme Farm, where Marianne herself had halted with her cart, and Liberté Dumont had described the army's deployment for them.

'Is he ill?' murmured Fabrizio.

'No,' she said. 'Just impatient. Waiting to launch the attack.'

Did she know him so well? Really? She admired him. His ability to speak with such passion in a voice that people understood. His grasp of those things that most angered the peasant and the city poor. His delivery of reforms to meet their needs and fears. Oh, she was no fool, understood that the number of those reforms was just sufficient to keep their demands dampened. Just sufficient. Nothing like the full promise of the Revolution, Maman Cholet had told her. But better than the life they had endured before. And she admired his foxiness. His ability to damn the aristos, the Church, the old order, while still keeping them sweet enough to soak up their wealth. He had strengthened the state, the

Empire, but he had done it in the name of the people. Whether it would ever truly belong to the people, she could not say. Bonaparte was their new Messiah. And if all Messiahs had the same questionable attributes, she did not really care.

'When will he begin?' said the boy.

'Let's go and find out, Fabrizio,' she replied, pointed up the highway towards the Hotel of the Beautiful Alliance, and the Italian kept up an endless stream of idle chatter, details of his background, his family, or vaguely foolish questions about the army.

'The hospital?' he said, as they passed the place where some brown-coated orderlies were burying a body. There was a tent already erected, a couple of two-horse ambulances standing alongside, most of the men sitting around, playing cards or smoking. 'Has that poor fellow been shot already?'

'We're too far back from the front,' said Marianne. 'That will be one of the fever cases, most likely. We lose plenty for other reasons. Not just the fighting.'

'It's not very big. The hospital, I mean.'

'Every Division's got its own,' she replied. 'There'll be a couple of dozen hospitals dotted about.' But she was thinking of that damp grave where they had left Suzanne Prairial and her baby boy, the daughter and son that she herself had left by the pathways of Spain. This idea of Dumont's – her sister's idea, she corrected herself. She would make it work for their sake, as well as for Poppy. And here came a few sous more to add to the pot, as the orderlies bought some of her dog-dog.

It was a fair step further forward to the guns. A thousand paces. And even then it was difficult to get close for all the clamour and bustle. Gunners still heaved on wheels and trail spikes to put the last of the pieces into line, but that line stretched away over a thousand muddy paces more, along the forward lip of the French ridge.

'It's magnificent,' said Fabrizio. 'And these, the Emperor's Daughters?' There was a pair of six-pounders closest to them.

'No,' she replied. 'Those big buggers over there. See?' She pointed further along. 'Only the twelve-pounders count for the Shaveling. But they are beautiful, are they not?'

'Have you ever seen so many before? There must be seventy? Eighty?'

Marianne had no idea, but she had, indeed, seen larger Grand Batteries. Not often. But she had seen them. And she watched as the Italian took in the whole glorious scene. Not just the guns themselves but, thirty paces back, the limbers, the horses, the horse-holders. Further back still, the ammunition caissons, long and olive-green. Perhaps two hundred of them or more. And all that ground churned up, not just by the rain, but by the very deployment of the artillery train itself, all those hooves and wheels.

'And those poor sods will have to plough their way through this swamp to reach the Goddams.' She thumbed over her shoulder at the infantry battalions stretching away behind the ammunition wagons.

'The English?' said Fabrizio. He turned to his left, peered across the valley. They were perhaps six hundred paces from the opposite ridge, but there were only a few scattered lines of skirmishers visible on the forward slopes. 'Where are they?'

'Oh, they'll be there,' she told him. 'It's what the buggers did in Spain. They'll be hiding just out of sight.'

'The cowards,' cried the boy.

'No,' she said. 'They've just got more brains than us. They're not cowards.' She had seen enough of them to know how well they could fight. Yet she remembered Saint-Sébastien too. Those scum. 'Most of them, anyway. And not all Roast Beefs either. They'll have as many Dutchies fighting for them. Or German Nassauers. Or Scotsmen. Or Brunswickers. They don't like to do their own fighting if they can get somebody else to do it for them.'

'How will the guns hit them if they can't see them?' said Fabrizio.

'The howitzers will drop shells on top of them. And the rest will try to pitch their balls so they hit the slope and bounce over into their lines. Not much chance of that with all this mud, mind. But that's not what the Grand Battery's all about. Not really.'

'Then what...?'

But the guns themselves gave him his answer.

It was finely timed. A sudden silence when even the birds stopped singing. One clear command. Hundreds of blue-coated gunners standing back from their pieces. Eighty port-fires stretching for the muzzle vents. Every gun leaving the ground and leaping backward from the smoke that spewed through their barrel mouths. Great gashes of yellow and orange flame stabbing out at the enemy positions. Spitting black flecks of the shattered wooden wadding shoe and powder bag. A thunder, roaring and bellowing as though they stood at the centre of the world's worst ever storm. It shook the ground so much that Fabrizio's nag almost stumbled and Marianne clung to the stirrup to help keep her own balance. The sulphur-pit stink. And then the gunners moving back even before the pieces finished that gravity-defying recoil to begin setting them afresh.

Now, she thought, *it truly has begun*.

Chapter Thirty-One

Sunday 18th June 1815, 1.30pm

By the time Marianne and Fabrizio had retraced their steps to the Battalion, the Grand Battery had fallen silent.

'What was that?' she said. 'A half-hour? That should have given them something to think about.'

But, in truth, it did not feel like much of a barrage. *All those hours spent waiting for the guns to be worked into position*, she thought, *just to give them shit for thirty minutes?*

'Look,' said the boy. 'Prisoners already. That's a good sign.'

There were Gendarmes pushing a little string of sad-looking fellows along the highway, south towards the Emperor's command post that, she assumed, was still on that mound at the Rosomme Farm. She had certainly seen no sign of his entourage on the move again. The prisoners themselves were Hussars, mud-streaked, green-coated and one of them, short and stout, was being hoisted aloft at regular intervals, his feet pedalling in the air, by a red-breast who gripped the shoulder of his pelisse, shouting abuse at him.

'Come on, you Prussian pig,' the Gendarme cried. 'Can't keep the Emperor waiting.'

'Prussian?' Fabrizio said. 'Did he say Prussian?'

'He must be mistaken,' she replied. 'And the red-breasts aren't very smart. They're policemen, for Marat's sake. That little runt's probably a Dutchie or something. Anyway, there's no Prussos within a dozen leagues from here.'

But among the ranks, the rumour-mill was working overtime.

'Prussians at Saint-Lambert,' said Cazajus. 'You heard?'

'We just saw some Prussian prisoners,' Fabrizio spat out.

'There,' said Muhler. 'What did I tell you? If Blücher's not done for after all, this could all turn out a right bloody mess.'

Marianne almost laughed. She remembered the raving old fool on the floor of that hovel in Mellery.

'They probably weren't Prussos at all,' she said. 'The boy just overheard some stupid red-breast. That's all.'

'Well, all the same,' said Fronsac. 'The lads in Second Company just picked up word that a whole Infantry Corps is being sent off to hold them.'

'And I suppose we'll be going with them?' Marianne sneered. 'By the Host, have you lot got nothing better to do than waste time on all this nonsense?'

Here we go, Liberté Dumont thought to herself as the Grand Battery fell silent, its smoke still drifting along the ridge in front of her, obscuring the view. *Diversion on the left, hit them on the right. That's the normal thing.* Yet the diversion, as she had thought earlier, seemed to be developing into something else. She could not see the orchards any more, for the smoke, but the sounds of firing, there ahead of them, had intensified. A lot. And it was static. Neither becoming more distant, which might have signalled a French advance towards the English, nor slackening in the way that normally meant a retreat. There was simply a greater volume of musketry, but all of it still apparently emanating from those trees. *Or that bloody big house behind them*, she thought.

'Hey, Fancy Hat,' she heard Falco call to their own canteen-mistress. Liberté ran the grooming brush down Lucette's right stifle and gaskin one more time, then straightened, looked over the Percheron's back to see the woman coming down the line. 'Don't forget your favourite Section,' Falco shouted.'

I don't even know her real name, she thought. She had been with them, and only ever known as Fancy Hat, since the early days in Spain, but Liberté knew nothing about her. Except that she was a surly bitch.

'Croaker's four sous a shot,' the woman called back.

'Four sous for rotgut?' Bertine protested. 'That's twice what you were charging yesterday.'

'Well, we ran out, didn't we?' said Fancy Hat. 'You thirsty buggers drank it all last night. Had to walk god knows how far to find more. An' then I finds the price gone through the roof. Got to pass on the increase, Trooper. Wouldn't expect me to give it away, now, would you, sweetie?'

Liberté wondered what Marianne would be doing now.

Not selling her stuff at rip-off rates, that's for sure, she thought. They were a mixed bunch, these canteen-mistresses. Some of them just miserable profiteers like Fancy Hat. But some of them now household names across France. Like Kintelberger, who had become a bit of a legend after Austerlitz, cut off with her kids by Cossacks, held them off with a sword she picked up. Fought like a demon, so they said. Lost an arm in the process. Shot in each leg. Pregnant with twins at the time. Taken prisoner, then sent back to France with her children to a hero's welcome by the Shaveling himself. *Well*, she said to herself, *my little sister might not be as famous as Kintelberger, but at least she'll be safe back there with the Guard.*

'What d'you think?' Falco said to her. 'We going to pay those prices?'

'Makes no difference to me,' she replied. 'I'm fresh out of coins anyway.' But the fact was that she had a really bad craving for the brandy just now. The lads began to haggle with Fancy Hat but did not get very far, and they ended up shelling out the four sous that she demanded, while Liberté went back to the grooming.

'I'm sorry we can't do it properly, my beauty,' she murmured, as she took some of the filth and dust from Lucette's shoulders. But they could not off-saddle and she was forced to work around most of the tack, only unfastening those parts of the headgear or saddle straps that the watchful eye of Sergeant Tranchante might take for adjustment. Yet she stopped work, as they all did, when the bands struck up the *Veillons au salut de l'Empire,* off to the right somewhere.

'Well,' said Bertine, 'that's a turn-up for the books. Thought we were going to hit their flank.'

We all did, thought Liberté. *Diversion on the left...*

But it was the centre that seemed to be on the move. An Infantry Corps moving up through the Grand Battery.

'Going to smack the Goddams right in the belly,' laughed Falco. 'Well, if *we* weren't expecting it, neither will they, I suppose.'

And over there somewhere, she imagined, *is that purple-faced sergeant that Marianne wants so much to see dead.* That conjured up a vision of the woman – the only mother, she reminded herself – that Marianne had really known for most of her life, and Liberté cursed Cholet. *Why could she not have done more? Didn't Marianne say that Cholet had taught her everything about birthing? Why then take Maman to those saw-bones? Why...?*

Bertine punched her arm.

'That's neat enough,' he said, showing her the lines of distant footsloggers filing between the stilled guns and out of sight, down into the valley. It was no small thing, to move that many men efficiently through those hundreds of obstacles and yet keep them orderly.

I will have to try to maintain some order too, Liberté thought, *when I bring Marianne back to her family.* She doubted Papa would even understand it. Their brother, however, was a different matter. At thirty-eight, he had become one of the most noted lawyers in Paris. A mean-minded little man who would interrogate all of this. '*You had a vision?*' she could hear him sneer. '*And on that evidence alone you seek to establish this creature as a member of my family?*'

Her other sister, ten years younger than Liberté, would be a different case entirely. But she had returned to Arcachon with their father, to the family's roots, her husband now running the freighting business on behalf of Uncle Pierre. Yet Liberté imagined her swooning with delight at some future meeting between the three girls, and she thrilled at the thought of it all, her blood racing fast and a choking sensation in her throat. Did she love Marianne like a sister? Not yet perhaps. These things took time. But there *was* something.

A good ten minutes passed before Liberté caught sight again of that Infantry Corps sent forward to strike the enemy's centre. And during those ten minutes the Grand Battery resumed its barrage while, from their own ridge, the English guns replied. Ahead of her, the firing was unabated and still spoke of deadlock around the orchard and its big house. But over there, to the north-east, whenever the powder smog parted she could see two attack columns, each probably battalion strength, making for that other farm, its roof tiles just visible, which stood where the Brussels highway sliced into the English positions. Exactly opposite the Beautiful Alliance Hotel, she recalled again. There were skirmishers in action, tiny figures in small groups, running ahead of the advance, puffs of white here and there, betraying their firing positions. But it was the units behind these columns that drew Liberté's attention.

'Look,' she said. 'Lobsters.'

The breastplates of those Cuirassiers shone like four hundred mirrors.

'Lucky buggers,' said Bertine. When do *we* get a chance? That's what I want to know.'

Yet Liberté was thinking about hotels. *Why settle for a simple cabaret, a soup house, when we could have a proper inn?* She could see the name. *The Three Sisters.* And she could picture their names above the door. *Liberté and Marianne Dumont.*

'What the hell sort of formation d'you call that?' said Falco.

Beyond the two columns and their Cuirassier escort, the rest of the Infantry Corps was coming into sight. A real swarm of *Voltigeurs* leading, of course, as usual. Clearing away the enemy's own skirmishers. Then aiming to keep up enough fire on the English lines to keep their Goddam heads down. Pick off any officers stupid enough to show themselves. Allow the main force to get close without too many casualties and deliver the hammer blow. But, from what Liberté could see, this was not their normal way of landing that punch.

On the far side of the Brussels road, the valley floor was changing colour, the dark ink of attack columns bleeding into the yellow wheat and rye until all the visible ground was stained with it, and Liberté knew from the depth and breadth that the blue must spread away, well beyond the curve of the French ridge that prevented them seeing the farthest right of the field from here. *Yes*, she thought, *attack columns*. But they must have had a longer frontage than anything Liberté had ever seen. Unfamiliar formations. Each battalion, she guessed, in extended line. If so, how long? One hundred and forty men across, she estimated. Seven or eight battalions, one behind the other. Twenty-four ranks deep. These were formidable.

'Column of Division by Battalion,' smirked Bertine. 'That's what I'd call it.'

It was something of a play on words, a joke, since their normal infantry attack formation was Column of Battalion by Division – columns only two companies wide. As it happened, a pair of companies was also called a Division, the same as two regiments matched within a Corps.

'Well,' said Liberté, 'whatever it's called, it looks like some bugger's muddle. Some bright spark of a general playing around with a new idea.'

'Bloody generals,' said Falco, and spat on the ground.

'Don't count your chickens, my lads.' Tranchante had ridden up behind them. 'This could be good. You remember how many times in Spain the Roast Beefs stood in line and mowed down our columns? Well, this time maybe somebody's been sharp enough to fight fire with fire.'

Yet, as those strange shadows darkened the valley, Liberté caught the first movement of the Cuirassiers she had been watching. Above them, a trickle of green-coated soldiers had been angling down from the English ridge towards the back of that part-hidden farm, moving to reinforce its garrison, she assumed. They seemed absurdly exposed. Neglectfully so. And the Cuirassiers must have known it too, moved off smartly at the Walk, and the Trot, maintained that steady pace all the way uphill while the Englishmen – or their Germans, or Dutch, whatever the hell they were – seemed entirely oblivious.

'You think those Lobsters are using the lie of the land, Sarge?' she said.

'Can't tell from here,' Tranchante replied. 'But if the Goddams can see them, they don't seem much bothered.'

Yet the moment they *did* realise their danger was plain to see. They simply disintegrated, broke up into fleeing groups that ran in all directions, the Cuirassiers still at no more than a trot, hardly working up a sweat at all, just lazily cutting down the fugitives in casual droves. Nor did they stop when there were no more greencoats left standing but, in the same strolling manner, headed up to the crest and, in minutes, had disappeared over the top.

'They'll be in Brussels before they know it,' laughed Falco.

'Maybe not,' said Liberté as a long smudge of smoke showed a storm cloud just over the ridge and, seconds later, the rending crackle of muskets firing in volleys. She kept expecting to see the horsemen come back, their point made but tails between their legs, proud to have scored first blood. Then, when they failed to show, she feared they must all be dead. But it was fifteen anxious minutes afterwards when those bloody heroes came surging back down the hill and regrouped precisely where they had begun.

'Well,' said Tranchante, 'it looks like they must have found where the Goddams have hidden themselves, at least.'

The Grand Battery ceased fire for the second time when, with the two smaller left flank columns already soaked into the chaos of battle around the farm, the first of those strangely elongated formations reached the rolling smoke line created by the English guns, which were doubly hidden behind a hedge delineating the slope's crest along that part of the field. The second of the large attack columns was still creeping through the crops across the valley's floor, while yet another – this one smaller, in the normal form – had come into sight and could be seen snaking across the very farthest right, though Liberté had no idea what its target might be.

'Hey,' said Falco, 'have you heard the one about the Belgian farmer?' They all groaned. 'He went out one morning just before harvest time and spotted his neighbour, sitting in a rowing boat, way out in the middle of his own field.

"What are you doing?" shouted the farmer. "Rowing my boat through this ocean of wheat," the neighbour told him. The farmer was really angry. "It's people like you that give us Belgians this reputation for being stupid," he said. "If I could swim, I'd come out there and kick your arse!'"

Not bad, thought Liberté though, like the others, as usual, she refused to laugh. It only encouraged him, after all. Yet she guessed that they were all thinking the same thing. That it must be a nightmare down there. Not just the mud but shoulder-high crops to struggle through, all the way across the valley and right up the slope. Over the top of it too, in fact. And that first large column was at the top, with the fire from the English guns now frenzied. Case shot. The lads would be facing case shot, those canisters of large musket balls that exploded at short range in the face of an advance and rained down more death than a company's volley. It was wicked stuff that ripped through the ranks and tore men apart. And while it looked as though the column was advancing into the smoke, Liberté knew that, in practice, the leading ranks were simply being chewed up there, mangled into eternity. She knew because, at various points, the entire formation would stop, seem to shake itself, and suddenly shrink in width as they received and followed the order to Close Ranks.

It happened three times before the guns finally began to fire in more ragged fashion, or cease entirely, a sure sign that the column had been broken past that magical point where the artillerymen would be abandoning their positions. And, as if to confirm this, the French lines seemed to surge suddenly forward. There was musket fire over there now, quite distinct from the background noise just ahead.

'We've broken through,' shouted Bertine. 'We must have done. Look.'

'No, they've stopped again,' said Falco.

'Waiting for that other Division to come up, maybe,' Liberté offered.

And that second 'Column of Division by Battalion' was, indeed, coming up, making good progress, still taking fire from the guns along the right of the hedge but, it seemed, receiving less punishment than had been meted out to the others. The whole process was repeated. Their thick skirmish line came up, the column reached the smoke, closed up, but only once, then halted at the hedge, the guns before them struck mute.

'Press on,' said Bertine. 'Go on, boys. You've made it. Press on!'

But they did not. Something was blocking the way, though at this distance, the watching Dragoons could not make it out. Yet they could see the second Division shift sideways, to the left, until the two columns almost touched.

And then the ripping screech of massed musketry suddenly drowned even the battle's din before them. The left corner of the French line seemed to stagger back, and then again, while the opposite end lurched forward, through the hedge or over it.

'What the hell's happening?' said Falco, and he mounted in the hope of getting a better view, trying to pierce that fog of war with his staring eyes.

'They need to push,' said Bertine. 'Now. Surely. Push right through the Goddams' centre. Oh, come on!'

'There,' Liberté pointed. 'There's their problem.'

Through the smoke, there was an indistinct smudge of scarlet. The English coming forward from wherever they had been hidden. Not just musket fire now but the guns again, perhaps those they had succeeded in pulling back in the face of the French attack.

That left corner began to break apart, fall back, the redcoats following behind, forming their own line at the hedge, while the French centre – the first of the big columns – remained in place along the ridge line. And the right, the second big block, was still pressing forward through the hedge and beyond to whatever unknown hell awaited them there.

Everything hung still.

'They're not going to make the same mistake twice, surely,' said Falco.

Remarkably, a second body of green uniforms began to cross the slope exactly as those others had done earlier, yet this time followed by units of redcoats.

'Watch your left, boys!' Bertine was yelling. 'Watch your left, for pity's sake.'

They did, too. Liberté could almost feel the moment when that nearest corner of the French advance realised they were about to be hit by an English flank attack. And the corner suddenly began to fall apart. But she understood – they all did – the mistake to which Falco was referring. For the same Cuirassiers who had savaged the Roast Beefs earlier were still in play, now casually trotting back over the same ground they had covered before.

'Oh, you lovely Lobsters,' Falco grinned. 'Fancy being that lucky twice on the same day.'

Liberté was convinced that the English must this time understand their danger. Had the fools not seen what happened earlier? Yet it was almost an exact repeat of their former success. The Cuirassiers took their time, cool and casual, caught the nearest redcoats in confusion and hacked them down.

'Move on,' she shouted. 'By the Host, move on!'

For she could see that, successful as they might be, the Cuirassiers' lack of haste was allowing those other red and green units further away to form square up on the crest. An opportunity lost. And worse. There was a new danger.

Trumpets. Not their own familiar refrains. Hardly martial music at all. *Almost like… hunting horns*, thought Liberté.

'Oh hell,' said Falco, as the first scarlet waves of the Goddams' cavalry burst through that wall of smoke.

Chapter Thirty-Two

Sunday 18th June 1815, 3.00pm

The flower of that Infantry Corps lay scattered and trampled, hacked and slashed, reaped and harvested, all across the dreadful field.

The leading edge of the English Horse had slammed into the Cuirassiers without even pausing, the charge driving the entire mass out of sight behind the farm, only to reappear as it rolled into that already fractured corner of the French left. Yet there had seemed no end to the Goddam squadrons that came up behind, pushing their mad dash on and on, so that the French columns, caught in those unfamiliar long lines, had given almost the appearance of being tossed blithely aside.

And the lads had run, the same fever gripping them in their thousands.

They had run back down into the valley, those that were able, the English Horse cutting them as they went, riding them down even as they fled headlong into the artillery pieces being sent forward to support the breakthrough which, minutes before, had seemed within their grasp.

More artillery was on the move too. Sections of the Grand Battery that had begun to move forward to another ridge, lower than their own but closer to the English positions, in preparation for what was surely the final advance. And this easy target of limbered cannon and their caissons was too much for the Goddam cavalry to ignore.

Liberté had found herself whistling in reluctant admiration as they came across the divide. Magnificent. A whole regiment among them mounted on nothing but greys. These were Heavies, but they had charged like madmen, like Hussars. Yet, as wild as they were, for all the gunners they may have cut down, they had not been able to withstand the massed musketry that slaughtered so many of them when they reached the French lines. Nor the Cuirassiers that came at their flanks and took a rich revenge for those of their fellows killed up on the ridge. Nor the Lancers who, when the Goddams began to fall back, had swung around from the right like a swarm and stuck them like dogs by the hundred.

For once, there seemed nothing to say. Even the well of their blackest humour had dried. And had it not been for this interminable racket to the Dragoons' front – that bloody orchard and its big house – the entire battlefield would have been shrouded in silence, as though each side considered the enormity, the futility of its losses.

'God alive,' said Falco. 'How many men does it take to capture a few trees?'

For the ridge ahead of them was now even more deserted, as further battalions were thrown into that section of the fight.

'It will be the house,' said Liberté. 'I told you. It's like a fortress behind there.'

'Then why not send some twelve-pounders to smash the bloody place to bits?' Bertine said.

'Looks like somebody already thought of that,' said Falco as, above the trees, a pall of black smoke began to rise. But there were still more English units moving down the far slope. And away to the right, two more columns could be seen crossing the valley once again, yet another attack commencing at that farm on the Brussels road.

'Christ's Teeth,' said Bertine. 'Are we going to hang around here all afternoon?'

'It's just more rumours,' said Marianne Tambour.

'Then why not go and look for yourself?' said Cazajus. 'Take the boy with you again.'

It was impossible, she knew. A whole Infantry Corps destroyed? Thousands dead or taken for prisoners? Two of the Shaveling's Eagles captured? More Prussian captives seen here and there. Nonsense, surely.

'That's the way the game goes sometimes,' said Muhler, the *Peloton*'s resident chess player and tactician. 'And what about the Roast Beef cavalry? Completely destroyed, I heard. So what's that? Black King's Tower takes White Lady's Jester. Black Lady's Knight takes White King's Jester. White King's Knight takes Black Lady. We're doing fine.'

'I'd still like to see,' said Fabrizio.

'I'll come too this time, Maman,' Florisette insisted.

'No, girl,' she said. 'You stay with your Aunt Argonne again. Here, take these two bottles and see if you can help her sell some while I'm away.'

'You're going with the cart?' Poppy said, and looked balefully at the goats.

'Untie them then,' Marianne told her. 'And keep them safe until I get back. But remember, they go in the soup tonight.'

She had no doubt at all that the creatures would have pulled off a miraculous escape and disappeared by the time she returned. But that was fine. They would not need them again, she had decided. This would be their last campaign. Their last battle. She just needed a way to break the news to Fronsac. And to Hawk-face too. Though she thought that she might take the coward's path. Simply slip away before Liberté could find her again. After all, she now realised, this nonsense about a cabaret in Paris was just a wicked illusion. A family reunion in Arcachon. Another stupid dream. *Imagine*, she thought, *I turn up on the doorstep of this fancy bunch.* She remembered the details from that shared vision with an accuracy that was barely natural. *Guess who's coming to dinner? The canteen-mistress from the 2nd Battalion, 4th Foot Grenadiers. Aren't you the lucky ones? A new daughter for you, Monsieur Dumont. I mean, Papa.* She could picture every pitiless remark, feel the rejection cut her like a knife, worse than anything that Lomballe or Bufanda might have dealt her. *And here's your granddaughter too. Come to stay with you. Just wait while I wipe the snot from her dainty little nose.* It had become an agony for her. She would get Poppy out of this before it was too late. But she would do it her own way. After all, she had a fine silk purse of diamonds in her *tonnelet.* What else were sisters for, if not to help each other in a jam? *She'll understand,* Marianne told herself. *Hawk-face will understand.*

'Tell me about your family,' Fabrizio said to her as she steered the cart up the highway and came to a lane that turned off to the right. It was probably two hundred paces south of that inn where Liberté had made her take the journey, not far from the rear of the Grand Battery where they had stood earlier and that still maintained its ground-shaking thunder.

'I have no family,' she replied. 'Apart from the girl.' But she thought about Maman Cholet. Saint-Sébastien. *My fault,* she thought. *I should have gone back for her earlier. When I had the chance. When that purple-faced bastard dragged her off. I could have saved her. And then all this nonsense about the locket...* 'What about your own? Rich, I suppose?'

'You have me nailed as some grandee?'

'And are you not? Run away from home to fight for the Shaveling? For the Revolution? How romantic. Well, rich boy, romance will get you killed. And then what will your royalist rosary-rolling old man say?'

'Who says he's a royalist?'

She laughed.

'Rich boys who run away from home are always trying to prove themselves the opposite of their fathers, aren't they? At least for a while. But you can't escape what's bred in your bone, boy. None of us can.'

None of us can? she said to herself. *Then what's bred in your bones, Marianne? That same wealth that your real mother was married into? No, that's not me. I'm the abandoned babe found on the drum skin. I always was. I always will be! Blood thicker than water? Bollocks.*

'It's no crime to be rich,' said Fabrizio. 'And no sin to be poor.'

'It's no blessing either, boy,' she replied, and turned Cocotte's head up a ridgeway that ran south-east from the rear of a large formation of Cuirassiers, resting their mounts next to a hospital tent. 'But just think what luxury you have. To be able to escape all this at any moment you choose. Run all the way back to Milano. You get robbed then you find the nearest banker and draw a note on your father's name. You'll not despise him quite so much at that moment, will you?'

She saw the lad's head go down, as though she had whipped him senseless. *Well,* she thought, *Hawk-face may have talked a load of nonsense to me about family and all, but she was right about the boy. I need to get rid of him. He's a liability. A liability to himself. If he doesn't get out of here, he won't live to see another day.*

And then the cart jolted to a halt. If she had been paying more attention, she may have seen the quagmire into which the pony was taking them but, as it was, the wheels were sunk deep in the mud.

'Wait,' said Marianne, staying on the cart long enough to remove those new shoes. Then she eased herself down into the oozing sludge. 'Come on,' she told him. 'Time to get some muck on those bright new breeches. At least you'll look a *bit* more like a trooper.'

But Fabrizio said nothing. He was struggling to control the horse and she assumed it must be worried about sinking in the stuff for it had finally become animated, trying to reverse back the way they had come, its eyes wide and nostrils flaring. Then she realised that the lad was staring down at a point just ahead of them. At first she could see nothing, though finally she spotted the splash of colour in all that churned and puddled earth. Barely coloured at all though. It had once been scarlet, she thought, but was now hardly even the palest of rose pinks, faded by too many campaigns of sun and rain. A tunic arm, or at least the elbow, the rest of the body sunk into a water-filled furrow and invisible until she stood at its side.

'Not one of ours,' she said. 'Come and look.' The lad had steadied the nag now but did not dismount. 'What's the matter? He can't harm you now, boy. It's not the dead you have to fear in this place.' *No*, she thought, *but it's all those you can't save that shape you.* 'Come down, my young friend, and see what the glory of war is all about.'

Fabrizio climbed off the horse, gave the reins a turn around the cart's wheel, then ponderously crossed to where she stood, at each step having to heave on the well-stitched silk tassels of his Hessian boots, pulling them free of the sucking filth.

'Is he…?'

'There's only one way to tell,' she replied. 'Shake his hand and see if he returns the compliment.' He looked at her as though she was mad. 'Go on,' said Marianne. 'I mean it. You'll never be able to survive any of this unless you can look them in the face and touch them.'

He took the last two difficult strides to join her, and though the skin of Fabrizio's face was drawn tight, tinged with palest pistachio, he slowly stretched out his fingers to grip those of the dead man. He recoiled at once, but the contact had been enough for the water in which it lay to roll the corpse onto its back with a gentle splash, the arm still bent over the head.

'Oh, Saints preserve us,' muttered Fabrizio, as he saw what the ball had done to the man's face.

'There,' she said. 'Your first Goddam. Must have ridden clear through our lines before we got him.'

'Somebody's taken his boots,' said the lad. 'Already.'

'Waste not, want not,' she told him. There was nothing left that was worth taking. Except those teeth maybe. At least you could see them all. On this side, anyway. Not a bad set. But she had never been taken by that particular trade. So she unhooked a cup from her shoulder strap, poured the boy a shot of rotgut. 'Here,' said Marianne. 'This one's on the house. Now listen. You want to end up like him? Because that's what will happen. You're not made for this, Fabrizio. So do me a favour. Help me get the cart out of this and then ride away. This fight won't be finished today. And if you still feel like playing the hero tomorrow, come back and find me.'

'There'll be a second day? You're sure?'

'A second? You cheeky pup. This is our fourth day already. We've all been at this game so long now that we can fight for a full week before exhaustion or sheer numbers make us give up the field. There's *always* another day, d'you see?'

And there's the problem, she thought. *Always another day.*

Between them, they pulled the cart clear while, just to the north, the artillery duel continued, squadrons of horsemen wheeled into new positions, and groups of fine-braided generals galloped across the skyline.

'You're right,' he said. 'This isn't for me. Not yet awhile. But I've seen him, Marianne. The Emperor. He'll always be the Shaveling to me now. And I've ridden with his army like I said I would.'

Marianne stretched out her legs, admired the shoes that were now safely back on her feet, snug and dry.

'If there'd been more time,' she said, 'I would have introduced you to him. We're on speaking terms, you know?'

'I'll have some tales to tell, won't I?' Fabrizio smiled.

'Make them tall ones, boy. About how you stood with us when we smashed Wellesley and Blücher both. I know old Blücher too, by the way. Did I say? Well, come on. Let's see if we can find your way home.'

'On this thing?' he said. 'I'll never make it.'

But they carried on and found the track once more. It continued to rise steadily until they neared the top of this other slight ridge, heading east but, strangely she thought, with the sound of sporadic artillery fire coming from their front as well as to the north and west. She looked up into the sun that was streaked and dimmed by a dismal haze of dark smoke, checked that they were, indeed, still heading in the right direction.

'Sounds like fighting up ahead,' she told him. 'If anything comes at us, try to get that nag moving and run for your life. They won't bother me.' She was not certain this was true but she thought she might stand a better chance alone.

'And if I can't get away?'

'Then for Marat's sake, remember to use the *pointy* end of that bloody sword.'

Yet they were not alone on the path. There were four soldiers. Their own. Skirmishers. *Voltigeurs.* And one of them was trying to ride a skittish horse, pale grey, with a squared blanket, red cloak rolled in front of the saddle and a portmanteau hanging loose from its broken straps.

'Hey, Jacques,' she called. The old Revolutionary greeting. 'You're not having much luck with that bugger. Want to sell him?'

'For you, beautiful, or your boy?' said one of the men.

'It's a general's horse,' said the fellow who was trying to ride the nervous mare. 'You can tell.'

'It's a Goddam's horse,' Marianne replied. 'We found the poor sod back down the way. How much do you want?'

They wanted ten gold Napoléons. She offered them five francs. They settled on a single gold piece and a shot of brandy each, though one of them in particular was a bit too frisky with his hands. Yet at least they confirmed the rumour. D'Erlon's Corps had been destroyed on the slopes opposite. A great charge by the English cavalry repelled. Everybody waiting for the Shaveling's next move. The killer blow, they reckoned.

'I should have challenged him,' said Fabrizio, when they were on the move again, topping the ridge.

'What, a gentleman's duel?' she laughed. 'To protect my honour? Oh, Fabrizio. What will we do with you?' She had grown fond of the boy, fool that he was, and she reached inside her blouse, took out the *salvavirgo*, waved the knife at him. 'He'd have been carrying his dick in his hands long before you had the chance to slap his face, lad.'

She chortled for much longer than the image deserved, but that was due more to the fact that her own agonies of indecision seemed to be ebbing away. If Fabrizio could escape, then why should she not do so too? And with the diamonds she would have more than she needed. Perhaps one day, when she had made some money, established herself, she would feel better about finding that new family and her sister again – if Hawk-face was, indeed, her sister. But first she needed to decide what she would do about Fronsac.

'What's all that?' said Fabrizio. He was mounted on the strong English grey now, a horse not much different from Liberté Dumont's Lucette. The lad's old nag was tethered to the cart's tail and he had decided that the creature might still suffice as a second string for the long road home. The boy was a good rider too, she'd give him that. Handled the skittish mare as one born to it.

The ridge angled away from them, down to the right and, nestled in its lee, below them, was a village formed like a crucifix along two streets, a stream running close to their crossroads. To the north, a second stream was marked by a tree line, with the undulating thousand paces between the rivulets bright with crops, and marred only by the dark blue swatches of their own infantry battalions, set here to protect the army's right flank. There were cavalry too, at each end of the position while, here and there, a gun battery would fire a salvo, though seemingly at random.

'You need to go now, Fabrizio,' she said, quietly. And something in her voice, she guessed, made him suddenly alert. 'Ride like the Beast of Gévaudan was on your tail.'

'They're not our own?' he said, peering past the French troops to those patches of forest that filled the middle distance, and the deeper shadows between.

She offered him no response, simply pressed her tongue against the backs of her lower teeth and sucked hard on them.

'Where's Fabrizio?' Poppy demanded, as Marianne drove the cart back to the Battalion's position.

'Gone home to his family, I hope,' Marianne told her, saw the pout of disappointment. 'And where are those damned goats? Ready for the pot, maybe?'

The girl made a running jump that fetched her up alongside her mother.

'Maman,' she said, breathless. 'You'll never believe what happened. Something terrible…'

Florisette prattled away happily with some nonsense about the goats being stolen, until Fronsac also came up to meet her, took the pony's bridle, steered the beast around to his platoon's resting place.

They look as though they're on a Feast Day, she thought. For, despite the hammer of the guns, the proximity of the barrage, the coming and going of horsemen all around them, the Grenadiers were at their ease, playing cards or dominoes, insects buzzing, flitting among the poppy heads, and the air stiff with the scent of ripening corn.

'You know what makes the difference, Marianne?' Fronsac looked back at her from between the pony's ears. 'With men and women? Whether they stay together or not.' As it happened, she could think of many things that might be on Fronsac's list, but they did not include his chosen answer. 'It's sharing things that happen to them. All those things we've been through together. I used to think about it a lot when I was on that bloody hulk.'

'We've seen some things, haven't we?' she replied.

'More than most people get to see in a whole lifetime. Don't you reckon? Too many things to just walk away from.'

It was the closest she would ever come, she knew, to anything like a confession about that Spanish bitch.

'I've been thinking,' she said. 'When this one's over. I reckon we've got enough to maybe think about a stake somewhere. Maybe an inn. Soups and bread. Poppy can help. You can serve the wine. But if you touch any of it, I'll cut your balls off.'

Fronsac smiled. The old Fronsac. The nose seemed less bulbous. His skin less blemished by those liverish spots.

'That's fair enough,' he said. 'One condition though. The name of the place. It's got to be *The Old Grenadier*, no?'

Well, she thought, *what else would we call it?*

'What's that?' shouted Marle. 'You going to retire, Fronsac?'

'And become an inn-keeper,' Fronsac smiled. 'What d'you think, boys? Just need to settle with the Goddams first, of course.' He brushed his hands, as though dusting the English from them with the same gesture. 'After that...'

'Just rumours then, Marianne?' said Muhler. 'All that about the Prussos?'

'Not quite rumours,' Marianne told him. The memory still disturbed her, damaged her dream of the future. Ran a knife through its heart, in fact. Those shadows between the distant trees. Not just dark. But black. Prussian black. 'They've arrived,' she said. 'Hordes of them. And less than a league away.'

Chapter Thirty-Three

Sunday 18th June 1815, 4.00pm

The lull that seemed to have spread like a depressive blanket over the entire battle, at last even reached the orchards opposite Liberté's 2nd Regiment of Dragoons. There were no accompanying cries of victory and no reappearance of shattered units that might mark a defeat. It all simply petered out. Or almost. As though the participants had now tired of the place. It still burned. And there was still firing. But it was much reduced. The Dumonceau Farm, somebody said it was called. Others that it was the Gum Hill Manor House. And a third faction simply called it by the local Walloon equivalent, Hougoumont. Yet it mattered little. Their proximity to this conflict within a conflict, which had now lasted more than four hours, chafed on the nerves of those frustrated by the regiment's lack of activity.

'It's always like this,' said Liberté. 'Are you not used to it yet? How many times have we stood around like gargoyles for a whole day, or longer, and our blades not even tasted fresh air?'

'Well,' said Falco, 'somebody said earlier that the road to Brussels is full of Roast Beefs running like rabbits. Deserters and stragglers, thick as fleas.'

'As thick as your head, Falco,' said Bertine. 'And who, precisely, would have been in the fortunate position to see this little miracle?'

'It's certainly quiet though,' Liberté suggested. 'And you know what they say about the hush before the storm.'

'They should send us in,' Bertine insisted. He punched one clenched gauntleted and fist into the open palm of the other. 'They should just send us in.'

'Against the English in squares?' she said. 'Waiting for us over there? I don't think so. If we go in, it will be as part of a combined attack. Foot, artillery and cavalry. You know the score, Bertine.'

'We've done it before,' he replied. 'You can smash squares easily enough. Remember Eylau? And look at Friday.'

'We didn't break anything at Eylau,' said Liberté. 'We just bought time for the reserves to come up. Anyway, that was the Russians. They don't count. And on Friday the Goddams weren't ready for us. Now they're just sitting over those ridges somewhere, asking themselves why that idiot, Bertine, doesn't come over there and get his arse shot off.'

'Smart-mouth bitch,' Bertine sneered. 'So what d'you call that then?'

But she had already seen it. Like wind rippling across a sunlit lake, so that the brilliance reflected from the wavelets' tips. That glittering spectacle of an entire Cuirassier Corps on the move, their trumpets sounding clear across the intervening ground and their nickname – the Shaveling's Big Brothers – well-deserved today as they filled Liberté's field of vision.

'Milhaud's lads,' said Falco. 'And coming this way. Reckon we'll be joining them?'

But the Cuirassiers, merely advanced across the Brussels road, exciting the English guns into opening up once more, their shot falling within Milhaud's ranks but not preventing them forming up out there, less than a thousand paces away. And not the Shaveling's Big Brothers alone.

'Is that the Guard?' asked Bertine.

There were Lancers following the Lobsters out: the scarlet tunics of the 2nd; the blue and crimson of the 1st. The Imperial Guard's Horse Chasseurs too, in green and red.

'God's Hooks,' said Falco. 'Who's leading?'

There was some sort of review taking place, one of the senior commanders riding up and down the front, hat in hand.

'Old Redhead himself,' said Bertine. 'That's good, isn't it?'

Ney, whom the Emperor had dubbed his Bravest of the Brave. Ney, who commanded that rear-guard from Moscow and left something of his soul, they said, in the Russian wastes. Ney, who had been chief among those persuading the Shaveling to abdicate the previous year, and then turned his coat almost immediately to take up service with Fat King Louis. Ney, who – as everybody knew – had promised to bring Bonaparte to Paris in an iron cage when he heard of his return from Elba. Ney, contrite and back in the Emperor's favour by the time Liberté attended the Tuileries dinner back in March. Ney, entrusted with command of the entire Left Wing only a few days before. And Ney who had failed to take Quatre Bras.

'If you say so,' she murmured. But the dice were cast and they heard the cries of five thousand voices go up.

'Long live the Emperor!'

Trumpets again, and they could feel the ground shake even from here.

'Why are we left here?' Bertine groaned. But nobody paid him any mind. It was a hell of a spectacle, after all. Five thousand horsemen at the Walk, and then the Trot. Never faster than the Trot. Forty squadrons abreast. The longest single line of Horse that Liberté has ever seen. Sun on armour steel. On flourished swords. Horsehair helmet tails flying behind. Black soil heaved into the air as the English gunners blasted them with shot and howitzer shell. Yet nothing stopped them.

'With a bit of luck,' she said, 'they'll just scare the bastards off that ridge.'

They had to watch the slaughter though, as the first ranks went down together in the smoke when case shot caught them. But that could not stop them either.

'That's it, my beauties,' Falco cheered. 'On you go! On you go!'

And they were gone, passing through that line of cannon, over the top, out of sight. They could still be heard, however. That distant thumping upon the earth, which Liberté could also feel through the soles of her boots. Then musketry. Crackle and growl. That went on and on. For how long they could not really say. But fifteen minutes, at least. Twenty perhaps. Until the watching Dragoons exhausted even the most banal of their commentaries.

It was thus that they watched in silence when, at last, Milhaud's men came streaming back in the opposite direction, spreading over the top of the ridge and trotting – still trotting – down the slope once more, English cavalry on their heels, but unwilling, Liberté thought, to chance their arms too far.

'Is that it?' said Falco.

'They're not done yet,' Bertine told him. 'Hardly a dent in them. Look.'

It was nonsense, of course. For the line, as it halted and regrouped along the valley floor, turned to face the front once more, must have been reduced by a quarter.

Can that be right? she thought. *A thousand men left behind up there?*

There was another review. Copperhead Ney up and down the squadrons. But no shouting this time. Just the trumpets. The steady Walk and Trot. And Milhaud headed up the ridge for a second time.

'You recall telling me,' said Colonel Planzeau, his Provençal accent thicker than usual – due, Liberté considered, to the effects of brandy – 'that you knew nothing of Lieutenant Henry's whereabouts?'

'Not those precise words, Colonel,' she replied. 'But yes, sir.'

She had joined him, on Sergeant Tranchante's instruction, at the Regiment's head where, once more, the Colonel had drawn her aside from his assembled squadron commanders with their telescopes and tables.

'Well, I thought you should like to know. The Lieutenant took something of a fever, it seems.' The Colonel shifted his left arm in its sling. 'An ague. Caused him to swoon and fall from his horse. Damnable creature reared and trampled the poor fellow's hand. Mangled it badly. A saw-bones at Frasnes wanted to take it off at the wrist. Send him to the rear. But he refused to let them. Eventually found a remount and, when he was able, made his way back to us here. He has some bottom, wouldn't you say?'

She had wished him in the bottom of a ditch, in truth. And now he had returned. *I should have finished him*, she thought again, the fear returning that she would never be free of him. Or others like him. Or Fouché himself.

'Which hand, sir?'

'Oh, the right. Worse still, wouldn't you say? Neither use nor ornament in a fight. But useful to act as a galloper perhaps. I've sent him off to the Corps Commander. See if he can use him there.'

'If you don't mind me saying so, Colonel, you manage well enough with just the one.'

He rubbed at the ruined arm.

'Less problem with the left,' he said. 'Bit of a bugger in a scrap, but used to the thing now. And hopefully we'll have a scrap of our own soon.' He looked over at the ridge, where the firing and Milhaud's second attack had been raging, out of sight, for twenty endless minutes more.

'The lads all hope so too, sir,' she said, though her mind was full of Fouché.

'And you'll stay with us this time, Dumont?' said the Colonel. 'The fact is that you're a fine trooper. One of the best. I have no idea what all this secret mission business is about. Don't want to know either. And it's not easy, having a woman in the ranks at the best of times. I only mention Lieutenant Henry because... Well, the reason I thought you should know is that he claims he would never have made it without your help. Suggested I might mention you in my dispatches.'

Milhaud's Heavies came back into view exactly as they had done the first time. Slower perhaps. Thinned still further. The English squadrons yapping at their heels, steering them this way and that but always, inexorably, to their home lowland pasture, while the green and red of the Imperial Guard's Horse Chasseurs counter-attacked in their turn. Swirling mêlées eddying around the fringes of the cavalry's mass.

So what is he up to? she thought. *Lieutenant bloody Henry. Mention me in dispatches? Why?* Yet it occurred to her that this was a reasonable way to keep her in Planzeau's eye. Make it probable that, if something should happen to her, the Colonel would be more likely to take special note of it. That word would reach Paris. That Fouché should know his wishes were fulfilled.

'See there?' said Bertine. He pointed across to that modestly higher point, near the Hotel of the Beautiful Alliance, and where the Emperor's white stallion now stood like a marker stone.

'What's he thinking?' Falco snarled. 'Where's the infantry support? The guns?'

There were certainly battalions of Foot back in the valley, beyond Milhaud's Lobsters, but they seemed to be making for that other farm again, rather than support these mounted assaults.

And it's too early, Liberté told herself. *Too soon to throw in this much Horse. Why?* It felt almost like panic. Blindly throwing everything available at Wellesley in the hope that luck might lend a hand. *Well*, she thought, *the Shaveling has generally been blessed with good fortune.* But Minister Fouché still stalked the corridors of her mind. Nostredame. That First Quatrain. "*In the third month, at sunrise, the Boar and the Leopard meet on the battlefield. The fatigued Leopard looks up to heaven and sees an eagle playing around the sun.*" What had Fouché said? Was this not the third month since Bonaparte's return? Was the Boar not Bonaparte himself? And the Leopard was Wellesley? *Yet is the English Duke fatigued?* she wondered. *And if he looks up to heaven and sees an eagle, what does that mean? The Eagles of France coming to finish him? Or the Eagle of Prussia flying to his salvation?*

'That's a good sign,' said Bertine, as the Regiment's remounts were taken from the rear and were herded east, towards the centre. 'Somebody's had orders. You can bet your life.'

He was right. Within minutes, the Carabiniers' Brigade, two units of those burnished bronze breastplates, were following the remounts. A sure indication of reserves being established for their Corps.

'Those boys won't be happy,' Falco laughed. 'They're going to miss all the fun.'

But the talk soon swung to showing Milhaud's lads how the thing should be properly done, as the succession of Trumpet ditties called them to Assemble, to Mount, and for the Regiment, in Column of Line by Fours, to Advance, by Half-Turn, to the Right, March.

'Now, girl,' Liberté told the Percheron, slapping her hand against the mare's shoulder. 'Now we'll see what this is all about. Steady, my beautiful.'

The entire Corps swung behind the remaining battalions of the forward position's Line and Light Infantry, still in their long summer overcoats, the men waving their shakos and shouting either encouragement or obscenities. The formation remained as it had been before, though now with each squadron in column of march, the 2nd's sister regiment, the 7th Dragoons, to their right. Beyond them, two regiments of Cuirassiers, the 8th and the 11th while, over on the left, two more lots of Lobsters, the 2nd and 3rd. At their head, Lieutenant General François-Étienne Kellerman, hero of Marengo.

He's not the tallest general I ever served under, thought Liberté. *But by Christ's Teeth, I'd not wish to fight alongside a finer soldier.*

'You'd think he might sit this one out,' said Falco.

'Why don't you go and suggest that to him?' Bertine laughed.

'He's not going to miss this one,' said Liberté, and she looked over her shoulder. 'And look what he's been given to play with.'

Behind their own Corps, the Imperial Guard's Heavy Division had come up to join them. Only two regiments. But she had never clapped eyes on anything bigger. That great mass of the Empress Dragoons, their uniforms similar to Liberté's own, though immaculate, and the turbans wrapped around their helmets all of leopard skin. Next to them, the Horse Grenadiers, dressed in a similar style to the Emperor's Foot Guards and their blue tunics, but with thigh-length riding boots and tall bearskins that made them genuinely seem like giants, enormous men on the grandest of horses, furious blacks and darkest bays.

*

They formed by squadrons to the left of the spent ranks, Milhaud's horses dripping sweat, riders bent in their saddles with exhaustion. But they still managed a ragged cheer when old Kellerman wheeled his fresh troopers into line beside them. From this new position, Liberté's Section could now see the Goumont Manor House at closer quarters.

'That's what they've been trying to storm?' said Falco. 'It's like a fortress.' Smoke poured from the place and the grounds were filled with dead, but the defenders kept up their fire on some unseen further French assault.

Kellerman was riding casually along the front of his companies, delivering the same meagre message to them all.

'The English are three-quarters beaten, my boys. Time to finish the job.' But he looked frequently to the right, towards that ridge, and the message lacked conviction. All the same, as he left each company behind, the men began to shout, to punch the air with drawn swords.

'Long live the Emperor!'

Or they would sing, though they had no regimental bands with them here. *Veillons au salut de l'Empire* again, while groups of Cuirassiers along that second mass of snorting horses and tossing manes began to beat time, hammering the pommel buttons of their straight sabres against the steel of their breastplates.

No, thought Liberté. *Nothing in the world to better this.*

Then the trumpets called. The singing stopped. Replaced by a more discordant note, thousands of other sabres screeching from their scabbards. The Forward Walk. Gentle pressure of legs. Kick of heels. Clicking of tongues. The rise and fall of a rippling wave, to left and to right. Familiar feel of the saddle. Smell of leather and wax. Stirrup iron beneath the toes. A scent of wet earth. Trampled crops. Horse shit. The sibilant whisper of parting rye. Drumming of hooves that ran up through a trooper's whole body, shook their teeth. Helmet horsehair catching the breeze as they passed from Walk to Trot. The silly words of the trumpet call so that nobody ever forgot, the words heard in each man's head at precisely the same moment, binding them and keeping them as one.

They gathered speed. Soil thrown up now in clods. The wind seeming to gather. An illusion. A feature simply of their own pace. False zephyr. The enemy's cannons belching smoke and flame, all along the ridge. The ground fountained earth towards the heavens. Roundshot sheered through their ranks. Howitzer shells burst above, with shards of iron that flensed the living flesh from those they found. The slope reached. More heel to horses' flanks. And the heads of their mounts beginning to lift, necks turning from the noise and smoke, ears back, eyes growing wild. Some went down in a tangle of legs. Riders thrown forward, arse over tip.

Liberté looked around, checking that the other men of her Section were still safe. Still there. All fine. Bertine shouting something that she could not hear. Not over the noise. The relentless trembling tattoo of their passage. She could not remember the call. But her sword arm was stretched now. At the Guard. She was yelling. Kept yelling. While, ahead, the Goddams switched to case shot. Or double-shotting, peppering them with ball and canister at the same time, from the same barrel. Hailstones. It sounded like hailstones where the case shot's bullets clattered against breastplates. Or sometimes the sound of enormous raindrops splattering against a windowpane, whenever the balls slapped wetly through the wool of a Dragoon's jacket. The shot sometimes took down six horses at a time. The whine and breath-sucking howl of shot and shell. Screaming horses and men too.

They reached the crest, more mounts falling. But into a sunken road, invisible from below. Front ranks disappearing into the gulf as a lesson for those behind. Men clinging to the tails of others' mounts to haul themselves clear. Liberté saw it coming, lifted her backside from the saddle and stretched forward, gathering Lucette's mane in her bridle hand, shifting her weight onto her heels and lengthening the mare's stride so that she cleared the gap with ease. Good as gold. Up. Over. Through the sparse hedge, the gunners running before them, dodging and weaving. Running downhill, she realised. The ridge-top reached.

So now to see what's down the other side, she thought. Yet she already knew. Like so many times in Spain. The reverse slope that flattened slowly. To the place where the Goddams waited. Her eyes were stinging. Stinking smoke. The same for poor Lucette. Though the Percheron still swerved unerringly around the mounds of carnage left by Milhaud's earlier attacks. Liberté dimly perceived the writhing limbs, punctured breastplates and hacked flesh. Beyond them, a shifting scarlet shape that seemed more like some infernal machine than a body of men. A mechanical furnace that spewed flame and flashed an evil abatis of steel points, up and down, to bar their progress. She wondered how they could not be scorched and devoured by the thing. And her horse tried to turn from it, bewildered by terror so that Liberté had to force the mare's head forward again.

'On, beauty,' she howled. On, good girl.'

They had made that discovery, which those who went before had found in their own turn. Not just one square, but a line of them. And behind that, a second line. She could not see them clearly for the smoke and her stinging eyes. But many of the English also seemed to be down. The ranks far from drilled and precise. Ragged and less than steady. English redcoats, of course. Green-coated Nassauers and riflemen. Black-jacket Brunswickers. Casualties. Yet nothing like the shambles of horsemeat and shattered Frenchmen that lay at every turn. Horsemen still strove to leap the bayonet bristle of one square or another, while Liberté herself swung a few useless blows here and there. She checked on her Section once more. Still with her. Still all alive. But how? She had no idea.

There were horses ahead that had stopped entirely. Spent. Dripping. Flecked with spittle. And these seemed to share her immortality. For they merely stood, their riders watching, waiting, as though paralysed. Yet they remained untouched. So that she wondered if this was some stupid dream. For she rode in a form of figure-of-eight around the squares. A dozen of them? Fifteen? Nothing to slash at but thin air. Round and round. Until she lost all track of time.

'Shoot straight, you bastards,' Liberté shouted at those Goddams, until her throat was parched, and she heard the Recall, followed the other green coats ahead of her. Blind. Following each other like sheep. But back, at last, through the English guns.

Why the hell has nobody dragged those buggers away? she thought. *Or spiked the bloody things?*

But they had not. And this was... What? The third charge? So the gunners were practised at their trade now, with their pieces again almost before the last of the horsemen had gone by, pouring case shot that ripped into them even as they fell back down the forward slope.

'By Christ, Dumont,' laughed Falco, as they crossed the valley to their rallying point, 'you're a mad bitch, and no mistake. Me and the lads, we'd follow you anywhere. Our lucky cat, that's what you are.'

They were all wide-eyed, panting, drunk on survival, sweat pouring from horse and rider alike. A couple of the lads had lost their helmets, and everybody was smeared with mud.

And smoke, she thought, glancing around. Smoke rising from them all. *No*, she realised, *not smoke*. Steam. Rising in wispy clouds from each horse's rump or shoulder. She patted Lucette's neck again.

'That'll do, girl,' she said. 'That'll do.'

But as she looked up again, she thought she caught a glimpse. The ghost of a glimpse. A Dragoon officer's uniform. Nothing unusual. Just something that took her eye before the fellow disappeared, quick as a flash, between the Squadron's ranks. A heavily bandaged right hand, the arm in a sling.

Chapter Thirty-Four

Sunday 18th June 1815, 5.30pm

They were going to hit that ridge again. The trumpets told them so. And not just their own Corps, but Milhaud's boys as well, this time.

'At least those lucky buggers have had some rest,' Falco grumbled.

'This will be their third time,' Liberté reminded him. 'Only our second.'

But she was worried, all the same. Lucette's big heart was still racing. And Falco's black stallion, she now saw, was bleeding from its near-side stifle. A bayonet slash, she was certain.

'Well,' Bertine smiled at her, 'we'll just stick with you and we'll be safe enough.'

He reached over and slapped her back, but she knew he was touching her for luck.

It's more than luck I'll need, she thought, *if Henry's somewhere in this lot. A bullet in the back's just too easy on a day like this*. She stood in her stirrups, yet could see nothing to confirm her concerns. But she *could* see the length of their formation now. There must have been ten thousand men and horses. And how many squadrons? Seventy? Eighty?

'Yes,' she said. 'Lucky Liberté, that's me. Stay tight. And stay safe.'

At fifty paces from the slope's summit, the gunners hit them again. Canister and ball, double-shotted once more. Point blank. She saw almost the entire front rank go down in a terrible heaving confusion. Like grass beneath a scythe. Yet they would somehow have to get past. Liberté looked for a gap in the carnage. A passage that might take them safely through. *There!* she thought, looking off to her right, where a few riders had lost their nerve and veered away from the smoke and stabbing flames. *Lucky Liberté*. She turned, pointing, to show her Section the direction they should follow. Falco's eyes were wide and laughing, and she began to shout.

'Lucky...' she mouthed, as the man's entire upper body disappeared with a sound like ripping paper. And, in that very instant, the same roundshot carried whatever was left of him through Bertine's chest and shoulder.

Liberté looked away.

Nothing in the world to better this, kept repeating itself in her head, and the voice would not stop. *Lucky Liberté. Lucky girl.*

There was an English gunner ahead of her. Running. She had come straight through their artillery line without noticing. So she sliced at the fellow in his blue tunic. But not too hard.

Not too quick for you, bastard, she said to herself, as the Englishman tried to protect himself, mumbling something in his stupid bloody language that she did not understand, and as she determined to pay him back with pain on pain for Falco, for Bertine, for...

'Hiding behind your sodding cannon, you cowardly *bugger*!' she screamed.

But there was nothing left of him to kill any more.

Lucky Liberté. Lucky girl.

She looked for something else that would help make the voice stop, found the remaining six men of her Section halted close behind, watching her carefully. And she saw the square of redcoats ahead.

'There!' she yelled. 'There!' Liberté levelled her blade, spurred Lucette forward.

But this was no steady trot, for she pressed the Percheron straight to the canter, leaned forward over the mare's neck. Screaming. The gap closing. Waiting for them to fire. Why did they not fire? Their muskets were levelled. Closer. Nothing. Closer still. She could see the colour of their eyes. Felt fear. For the first time, fear. They were too steady. When it came, it would be...

Her world erupted. The crack of a hundred flints on frizzen pans. A hundred firefly sparks. That cliff face of smoke and ear-splitting sound so solid that any ship of the line would shatter upon it. Five score flashes of flame that lashed out to whip and burn them. As burn them they did. Saddles emptying all around her and the musket balls flicking and snapping past her face like gnats in the night.

Liberté cast about but recognised none of her own. None of them. Yet she saw Sergeant Tranchante, caught in the middle of a mixed group – their Regiment's Dragoons, a couple of Cuirassiers, a Horse Grenadier – that seemed to have been swept away, a wave broken by the same barrier, foaming to the right past that terrible volley, horses almost beyond control, rushing headlong towards the face of a second square. There seemed nowhere else to go. So she nudged Lucette in the same direction, allowed herself to be caught up by the stampede. *Lucky Liberté.* Certain that the next volley would get her. Yet she passed this next batch of redcoats without them firing a shot. The horses kept running. A third square. Some scattered firing. But negligible.

She looked over her shoulder. *Perhaps lucky after all*, she thought, though with bitterness now. To have passed each square while the Goddams were reloading. But the troopers coming up behind seemed also untroubled. The whole mass slowed to a trot, the ground uneven. They must be moving, she knew, towards the English centre, for the top of the ridge was still to her right. Sometimes higher, or dipping on occasions to allow glimpses of the valley below. But it was always to her right.

'Dumont,' shouted Sergeant Tranchante, when they finally reined to a halt. 'Where the hell is your Section?' She felt like taking her sabre and slicing the fool, but the madness passed and she simply shook her head, unable to speak for fear it might grip her again. 'Well,' he said, 'we've still got work to do.' He looked around the men who had rallied to him, as though searching for the most senior among them, an officer perhaps. 'Looks like it's me, then.' There were Lancers with them now, more Cuirassiers too. 'But let's try something different this time, eh, lads? It looks like the Roast Beefs are running low.'

He explained his plan, while Liberté took her bearings. They were almost alongside the Brussels highway. *And that farm*, she thought, *must be the one we could see earlier.* But then she had only been able to make out the roof tiles. For it did, indeed, sit in a hollow. Bigger than she had imagined. High white perimeter walls pocked and peppered with shot. A sand quarry – the district was riddled with them, to keep the roadside bridleway verges properly maintained – on its farther side, the enemy sheltering against its banks. French skirmishers beyond, keeping them and the farm's defenders pinned down. Above the farm, a knoll, from which the ridge continued eastwards, away from them, with the rest of Wellesley's might still hidden there. More squares, though none of them touched as yet by these charges. She could hear the wail of bagpipes, just about see a block of those skirted Scotsmen, believed she could almost sense them staring back at her, wondering when it might be their turn. But there were drums too. *TAN-tra-tran. TAN-tra-tran.* French battalions coming into view through the valley's crops in a determined attack on the place.

That's more like it, she thought. *Smash through them while they're in square.*

'Forward…' yelled Tranchante. 'Walk!'

They moved steadily. Towards the nearest square. But passing more rapidly through any gaps that presented themselves in the almost endless stream of squadrons and companies riding through and around the English positions. Yet this square stood as fast as those Liberté had passed earlier. And then Tranchante found the thing he sought. A fold in the ground. Not deep enough to hide them entirely, but sufficient to allow some shelter from a volley, or from the random bullets that whined and ricocheted in every direction.

'Why don't they fire?' she called to him when they were all within the hollow's protection.

'Nearly out of cartridges, I reckon,' said Tranchante. 'Just need to test that idea though.' She was the only one still mounted, so she wheeled Lucette about and scrambled her back out of the dip. 'Dumont…!' he shouted, but she was already gone, making the Percheron cavort up and down in full view of the Englishmen. She even unfastened the helmet, threw it aside, shook her hair loose so it flowed free.

'Want some, Johnnie?' she spat at them. The only three words of English she possessed. Yet she kept the horse moving, side-passing one way, then the other, irregular steps to make herself a more difficult target. Nothing. So she unslung the Dragoon musket on its swivel, checked the priming, steadied Lucette, and fired. One of them fell. A flurry of activity. Angry shouts from the rankers. Muskets raised. And a frantic officer running down their line. Desperate commands.

'You're right, Sarge,' she called back over her shoulder.

'Get down from there, you bloody idiot,' he shouted back, though, at the same time, organising his tatterdemalion command into sections. 'You lads,' he said, tapping several of the Dragoons on their shoulders, 'skirmish line. Lancers to stand ready. You two, horse-holders. The rest, follow me when I give the word.'

The skirmishers were up and out, on foot, alongside Liberté. They worked in pairs. One loading, one firing. Picking off Goddams whenever there was a clear shot. No response.

'Do we take the officer down?' one of them called.

'Christ, no,' Tranchante told them. 'He's holding them nice and tight for us. Just keep it up. And Lancers... get to it. The rest, saddle up.'

The Lancers spurred out of the hollow, one of them in the scarlet that had formerly marked out the 2nd Regiment, the other two from their Polish Squadron, in their blue and crimson. And, by God, she had seen them work some miracles in the past. Spain. Leipzig too. And Brienne.

They have no fear, those lads, she said to herself, as the three men waited for their path to clear, then walked their horses forward, chatting amiably enough to each other. Sharing a joke. It seemed they would simply walk straight through the square's front line. She held her breath. For that front line, the men all kneeling, was edging back into the fellows behind them. Some stood, looked around for instruction. And then a lance snaked out. A fisherman making a strike. One of the redcoats speared through the guts, the Pole pulling his catch out through the ranks.

No firing. Though a couple of the Goddams, ignoring orders, sprang up, ran forward with the bayonet, were cut down in their turn while the officer tried desperately to plug his gaps, maintain discipline.

'Now,' Tranchante shouted, and the rest of his group were riding out of the hollow too, Liberté setting her heels to join them, her musket still in her hand and useless to her unless she stopped to reload. But that was not the point. The skirmishers were running too, firing when they were able, and the Lancers speared one more fish, hauled the fellow kicking and screaming to one side while one of their shafts was hurled like a javelin, piercing a redcoat's leg and pinning him to the ground, upright in his place.

They must break, she told herself. *They must!*

She saw their front line fold upon itself. Just one split and they would be through. And she knew that once inside a broken square, twenty troopers could take out a battalion. Yet they did not fold enough. Maybe reinforcements brought from one of the other three faces. Perhaps just the personality of that damned Roast Beef officer. But the volley hit them from fifteen paces and, when the smoke cleared, she was alone. Only two horses left standing apart from Lucette. The Red Lancer still in his saddle, fingers twitching at the reins, his face missing. The rest were dead or trapped beneath their dying horses. And Tranchante was on his knees, his arms stretched out towards the square, fists bunched, but now entirely without life.

Liberté recalled a favourite tale from her childhood, saw herself back in that family apartment, her mother sitting on the edge of her bed and reading by the candle's dim light. Voltaire's *Zadig*. Much of it she had not understood, but the poetry of Voltaire's language had been like music to her. She had taken especially to the chapter in which the eponymous hero wanders aimlessly on the banks of the Euphrates and meets a hermit who introduces him to the Book of Destinies. And Liberté felt like Zadig now, as she drifted without aim, searching for her Company, her Squadron, anything that might help anchor her in this bizarre world. And for a moment she thought she too must be dead, destined to wander in this after-life searching for her fellows for evermore. *Lucky Liberté*!

Yet all she found were more squares of the enemy. Though here, strangely, she seemed to find the familiar, and her absurd heart skipped a little. Not redcoats. No, these were the green jackets of the Jägers she had last seen in the yard of the Gémioncourt Farm. But, like the English, these fellows refused to fire when she rode at them. And through the haze of the shock and stupidity now confounding her, she thought briefly that she might lean on her old acquaintance with them to beg a few drops of water. *Or brandy*, she thought. *What I would not give now for a shot of Marianne's rotgut*. For her thirst, her need for liquor, was terrible, burning through her innards.

'Hot work, Liberté,' sneered a voice at her side. 'But I doubt those boys will be too inclined to help you.'

She turned to see a face she recognised, though she had to dig among a whole pile of rubble in her mind to attach a name. For the features seemed somewhat altered.

'Ah, Lieutenant,' she said at last. 'How's your arm now?'

He had to use his left hand to lift it, even in its stained sling. And she idly noticed that the hand held a cavalry pistol.

'It stinks a bit, does it not?' said Lieutenant Henry. The skin was stretched tight across his cheeks, the eyes darkly ringed, febrile sweat upon his brow,

'You should have let the saw-bones take it while you had the chance,' she murmured.

'But then I could not have done my duty,' he said. 'I had thought the English would have finished you by now, yet you seem to have a charmed life.'

Lucky Liberté, she thought. *Lucky girl*.

Her feet were hanging loose, aching, from her stirrups, and she wondered what she should do next. Henry was resting the pistol on the saddle holsters, which were covered by his sheepskin shabraque. The weapon was cocked and aimed at her chest, shaking a little but, at this range, he could not miss.

'Dumont, is that you?' somebody shouted, in perfect French.

She looked towards the Dutch-Belgians' square, just as Lieutenant Henry did the same. But, unlike Fouché's assassin, she did not let the moment linger. Rather, she rolled back in her saddle, bringing her left leg up, bending the knee to her chest, and kicked with all her might, jarring the heel of her boot into his injured arm. The hurt must have been terrible, for he dropped the pistol, leaned sideways to catch it, fell heavily onto the trampled earth, squealing with pain.

She imagined she heard a cheer and laughter from the Dutchies' ranks as she pulled back on Lucette's reins, turned the mare in a tight circle. Her head cleared a little. She threw down the useless musket, pulled aside her own sheepskin saddle cover and reached for a pistol of her own. *Stupid bitch*, she thought. Not to have unbuckled the flaps. She fumbled with the fastening, saw Henry on his knees, his mount bucking sideways, its nerve gone completely. But her holster flap came open just as he picked up his pistol, cocked and levelled the thing at her.

Lucette reared wildly as the gun discharged. Nothing. Liberté had expected to feel the impact. But she felt nothing. *Lucky Liberté*. Her own pistol was in her hand and she pulled back the hammer's head. No need to check the priming. There had been plenty of time for that during the long hours of waiting.

'He will find you,' said Henry. 'And you can't very well shoot me here, can you? In full view of the enemy? What would your Little Shaveling say?'

She thought for a moment, then squeezed the trigger.

'He'd probably say something about victory belonging to the most persevering.'

But in the midst of her own small victory, she felt Lucette shudder, stumble forward towards the waiting bayonets and levelled muskets.

She sat in the mud at the corner of the Dutch-Belgians' square, with the Percheron's head in her lap. And while she had never felt anything but wild rage at the battlefield death of friends and comrades in the past, now she was filled with an uncontrollable grief, a deep pit of agony that sat like a lump of iron in her guts, her chest and her throat. In all her strangest dreams, she had never imagined anything but her own end, as though Lucette must be immune from any danger.

'All those places we have seen, my beautiful,' she said. 'The things we have done.'

Liberté saw herself reflected, distorted, in that exquisite dark glass of Lucette's eye, and she knew that she should have ended this. But the old girl did not seem to be suffering. She was perfectly still, showed no sign of distress apart from that quiet snicker that she gave sometimes when she did not quite understand an unintended pressure on her bit or contact with some part of her rider's form.

'You should let her go now,' said Rebecque. It was Thin William's Chief-of-Staff who had recognised her, called her name, distracted Lieutenant Henry.

She felt that she should have been grateful to him, but could not find it in her heart.

'You should have let your men shoot,' she said.

Another debt. For when Lucette had tumbled towards the square, with the assassin's bullet intended for Liberté deep within her, the Dutchmen, muskets levelled, would have wasted an entire volley on them had Rebecque not ordered them to Hold Fire.

'That would have been a terrible waste,' he replied. 'Almost down to our last *cartouche*. And no chance of any more until we can shift you chaps off this plateau and get ourselves back into proper formation. And I dread to think what would happen if these fellows had nothing left in their pouches. They are pure gold, the bunch of them. And you saw how they fought the other day. But they've had enough now. We all have, don't you think?'

Had enough? she thought. *There's never enough. Not for us.* She remembered a priest once, back in the early days, who had told her his belief that war was God's gift to mankind. That He had bestowed on all other creatures some mysterious way to keep balance and order in their numbers. Extraordinary ways. Pestilence. Famine. Yet, to mankind, cursed with the power of invention to conquer those other controls, he had added the unique thirst for warfare.

'Then let them run, Baron,' she said. 'You saved Wellesley's bacon at Quatre Bras, did you not? The least you can do now is allow your men to live.'

She stroked Lucette's jowl with one hand, the mare's gentle face with the other.

'Well, I've rallied them three times already,' Rebecque said. 'It would seem such a waste of effort if I stopped now. And the Prince, I'm sure, would not approve. There are strange chains, at times, that bind us, don't you think?'

Yes, she thought, *strange chains*. Lucette shivered. Just once. As though cold. And the light went out in that loyal and loving eye. And Liberté, who never cried, found she was weeping silent tears.

'I can't promise anything,' Rebecque told her. 'But if we hold this place, if we are responsible for burial details, I shall try to ensure that she remains safe.'

Safe from the scavengers and the knacker-men, she thought.

'No need,' she said. 'We'll be back to claim this ridge soon enough. I'll make sure she rests as she deserves.'

Rebecque looked around at the hundreds of other mounts that lay dead and dying between the squares. There was disbelief in his eyes.

'Why don't they stop?' he said, waving a hand at the horsemen still thundering past.

'Fall back without instruction?' she asked him. 'Without the trumpets' Recall? It would look too much like a rout, don't you think? It might spread. And then we should be deprived of the honour of pushing Wellesley into the sea. So we cannot retreat. But it seems that we cannot fight either.'

'And why should one of your own want you dead, Trooper Dumont?'

'It seems,' she said, 'that I have upset people in high places. Why do you ask? You plan to have me shot as a spy again?'

Rebecque smiled.

'No,' he said. 'You may go with God. For if Fouché is so intent on murdering one of his own spies, I can only collect that it must be in *our* interests to keep you alive. Besides, the Lord may not be best pleased if I were given the chance to save such an astonishing daughter of Eve and passed up on the opportunity.'

'You felt no such compunction two days ago,' she said.

'Ah, but two days ago I was under orders and had no choice in the matter. At least your face looks better than it did then. Amazing what forty-eight hours of healthy living can do for you.'

And where, she wondered, as Rebecque retired back to the centre of his square, *is Thin William himself?* Yet there was no sign of the pederast Prince as she took the second pistol from Lucette's holsters, buried her face in the white-grey mane for the last time, and began to make her way across that field so unlike any other that she and the Percheron had battled over. Liberté knew she must make a strange sight herself, of course. No helmet to cover her hair, nor its visor to mask her distinctive features. So was not surprised by the puzzled glances she attracted as she passed among the riders. A woman in the ranks was not unique, but unusual enough to turn heads. And many knew her name, her reputation, if not her face.

'Liberté Dumont?' they would call. 'You need a stirrup.'

She ignored them for the most part. Too wrapped in her own sorrow. Biting back tears. She would not ride again. Not for a while. Maybe never. Though there was the Emperor's letter to deliver. The journey to Vienna that she hoped never to make. Yet, if make it she must, the idea of travelling without Lucette was unbearable. Yet a stirrup? To where?

There were still horsemen continuing their lunatic hippodrome circuits, and she had even seen Redhead Ney among them, hatless, waving his sword around, shouting like a madman. *But why is he here?* she thought, bitterly. *Why not acting like the commander he's supposed to be?* It may have been heroic, but it was a gesture, and she cursed him for it. *Why not organising the battalions of foot to follow up here? To smash these squares. Why no batteries of guns brought up to pound the buggers?* She could almost taste victory, see a ragged line of English fugitives streaming up the Brussels highway in reality now. The enemy cavalry in no position to intervene either. Standing aloof over there, their own numbers reduced, fit for nothing but pursuit if the chance arose. Though doubtless burning to chance their hand with this tempting target.

Tempting indeed. For many of Liberté's comrades were not even bothering to move now. Half of the French squadrons seemed to have dismounted, resting their horses within easy musket-range of the Goddams. The two sides simply gazing at each other, twenty or thirty paces apart. And she even felt sorry for the English bastards, many of them so weary they could no longer stand, their officers hauling them back to their feet again.

Their officers… or their sergeants.

She had passed four or five squares already, trying to find some sign of her own Squadron or its remains, but as she turned a corner of the next – this one badly depleted too – Liberté saw him. He was kicking a soldier too exhausted to even respond. And the rogue was unmistakable, as he had been in her visions, and at Quatre Bras. The same purple-blotched face. She realised she had halted in her own tracks, bewitched by his proximity. And he, in turn, knew that he was observed. He straightened, hefted his musket, yelled at her through those blackened teeth. She did not understand the precise words but his intention was clear enough.

And you're the creature, she thought, *that killed the woman who stole my sister.*

She laughed. Something of hysteria in it. A madness that was part the result of this irony, part borne by Marianne Tambour's thirst for vengeance against him, part outpouring of her own losses, and part the consequence of this day's opportunities squandered. For behind her, on the ridge-top, two French twelve-pounders were being manhandled through the mud and chaos. They would bring wrack and ruin to some of these Goddams. But too little. Too late.

And this one was still shouting obscenities at her. Not just shouting, but gesturing with his hand on his thrusting groin.

So she took the second pistol, cocked it, took aim. At his balls.

He stopped his capering at once, the idiot grin slipping from his face, and he raised his musket.

Not quick enough, she thought, squeezed the trigger. The hammer fell. But nothing more. *Lucette's fall*, she thought. *The priming.* And as, for the second time today, she faced certain death, the sergeant's company commander ran forward, knocked the musket aside. *Why?*

Then the trumpets called at last. The Rally.

Lucky Liberté, she said to herself. And looked around for a stirrup to take her away from here after all.

Chapter Thirty-Five

Sunday 18th June 1815, 6.30pm

Fronsac's Company was moving fast, at the Double, towards the first houses of that same village Marianne had seen a couple of hours earlier from the ridge, with Fabrizio. They were marching towards the sound of the guns – but these were Prussian guns. And the Prussians were not supposed to be there.

'We should have finished the buggers while we had the chance,' said Muhler. 'The horse-boys should have cut them down.'

'They can only go where they're sent,' Marianne told him, flicking her whip at the pony's shoulder to keep the cart moving. She felt a sudden and unexplained need to put a protective arm around the cavalry. 'It'll be some idiot general. Fallen down in his duty again.'

'If I was the Shaveling,' said Marle, 'I'd have them shot. The bloody lot of them. But here we are again, having to clean up the mess they always leave behind.'

'Shooting's too good for them,' said Fronsac. 'We could have been sitting nice and snug in Brussels. If they'd been doing their job properly.'

But nobody really spoke of Brussels any more and Marianne had the sense that, instead, they would all find themselves back in Charleroi before too long, with this battle neither won nor lost. *Always another day*, she thought. *Another fight. Though not for me. Not for Poppy neither.* Yet when she looked at Fronsac, she could see that light in his eye, and knew he would never leave this.

'Never mind, Fronsac' she said. 'We'll not have to worry about colonels and generals much longer. Just think about that inn. *The Old Grenadier.*'

He nodded enthusiastically enough. *Too enthusiastically*, she thought. *And anyway, who am I to talk? Look at me. I could have stayed back there with the girl and Argonne. But the first whiff of gun smoke, and here I am. Like the bloody fool I've always been.* For this was not even a battalion action. Only the Fourth Company detailed for this one. *But Fronsac's Company*, she told herself. *What was I going to do? Let him out of my sight again?*

'Look,' snarled the corporal, Poncet, 'more splitters.'

They were approaching a farm track that cut across their own lane. The men straggling along it, however, were not marching to the sound of the guns, but away from it. Some of them wounded. Yet the rest simply trudging south, most without weapons and packs. She saw Captain Vicquot break away from the column, try to remonstrate with the deserters, but he was having no success.

'Ah, they're all just lads,' said Fronsac. 'Wet behind the ears, most of them. Not worth worrying about.'

But then another batch of fugitives was streaming towards them, directly away from the smoke and fire of Plancenoit itself. And these were not raw recruits. These were men of the Imperial Guard – admittedly the Young Guard, the recently formed *Tirailleur* and *Voltigeur* regiments, but they carried the Emperor's honour with them all the same.

'You useless bastards,' Marle shouted at them. 'Get back in there.'

And some scuffling broke out, the Battalion's advance halted while they tried to push the deserters into a semblance of order.

It had begun some time before, the Battalion still waiting near the highway, at the Rosomme Farm. The rumours had continued, the mood among the men darkening, and then that trickle had started. Ones and twos at first. Then more and more. Attempts made to turn them, but usually without result. There were threats to execute them. A few pressed back into action. But most simply hurried past while, away to the east, and growing louder by the minute, the sounds of a second battle developing on their flank. There was no time, really, to worry about a few cowards. No real issue though, they had said to each other. And Lobau's Corps was over there, was it not? Marianne had seen them, holding the village. Plancenoit, that was the place. Only twenty *arpents* away though. A couple of thousand paces.

Then word that Lobau had been driven out of the hamlet. Reinforcements needed. All eight battalions of the Young Guard's *Tirailleurs* and *Voltigeurs* sent off to support them. And here was the result.

They had known, of course. Known it must have all gone sour, when one battalion of Foot Chasseurs, and then a battalion of Grenadiers, had marched off as well. But they had been surprised when their own Company had been sent after them too.

'I still don't understand why it's just us,' said Cazajus. 'Why not the rest of the Battalion.'

'We're just lucky that way, I guess,' said Fronsac. 'The others must have got themselves in the shit,' he went on, 'if they need us to go in and wipe their noses. After all, we're the best of the rest, aren't we?'

Captain Vicquot had his orders.

'We cross the stream here,' he said. 'Then straight up that main street. Steel only, boys. There's Prussos between us and the church. We don't want to give them any warning. And, for pity's sake, when we break them, no chasing the buggers.'

'Prisoners, sir?' Marle shouted.

'What about them?' Vicquot replied.

Well, that's clear enough, Marianne thought. They had approached by trails that brought them south of Plancenoit, so the ridge on which she had stood with Fabrizio rose ahead of her, beyond the village. There were French units up there. The remnants of Lobau's battalions in square, guns and horse. Between, there was the ford, a cobbled lane on the far side leading off to the left, lined with houses, and each house a battlefield of its own. Screams, smoke and musket fire. Beyond the lane, and straight before them, the road climbed into the centre of Plancenoit, some larger buildings, and the church that was their target.

Vicquot nodded at Sergeant Flambert.

'Company…' bellowed the sergeant.

'What about the moans and groans, Sarge?' said Fronsac, masking his voice and keeping his head low, hoping to remain anonymous.

'That'll do, Fronsac,' Vicquot told him. 'Carry on, Sergeant.'

'Company… Charge Bayonets!'

The men's muskets came down from the Shoulder, bayonets levelled.

'Company will advance by Column of Sections. At the Double…'

The First Section marched across the fording place, four ranks, each a dozen or more men abreast. And the Second Section followed just behind, Fronsac's *Peloton* A, forming the front rank. Twelve of them, now that they had lost Pons and Senent. Bringing up the rear, Marianne and the canteen cart.

'Not you, Tambour,' Corporal Poncet told her. 'Captain's orders. No further than the stream,' he said.

'Just you try and stop me, Poncet,' she spat, 'and see what happens to you, my lad.'

Stay here? she thought. *With the Prussos running around? And a fortune hanging about my neck? I don't think so.*

And, apart from the creaking of the cart's hub spindles and the steady tramp of the men's boots, the advance proceeded in total silence. It was the trick of the bayonet. You either screamed like a banshee as you ran forward, or you kept it as silent and slow as an ice floe. All a matter of nerve. Nobody in his right mind, Marianne had long since realised, truly wanted to face that cruel fifteen-inch piece of wickedness. So it was always about resolve. It was the thing that the Imperial Guard did better than any army in Europe. Prove that your resolve was always steadier than the other fellow's, create that reputation, and your enemy would run. Somebody *always* ran. As the Prussians who suddenly found themselves with this bristling phalanx at their backs did now. They turned to see the famous bearskins and blue summer coats of the Guard bearing down upon them, recognised the futility of every other option, and they ran. Not a shot had been fired. Not a word spoken. Not a single enemy stood against them. But, against their orders, the Grenadiers broke ranks and ran after them, stabbing and clubbing as they went. They drove them through the houses, into the grounds of a rectory that had already seen much fighting, bodies thick around its garden, among the apple trees.

'There's work for us here, Cocotte,' said Marianne and drove the pony on past thatched cottages, to a farm that stood beyond the church. She turned in through the main gate to find the yard serving as a dressing station, a two-wheeled ambulance loading up with its pair of stretcher cases, and the low background drone of crooning agonies, whispered weeping.

'Can you dress wounds?' a man in a blood-soaked apron shouted to her above the cannons' roar and the musketry's insistent chatter.

'Is Fat Louis a Bourbon?' she replied. 'Of *course* I can dress wounds.'

They were coming in thick and fast. Their own Foot Chasseurs and Grenadiers. Some Line Fusiliers who had been here since the Prussians' first attack. And the nature of the fighting was evident from their injuries, the way men bore them, many shocked into silence. A young lad's eyes had been gouged out, yet he made not a word of complaint when she bathed the sockets. A soldier of the 107th had lost both feet at the ankles yet demanded to know only whether the Emperor was yet victorious. Every muscle of his face and body spoke of intolerable pain, yet his voice murmured only the language of martyrdom. Though such stoicism was not universal.

'Can't you shut them up?' demanded a man that she took for a veteran. 'All their whining.' Yet he screamed when she probed the bayonet wound to his arm that looked, to Marianne, only superficial. 'Well,' he said, 'I expect this will at least be worth a discharge and a pension.'

The Prussians' wounded were here too. She was busy tending one of them, wrapping a badly gashed temple in a linen dressing, when she noticed old Cazajus carrying another of Fronsac's platoon members, Abnet, into the yard.

'Can you help him?' said Cazajus, but she could see that his friend was already dead.

'Fronsac?' she said, as they laid Abnet's body against the wall, another addition to the line of corpses.

'They're not making it easy for us,' said Cazajus, and he crossed himself, helped usher Abnet into an afterlife which, she knew, did not exist. *Old habits die hard*, she thought. 'But our friend Fronsac's still frightening them. We could all do with a wet, though.'

She dragged two spare water bottles from the cart, then grabbed the *tonnelet* and followed Cazajus down the cobbled road, through the two-storey lych gate and around the church mound, up past ancient gravestones strewn throughout the cemetery and enclosed by a shoulder-high stone wall.

Captain Vicquot had managed to regroup the Company and they now held the far left, the highest and north-eastern stretch. Yew trees grew all around the inside of the perimeter wall and Fronsac was perched here among sturdy branches, sniping over the wall while Catherine Argonne's man loaded for him below. There were casualties everywhere. Though, thankfully, the rest of *Peloton* A seemed all present and correct apart from poor Abnet.

'How is he?' Fronsac shouted to her, and she shook her head. 'Bastards,' he said, and hefted up the loaded Charleville that Argonne handed him. 'Oh, shit,' he cried, as he looked over the wall. 'Here they come again.'

There was no real order, she saw, just the mingled platoons and companies running for the wall, to the fire steps they had built from whatever shrines, tombstones and grave markers could be rapidly employed for the purpose, and some wooden pews from the church itself. Marianne went from place to place, selling the croaker at two sous a shot, while the wall began to rattle and vibrate with balls that bounced from the flint and limestone, the evening air filled with the war cries of a thousand barbarians.

'Water!' some of the men shouted. For lack of coins to buy the brandy, she thought.

'You'll need that later,' she told them. But they already knew that, so would not press the point.

'Can you spare some of your rot-gut for me, my dear?' called a Colonel whom she did not recognise. He was sitting at the base of the grassy hillock on which the church had been built, his leg heavily bandaged but still bleeding badly. He was surrounded by his officers, an Adjutant-Major, a couple of captains, each of his staff sporting one or more serious injuries. 'Go on, Paton,' he said to one of these, a man with his arm in a sling, 'hold their fire until the very last. You understand?'

By Marat, thought Marianne, *they don't have a sound set of limbs between them.*

'Of course, Colonel,' she replied. 'Four sous each shot, if you please.'

'That's daylight robbery,' said the Colonel.

'If you have any complaints,' she told him, 'I suggest you take them up with the Shaveling. He's always happy to pay my prices.'

The Prussians were coming over the wall like wounds that bled too fast to be staunched. The third assault in thirty minutes and, between each new onslaught, the buggers had been dropping howitzer shells with terrifying accuracy, so there were now more dead here above the ground than below it. Agide and Daubanne looked set to join them, both beyond her skills.

It's all those you can't save that shape you.

Yet that meant the platoon had now lost fully one-third of its number. And whether the rest of the Company fared any better, she could not say, for Captain Vicquot had taken the First Section to help plug another hole, just up the road, where the Prussos had sent in a flanking attack. She had no idea by what mathematical ratio they might be outnumbered, but she knew it was hopeless; simply kept low and kept running, stretching the last drops of water as far as she was able – now they were needed – and the final dregs of her energy too.

'You know,' said Fronsac, 'just at this moment, the stuff tastes better than the dog-dog. And we're not charging for it?'

'I'll pass the hat later,' she said, then saw that Trinquart and Lejeune were each rummaging in their cartridge pouches for the last rounds. She had just picked up some spare ammunition from Daubanne.

'Here,' she said to the two men, 'take these.'

They were being pushed back towards the lych gate, a thin line now, but unshakeable, the Prussos crowding at them and so close that the bayonet points of each side were almost touching whenever they fired. "Point blank" barely did the thing justice, and the wounds, at that range, were some of the worst Marianne had ever seen. Red-rimmed eyes stared wide and wild through blackened faces. Powder-stained teeth clenched and ground in mouths too parched to even raise spit. So she barely recognised Sergeant Flambert when he hobbled up behind them, through the smoke, blood staining the hip of his trousers.

'Tambour,' he said, gripping the cask strap, 'what the hell are you doing here? The Captain said...'

'Sod the Captain,' she told him. 'What's happened to your leg?'

'One of our own, I'm ashamed to say. Captain will explain.'

'Where is he anyway? What's happening?'

'We're pulling back. He's had orders. Where's Poncet?' But Corporal Poncet could not be distinguished any easier than the rest, so she helped the sergeant, going along the line and tapping on the shoulder each member of the Section they could find, trying to make it clear that they should drop out. Some refused, of course, and she doubted she would ever see those fellows again.

'I thought we were finished that time,' said Fronsac, as they stumbled onto the road. He looked back into the graveyard once more. 'And those poor sods...'

'For the Glory of France,' she murmured, then ran through the farm's gate, her arms and legs like lead, her head dizzy with fatigue, dragged Cocotte behind her and climbed the street in the wake of their survivors.

'On your guard here, boys,' Flambert told them, and they kept their muskets trained on the Prussians, those who were pressed low against the walls of a green-shuttered house to their right, who would occasionally risk a shot through the open windows at the French Chasseurs barricaded within. Then bullets flicked at them, struck the cart, shot from a single-storey cottage on the left, filled with Prussian blue, while a platoon of Grenadiers kicked in the front door and died in the attempt to recapture the place.

They found Captain Vicquot sitting on a milestone that marked the distance to Brussels. He was weeping.

'I couldn't save them,' he said, as snot trickled down his upper lip. There were Prussian dead behind him, sprawled against a wall. Prisoners. Each of them had a gashed throat.

'Lads from the Second Chasseurs,' said the sergeant. 'They reckoned the Prussos had killed some of our boys who wanted to surrender. They weren't best pleased when the Captain and me tried to stop them.'

'They're only Prussos, sir,' offered Fronsac. But most of the men looked away. *Standing guard against the enemy,* thought Marianne, *though, in truth, they're all ashamed, like me. That an officer of the Imperial Guard should be whinging about the fate of a few prisoners.*

'No worse than they've done to us in the past, Captain,' she said. In truth, there were more scores to settle against the Prussians, she reckoned, than even against the Roast Beefs. *And anyway,* she thought, *he wasn't so prissy before. "What about them?" Wasn't that what he'd said.*

'And not safe to stay here, sir,' Sergeant Flambert told him, hoisting the captain to his feet.

'Where to, Sarge?' said Fronsac.

'It seems like the Shaveling's had enough of all this nonsense. The whole of the Guard's going in, they say. These lads will hold the back door.' He stabbed with his thumb, over his shoulder. 'Now then. Any moans, groans, beefs or bones?' There were none.

They wheeled left at the end of the street, near another apple orchard, and were climbing the track up the ridge as another battalion of dark-coated enemy infantrymen, black and white flags flying, were charging into the village behind them. *Close,* she thought. *Five more minutes and we'd have walked into the middle of that.* She swung her legs around on the cart so she could watch, and she gave a little cheer as a group of Grenadiers was rallied alongside the orchard wall, pushed and pulled into line by a bare-headed officer in an ankle-length coat, who had even managed to find himself some drummers. The odds were absurd. Perhaps forty French against ten times that number, but as the *Pas de Charge* was beaten, she knew that they could do it. The first section of the Quick drifted up to her – *TAN-tra-tran, TAN-tra-tran* – but then she also saw the battery of Prussian Horse Artillery sweeping in front of their own column, unlimbering in seconds and, before the Grenadiers had taken twenty paces, firing their first salvo. Case shot. Into their faces. And when the smoke cleared, the Frenchmen had all been blown to hell.

The lump of leaden loss that filled Liberté Dumont's soul had not diminished. If anything, its weight had become a physical thing that filled her boots and made every step intolerable. A tiredness that defied description and erased the heart-lifting memories of all she had seen this past hour. The fall of that farm near the sand quarry – Holy Hedge, it was called – and the raising of a French battle standard upon its roof; the English battalion sent to recapture the place and entirely destroyed by Cuirassiers, who had remained out of sight until the very moment they fell upon the Goddams; and that troop of the Guard's Horse Artillery deployed to the left of the farm and, along with the Grand Battery's continued bombardment, wrought so much damage on the enemy that their guns along the ridge had fallen silent one by one.

She should have been elated.

But as she mingled with the survivors of her own Regiment, the talk was all sombre. She had fought among the English squares and wondered at the lack of infantry support. And now she discovered that entire Divisions of Reille's Corps had indeed been marched to their aid. But, once again, too little, too late. Destroyed. Then, while the rest of their horsemen had been pouring back from the futile attacks against the ridge, Kellerman's reserve, that burnished bronze Carabinier Brigade, had been sent forward alone and returned in tatters.

'Ney should be hung,' men muttered.

'Traitors!' they said. 'Those damned generals have betrayed the Emperor again.'

Not all generals, naturally. Their own Kellerman, hero of Marengo, had been wounded yet again. Milhaud, who had led the first two charges, had been unhorsed, the beast shot from beneath him, and barely escaped with his life. Yet, while she blamed the Marshals and generals collectively as much as the rest, Liberté reserved the greatest condemnation for herself. It was almost a litany.

What else can you expect from generals? she thought. *But it was me. I betrayed the Emperor. I should have done more. If I had killed that English sergeant, or others like him, perhaps that square would have folded. And if that one had gone, maybe others would have broken too.*

And if she'd killed Wellesley…

She envisaged a house of playing cards, like those that some of her Section had built, at times, for amusement… *But they will build them no more,* she recalled. *I led them to destruction as surely as Ney led the rest of us. It was me. I betrayed the Emperor.*

Then her fevered brain turned to the Shaveling's other Marshals. His Chief-of-Staff, Soult. They all knew that he would have been better utilised in a field command. That Berthier should have been here to act at the Emperor's side.

Yet, with your help, Dumont, she said to herself, *old Berthier fell from that window in Bamberg. It was me. I betrayed the Emperor.*

And her mission for Fouché.

It was me. I betrayed the Emperor.

The words of Lieutenant Henry still rang in her ears too.

'*He* will *find you.*'

Oh, she was sure of that. She would end her life in a ditch somewhere, shot down or knifed by an unknown hand. She deserved no less.

The Regiment was back where it had begun, to the south of that Gum Hill House where, despite everything else, fighting still continued. But the Dragoon Squadrons were broken. Many, like herself, had lost their mounts, and not bothered to replace them were sat upon the ground, telling sad stories of the fall of friends while, around them, the Cuirassier units of Kellerman's Corps did the same. None of these would fight again this day, and nobody even bothered about those who were drifting off, in twos or threes, towards the south.

And then a galloper was racing towards them.

'Oh, no,' chorused the men. 'Not again.'

But the Aide was grinning like a fool, not what they had expected.

'Grouchy,' he was yelling. 'Grouchy is coming. Thirty thousand men. Listen, you can hear them.'

She listened. And yes, there was fresh cannon fire. Away to the northeast. They could all hear it. Fresh hope. The tiredness beginning to fall away. From Liberté, and from many of those around her.

Well, I shall betray him no more. And perhaps a fresh horse, after all. I'd better report to Tranchante and...

But Sergeant Tranchante, she remembered, was dead upon that ridge with all the rest.

She began to trudge off towards the Hotel of the Beautiful Alliance, then thought once more about Marianne. *Yet I have a sister to protect too*, she thought. *And my sister has a debt to settle. That English sergeant.*

So she swung south, ashamed to be seen with those fellows who were still heading that way despite the news about Grouchy, but knowing that the Imperial Guard was still clustered in that direction too, around the Rosomme Farm. Knowing that she could just as easily find a remount there as among the Regiment's picket lines.

There must be a way, she thought. *To settle with that English pig on Marianne's behalf. To keep my sister and her child from harm. To help build the girl a better life. To atone for my betrayal of the Emperor. I will serve him now as I have never done before. And, at the end, I shall return to him the letter he intended for his son. For he will not need to send it now. But I must find a way to escape Fouché's clutches. Even if it means some sacrifice to do so.*

Chapter Thirty-Six

Sunday 18th June 1815, 7.30pm

'Where is your Maman, girl?' Liberté demanded.

'With Fronsac, of course,' replied Florisette. The canteen tent was here, but no sign of the cart. 'My Papi.'

'Yes, but where?' said Liberté, her patience running thin. And she could not help glancing over to the east, where another battle was plainly raging. Too close for comfort, as well.

'Why do you want to know?' Poppy asked her. She was sitting inside the tent flap, playing with some mop-topped wooden figure.

'Your father made that for you?' said Liberté

'That useless bugger?' Liberté spun about to find the one-legged woman behind her, propped on a crutch and wiping greasy hands on her apron. 'I carved it for her,' said Catherine Argonne. 'Mine are all lads.' Liberté could see the boys, some at their chores, a couple romping in the tall crops. All fated for the army when they grew. 'What is it you want with Tambour, Trooper?'

'Absolution,' said Liberté, and began listing items on her fingers. 'Confession. Protection for her. Salvation for me.'

'And the girl?'

Liberté kept the four fingers raised.

'The same four things, it seems,' she said. 'And a family bond for us to seal.'

'I could see it the first time I set eyes on you,' Argonne told her. 'You could almost be sisters, you and Marianne. But the poor dear sometimes can't recognise the forest for the trees. What are you? Cousins?'

'Not exactly,' said Liberté, deciding that she did not know this woman enough to trust her with the truth, yet still needing her help. 'But I must find her. She wasn't with the Battalion when I passed them on the road. The fellows I asked said they'd not seen her.'

'The Company went off to Plancenoit,' said Argonne. 'My own fool of a husband with them. And Marianne too. They've not come back.'

'They sent a single company?' said Liberté.

'Two whole battalions *and* a single company,' the one-legged woman replied, pointing towards the sounds of musketry and cannon. '*None* of them have come back.'

Plancenoit? thought Liberté. *Wasn't that the place we went foraging this morning? And what was it that Bertine had said to the priest there. "With a bit of luck, you can then settle down to a nice peaceful day. We'll try not to disturb your Sunday too much." Wasn't that it?*

'What's she doing there?' she said. It was a stupid question.

'Making money, of course,' said the woman. 'Same as the rest of us. The girl tells me Marianne's got her head full of ideas about opening an inn, all of a sudden. An inn. Can you imagine? With Fronsac splashing her profits up against the wall every night. But you know Tambour. If there's a sou to be made, she'll always be first in the queue.'

As it happens, thought Liberté, *I don't really know her at all. And an inn?*

'I'm going to try and find her,' she said. She would need the horse now, of course, but there were plenty here.

'Are you coming back, lady?' The girl held up the ragged doll as though she had not asked the question herself. 'And bringing Mami with you?'

'I'll do my best, Florisette,' Liberté told her.

'If you do,' said the child, 'I'll try to like you. And then you can call me Poppy.'

She found a remount, and more besides, at the farm itself. It was now serving as a general supply depot and hospital too, but as Liberté trotted onto the road, on an unfamiliar but biddable chestnut stallion, she found a fresh team being harnessed to the Emperor's dark blue dormeuse. His open carriage was there too. But the normal escort of Imperial Guard Horse Chasseurs was missing, only the drivers and a single postilion in attendance.

'Are you not staying with the Emperor then?' she asked the fellow. It was irregular for the vehicles to be so far removed from the Shaveling, and she had never known them left unguarded.

'Somebody's got the wind up and no mistake,' the postilion replied. 'We're being sent back to the Pebble Farm, and if the Prussos are there too, we've been told to carry on. The Shaveling's fond of his wheels.'

I should think so too, she thought, *with half the treasury of France hidden in there*. But terrible suspicions began to assail her as she turned north. Suspicions that heavily featured Fouché. Though, for now, she had Marianne to worry about. She rejected the more direct route she had taken earlier to Plancenoit in favour of the lanes closer to the Beautiful Alliance. She reckoned, reasonably, that with the rest of the Imperial Guard moving up, Fronsac's company – and her sister too, she assumed – could easily find themselves rejoining their battalion, in which case they would not return here until the battle was won.

Yet when she arrived on that ridge above Plancenoit she hardly recognised the village as the same peaceful haven to which she had ridden earlier in the day. It was not just the exhausted remnants of retreated units formed in straggling defensive squares along the crest, but the memory evoked of that painting she had once seen in a Spanish Royal Palace. At La Granja de San Ildefonso. Another mission for Fouché. Secret messages delivered to Maria Luisa of Spain. And there had been the picture. By a Flemish artist. Brueghel, she recalled. *The Triumph of Death*. And here, too, hordes of diminutive demons, Prussians, ran this way and that, swept through the smoke and flame of burning houses, the church, the graveyard while, against them, the much smaller legions of the righteous tried to hold them at bay, to defend the freedom of France. There were collisions, clashes, between the forces of Evil and Good, at street corners, in fields, at crossroads, and then the two sides would interfuse, the satanic mob grappling with the divine seraphim, climbing over each other, or spinning in a fatal embrace, a macabre dance.

And Liberté knew that if Marianne was down there, trapped in that writhing tableau, her chances of survival were slim. Yet she could not be down there, of course. Liberté had no sense of her sister facing such peril, no sense of imminent danger, no sense that she might already be harmed. But she *did* have an entirely different sense. That if the Prussos were here, so close, so confident, in such numbers, with no concern for their backs, then what might she make of the word that Grouchy's 33,000 men were about to save the day? All her instincts screamed against the veracity of this news, though she longed, with more than just her heart, for it to be true.

She swung the chestnut's head north, rode towards that inn again, the Hotel of the Beautiful Alliance, passed the derelict outbuildings and gnarled apple trees where she had discovered her mother's fate in that dream journey with Marianne, rounded the wall painted with the inn's name in large black script, and expected to find the Emperor still here, directing their salvation. But he was gone. Still visible, however. Down there. Across the valley's floor. On the road leading all the way to Brussels. Perhaps half the distance to that other farm on the farther ridge. The Holy Hedge Farm. And, may all the Saints bless him, he was not alone. For to his left and to his rear marched six, maybe seven, battalions of his finest soldiers. Five thousand or more and, as Liberté knew only too well, many of the regimental women. The men may not have been at their parade ground best, with their long blue summer greatcoats, brightened only by their white cross-belts, the splash of red fringed epaulettes, their pride and joy. Many of them no longer even wore their tall bearskins. Yet, for all this, there was no mistaking the magnificent spectacle of Bonaparte's invincible Imperial Guard going forward to war.

'They must think we're stupid,' said Fronsac.

The gallopers had been up and down three times.

'Here is Grouchy!' they would shout, and point back towards the northeast.

And the massed ranks of their Middle Guard battalions would cheer.

'Here we go!' they chanted, until those not caught up by the magic, like Fronsac, began to grumble and allow the darkness of doubt to fall upon this little piece of vaudeville.

'Stupid?' said Muhler. 'The Shaveling doesn't think we're stupid. It's just that new boys like you, Fronsac, haven't quite got the hang of it yet.'

'New?' Fronsac retorted. 'New? D'you know how many times...?'

'New to the Guard, I mean,' Muhler told him. 'It's what makes us what we are. Makes us something special. What the extra pay's for. For knowing what makes him tick. Just as much as he knows us. The Shaveling.' Muhler interlinked his first two fingers together. 'And the Shaveling's Imperial Guard.'

Marianne had understood this since the first day of Fronsac's promotion to the Battalion even if it had escaped her husband. That all promotions carried responsibility. In this case, nobody spoke the words, yet every one of them knew that it was not Grouchy's guns they could hear away over to the right. It was the Prussos. Yet an easily accepted self-deception. They *wanted* to believe. And they shared the Shaveling's desire to lift the spirits of the entire army. Just one more push and they could turn around this thing that still stood on a knife's edge. The final moments of the great game. And everything yet to play for.

'Here is Grouchy!' The messengers cantered past.

'Long live the Emperor!' shouted the Guardsmen, and Marianne joined them, weariness falling away from her, their comrades too. And even those with flesh wounds who had limped and slouched their way back from Plancenoit, they too straightened, their eyes brightened, miseries dropped from them, their hurts suddenly healed.

Yes, a vaudeville, she thought. *The best I've ever seen.*

And the Emperor himself had acted as Narrator for the Prologue.

'Who will follow me?' he had called after the Company caught up with their Battalion and he came riding past their assembly point around that inn – the place where Hawk-face had taken her. 'Who will follow me?'

His face was pale, and he rode upon his pale horse. Yet he still wore the old grey coat, the same cocked hat. He was the old Bonaparte. And they followed him. By battalion, in column of platoons. Down the slope. Into the valley bottom where, remarkably, crops still grew tall.

Marianne had the strangest instinct that perhaps they were already being fed and nurtured by the dead scattered across the valley's width, and more densely upon the slopes ahead of them where, they said, two entire Cavalry Corps had dashed themselves to pieces. Yet not her sister. Marianne had no fear for Liberté Dumont, was quite certain that her sister still lived, somewhere in this smoking, smouldering ruin of a place, black as a foundry yard, that stunk so much now of sulphur, and blood, and meat, and shit.

One last push, she thought, *and this will all be over.*

That push was led by the 1st Battalion of the 3rd Grenadiers, following the Emperor up the road itself. Then the 3rd's Second Battalion, immediately behind and just to the left of the road. And so they went until they were all on the march, in echelon, a diagonal line of columns, heading for the centre of the Goddams' ridge, with the farthest left and rearmost position taken by the single battalion of the 4th Foot Chasseurs.

Behind them, Marianne could see a second echelon, three further battalions, Grenadiers and Chasseurs, that descended the slope but did not go further forward, the Guard's own reserve and rear-guard.

'Well, at least our backs are covered,' said Fronsac.

And not just our own *backs, but my daughter's too.* For she had not wanted to leave Poppy there, at the inn, with Argonne and the cart. Not with the Prussians so close. But she knew she had no choice. The girl would be fine anyway, she decided, and smiled, remembering the tall story Florisette had spun about the goats' miraculous escape. *I wonder where she's hidden them,* she thought. *Little bugger!* Yet it was the cart itself she was missing too for, without it, she was forced to carry her spare brandy bottles in a canvas haversack, which was already cutting into her shoulder. She shifted it now to a more comfortable position, and then the first roundshot from the English guns carved its way into the nearest file of the battalion to their left, while the Grand Battery deafened them with its own salvo in reply.

This shouldn't take too long, Marianne thought, as they came to a halt just where the ground began to rise up the enemy ridge. Above them and to the right was a white-walled farm, riddled with bullets and smashed about by cannon fire, smoke drifting from black gaps in the tiled roof. There was musketry from their own lads who held the place, and a couple of artillery pieces too, blasting into those few units of the Roast Beefs that could be seen from here. *Not too long. And then, when we bivouac for the night, I'll break the news to Fronsac. I'll just tell him, whether he likes it or not. He can follow us, if he wants. When he's had enough of this. Catherine Argonne can have the commission. I'll resign the thing. To Vicquot. Take the girl, head back to Paris. Find somewhere in one of the villages. Belleville, maybe. Or Montmartre. Find a fence who'll give me a good price for the bloody diamonds. Then look for that inn…*

The bands struck up. *Let us protect the life-blood of Empire!* And the Emperor was waving his hat, leading the Second Battalion of the 3rd Grenadiers, that wheeled from the road and marched behind them, heading towards the large house with its orchards that Marianne could see over to the west. Another place in flames.

'There you go, Fronsac,' said Marle. 'Now you've not only got your arse covered by the lads behind, but the Shaveling himself guarding your left. We should have this wrapped up in no time.'

In truth, it looked as though they were, indeed, well protected. Not just the Guard's reserve battalions behind them, but more Line regiments forming by that big house and, above the farm, up to the right, still more battalions near the ridge crest.

'Long live the Emperor!' The lads all turned in their ranks to wave and cheer as he rode along their rear.

'Here we go,' they chanted. For, despite the close support of those Line boys, it would be the Guard that won the day. *En avant.* 'Here we go.'

The drums beat. Battalion Square. And Captain Vicquot was ordering them through the familiar manoeuvres of the drill, Sergeant Flambert limping along, keeping their ranks dressed, as the Company's Sections wheeled left or right and arranged themselves afresh to establish the formation's forward-facing rear wall, while the First, Second and Third Companies marched and turned to respectively create the leading edge and each of the sides, both in column of platoons.

'This too,' shouted Muhler. 'This is what makes us what we are. Long live the Guard!'

He was right. To use Square for anything other than defence was beyond most units except those gathered here. Oh, most battalions were capable of moving in Square, to fall back or slowly position themselves somewhere else. But to attack? To march at the Double and keep that hollow rectangle precise and intact? By the Host, no. That was a miracle that only the Guard could truly perform.

'Well, woman?' Fronsac called to her. 'What are you waiting for? Now's your time.'

'What the hell, d'you think I'm doing?' she shouted back, for she had already sold a dozen shots from the cask. 'And a bit of help wouldn't have gone amiss. What a shame our little Spanish friend's been turned out upon the road.'

Fronsac's head went down, while the rest of *Peloton* A, what was left of them, ragged him about his infidelity and the alleged size of his private parts. But Marianne thought about Suzanne Prairial and her baby, buried in their shallow, muddy grave. So far as Juanita Bufanda was concerned, she did not regret the absence of the *manola* herself, but this Battalion was too big for just one canteen-mistress.

But, she thought, imagining the money to be made, *I shouldn't moan too much, I suppose.*

By the time the drums rattled out the Advance, the two squares to the right had, each in turn, begun to climb the slope and Marianne had worked her way through half the platoons in the Battalion's left-hand side column. Spirits among the men were high and her own particular brand of spirit selling very nicely, the pocket of her russet jacket already beginning to bulge with small coin.

From time to time, the terrain allowed her to see the leading battalions with Redhead Ney riding at its front alongside a brace of generals. Yet, mostly, she could observe nothing but the shouldered muskets, backpacks, shakos and bearskins of the men in the ranks through which she was passing with her wares, weaving skilfully among them so she might not break their step. *Do I stink as badly as they do?* she wondered. The prevailing scent was that of wet dogs, but it was laced with stale sweat, garlic, onion and a hundred other things besides. Though it was strangely peaceful, this first part of the ascent. They were taking fire, but only an occasional roundshot, some musket fire from thinly spaced English skirmishers. Much less than anybody had expected.

'Calm before the storm,' said First Company Sergeant Wybicki when she reached the end of the very front rank. Marianne had not spoken with him since they buried Prairial and his boy. 'I not like it.' He looked grim, morose. 'But I thank you, Tambour. For help her.'

It's all those you can't save that shape you.

There was grumbling too, elsewhere in the First Company's platoons, about the lack of their own skirmishers. This front face of the formation - three ranks deep – would, after all, bear the brunt of any determined response from the Roast Beefs.

'Ah, to hell with that,' she kept telling the men, 'we won't need them.'

Halfway up the slope now, and a few howitzer shells exploding, men going down close to her. And, she noticed, they seemed to be swinging to the left a little, no longer heading straight for the crest but angling across it obliquely so that, as she began working her way down, front to rear, of the right-hand side column, balls were taking them in the flank. Still not enough to trouble them though, and the men simply closing ranks, while Marianne wasted little time trying to care for the fallen. Roundshot casualties were generally a lost cause, their amputations and injuries, the shock that went with them, almost always too grave for anybody's ministrations.

The drum beat changed. *TAN-tra-tran. TAN-tra-tran.* The pace picked up to the Quick, and Marianne took the chance to look after the musicians themselves. Thirsty work, drumming. And no chance, normally, to down a cup. But with this *Pas de Charge*, they would hammer out the tattoo for thirty paces, then pause, silent, while the men would fill the four-pace interval with their own rhythmic chorus.

'Long live the Emperor!'

And she would have a shot ready for each break, a drummer knocking back the welcome liquor, returning the cup in time to bring his sticks into play again at the correct moment, Marianne telling all eight of them the same thing.

'Pay me later,' she would say. 'It's no problem. Pay me later.'

A troop of Horse Artillery came struggling up the slope, passed them, and headed for the point where the lead battalion, the 1st/3rd Grenadiers, was just cresting the ridge. She saw men fall, and a cry went up.

'Redhead's down!'

Ney's horse shot from beneath him, they reckoned, though she could not see it herself. But that first square halted, the muskets of the front ranks came up, and spat out a rolling volley.

So the Goddams are really there, she thought. And then she did see Ney, back on his feet, sword in hand, his hat gone, waving the troops forward. Waving them on. So on they went, until the Halt, the first three battalion squares all now atop the slope, volley after volley, along the whole line, smoke filling the space between the opposing forces. Yet still she could not see the Goddams. Just the stabbing yellow flashes that pierced those boiling grey clouds from the English side. How far away? Fifty paces, she guessed. But it was slackening, was it not? The enemy fire, no longer in volleys. Shouting too. She could hear them shouting now. Sometimes frantic. And from all along their positions.

'The bastards are going to break,' she yelled, running from the drummers back to Fronsac's place behind them and to the right, in the front line of the rear three-rank wall, the platoon not engaged here, of course, but the lads all cheering.

'Here we go! Here we go!' *En avant.*

Marianne allowed herself a slug of brandy, raised the cup high.

'Long live the Emperor!' she yelled, toasting him at this place, whatever it was called, as he had toasted her at Beaumont four days earlier.

'The 3rd are on the move again,' said Fronsac, as that other battalion took up the *Pas de Charge* once more, started down the reverse slope.

'Now,' she said. 'Show them the steel, my lads.' And she was sure in her heart that it was over, for the smoke ahead was thinning. Red-coated figures there. But not in disciplined ranks, so far as she could tell. Men breaking and running, their officers trying in vain to hold them while, through their shattered ranks, horses and limbers, guns and riders, came into view, wheeling and screaming, sweat flying and hooves pounding. For a split second, the lads in the Platoon almost cheered, for the uniforms were French. Or almost.

'Dutchies,' shouted Marle. 'Bloody Dutchies. They were fighting with us, just last year.'

Too late though, thought Marianne. *They're just too bloody late*. But they were fast. She had to give them that much. Fast. So fast that she did not see them unlimber their guns. For she was pushing her way through the left-hand wall, through the Second Company, trying to get a better view of that nearest Goddam unit, doubting the truth of her own eyes.

'Tambour, where the hell are you going?' somebody shouted.

She was in the open ground now. Between her own battalion and another of Foot Chasseurs coming up on alongside.

Hawk-face had told her she spotted the devil two days earlier. That purple-faced bastard from Saint-Sébastien. Yet she never dreamed that their paths would cross here.

But why not? she thought. *I've been having those living dreams for so long now. Or whatever they are.* Whatever hocus-pocus name her sister chose to give it. Though she could not readily explain away the vision they had shared. The clarity of that day upon which Tambour and the Revolution had each been born. The fates that had brought herself and Liberté Dumont together. Here. The same fate, she assumed, that now set her down upon this ridge, within forty or fifty paces from the piece of filth who had butchered Maman Cholet.

She ran up the outside of the square, ran until she reached the First Company again, ignoring the stray bullets that whined like mosquitoes past her ears. The front rank was kneeling, the second also ready to fire.

'Shoot him,' she pleaded, pointing wildly at the Englishman. 'That bugger. With the purple face.'

'Tambour, back from there!' shouted Sergeant Wybicki, as the men fired. She felt the heat of the volley, the force of it pressing against her chest, pieces of burned wadding flicking at her face, ears ringing from the report, and nostrils stinging. And when the smoke cleared, there were even less of the Goddams left standing, even more of them creeping back towards Brussels, yet that bloody English sergeant still in his place, still trying to rally the dregs of his company.

'Christ's Balls,' she shouted. 'Are you all blind? Somebody give me a musket. I'll do the damned job myself.' She began to grapple with a third-ranker, whose name she did not know, but the man shoved her backwards onto her arse. And from this undignified position she saw the 1st/3rd Grenadiers halt again, just down the slope, no more than fifteen paces from that Dutch battery which, astonishingly, in those few moments, already looked set to fire.

'*PRESENT!*' she heard the command from that neighbouring square.

The muskets of the 1st/3rd came up. But they never fired. For, at that precise second, the Dutchies touched their vents as though they were all one.

'Hell's Teeth,' she heard somebody say as the salvo of case shot struck home and the front rank of their sister battalion trembled and fell. The whole formation seemed to stagger back, like the compression of a leather bellows. Ney was still there, though. She could see him. She could see the officers of the 3rd too, trying to close their ranks, form a new face.

But Marianne's own boys had reloaded now, and she scrambled to her feet.

'This time,' she said to the men closest to her. 'Look. You can't miss the sod.'

And, as she stretched her finger towards the Englishman, turned towards him, she saw that he was looking back at her, cocking the hammer of his own musket.

The Battalion's volley tore the evening air apart just as somebody smacked her arm with a heavy cane. Or something. She turned to see who it might be, but in the smoke she could see nobody. And when it parted there was still nobody. She looked to the men nearest her, but they were all busy reloading. Not one of them showed any sign that he might have struck her and then, as some sort of stupid jest, quickly looked away. Nothing.

Perhaps she had imagined the blow. And, anyway, beyond the Battalion, history was repeating itself. The 1st/3rd Grenadiers had regrouped, the order given once more to Present muskets, the barrels coming forward and down, but the Dutchies blasting another salvo before the instruction to Fire. And this time the case shot cut the French to pieces, tossed them aside, sent men reeling from their ranks.

'Tambour...' Wybicki was coming towards her, his hand reaching for her, and some stupid expression on his face. Concern? Pity?

'No,' she said. 'Look!' She tried to raise her left arm to point, show him what she had seen, but it would not obey her. And her hand was warm. Wet. Sticky. Yet she could not take her eyes from the apparition before her.

The regiment of Goddams had vanished almost entirely, except for that purple-faced bastard who was still there with a cluster of others around a yellow flag. He was just biting the top from another cartridge. But the broken English ranks had been replaced by completely fresh ones, and these were not broken at all. They marched as steadily as the Guard, bayonets lowered. And, to their left, there was a second column of the buggers, so that as the 1st/3rd Grenadiers saw them coming, it was their turn to fall apart. Slowly at first but, in moments, turned to a rabble streaming back over the crest.

Yet she saw this too. The Dutch gunners trail-spiking their pieces, slewing them round, bringing them to bear on her own Battalion's First Company.

'You are hit, Marianne,' Wybicki reached her. But she knew that already. Had worked it out. And not just her arm, either, but this burning dampness in her lung.

'It was him,' she said, looked back to see the English sergeant aiming at her again, watched the smoke from his gun, heard the sucking sound as the ball went through Wybicki's neck, tasted the salt of his splashed liquids on her lips. She caught a glimpse of the new Goddam regiment Present their muskets, heard the commands given within her square, the thirsty drummers beating out the *Pas de Charge* again. *TAN-tra-tran. TAN-tra-tran.*

'Here we go,' she cried. *En avant.*

The Goddams fired a volley but the lads marched straight through it, as though it were no more than a summer shower. Marianne trying to keep up. Thirty paces.

'Long live the Emperor!'

She felt dizzy. With the excitement of it all, she thought as, struggling to breath, she stumbled through the platoons of the Second Company.

I should tell Fronsac now, she thought. *About later.*

She heard the roar of those Dutch cannons, saw a swarm of case shot balls rip apart the men around her, broke through to the square's more open centre in time to see Captain Vicquot fall to his knees, drop flat on his face. Sergeant Flambert stopped briefly to see whether he still lived, grimaced, but hobbled on as the front rank of the Captain's Fourth Company stepped over the body. And then some other bugger hit her with that big stick again. Her leg this time. It folded beneath her.

Oh, Poppy, she thought. And she felt tears fill her eyes. *My sweet girl.*

Chapter Thirty-Seven

Sunday 18th June 1815, 8.00pm

Indecision had gripped Liberté as those battalion squares of the Imperial Guard disappeared, one by one over the opposite ridge, to the left of the farm, and she wondered why they had taken such a strange diagonal path rather than striking directly at the enemy's centre.

But my duty lies with finding the Regiment, she had told herself. There was little she could do to assist Marianne, she knew. It would have seemed absurd to go cantering after her in some gesture of sisterly protection. And, in any case, she would not have sought to deprive the girl of her glorious moment. Of being with the Guard when they smashed Wellesley's Goddams. Yet there had been the child to consider too. *Perhaps I should simply go and keep her safe until her mother returns. But then*, she had remembered, *I was also foolish enough to promise Poppy that I'd bring Marianne back to her. And you should never make promises to children without keeping them.*

She had been in the very moment of turning the chestnut's head when Colonel Planzeau called to her.

'Dumont,' he had said. 'I am so very pleased to see you alive. Remount?'

'I'm afraid so.' She had clenched her teeth, bitten down against the memory of Lucette's loss. 'And you, sir? How is the wound?'

He had touched the crippled arm, now in a completely fresh sling and blood oozing through the charpie bandage.

'It's the luck of the Provençal, Trooper. Shot in the arm that's already dead as a door nail. What more could a fellow ask, eh? And where are you headed?'

'Back to the Regiment, Colonel,' she had lied.

'The Regiment? There *is* no Regiment any more. Not for the moment And I promised to send some of the lads – any of my own troopers, I mean – over to General Jacquinot. That sergeant is gathering up stragglers.' He had pointed to a sergeant of Horse Chasseurs who was herding small groups of displaced horsemen – and there were plenty of them – into some semblance of a mixed squadron, and so it was that Liberté found herself now formed up with this ragged bunch near yet another small village at the northeast end of the valley. And here were Marbot's Fighting 7th Hussars again.

Liberté remembered the meeting with Bonaparte at Genappe. The

Englishman from that other 7th Hussars, Elphinstone. And it was a time for reunions, it seemed. For she soon picked up word that this insignificant hamlet, Papelotte, had held out all day against repeated French attacks. Holding Wellesley's left flank. Held by Sachsen-Weimar's Nassauers, who had already saved his bacon on the ridges between Frasnes and Quatre Bras. She almost laughed. How long? It felt like weeks. Though Gémioncourt had truly only been two days before. Yet she had been marching and fighting, almost continuously, for the past sixty hours. So had they all. And she could see the exhaustion on the faces around her. So, when masses of Prussians formed up on the slopes just beyond the village, she knew there was no will to fight them.

'The Guard will save the day,' men said.

Or, 'By the time the Prussos get here, they'll be too late.'

And, 'Why waste more lives when all we need to do is wait for the Old Grumblers to kick the buggers apart?'

But they made a fair enough show when squadrons of Prussian cavalry came probing their flanks and were sent off with a bloodied nose. Then a second charge, with Liberté almost too weary to handle her sabre. Yet they drove the Prussian horses back a second time.

It was during the ride back to their rallying point, though, that she felt it. The hair stood up on the nape of her neck, the pit of her stomach filling with a dread bile. Danger rose around her like a wall. She sensed pain and suffering. Something had changed, the world beginning to crumble about them. Rumours. But something more than simply grapevine gossip.

'The Guard's on the run.'

Or, 'The Grumblers have been wiped out.'

Or, 'That bloody traitor, Ney.'

And with no order given, no word of command spoken, the units of infantry and artillery each began to wheel away from Papelotte, to march back down the valley with the cavalry squadrons screening them. There was no panic, and no great hurry, Liberté thought. Just weary resignation. They marched until they reached the Brussels highway, the Hotel of the Beautiful Alliance coming into view on their left, and that farm, the Holy Hedge Farm, up the road to their right. There was still fighting there but, as she watched, she saw the French defenders simply leave their posts and march south too – towards the place where three intact battalions of the Imperial Guard, the Emperor's final reserve, stood in squares and provided a wall behind which the rest of the army might seek shelter.

But Liberté Dumont did not look for refuge there. For, in the centre of the valley, west of the highway, she could see some remnants of those other Guard Grenadier and Foot Chasseur battalions that she had earlier watched in glorious advance – only now that had begun to stream back down from the enemy ridge. The rumours were right. The Imperial Guard was on the run. Broken. Yet she knew she would not find her sister among those fugitive masses.

*

The Battalion roared like a wounded, baited bear. It still stood, but only just. And Marianne slipped again into that darkness where the pain subsided and where Maman Cholet no longer suffered either, but only offered her brandy from a golden cask.

'How many times have I slept?' she asked.

'A dozen, my dear,' said Cholet, then was swept away as the agony flooded back, Marianne convulsing into consciousness, choking back the blood that rose like vomit in her gorge.

The Battalion stood, but it was no longer in square. There was a drummer dead at her side. *He owes me two sous*, she thought, idly. Yet he was staring at her with guilty fish-eyes, and she knew she would never collect. And there must be plenty of other lapsed debts here for, from around the rim of his drum, past the skin's tuning keys, she could see nothing but an unbroken line of blue cloth hummocks, the occasional red epaulette, a patch of pale flesh. And, just above and beyond that escarpment of destruction, the backs of bearskin caps and shakos in a ragged block ahead of where their dead lay.

They have closed ranks, she guessed. *Formed a single line, perhaps.* It must have been a desperately reduced formation. *Yet it still stands*, she thought. *My brave boys still stand.*

Another convulsion, and this time she could not contain it. Her chest heaved. Flames ripped through her back and side. A racking cough spewed up blood until she drifted once more into another place.

That woman this time. The one she had last seen as a vision, limp and pale on a table at the Invalides. But now she lived again. Some sort of miracle, Marianne told herself. But the woman was beautiful. Like Hawk-face. Though bathed in a white light, arms stretched towards her. And though she longed to fall into that embrace, she knew she could not. Not yet.

'There are things I must do, Mami,' she said, but the tears of longing were almost as painful as the tortures she had left behind. Torments that dragged her, weeping and pleading back to that field, where her own eyes opened just enough so she could see the blue coat hems, the trouser legs and boots march past. A single drummer beat time. The Battalion, smashed to a fraction of its former glory, falling back. In perfect order. Precise as on the parade ground. But falling back.

She wept again. Left behind. Though that was not the cause of her tears. It was simply that she felt the most unbearable pain of all. The Battalion's unquenchable grief. For the Guard did not fall back. The Guard did not retreat. Yet peace, of a sort, came to her when they had gone. She could still hear the fighting that raged behind her. The rest of their squares, she assumed, still vainly pressing the attack, holding the crest. Though, here, the guns all seemed to have fallen silent and there was birdsong once more.

Fronsac, you bastard, she thought. *Left me and gone off with the lads then?*

It would be like him. Never even to give her a passing thought. But then she remembered seeing Captain Vicquot go down. She lay for a moment or two while the next agonising convulsions shook her, then began dragging herself, one-handed, through the crushed crops, in the direction she thought he had fallen. The leg did not trouble her much. She could not even feel it any more. But every tortuous *toise* that she covered felt like a league, stabbed into her spine and this pit of fire that now lived in her lungs. It seemed as though the sea swilled back and forth in her ears, and iron dribbled across her tongue. But, beyond her feet, unseen, she could still hear cannons, muskets, the *Pas de Charge*. Some of the squares still in action. Hope remained.

Marianne hauled herself past the Captain, found familiar faces of the Fourth Company's dead. Lads from the second section and, just beyond them, the remains of *Peloton* A. They must have been hit while the front of the square was open, so that the case shot had raked into their position, dropped them where they marched. Trinquart and Lejeune, gone down together, their arms intertwined. Muhler, who had saved poor Poppy's life.

How will I explain all this to her? she thought, coughed up more blood. Dug her fingers into the earth, heaved herself forward. Past Bloc and Corporal Poncet, who still lived, but both of them ripped and pitiful. Then Marle and Argonne, sitting back to back in a puddle of blood, shit and their own guts. They still lived too, and seemed to be mumbling the words of some madman's song. A duet of death. And, finally, Fronsac. He lay on his side, his back to her, feet digging into the ground as he tried in vain to push himself forward, or maybe brace himself against whatever hurt he had taken and upon which she could not bring herself to look.

'Oh, Fronsac,' she said, when she was close enough that she could just touch the hair above his neck. 'The whole platoon?' And she sobbed.

'You came for me,' he said, though he sounded as though he spoke through a froth of bubbles. 'Is there any dog-dog left?'

'I sold it all, my dear one. For the inn, you remember?'

'*The Old Grenadier*,' he murmured. 'That's a good one. But the Shaveling, he lied to us. About Grouchy. Didn't he?'

'Of course not,' she scolded him. 'Here they come now. Look, the Goddams are on the run. All along the ridge. They won't stop until they get to the sea.'

He tried to turn his head, but it took only the least pressure of her fingers to stop him.

'That's good,' he said. 'I owed them...'

She could see the spasm of pain that jerked up through the muscles of his neck and head as he died.

'I know,' she told him. 'For the hulks.'

It's all those you can't save that shape you.

She kept stroking his poor head as a column of Goddams marched across her field of vision, perhaps thirty paces away. But they were not heading for the sea, she knew. They were making for Paris, and they would not stop until they got there. Her pain turned to heaving sobs that did not cease even when somebody gripped her arm – the one that still obeyed her – and turned her roughly onto her back.

Through a mist of tears, she saw a familiar face and was glad to be alone here no more. She had so feared that she might die with nobody at her side. So she smiled up into the face, and the face smiled back. Black, rotten teeth, framed by a great purple blotch.

Not alone, she thought, when he knelt between her legs, lifted the musket so she could see it and, crooning some guttural English nonsense, began licking the tip of his bayonet.

Liberté Dumont glared at the two young ensigns, barely more than boys, who gaped at her as their disciplined redcoat column passed within pistol shot. But she imagined how she must seem to them. A lone horsewoman, dressed in the uniform green, the grey leather-lined overalls and boots of a French Dragoon, dark hair blowing in the breeze, sitting astride her chestnut stallion with one fist on her hip as though she owned the entire ridge. As if, by her mere presence alone, she could turn back the tide of this whole Goddam army.

And then they were gone, ignoring her, over the crest, with their fifes and drums receding into the vale of their victory, leaving behind them a scene that Liberté tried to imprint upon her brain. For she had never seen a battlefield like this one. Not in all her years. *I thought I had witnessed it all*, she said to herself. Hard to define her feelings. At first. Though she recognised the creature at last. It was awe. Pure wonder at Mankind's propensity for inventive self-destruction.

This was almost the same section of the slope on which she had stood when their charges failed. She remembered thinking, less than two hours earlier, that no further dead might be packed into that single stretch of ground. Yet she could not have been more wrong. She realised now that they had been parsimonious in their use of land, had left hectares lying fallow. And where Kellerman and Milhaud, or the defenders of the English squares, had left empty furrows, the Guard had now filled them with frightening efficiency. It was almost impossible to see where the corn had once grown for the carpet of bodies that in places writhed and groaned as though the whole fabric of the thing lived and suffered and breathed.

She thought about Lucette, scanned the ground of that lower plateau for any sign of the Percheron's beautiful grey hide, though she knew it was a useless exercise. But it was a distraction from her concern for Marianne. She could sense her sister's pain and presence here, but Liberté doubted her ability to find her in all this sprawling, heaving and mostly silent mass. Yet there was one point that drew her gaze. A splash of scarlet that moved independently of the other English formations now appearing, as though by magic, from the drifting saltpetre clouds. She watched as the redcoat stopped, reached down. To touch something on the ground, she thought.

Liberté squeezed the chestnut gently into motion, clicked her tongue and walked the horse forward, feeling that she should take a closer look.

What is he? she wondered. *A looter?* It was never too early for looting. Not for the English. Though the fellow was spending a lot of time on whatever he had found. A tooth-puller, perhaps? Like that bugger, Thénardier.

At ninety paces she saw the soldier kneel, lift his musket, touch the bayonet to his mouth. *What the hell is he doing?* she wondered, watched as he set down the musket again, started scrabbling at whatever was on the ground before him.

Sixty paces, and he turned for a moment to retrieve the musket and bayonet, so that she saw the purple blotch upon his face.

Liberté kicked the horse into a trot, but it made hardly any difference, for the beast still needed to pick its way carefully over the mounds of death, almost impossible to set down its hooves without stepping upon human flesh.

Forty paces. Liberté could see the familiar russet jacket and bonnet, the nankeen trousers ripped from Marianne's pale thighs. And she knew then exactly what he intended to do with that bloody bayonet.

'Want some, Johnnie?' she howled at him, felt herself tremble with rage. And he turned, stared for a moment. Grinned as recognition dawned, stood with the musket, and made that same old gesture with his crotch as he had done earlier.

Liberté hooked her left leg up and over the horse's neck, resting it on the saddle's pommel and holsters, right hand behind her on the cantle, ready to spring down. She knew this fellow must be a fighter. He was a survivor, apart from anything else. He had made and remained sergeant. He had stayed at his post in the square even when the rest of his unit had mostly fled. But was he good enough that he had remembered to reload after the Guard had been repulsed?

Well, she thought, *we'll see.*

She slipped from the saddle, made a performance of pulling the sabre free from the scabbard, allowing it to jar until the Englishman was sneering at her. *And, loaded or not*, she smiled to herself, *this bugger delights in the delivery of pain. The bayonet is his tool of choice.*

Liberté looked him in the eye, projected fear into her own features, remembering the pantomime that Lieutenant Henry had performed for her, so she let the tip of her sword drag a little against the bodies among which she stood, as though it were too heavy for her. *One chance*, she thought, *because he's no fool either.*

He was saying something to her, but the wild lunge she had expected did not materialise. The stock of his musket was braced against his hip, the bayonet itself charged at waist height. He feinted forward, feet stepping with speed and delicacy over the outstretched arm of a dead Sapper, the long blade flicking at her twice. *And he fancies himself the duellist*, she realised, as she retreated before him, making herself look as clumsy as possible without actually falling.

Most men, she knew, were taught nothing about the use of this weapon except its value in destroying morale, to advance with it, steadfast, until their unit's evidently unshakable resolve persuaded the enemy to run. It was the task of their officers, or sergeants like this fellow, to time the final advance so that they closed with the foe just as they were reloading, at their most vulnerable.

Like this!

She swung the sabre wide. The worst pass she could make. But sufficient that he must parry the blow, lowering the bayonet just enough to let her blade flash past, then following it, a tight circular motion. Fast. Smashing against the back of her steel so that it would prevent her recovery. Take her off balance. Exactly as she had expected. And, when his left side was exposed, she shifted her weight, brought up her right leg, and gave him a vicious kick in the ribs with the heavy toe of her cavalry boot.

The sergeant stumbled back over that outstretched arm, cursing and spitting. And the pantomime was over. He moved back to a more respectful distance. She guessed that his confidence was dented. For he was suddenly unsure of his ground. He looked around to check the new lie of the land, nursing those bruised ribs, as best he could with his left elbow, while tightening the grip on his weapon.

Just a heavy spear, after all, she thought. *No skill in hefting a spear, you bastard.*

He was mouthing mumbled promises to her now. So she looked him in the eye, allowed the hatred and cold venom to show. Then she dropped back into the hanging guard, left leg forward and bent, left arm stretched out straight, gauntlet fingers splayed like a tiny buckler before her face, sword hilt at the level of her right eye and the sharpened tip aimed at his chest.

He feinted again. She could smell his sweat. Her turn now to flick his blade aside. Steel on steel. Once. Twice. She was breathing hard, making her chest heave. More theatre.

The bugger's got to go for the deep lunge, she decided. *Sooner or later. Deep lunge.* For the only purpose of a heavy spear was to use its weight, driving your point home far enough to finish your enemy. And she gambled that he had not faced a backsword fencer before.

More feints with the bayonet. Parried again. One. Two. Three. And Liberté panting, the heavy Dragoon sabre lowering with each clash, until it was barely pointing at his toes. Her guard almost entirely down.

This was his moment, and he knew it. She could see it in his eyes. The excitement. Two sharp steps forward and he put his full strength behind the weight of his musket's iron, wood and steel.

The deep lunge.

Liberté barely sidestepped, simply braced herself, summoned every ounce of her own power as she closed her gauntlet fingers around the triangular shape of the bayonet when it came in, her muscles rigid so that the entire fifteen inches of its blade ran harmlessly along the underside of her arm, its forward thrust halted when her gloved hand jarred up against the bayonet's elbow and socket. The point just failed to reach her chest, and though the muscles of her arm screamed in agony at the punishment they had just taken, she knew that, without the gauntlet, she would also likely have lost her fingers.

There was surprise on that blotched purple face, however, as the Englishman tried to pull the blade free of her grip. But he was even more shocked when she slammed the knuckle guards of her sabre into those snarling black teeth, and she thought there was almost amusement in his eyes when he fell backwards, momentarily senseless. Yet his sense of humour seemed soon to leave him, for he squealed and screamed like a pig a long time, when she finally employed the bayonet upon him in the manner that he had clearly intended for her sister.

Liberté threw the blood-caked gauntlets aside and cradled Marianne's head in her lap as the poor girl struggled to hoist the nankeen trousers, one-handed, back around her hips. The wounds were bad, she knew, and Marianne's flesh had that waxen quality of somebody who is already dead but has not yet quite recognised the fact. The leg was smashed and broken below the knee and would certainly need to be removed. *How would she take that?* Liberté wondered. She had much to learn about this young woman.

'Is he...?' Marianne whispered to her. She was weak from loss of blood.

'The Englishman? He'll trouble your dreams no more.'

'No trouble. I had this for him.' She barely managed to lift her right hand, showed the *salvavirgo* she had palmed there. Then it slipped from her fingers.

'I might have known,' said Liberté. 'You didn't need me, after all.'

'I was going to take the diamonds,' Marianne gripped her arm. 'Go off and...'

'I thought you might,' said Liberté. 'But I said to myself, what the hell. What else are sisters for, eh? You should have done it, silly girl. Got out while you had the chance.'

'No chance now, then?'

The leg was not the real problem. Liberté peered down at the girl's left arm. It had been pierced by a ball, above the elbow. A ricochet, perhaps. Because, as she eased the arm gently from Marianne's side, drawing an agonised cry from those blue-tinted lips, she saw that the damned thing had left an exit wound and then ploughed straight up into her sister's armpit. Her cheek and chin were splattered with the blood she had already coughed up.

'Not now, little one,' she told her.

'Then will you lend me that fine coat?'

'Cold?' Liberté asked her. But Marianne shook her head.

'Always wanted a decent tunic. Some of the others have them. The canteen-mistresses. Hussar dolmans. Shakos. All sorts.'

Liberté unfastened her Dragoon's coat.

'I need to work out how we get you back to that child of yours,' she said, easing Marianne forward and wrapping the coat gently around her shoulders.

'Please don't move me,' Tambour replied, and a tear rolled down her cheek. 'It hurts me, lady. And my place is here. With the boys. Poppy will understand.'

'But I promised her,' said Liberté.

'That girl's life is littered with broken promises. One more won't matter.' She coughed, cried, spat blood. 'And tell her something for me. Tell her she can keep the goats.'

'I'll tell her.'

'Anyway,' said Marianne, 'maybe those who want you dead will think their wishes have all come true if they find me here. With your coat.'

'You're sure?'

'I'm sure. But will my spirit still fly? After...'

'I don't know. But I think it might. And you know where we'll be. Poppy and me.'

'Rue de Grenelle,' Marianne's eyes flashed for a moment in shared memory. Or perhaps just a final spasm of pain. Then they closed forever.

'Maybe not the rue de Grenelle, after all. But you'll find us somewhere, my sweet. I'm sure of that.'

The redcoats that passed probably took her for a looter too, and would not have recognised that she was dressing one of the fallen rather than stripping them. But she laid out her sister as nobly as she was able. She took off her overalls, pulled them on over the girl's nankeen trousers, before neatly arranging the belt, sword slings and scabbard. Then she removed Marianne's shoes and replaced them with her own cavalry boots. The green coat next, into which she now slipped Marianne's arms properly, knowing that she could not hurt her any more. Somebody might wonder why she wore an old russet jacket beneath her uniform, but it seemed proper to leave her with the thing. And, finally, the sabre, which she put into the girl's grip and settled it by her side.

'There, my dear,' she muttered. 'That is the best I can do for you now.'

But she could not bear to look and linger. There was too much pain inside her. So she took the precious *tonnelet*, slung it as she had seen Marianne do so many times, and she walked the horse south, following the carts and English women who trailed behind their own Goddam regiments. They regarded her with curiosity, of course, whispering among themselves, pointing and staring, yet nobody questioned her presence among them. There was already too much to occupy them.

*

She determined to aim for the Rosomme Farm again. It seemed the obvious place. For the valley between the two ridges was now being eaten alive by the general advance of the English. So Liberté swung to her right, dropped back down the slope up which she had charged with her Regiment, retraced their steps to the place where they had stood opposite that Gum Hill Manor House, which the Walloons called *Hougoumont*. It was still burning but, for the first time in the past ten hours, there seemed to be no more fighting there.

She had almost expected to find Colonel Planzeau with whatever now remained of the 2nd Dragoons and Kellerman's Corps, but they had gone. And she joined the stream of other French soldiers who also no longer had any unit; nor officer; nor organisation to guide them. Yet she stopped long enough for a final view of the tragedy's closing act, saw the reserve squares of the Imperial Guard Grenadiers and Foot Chasseurs being cut to pieces by case shot and skirmisher fire or - with only handfuls of Guard Cavalry to try and defend them - surrounded by the English Heavies who came pouring down upon them and simply washed them away in the flood.

But Liberté remembered that, at Rosomme, there were the two battalions of the 1st Grenadiers, the Old Grumblers, the toughest of the army's veterans.

They will hold the Goddams and the Prussos back, she told herself, *make sure that the Emperor is safe*. And, as she took the lane that led to the Rosomme Farm, to the mound where she had stopped with Marianne this morning, she knew they would also provide a wall behind which the rest of the army might fall back. It would be a shambles, of course. But, somewhere behind that wall, she would find a cart with a broken-backed pony called Cocotte. There would be a small child at the reins, heading south, a one-legged woman at her side.

Likely as not, there would be a pair of goats tethered to the cart's tail and, though Liberté feared the meeting, she also knew that no explanations would be needed. Not really. Marianne Tambour's daughter would already know the fate that had befallen her mother, because she would have felt it. Lived it. And the girl was sharp enough to know that, if her mother was not coming back, then neither would her father. So there would be no tear-soaked embraces. Simply the silent grief-stained journey that would see so many of their dreams and hopes fallen by the wayside.

At some point, the army would rally, stand again to defend Paris. But then what? Would it follow the pattern of the previous year? Bonaparte forced to abdicate. The Fat King Louis back with all his cronies. The work of the Revolution turned upside down once more. The people set in their chains again. She was sure of it. Yet she was certain of this too. That however harsh the winter, a new spring always followed close upon the thaw. There was consolation in this, but not enough to staunch the tears that coursed down her face.

We should have won, she thought. *It was so close to us. And snatched away. By what? The weather? Our bloody generals? Bad fortune? The prediction of Nostredame? Fouché's meddling?* She wondered where the Emperor might be at this moment. And she shed tears for him also, became inconsolable when she tried to imagine the bottomless level of his own grief. He *was* France, after all. Somewhere, there would be answers. Somewhere in the memory of all things that have come to pass, and all those that have yet to be. So she would return, continue to travel her dreams, seek guidance in understanding all that had happened to her, all that would happen in the future.

For the rest, she had a letter that she must deliver, for the Emperor's son, to that pencilled name on the envelope in her portmanteau, that trusted member of his wife's suite at the Schönbrunn. And the diamonds? The treasure of France? It was out of her hands now. Doubtless Fouché would have some other scheme to liberate them. Would he receive reports, she wondered, of the female Dragoon found dead upon the field? She imagined so. Marianne had given her that chance to escape his clutches. Begin a new life.

She would find Florisette and raise the girl as her own. There would be a cabaret somewhere. Or maybe an inn. In Arcachon now, she thought, rather than Paris. She would return there soon. When it was safe. Find her father, if he still lived. Share with him a sanitized version of his wife's fate and the other daughter he had never known. So she would need somebody to run the establishment while she was travelling. Perhaps the one-legged woman, Catherine Argonne. She thought that in her own bittersweet way, Marianne would have liked that. And the woman could tell tales to their customers about all the glory they had seen. About the canteen-mistresses she had known. About the greatest of them all. A young woman called Marianne Tambour, who had fulfilled her ambition and fought her last campaign for the Shaveling that she loved.

The place would need a name, naturally. But Liberté already knew what that might be. For she had a vision. Of fine food. Of folk that would flock for miles to eat and drink there. To share the best of entertainment…

And Marianne had just murmured the name in her ear. She would call it *The Old Grenadier.*

Aftermath

Monday 19th June 1815, 5.00am

The woman might be beautiful, but she was beyond help. And a dead woman, beautiful or otherwise, sprawled in the midst of those huddled battlefield masses, was a rare matter. Rare, and shrouded like the mystery of her presence in the dark and drifting smoke that still made the morning indistinguishable from the night just gone.

It was an Englishman who found her. At least, he was one of the Green Jackets that fought within the British ranks. Yet, regardless of chance nationality, he could be seen to wonder at her discovery.

'Beautiful,' he said again, 'despite it all.'

'She's French,' said his companion.

The Green Jacket glanced at him, uncertain whether the comment was a negation of his own, or a self-evident opinion of her valour. For the woman lay where the action had been thickest, in that fold of the field's embrace where Bonaparte's army fell in such generous abandon. And her beauty was more than simply physical, for it existed, despite the vacant pallor of her frigid flesh.

They said there were more than thirty-two thousand left sleeping in that Belgian soil. From just one day, regardless of the others that had gone before. From La Belle Alliance and Plancenoit in the south, to the village of Mont St. Jean in the north. Then west to east, from the château of Hougoumont to Papelotte. Thirty-two thousand sewn across those few square miles from that engagement which had demanded so much blood to still its ardour.

But it was over. A battle won. A battle lost. A battle close-run. A battle fated to failure. A battle with victory for Wellington's infamous army, defeat for the Imperial Eagles. A battle that would, he hoped, finally end so many centuries of war between English and French. Though now, for the Green Jacket and his companion, there was the woman to bury. The woman and all these others.

The End

Historical and Literary Note

The village of Waterloo (Vaterlô), of course, played no part in the battle at all. In fact, it is more than 3 kilometres from Waterloo to the nearest point on the battlefield. And that point, as it happens, is the hamlet and farm of Mont St. Jean, just behind Wellington's defensive ridge. So, for the French, the disastrous event of 18th June 1815 has always been known as the Battle of Mont St. Jean. For the Prussians, it is the Battle of La Belle Alliance. But Wellington spent the nights of 17th and 18th June at Waterloo's coaching inn. It was from there that he wrote up his victorious dispatches and, therefore, for the British, it has been the Battle of Waterloo ever since.

At the battle's end, the French squares that stood in the valley below the Hotel of the Beautiful Alliance (*La Belle Alliance*) were either cut to pieces by Allied artillery fire or cavalry attacks, or succeeded in retiring to those two other battalion squares of the Old Guard's 1st Grenadiers which had stood all day behind the front lines, at Rosomme.

It was within their ranks that the Emperor originally sought refuge once the general disintegration of his army began, and it was there, too, where many of the other retreating units – many still in good order, some totally routed – also looked for shelter.

Guardsmen from other shattered units joined them, swelled their numbers and then withstood several attacks by Allied cavalry in the gathering darkness. Even in their defeat, most of these Frenchmen would have "died a thousand times" before letting the enemy reach their Emperor.

It was Bonaparte himself who gave the final order to retire, and the two enlarged squares began an orderly retreat, while the Emperor himself rode for the Pebble Farm (*Le Caillou*), and from there towards Genappe. Those riding with him confirmed that he showed no trace of personal fear, and that their progress was slow and measured – contrary to the normal depiction of Bonaparte in headlong flight for Paris. At the same time, the rest of the defeated army also dragged itself south, many of the wounded, or those attempting surrender, butchered by the pursuing Prussians.

In Genappe, all was confusion, and it was there that the Allies overtook and captured Bonaparte's carriages – and a fortune in diamonds hidden within

– but not the Emperor himself. And the French retreat did not put an end to the fighting either for Grouchy's 33,000 men (who could have made such a decisive difference at Waterloo itself) finally saw action at Wavre where they defeated the Prussians in a two-day battle (18th and 19th June, 1815).

Yet it was too late for Bonaparte. He returned to Paris on 21st June, where pressure from the Chamber of Peers and Deputies, as well as some of his key Marshals, forced him on the following day to abdicate for a second time, and then to leave the capital. He spent several weeks trying to find ways of escaping by sea, but British blockades made this impossible and, on 15th July, he eventually surrendered to the Royal Navy. He was exiled to the South Atlantic island of St Helena, where he died six years later. He never saw his son again.

The boy, Napoléon François Charles Joseph Bonaparte, had been born in 1811 to the Emperor's second wife, Marie Louise of Austria. With Napoleon's first abdication, in 1814, his son became, briefly, Napoléon II. However, with Bonaparte sent to exile on Elba, mother and son took refuge at the court of her father, the Austrian Emperor Francis I. The boy was brought up as Franz, Duke of Reichstadt. He died of tuberculosis at the Schönbrunn Palace, Vienna, in 1832.

In 1840, Bonaparte's body was returned to France and interred at Les Invalides, with more than a million French men and women lining the route of the procession and 150,000 soldiers taking part – although pride of place was reserved for the last survivors of his Imperial Guardsmen, who marched behind his hearse.

Meanwhile, following the Emperor's abdication, a Provisional Government was established and, after considerable Machiavellian plotting, Fouché placed himself at its head. And with the restoration of the Bourbon King Louis XVIII, the final dreams of the Revolution dashed, Fouché insinuated himself back into his post as Minister of Police, though he did not last long in that position. A Royalist backlash resulted in a new White Reign of Terror, a purge of leading former-Republicans that, among other things, resulted in Fouché's dismissal and exile in 1816. He died in exile too, in 1820.

Yet this White Reign of Terror also took some notable lives, including that of Michel Ney, Bonaparte's field commander at Quatre Bras and Waterloo. Ney – Duke of Elchingen and Prince of Moskowa – had been nicknamed "the bravest of the brave" by Bonaparte, and in December 1815 was tried for treason, before being executed by firing squad a few days later. I like to think of him leading those futile cavalry charges against the British squares while waving the sabre that the Emperor had gifted to him upon Ney's wedding day. It was almost certainly the same sword that eventually was also presented by Ney's descendants to the French Prince Imperial, Louis Napoleon (the Emperor's great-nephew and son of Napoleon III) before he went to Zululand in 1879 and was killed there, vainly trying to defend himself with that very blade. (Prince Louis Napoleon, his death and his sword are featured in my third novel, *The Kraals of Ulundi*.)

So far as the novel's other historical characters are concerned, the death of Berthier is still shrouded in mystery. He died as a result of a fall from the window of his house at Bamberg. There was only one alleged eye-witness. However, in the Memoirs of Colonel Maceroni, the author claims to have been in the company of Fouché when the latter boasted of the killing being "by order."

There are various legends alleging that Nathan Rothschild not only received early news of the victory at Waterloo, but then lied about the outcome to force the price of government bonds down still further, bought all that he could and then "made a killing" when the price rose again once the actual outcome became known. I could find no documentary evidence of this whatsoever, and the legends are suspect since they have variously been used and embellished as part of several anti-Semitic "conspiracy theories" about Jewish bankers and world domination – including one perpetrated by Hitler himself. But international bankers certainly made enormous profits from the various government loans and other financial arrangements that resourced and fed the Napoleonic Wars in general.

General Letort, that fine cavalry leader who might also have made a difference at Waterloo if he had not been wounded at Gilly, eventually succumbed to his awful abdominal injury and died in the house at Charleroi on 17th June.

Willem Frederik George Lodewijk van Oranje-Nassau – Prince William of Orange ("Thin William") narrowly escaped capture at Quatre Bras only to be seriously wounded at Waterloo, two days later. But he survived and, in the following year, married the Grand Duchess Anna Pavlovna of Russia. The marriage, of course, did not prevent further scandalous rumours about his "shameful and unnatural lusts" although he seems to have survived them all. Then, in 1830, revolution broke out in Belgium, a movement springing up to demand the country's independence from the Netherlands and electing their own Belgian king, Leopold. Thin William was sent with an army to restore order in 1831 but was unsuccessful. Eight years of border warfare ensued, as a result of which, in 1839, the Treaty of London was signed and Belgium's independence finally established. Thin William's father abdicated soon after, and the Prince acceded to the throne in October 1840 as William II, King of the Netherlands. He died in 1849.

Jean Victor, Baron de Constant Rebecque, did indeed countermand Wellington's orders on 15th June to pull allied troops from Quatre Bras and concentrate at Nivelles. His decision to countermand the order, and the subsequent holding of Quatre Bras by the Dutch-Belgians against Ney's forces, allowed Wellington to change his plans, bring up the rest of the Allied army, and then fight the successful battle at Mont St. Jean. He became Chief of Staff for the Netherlands Army in 1816 and had a relatively distinguished career until his involvement in attempts to quell the 1830 Belgian Revolution. He retired from service in 1837 and died in 1850.

Sir Arthur Wellesley, 1st Duke of Wellington, had already begun a political career, as a Member of Parliament, between 1806 and 1807, and he resumed these ambitions when, in 1818, he accepted a post in Lord Liverpool's Tory Government. In 1827, he was appointed Commander-in-Chief of the British Army, but he resigned this position the following year when he became Prime Minister. He served until 1834, when he was superseded by Robert Peel, although Wellington remained at the centre of government as Foreign Secretary. In 1842, he was also re-appointed as Commander-in-Chief of the British Army. He died in September 1852, aged 83. He was given a state funeral, the procession one of the largest in British history.

But what about the non-historical characters in this story? A few of them, I thought, at least deserve further mention. First, the Thénardiers. As you will know, in Victor Hugo's *Les Misérables*, we first meet Thénardier himself scavenging in the aftermath of the Battle of Waterloo. When we next encounter him, he is running an inn at Montfermeil and has two daughters, Éponine and Azelma, and a son, Gavroche. Those who love to make such calculations seem divided on whether Éponine would have been born just before, or just after, the battle – but I have gone with the former and concluded that, on 15th June 1815, Éponine would have been a baby and Madame Thénardier would probably have been pregnant with the second child, Azelma. Fans of the film versions and the musical will know that both Éponine and Gavroche are each fated to die on the Paris barricades of 1832, but only readers of Hugo's expansive novel will know that, by then, Madame Thénardier will have given birth to two further sons and then died in prison. At the novel's dénouement (hopefully, I'm not giving too much away here), Thénardier takes Azelma – we never really discover what happens to the two younger boys – off to America where, perhaps predictably, he becomes a slave trader. The other "famous" fictional Waterloo-related character who appears in the story is Fabrice (Fabrizio) del Dongo, from Stendhal's *The Charterhouse of Parma*. After his quixotic adventures on the field of Waterloo (I think Stendhal, or perhaps Fabrizio himself may have embroidered his part in the battle), he returns to his home at Lake Como and then Parma, where his Aunt Gina has an ingenious plan to send him to a seminary in Naples. He has no real interest in religion but sees that the priesthood might hold some advantage for him, but it does not prevent his involvement in a series of love affairs, intrigues, a duel, imprisonment and the birth of a child, the tragic death of both child and its mother, and Fabrizio's retirement to a monastery – the eponymous Charterhouse of Parma – where he dies also.

November 2014
Wrexham, North Wales

Glossary

Bayard – Mythical horse of Old French legend, capable of carrying the four sons of Aymon

Cantinière – a female auxiliary, officially attached to French (and some other) army units, for the purpose of selling provisions as a supplement to normal rations; there were also vivandières, serving a similar purpose

Cornarde – a French insult, literally meaning "horned one" – so here perhaps meaning "Cow!" though, like most French insults, it is multi-layered

Charpie – a simple surgical dressing made from linen thread

Charrado – a Provençal word, meaning chatter, or prattle – the possible origin of "charade"

Chasseur – the French word for "hunter" and applied to various groups of both light infantry and light cavalry

Dormeuse – a travelling carriage, the seats of which can form a bed

Horizontale – a slang word for a prostitute

League, or *lieue* – a measurement of distance, equivalent to approx. 4.5 kilometres, or 2.7 miles, although the way in which the league was defined and calculated changed according to circumstance and at various periods

Manolo/a - French Napoleonic slang for a Spanish man or woman

Peloton – French for Platoon

Poque – a French precursor of poker

Puncheon – a large barrel

Prairial – the ninth month in the new French revolutionary calendar, and the third month of the spring quarter, so roughly mid-May to mid-June, and literally meaning "meadow"

Reticule – a small bag, or purse

Salvavirgo – Spanish word for a "chastity knife"

Sans-Culottes – a word for the French working class, which refers to the fashion among the bourgeoisie of wearing knee-breeches, or culottes; poorer workers wore trousers and thus were "without culottes"

Sou – a French coin, equivalent to 5 centimes, and there were 100 centimes to a franc (20 sous); there were 5 francs to one écu and 20 francs to a gold Napoléon

Tirailleur – literally meaning "shooter" but used as another term for a light infantry skirmisher and, in the French Napoleonic army, usually to mean the light infantry regiments of the Young Guard; later in the 19th Century, tirailleurs were generally colonial troops

Toise – a measurement of distance, originating in pre-revolutionary France, equivalent to six feet, or a fathom; there are 36 *toises* to an *arpent* (approx. 67 metres)

Tonnelet – a small, portable cask

Veuze – Breton bagpipes

Voltigeur – elite skirmishers, literally meaning "vaulters" since originally intended to be carried into battle by cavalrymen; each French line or light infantry battalion had a dedicated company of voltigeurs

Acknowledgements

I owe much of the background for this latest novel to many online resources, which predominantly included:

The campaign of 1815: a study by Pierre de Wit (www.waterloo-campaign.nl) for its scholarly examination of the action at Gilly on 15th June 1815; for further details of Gilly, the excellent French-language site, *Napoléon a Gilly en 1815* (www.gilly.be/VVV/Napoleon_Gilly_1815.html); for the siege and rape of San Sebastián, *When Soldiers Quit: Studies in Military Disintegration* by Bruce Watson, and also Thomas Hardy's fine poem, *San Sebastian*; for Napoleon, His Army and Enemies, the site at www.napolun.com; for countless academic papers on subjects too numerous to mention, the remarkable Napoleon Series (www.napoleon-series.org), and their main editor, Bob Burnham); for the research on French drum calls and their rhythms, the *Fifing: Historical Music and Re-enacting* site, and especially its sections on *French Napoleonic Ordonnance, 1813* (www.fifemusic.wordpress.com); for more on French military music, the Gallica Biblioteque Nationale online version of Bardin's *1813 Infantry Manual*; for the French trumpet calls, the wonderful site of the *Fanfare du 2ème Hussards* and its section on the *Sonneries Reglémentaires* (fanfare2rh.free.fr/sonneries.htm); and, for details of battlefield surgery and wound treatment, several posts by former surgeon Michael Crumplin.

The books on which I principally relied were:

Andrew W. Field's *Waterloo: the French Perspective*, which brings together so many primary French sources never previously published in English and which shed such an entirely different light on many aspects of the battle. I also owe a huge debt to Andrew for the considerable time he took in reading my drafts and offering technical advice. In addition, the following books were particularly helpful: J. David Markham's *The Road to St. Helena – Napoleon after Waterloo*; Mark Adkin's indispensable *The Waterloo Companion*; Thomas Cardoza's *Intrepid Women: Cantinières and Vivandières of the French Army*; the illustrated history, *Armies of the Napoleonic Wars*, edited by Chris McNab; Andrew Uffindell's *The Eagle's Last Triumph: Napoleon's Victory at Ligny*; and Peter Hofschröer's *Quatre Bras & Ligny*. Finally, I have taken it as a good omen that, on the day I put my very last touches to the second draft of *The Last Campaign*, Bernard Cornwell's non-fiction account of the battle landed in our local bookstore. Therefore, *Waterloo:*

the History of Four Days, Three Armies and Three Battles was published just too late to help me as a resource, but it makes fascinating reading, all the same.

My eternal thanks to all the various authors, archivists and website writers mentioned above, as well as the following organisations: the International Napoleonic Society (www.napoleonicsociety.com); the Napoleonic Association (www.napoleonicassociation.org); the Portsmouth Napoleonic Society; the Napoleon Guide (www.napoleonguide.com); and the Fondation Napoléon (www.napoleon.org).

It seems unfair to single out particular re-enactment groups, so those listed here are simply a few of those who have provided particular inspiration, one way or the other: the 2ème Régiment de Dragons; the Brigade Napoléon; the 16ème Régiment de Dragons; the 2ème Bn/1er Régiment de Grenadiers à Pied de la Garde Impérial; and the 7ème Régiment de Hussards. It may be worth noting for those who know little about such groups that, apart from the astonishing displays that they organise, their members are all wonderful historians in their own right.

As usual, I need to thank the exceptional team that helps bring my books to publication – my editor, Jo Field; cover designer, Cathy Helms, at Avalon Graphics; our family artist, Sharon Povey; my ideal reader and travel guide companion, Ann McCall; another family member, Brian McCall, for his German linguistic expertise; and the fabulous bunch at SilverWood Books.

I am also frequently staggered by the kindness of those who write and post reviews of my books. But that process is at least fairly easy now, and it's a very simple process to go on the various selling site pages for the particular novel (Waterstones, Foyles, Abe Books, Amazon.co.uk, Amazon.com, Kindle, Kobo, Nook), or book club sites like Goodreads and Librarything, and leave a few comments. So, if you feel that way inclined, please scribble a few words about *The Last Campaign of Marianne Tambour* and let the world know what you thought about it!

Supporters

I want to acknowledge the support that I've enjoyed from all my other supporters, and a special mention here to those who contributed to the crowd-funding resources that made this publication possible. Thanks to all of you!

Maija and Simon Robinson, Len Boulton, Judy and Bob Jones, Joan and Tony Roberts, Heidi Chapman, John Haywood, Ben Cameron, Nina and Keith Roberts, Lorna Eccleston, Jake and Marilyn McCall, Julie Madigan, Annemarie Neary, Chris Richardson, Nina Davies, Peter Booth plus those individuals who preferred to remain anonymous.

The Battlefields Route

I always check out the locations for all of my novels and have never yet failed to make positive changes to the text as a result. So, early in September 2014, I drove to France and Belgium with Ann so that we could travel the routes followed by Marianne Tambour and Liberté Dumont in the novel. While doing so, it occurred to me that this is a much more logical way of seeing the sites and battlefields associated with the Hundred Days than the more "traditional" option of beginning in Brussels. It also follows, more or less, the route signposted at regular intervals by *La Route Napoléon en Wallonie*, a development by the Belgian Tourist Board. We used Namur as a base and adopted the itinerary listed below, but it's just as easy to reverse or change the order.

Please remember, though, that the following maps are intended for guidance only, rather than accurate navigation.

Map Overview

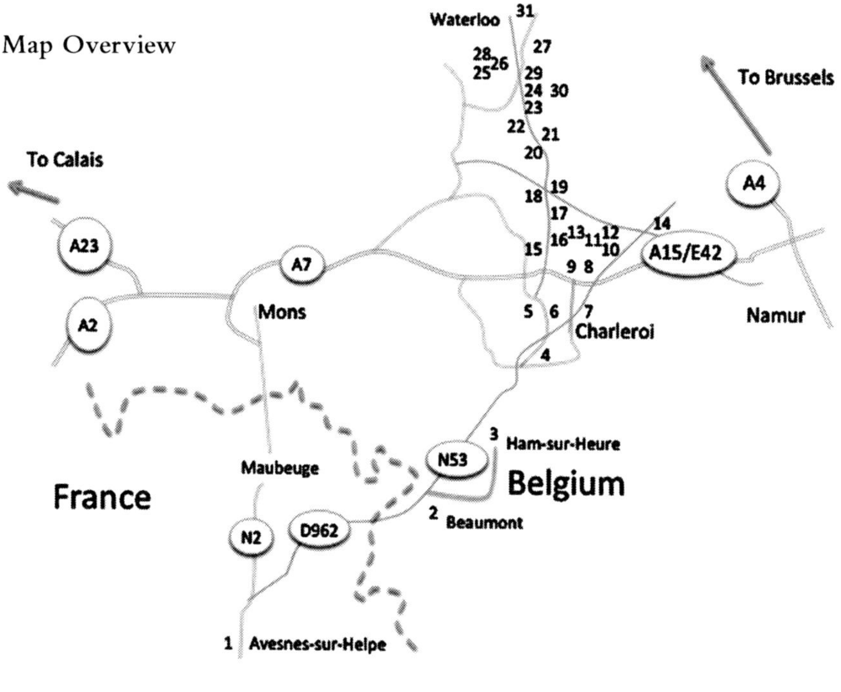

Day One

We drove from Calais, through Dunkerque, Lille, Valenciennes and Maubeuge to Avesnes-sur-Helpe (1) and the former residence of the local Prefect (next to the impressive St. Nicolas Church and down the alley at the side of the Tourist Office) where a plaque marks both the overnight stop that Bonaparte made there on 13th June 1815 as well as the visit by the Emperor's great-nephew, Louis Napoleon, at the end of August 1870 before his own exile to England and subsequent death in Zululand. Then 30km northeast, along the D962 through Hestrud to Beaumont (2), now in Belgium but, in 1815, just on the French side of the border. The Emperor spent the next night (14th June) at the current town hall, while the Imperial Guard was bivouacked in the town itself and in the area immediately to the south. Continuing northeast, you can follow the lanes to Ham-sur-Heure (3) where Bonaparte dozed at the crossroads while the army marched past, or take the N53 straight to Charleroi. These are all lovely locations and deserve some exploration. But the next stage, through Charleroi itself, requires a fair bit of imagination. The bridge where the French drove back the Prussians is no longer there and even the Sambre river itself has been diverted but, at the Gare du Sud railway station (4), there's a Drum Memorial to those who fought here in 1815 and, just across the new bridge, the Banque Nationale building (5) stands on the site of the Puissant house where the Emperor spent the night of 15th June. Two streets further on, at 88 Boulevard Tirou (6), is the house where General Letort was treated and died after Gilly. And so, on to Gilly itself (7), along the busy N29. Gilly is now a mere suburb of Charleroi, but we looked out for the church, just to the left, off the main road where it begins to dip down into the valley, and stopped there to look across at the steeply sloping high ground opposite, where the Prussians took up their positions for the battle on 15th June. Then we continued along the N29, climbing up the hill towards Fleurus and past the Abbey of Soleilmont (also on the left), still surrounded by woodland, as it was in 1815, when it anchored the right of the Prussian line. We ended the first day by following the road almost as far as Fleurus but turned east on the E42/A15 for a comfortable night and good food in Namur.

Map – Charleroi and Gilly

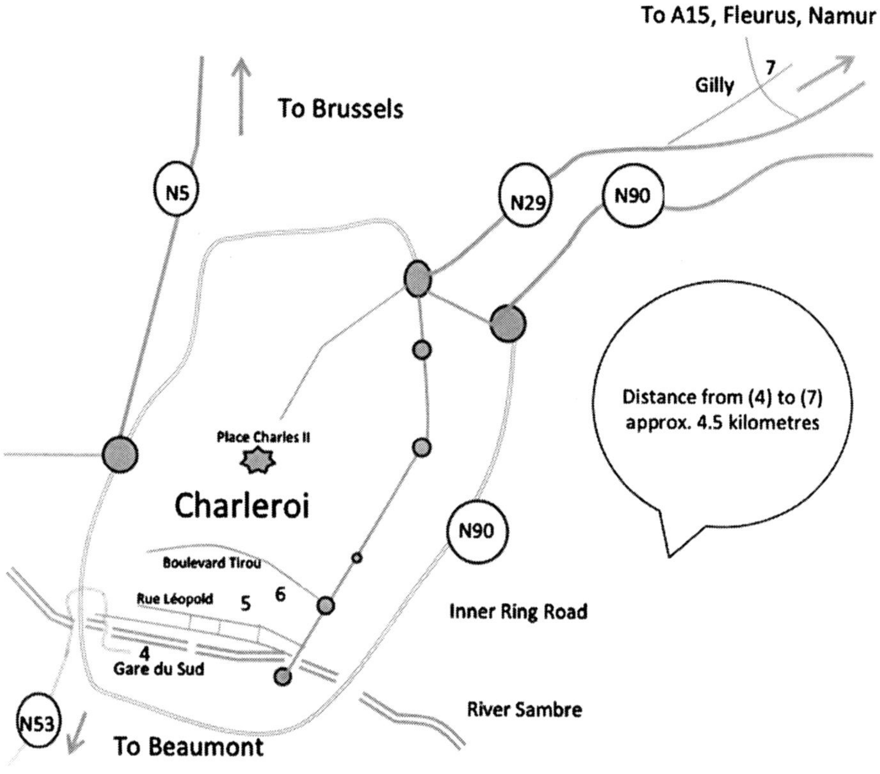

Day Two

Retracing our steps along the E42, we began today in Fleurus where, on 16th June, Bonaparte's Central Column, Reserve and Right Wing had marched in an effort to bring the Prussians to a more decisive battle. On the left of the N29 (opposite a Ford dealership) stands the monument (8) at the Naveau windmill, which Napoleon used as an observation post before the battle at Ligny. The Naveau monument actually commemorates three French victories on this ground, in 1690, 1794 and 1815. Further on, at the very edge of town, left along the Mons road, is the Chateau de la Paix (9), which served as Bonaparte's headquarters until the following morning. From here you can either follow the *Route Napoléon* signs, leading to St. Amand and giving a good view of the whole battlefield, a panorama of Wagnelée, St Amand, Ligny and Tongrinne – the villages in and behind which Blücher had drawn up his army. Alternatively, you can carry on up the N29 and then turn left towards Ligny on the N273. As you drive through Ligny, there is a road signposted St. Amand, to the left (at a large cannon barrel memorial of the bicentenary) with a car park next to the Farm d'En Haut and opposite the church (12). A sign at the church will lead you to the Farm d'En Bas (11) - both church and farm have been rebuilt since the battle but each was the site of horrific hand-to-hand fighting. Back on the N273, at the north end of the village, is the Centre Genéral Gérard Museum (10) – open most days but only afternoons – with its wonderful collection and large-scale map of the battlefield. There was plenty more to see around Ligny, and particularly the neighbouring villages of St. Amand (13) and Tongrinne (14) where, from the original church, you can get a good impression of this section's terrain. The sloping ground north of Ligny, along the N93, from which Blücher commanded his forces, also marks the line of the Prussian retreat towards Wavre and the area where the Imperial Guard later rested.

In the early afternoon, however, we headed back towards Charleroi, looking for the N5, which would lead us to Frasnes on the roads followed by Marshal Ney, with the French Left Wing, who had been instructed to take the village of Quatre Bras and keep Wellington's army in that area from joining with the Prussians. Ney had already been held up, just north of Frasnes, by stubborn resistance from Dutch-Belgian and Nassauer units. So we started there, vainly looking for the suburb of Le Balcan (15). Roadworks and poor signage thwarted us here, but we managed to find the site of the Grand Pierpont Farm and, to the right, the L'Erâle Farm – between which the Netherlanders established and held a thin line against Ney's forces with such determination that he was convinced he faced the whole of Wellington's army. The Dutch-Belgians were eventually pushed back to the Gémioncourt Farm (16), which has changed little since 1815. A plaque on the farm's wall apparently marks the severity of the fighting, both here and across the Gémioncourt Brook that ran beyond, but at the time of our visit there were unfriendly "Private Property" signs everywhere, though we took some good photos from the roadside. From Gémioncourt, the road passes two monuments, one of them to the Duke of Brunswick (17), and these also mark areas of heavy fighting, where Wellington's squares turned back the French cavalry, though at considerable cost to themselves. There are more memorials in Quatre Bras (18) itself, and the old farmhouse (19) still stands at the crossroads, though in the middle of a major refurbishment.

The evening took us further north on the N5 but turning off for the centre of Genappe, parking next to the Carrefour supermarket, then up and across the Dyle bridge to find the site of the former King of Spain Inn (20) – along the main street, past the square and church, in the Place de l'Empereur – where Wellington stayed on 16th June and Blücher spent the night after the battle. Immediately north of the centre, before rejoining the bypass and heading back to Namur, is the ground (21) on which Napoleon and his cavalry made a final attempt to overtake Wellington's rear-guard as the Duke's forces fell back from Quatre Bras towards the ridge of Mont St. Jean. It was here that the pursuit petered out and set the scene for the following day's monumental confrontation.

Map – Fleurus, Ligny and Quatre Bras

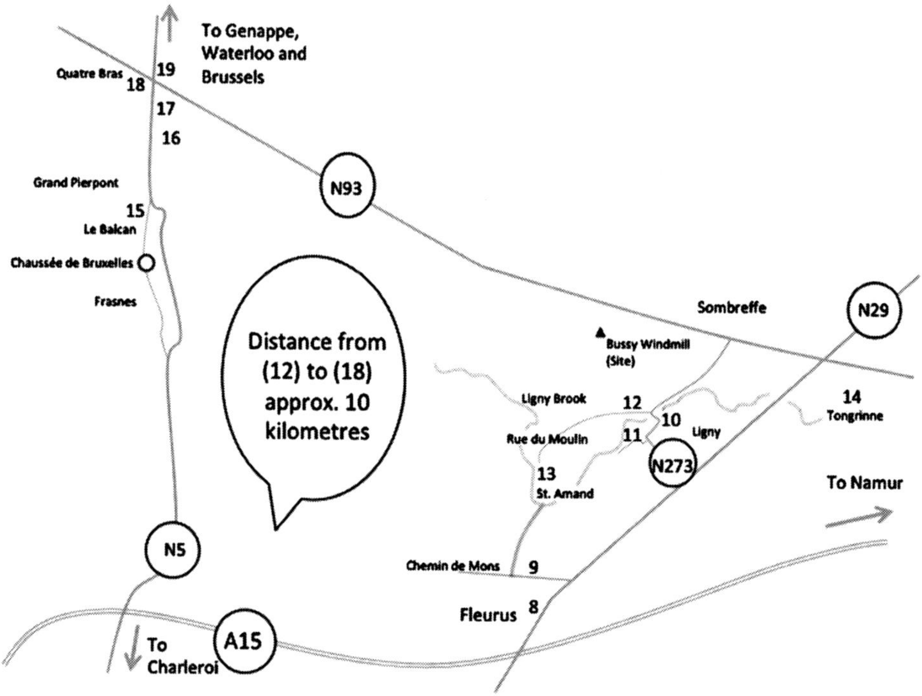

Day Three

The Waterloo battlefield is relatively compact, but it's still best to visit the main viewing points in some sort of logical order, though bearing in mind that parking is either limited or even non-existent at some of those locations. In our case this was fairly easy since we were following in the footsteps of Marianne Tambour and Liberté Dumont, so we drove from Namur back to Quatre Bras on the N93, broadly along the route taken by Bonaparte's Central Column and Reserve in order to catch up with Ney's Left Wing. Grouchy and the 33,000 men of the Right Wing, of course, had been sent off to pursue the Prussians. So, Quatre Bras and Genappe again, then to the Pebble Farm – Le Caillou (22) – where the Emperor spent the night of 17th June. There is a great little museum in the old farmhouse, which is well worth a visit, and includes the Emperor's campaign cot. About 1 kilometre north of Le Caillou on the N5 is Rosomme (23), around which the Imperial Guard was assembled and where Bonaparte spent a chunk of the 18th, though unable to see a great deal of the action. As it happens, it's virtually impossible to spot the place, which is now surrounded by high hedges. But if you get to the Victor Hugo monument without noticing it, you've gone too far! And, beyond Rosomme, the farm/inn called La Belle Alliance, or the Beautiful Alliance (24), from which the Emperor reviewed his army at 11.00am on the morning of the battle, and to which he returned only late in the day, even though it was the obvious place from which to command the attacks. There is a viewpoint here, marked by a plaque on the right side of the lane that leads to Plancenoit. The N5 is a very busy road, by the way, so you need to be careful here.

Just to the south, off the N5, a lane (the Chemin de Remyval) runs westwards, and we walked two hundred yards along this track to roughly the position in which Kellerman's cavalry were deployed and from which Liberté would have seen the opening action of the battle, the attack on the Hougoumont Farm (25), hidden in 1815 among trees opposite, at about 11.30am. This was supposed to be a diversion, but the farm, its gardens and orchards, remained the scene of horrific fighting and burning barns until late in the evening. We walked back to La Belle Alliance and drove on up the N5, turning left to the Lion Mound (26). Needless to say, neither the mound nor the buildings were here in 1815. But in the Visitors' Centre, at the foot of the Mound, there's an excellent audio-visual presentation while, in the adjacent building, there's the dramatic and not-to-be-missed Panorama. We then climbed to the top of the hill (226 steps), from which the whole battlefield can now be surveyed. It stands almost in the middle of Wellington's line, which ran along the track and low ridge immediately behind the Mound and the road away to the east. Across the shallow valley, to the south, is the opposing and equally modest ridge along which the Emperor drew up his own forces. Looking that way, we could see the rooftops of Hougoumont ahead (to our right) and, just to our left, the farm at La Haye Sainte on the Charleroi-Brussels road (N5), which was captured by the French though only late in the day. But it was easy to picture the three main French attacks from here. First, the valley filling with Bonaparte's advancing infantry battalions on the far side of the N5, turned back by Wellington's own infantry on the East Ridge and then pursued by the British cavalry counter-attack. Second, the massed ranks of the French cavalry coming almost straight towards our current position, wave after wave for almost two hours, only to be dashed against the Allied squares. And, third, the proud regiments of the Imperial Guard marching to their doom also on this same ground.

In a way, there was no need to view the site from anywhere else, but I wanted to see the terrain from the perspective of those taking part. So we headed for the Viewpoint on the East Ridge (27). As we walked along the lane in that direction, from the Mound, we had to remember that, in 1815, there would have been a high bank to our right (the earth was removed to make the hill) so that the road passed through a cutting. But, when you come to the crossroads with the N5 (there's a memorial to Lieutenant Colonel Gordon just down the main road from here) and continue, the terrain is much more recognisable as it would have been on the day of the battle. Two hundred yards further took us to the Viewpoint, at the heart of the positions in which the British Rifle Brigade and Picton's Division stood, and from where they would have seen the French Grand Battery's 80 big guns wheeled into line on the opposite ridge before opening their bombardment at 1.30pm. This is where those battalions held back three huge phalanxes of Count d'Erlon's French infantry, over 10,000 of them, before Sir William Ponsonby's Union Brigade with their Scots Greys came up at the gallop to chase off the enemy, but then continued too far and were ripped to shreds in their turn by French Lancers coming up on their flank. The whole thing took no more than half an hour and left the valley's trampled crops strewn with corpses. It was from this direction, too, that the bulk of Blücher's Prussians arrived in time to save the day, later in the evening.

But what about the West Ridge? There is a Viewpoint here (28), back towards Hougoumont, past the Lion Mound. But at the time of writing and our visit, there were large-scale building projects taking place in preparation for the bicentenary events, which prevented access to that section of the ridge. Yet you can normally look down into the valley from here, picturing the scene from about 4.00pm onwards as the French cavalry began to form up, 500 horsemen abreast and 12 ranks deep, then coming forward at a slow trot, up and over the ridge, swarming around the Allied squares lined along the lower ground behind, but unable to break them. The French fell back down the slope to regroup, to attack again and again, perhaps ten times over the next hour and a half, before finally giving up on the stalemate. But at 7.30pm, the now critically stretched British position here was attacked once more – this time by Bonaparte's Imperial Guard Foot Chasseurs and Grenadiers, his élite troops. Wellington kept his own thin lines, his own guardsmen, concealed until the last possible moment but then raked the advancing Frenchmen with musket and case shot. Many of the Imperial Guard battalions were torn apart, and the rest fell back towards La Belle Alliance. The Guard was defeated and Wellington signalled a general advance.

From the Lion Mound, however, you can still skirt the building site and take the access road, just before the bridge over the highway, which runs down to Hougoumont itself (25). This road takes you to the main north entrance that, in 1815, was secured by the solid wooden gate – focus of so many images of the fighting here. But the fighting was also intense and continuous around the courtyard and great barn, the chapel, the high surrounding walls and gardens, though the thick woodland south-east of the farm has now disappeared. It is estimated that 6,500 men of both sides died around Hougoumont.

Heading back towards the Lion Mound there is a lane which cuts diagonally across the valley towards La Belle Alliance and the area (29), where squares of the Imperial Guard made their last stand before beginning to retreat in good order towards Charleroi, providing a moving wall behind which the Emperor and the rest of the French army could fall back.

From La Belle Alliance, the rue Du Champ de Bataille took us to the neighbouring village of Plancenoit (30) where, from late in the afternoon, other units of the Imperial Guard also tried to hold back the tide of Prussians attacking from the east. The old church has now been replaced but this whole area was, once again, the scene of bitter hand-to-hand fighting for several hours until the battle was lost and the defenders also joined the general retreat. Plancenoit is certainly worth a visit though, with its original steep and cobbled main streets, its old farm and Prussian monument, so that it's very easy to imagine the action that took place here in 1815.

But we ended our own long day by picking up the car again and driving to the town of Waterloo (31) itself – actually a few kilometres north of Mont St. Jean – to visit the battlefield museum there, housed in the former coaching inn where Wellington stayed as his headquarters on the nights before and after the battle, thus providing the name by which English-speakers have subsequently always called the conflict: The Battle of Waterloo. The town of Waterloo seems to stretch forever along the N5 but it's very lively and you'll eventually come to a set of traffic lights with the domed Church of St. Joseph on the left (there's also a memorial to the battle's fallen British soldiers at the church) and the Wellington Museum on the right (if you're heading in the direction of Brussels, of course). Another worthwhile visit and there's good parking just behind the museum too.

Map – Le Caillou, Rosomme, Mont St. Jean, Plancenoit and Waterloo

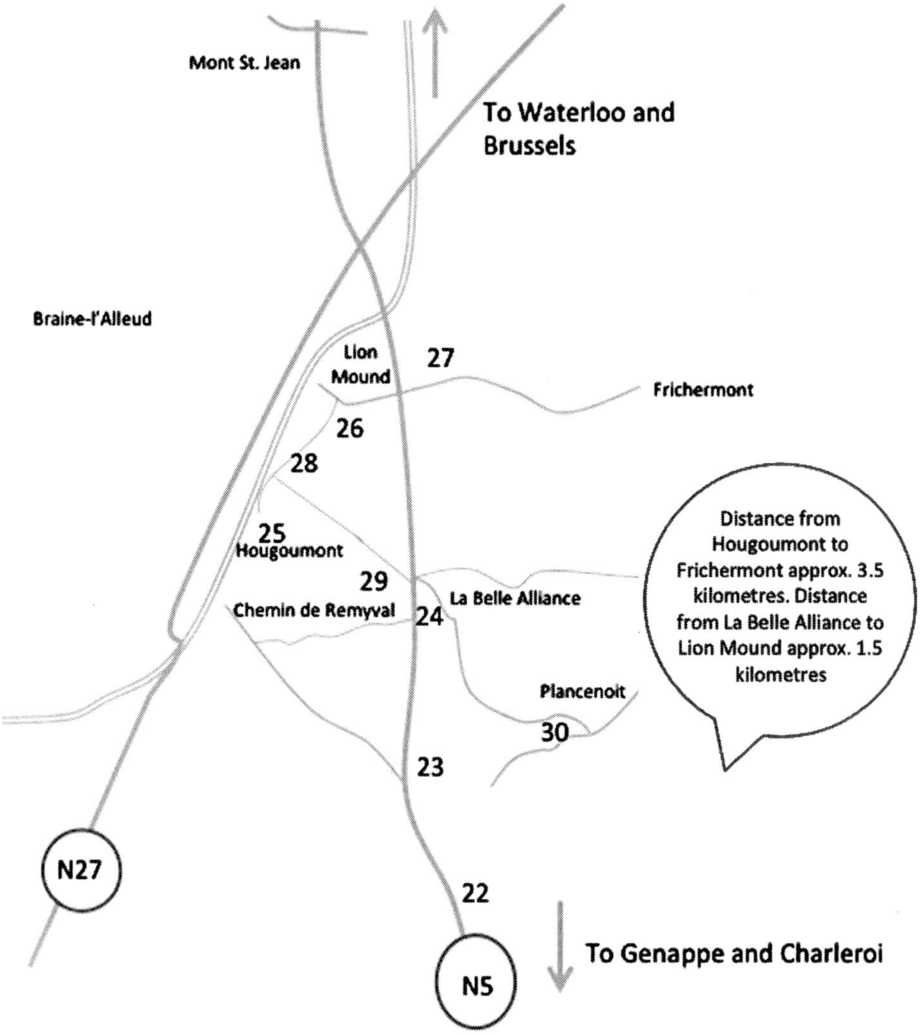

Day Four

I've not included this section on the route maps but it's worth mentioning that Brussels (an attractive city to visit in any case) has some interesting sites for those who wish to complete their Waterloo pilgrimage. The Grand-Place is the open square to which many of the Allied wounded were brought for whatever limited medical treatment was available to them, while the Hospital of the Augustine Sisters (rue de la Blanchisserie) has now replaced the building in which the Duchess of Richmond's ball was held on the night before the battle. Wellington's headquarters was located in the building still standing at 54-56 rue Royale.

This short guide is simply intended as a supplement to my Marianne Tambour novel, so I hope that readers will forgive details that may be missing due to its brevity. All the same, I also hope it might inspire those interested in the period to explore the area themselves. For those using public transport, the Rough Guide to Brussels *(Martin Dunford and Phil Lee) gives good instructions. I've also been asked to say what the "highlights" of this trip may have been and, for me, the best bits were definitely (in no particular order) the Wellington Museum (31) in the town of Waterloo; the Lion Mound, Panorama and Visitor Centre (26) at the battlefield itself; the wonderful Napoleon Museum at Le Caillou (22); and the General Gérard Museum (10) at Ligny. Happy travelling!*

David Ebsworth
Namur, September 2014

David Ebsworth maintains a website at www.davidebsworth.com
and welcomes direct contact from his readers, for whom
he writes a monthly e-newsletter.

To receive the newsletter, or for further information,
he can be contacted by email at davemccall@talktalk.net

Lightning Source UK Ltd.
Milton Keynes UK
UKOW05f1638211114

241957UK00004BA/49/P